TALL GRASS

A GENETICS INVESTIGATION TEAM THRILLER

RUSS TILTON

Copyright © 2022 by Russ Tilton.

Cover by Alex Perkins, Perky Visuals.

Edited by Mia Kleve and Zehron Stroud.

All rights reserved.

No part of this book may be reproduced in any form or by any means without written consent, excepting brief quotes used in reviews.

eBooks cannot be sold, shared, or given away because that's an infringement on the copyright of this work.

This book is licensed to the original purchaser only. Duplication or distribution via any means is illegal and a violation of International Copyright Law, subject to criminal prosecution and upon conviction, fines and/or imprisonment. No part of this e-book can be reproduced or sold by any person or business without the express permission of the publisher.

This is a work of fiction. Names, places, characters, and events are entirely the product of the author's imagination or are used fictitiously, and any resemblance to persons living or dead, actual locations, events, or organizations is coincidental.

1

Jengtang Yusef kicked in the door and stormed into the hut, spitting out a string of curses and looking to catch someone's eye to vent his rage. No one dared look up. They were not fools; they knew the man's wrath. Humble yourself, keep your head down, and perhaps keep it attached.

"How could this have happened?" he screamed, sweeping his eyes about the room but seeing only the tops of bowed heads. "Somebody answer me, or so help me I'll have you all skinned!"

Akin glanced at Chuk, who tightened his eyes and gave a slight shake of his head. Heedless of the warning, Akin cleared his throat and said, "Captain, none of our sources knew anything about the raid. Whoever they were, it wasn't government troops, or we would have known about it."

Yusef spun and kicked him in the side, driving him into the corrugated metal wall.

"I know it wasn't government troops, you idiot!" he said, standing over him, his body trembling with anger. "I want to know who it *was*. And I want to know how they found us. You are my head of security. You are supposed to make sure these things don't happen!"

He spat at the floor, then said, "You four are the only ones who knew where they were being held. One of you leaked that information and I'm going to find out who. Up against the wall!"

Two machete-bearing guards took a menacing step forward as the four advisors glanced at the bullet-pocked wall, the blood still sticky from an earlier purge. Chuk took a place at the end of the row.

"You will look me in the eye, then I'll know who it was." The rebel commander brought his face within two inches of the first man in line. "You, Kwento, look me in the eye or I'll shoot yours out!" he said, spittle flying from his khat-stained teeth.

Lips trembling, the terrified man raised his head and locked eyes with his leader. Yusef claimed he could judge a man's heart by looking in his eyes, a gift given to him by a witch woman. That these divinations often proved less than accurate after justice had been meted out did not seem to deter the leader. He snarled and moved to the next man.

Suddenly, Chuk bolted, knocking aside a guard and lunging through the door. Yusef charged after him.

Chuk ran through the courtyard, past soldiers cooking their breakfast. The men scattered when they saw their commander aiming a pistol.

Yusef fired.

The round slammed into Chuk's lower right side. He grunted, threw his arms wide, and tumbled to the ground. He moaned, rolled over, then scrambled backwards as Yusef pulled a machete from its scabbard.

"No, Commander, it wasn't me!" he screamed as the blade came down.

Yusef stood over the body, sucking air like a raging bull. Then he spun around and stabbed the bloody weapon toward his three remaining advisors. "Who's next?"

The commander took a step forward, then paused. He turned his head and listened as an electronic whine grew louder.

A brown object shot over the treetops and headed for the clearing.

"Drone!" Akin Ibrahim shouted. "Run!"

Chaos erupted as the soldiers scattered, tripping and slamming into each other, some firing rifles at the machine adding to the confusion and fear.

The three-foot round disk came in fast, fifty feet above the ground, and flew straight down the middle of the courtyard. Suddenly, four objects shot out from beneath it. *Fhhht, fhhht, fhhht, fhhht!* The projectiles impacted the ground twenty feet apart, and before the last one hit, the UAV was gone, leaving four black tubes protruding from the ground in its wake.

The jungle was silent. Everyone watched from behind shelter, waiting for an explosion—but nothing happened.

After a minute, Yusef peered out from behind the pickup truck where he and his three advisors had taken cover.

"What are they?"

When he got no response, he glared at the men, then locked his eyes on Amandi Musa, his "weapons expert," a title given because he knew how to disassemble, clean, and reassemble all the unit's rifles.

"Well?" Yusef said, his eyes tightening.

Musa's eyes went wide. "I—I don't know, Commander."

"Then, go find out. Unless you'd like me to find someone to take your place?"

Musa's eyes drifted to the machete, still dripping with Chuk's blood.

He swallowed, then slowly approached the nearest cylinder.

He stopped ten feet from the object, looked back as if reconsidering, caught Yusef's glare, and stepped forward.

The black tube looked like a road flare but with a spiked end embedded into the ground. Musa walked around it and examined it from different angles. Then, glancing back at his comrades again, he reached down and plucked it from the ground.

Nothing happened.

His shoulders slumped in relief. He studied the cylinder. After another minute, he looked back at the rebel leader and shrugged.

By now, the soldiers had returned to the camp and were gathering around the other tubes.

"Get away from them, you fools," Yusef yelled as he strode into the courtyard. "We have no idea what they are." He flipped a hand at Musa. "Get someone to carry them out of the camp until we can figure this out."

"Yes, Commander," Musa said, but as he turned to give the order, a green LED at the end of the tube lit up and started to rattle and thump.

"Yiii!" Musa dropped the tube like it was a snake and scrambled back, his eyes wide. He watched the cylinder jump and vibrate across the ground, emitting a rapid *thump, thump, thump, thump, thump.* The other three tubes lit up and matched the pulse.

Some soldiers jumped back in fear, while others pointed and laughed. One man picked up one of the vibrating tubes and shook it at his fellow fighters.

A rumble came from behind the huts like the sound of vehicles crashing through the brush. There was a shout, then a scream, followed by gunfire as men rushed into the courtyard and grabbed their rifles.

"Get your weapons and—" Yusef shouted as the hut next to him exploded, showering him and his two bodyguards with wood splinters.

He turned expecting to see a tank, and his eyes widened as a massive creature slammed into the nearest guard. It hooked the man with a twelve-inch-long tusk that jutted up from its lower jaw and with a flick of its neck, tossed the screaming soldier through the air. Blood flew from the torn femoral artery. While the dying man was still airborne, the animal spun, knocked the second guard to the ground and tore out his throat.

Then it turned on Yusef, who was scrabbling backward on his butt, screaming, "Kill it! Kill it!"

A pair of soldiers sprayed the monster with their AK-47s. It bellowed, spun towards them, and charged. As big as a rhino, the thing squealed and grunted as the rounds smacked into it, but it kept attacking, swinging its head back and forth, using its deadly tusks like a sickle cutting grain.

Yusef got to his feet to run, but two more of the creatures stampeded into the courtyard and cut off his escape. The rebel leader spun in a circle, looking for a way out as bullets zipped past and ricocheted at his feet.

One fighter hollered and jumped in front of one of the monsters, aimed his rifle, and *click!* He tore the empty magazine from his weapon. The creature dragged its head across his stomach, the bayonet-like tooth ripping flesh and dragging the man's intestines from his body.

The thing flung its gigantic head in the opposite direction and shattered another man's ribcage. Blood erupted from the fighter's mouth and his eyes went wide with shock.

In the pandemonium, soldiers screamed and ran or stood frozen in terror as the monsters tore a bloody swath through their ranks, trampling bodies and slinging full-grown men over their heads. For every man killed by one of the creatures, another was hit by friendly fire as every man frantically fought for his life.

One animal stood atop a pile of bodies, faced its opponents, and roared a challenge, seemingly immune to the 7.62 rounds slamming into its body.

There was another roar as a Nissan pickup and a battered Toyota Land Cruiser tore into the camp, their gunners clutching the machine guns mounted atop each. With earsplitting blasts, the soldiers opened fire. The creatures stood no chance against the .50 caliber rounds that ripped through their bodies. Half a minute later, all three were down.

The smoke cleared and Yusef walked from behind a line of men to survey the carnage. Half his rebels lay dead or dying from animal injuries or gunshot wounds.

A soldier walked up to a fallen creature and kicked it in the head. The beast reared up and with a grunt, ripped an eighteen-inch gash along the inside of the man's left leg. He fell to the ground, screaming, as a comrade ran up and emptied a magazine of rounds into the thing's head. With a mighty huff, the animal released its final breath.

The soldiers finished off the other two creatures, then stood atop them, raising their weapons in a display of victory.

Yusef approached the largest animal.

Lying on its side, it came up to the commander's waist. It was ten feet long from snout to tail and was covered in coarse brown fur; the beast was the size of a small car. A thick tuft of hair, like a mohawk, ran from between its ears to the middle of its back.

He pulled out his pistol and fired two rounds into its skull. When there was no reaction, he went to a knee, grabbed the twelve-inch-long tusk protruding from its mouth, and gave it a shake. He turned to his lieutenants. "What are they?"

"They look like pigs," one said.

Yusef snarled in disgust and spat on the ground. He looked closer and saw a brown strap circling the creature's neck, buried beneath the thick fur. The other two wore similar straps.

He grabbed it and followed it around to the base of the neck and found a small black plastic box with a lens.

"A camera," he growled. He stood and scanned the treetops for another drone.

"Get these filthy animals out of here and burn them but put the head of this big one on display for all the infidels to see." He turned to Musa. "And bring these cameras to me. They may lead us to whoever spawned these desecrations."

Yusef spun to leave when Ibrahim called out, "What about the wounded, Commander?"

He spat a curse and turned back just as Musa dragged his knife through the neck harness.

With an earsplitting *crack!* all three harnesses exploded in a burst of red mist and body tissue. Men screamed as those closest to the animals were knocked off their feet.

Yusef, ears ringing and eyes wide with astonishment, struggled to his feet. Around him, a half dozen more men lay unmoving. The explosions had completely severed the heads from two of the pigs, while the big one held on by a strip of flesh.

He heard a moan and saw Musa on his back, ten feet from the animal, holding aloft stumps where his hands used to be.

Shaking with rage, the rebel leader stalked over, pulled out his pistol and screamed, "You idiot!" He shot his weapons expert five times in the face.

Yusef's hand tingled from the recoil, then he noticed his other hand also tingled. He ignored it, thrust his pistol into the air, and shouted, "The infidels will pay for this attack! Allahu Akbar!"

"Allahu Akbar!" the men chanted and fired their weapons into the air, not realizing their jihad was over.

2

─ ● ─

April Flowers headed west on Interstate 10 from downtown New Orleans, still holding her breath and waiting for the other shoe to drop. The other shoe was discovering she hadn't really been transferred.

Her coworkers said being reassigned from Washington DC to the New Orleans Field Division of the Food and Drug Administration was the kiss of death, but for her, it was a godsend. When her supervisor broke the news, it was all she could do to keep from jumping up and down for joy. Flowers had always hated DC, the traffic, the hustle, the politics. She had done her best to appear saddened and disappointed, while in her mind, she was already packing her bags.

Her bosses had never been happy with having what they called the FDA version of the X-Files shoved down their throats. They didn't understand why one of their investigators was involved in something not even covered under federal regulations. Whenever she pointed to "the unethical treatment of animals involved in drug testing"—clearly in the venue of the Food and Drug Administration—they always said "Prove it." But after a year and a half, she had plenty of firsthand knowledge but no proof.

The drug trafficking allegations hadn't helped. Everyone knew the charges were bogus, designed to pull her and Jake Jessup off the investigation. But in DC, optics were everything. People heard, "a federal agent was arrested in Memphis, TN, for narcotics trafficking." But they seemed to miss, "the charges had been fabricated."

She still had her two hooks on Capitol Hill thanks to the short video of the giant mutant pit bulls she'd been able to scavenge from the operation, but she still couldn't prove the animals were being used as bioweapons. And while those congressmen knew it would be catastrophic if the United States was caught using germ warfare, even to fight terrorism, the funding faucet would eventually snap shut on the Genetics Investigation Team if she didn't come up with something tangible, soon.

That's why she'd hit the ground running. This was the most detailed tip she'd gotten from her mystery informant since he'd first contacted her six months ago. That information had led to the discovery of the giant mutant pit bull dogs in Memphis—a discovery which nearly cost Flowers and Jessup their lives.

This latest information was that animals were scheduled to arrive at a laboratory supply company in Alexandria, Louisiana, and that they might be a part of a government animal cloning project. From these one-sided interactions, Flowers assumed the informant worked in the cloning lab that produced the animals for Section 17, though she didn't know what his role was there. She guessed it was a "he" from the way he wrote his texts and secure emails.

Her phone rang. She looked at it and cringed. "Hello."

"Spock, here."

She dropped her head. "Hey, Greg."

"How's the search for the abominable snowman going?"

"Uh, it's a bit warm for that. He's probably inside enjoying the air conditioning right now. It's eighty-six."

"October in Louisiana. Lovely. It's a balmy seventy here in DC. Don't you wish you were back?"

"Let's see, traffic jams, motorcades, muggers, hour-long commutes. Uh, no, I'll pass."

"Speaking of... you didn't waste any time moving."

Flowers had had four weeks to report to New Orleans, but once she received word of the transfer, she'd packed everything into one U-Haul trailer the following day and was heading south after her going away party that Friday.

"Yeah, well," she said, "had a couple of hot leads to follow up on down here."

"You sound like you're on speakerphone."

"I am, and I'm very excited," Flowers said. "They gave me a 2018 Ford Focus to drive. It has Bluetooth, GPS, everything!"

"Welcome to the twenty-first century," he said drolly.

"Be nice. Compared to my old Ford Taurus, this is like brand new. Only thirteen thousand miles. The only problem is its bright red. I feel like I should pull over every time I see something burning."

"Well, I haven't come up with any fires for you to put out. I ran another ALERT search for Louisiana, and nothing jumps out other than alligators and snakes, of which there are thousands of complaints. Why in the world would anybody want to live in a place like that?"

Flowers smiled. She could almost see him shivering. Greg Crandall, certified genius and head computer technology person for the Food and Drug Administration, was a city boy who preferred to hunt with a computer screen. He'd created the "ALERT" program, which scoured the internet for animal-related incidents across the United States, searching everything from Facebook posts to emergency services broadcasts. The program was so powerful he had to run it through the FDA mainframe, a definite no-no. It was his program that had intercepted the police dispatcher call about a giant pit bull attack in Memphis.

"Thanks for checking, Greg, but be careful. I don't want you to get in trouble."

"What? This is work related, isn't it? Besides, I *am* the FDA mainframe. If I shut down, it all shuts down."

"How modest of you."

"Flaunt it if you got it. Besides, even the NSA couldn't track me."

"Don't even think of messing with them. Just be careful. I'm on my way to central Louisiana to check on a lead. Wish me luck."

"Live long and prosper, Earthling." The phone disconnected.

Flowers rolled her eyes. Crandall was one of the few people she had regularly hung out with in DC, and she suspected he had a crush on her, though he always ragged her about the way she dressed and her lack of a social life. But he drove a motorized skateboard from the Metro to work every day and roleplayed as Spock at Star Trek conventions. They had nothing in common.

She was surprised he hadn't mentioned Big Foot. At least once a week, somebody reported a sighting somewhere in the country, and as she drove past the swamps, she wouldn't have been surprised to see the elusive man-ape tromping along. The marshland was so thick, there could be a hundred Big Foots or Yetis or whatever just inside the tree line and you'd never know.

She knew there were plenty of gators, though, having already spotted half a dozen of them. As soon as she had time, she planned to take a swamp tour, but first things first.

3

Twenty miles west of Baton Rouge, Flowers drove over the Little Tensas Bayou and onto the Atchafalaya Basin Bridge. On the drive down from DC, she had listened to a podcast about its construction. The eighteen-mile-long bridge crossed the remote and treacherous Atchafalaya Swamp, the largest wetland in the United States.

Officially known as the Louisiana Airborne Memorial Bridge, it was the third longest bridge in the country, and was, ironically, just an hour and a half away from the two longest bridges: the Manchac Swamp Bridge and the Lake Pontchartrain Causeway Bridge, both of which led into New Orleans.

The forbidding landscape seemed to go on forever, and though the road appeared to float a couple dozen feet above the water, some of its pilings had to be driven over 140 feet down before finding stable sand. Getting the material and equipment to the building sites had been an engineering nightmare, but the resulting structure now carried over thirty thousand vehicles across the swamp every day.

"And all of them are on the bridge right now," Flowers groused as she jockeyed past a tandem-trailer semi.

"*G'day, mate,*" came a chipper voice over her speaker. "*In one mile, turn right onto exit 103B, merge onto I-49 and stay on it for eighty-three miles.*"

Flowers grinned. The built-in GPS voice program offered a James Bond British accented voice, or the Crocodile Dundee Australian one, for directions. The Outback seemed more appropriate under the circumstances, and a minute later she was headed north on I-49 toward Alexandria.

She thought about the information from her informant. Standard Laboratory Supplies Wholesalers was in a multi-rental warehouse building on the west side of Alexandria, one of a hundred such complexes in the area. There was no information about SLS online, which was unusual for a commercial venture. The warehouse building came back to a commercial real estate company in Baton Rouge.

Why would Section 17 set up a warehouse to receive animals when they could ship them directly to the training areas? Secrecy, she supposed. But would they go through all this trouble just to transfer animals to one training site? Or was this business being used as a drop for other locations?

She was running blind, and it was frustrating that she couldn't contact the informant for clarification. His emails and texts were dead ends, which meant he was tech savvy as well as cautious—or paranoid. But when dealing with Section 17, it paid to be paranoid.

Don't look a gift horse, or a mutant animal, in the mouth, she thought.

"Blimey, mate! Ya missed your exit!" a voice suddenly shouted.

Flower jumped in her seat and watched as her exit flashed by.

"Well, now you'll have to get crackin' and take the next exit in two miles if you want to get back on track, mate," the electronic voice said.

"How about a warning next time, huh, mate?" She stabbed the volume button, got turned around, then headed west.

Ten minutes later, she was in an industrial area near the airport. After passing fifteen blocks of cookie-cutter single-story metal buildings, Flowers saw the sign for the Ivanhoe Industrial Complex.

The sign out front bore a list of names, presumably of the companies renting space there. Standard Laboratory Supplies Wholesalers was not on the list. She drove down the driveway past the businesses, which lined both sides of the drive. They included everything from pest control companies to laminate flooring distributors. There was even a private security company with a small fleet of patrol cars parked outside one of the mini warehouses. Each had their name displayed either on the door or on the small lobby window.

She continued down the row looking for unit eleven; it was the last space on the left-hand side. There was no sign or markings other than two black plastic "1's" fastened above the front door. There were no cars out front, and reflective tint covered the lobby window.

"You obviously don't cater to walk-up traffic."

She noted the surveillance cameras above the front door and at the top corner. The other businesses did not have them, though a couple had doorbell cameras.

"Hmm, interesting."

She drove around to the back, which had a walk-in door and a roll-up garage door for each business. Unit eleven had surveillance cameras covering that side as well.

Most of the businesses were open, with people and vehicles moving about, but there was no activity at number eleven. Being the middle of the week in the middle of the day, Flowers hadn't expected the place to be closed.

She wondered how often it was used, if there was anything to the tip. Was this a wild goose chase? The information had sounded good, and while the surveillance equipment might mean something, the previous business could have left it behind.

If she knew anything about cameras, she knew she could set one up and monitor the site remotely. She chuckled to herself. This was the FDA not the DEA. They didn't have that kind of equipment. She thought about Frosty Williams, Jessup's old partner and AA sponsor, who had saved their butts by wiring Jessup's boat and her hotel room with video cameras. If it hadn't been for him, they'd both be facing felony narcotics charges.

I wonder if he makes house calls? she thought, smiling.

Flowers pulled around to the front of the complex and parked in the lot. Hidden behind the business sign and some bushes, she pulled out her lunch and Diet Coke, and considered her options.

After she finished her sandwich, she pulled out her flip phone and called Jessup.

"April Flowers," he said. "Getting a call from the Feds is never good."

"Nice to talk to you, too."

"So, how are things in the Big Easy? Made it down to Bourbon Street yet?"

"No, but I made it to Café du Monde for coffee and beignets. Jealous?"

"Oh, my God, that's the first thing I do whenever I go there. It's like a pilgrimage." He was shouting over a whining noise that rose and fell in the background.

"I'll treat next time you come down. What is that noise?"

"That's Davie. He's doing laps around me on his dirt bike. I think he's trying to tell me something."

"Dirt bike?"

"Yeah, it's a big deal out here. I mean, what else are you gonna do in Arizona? It's nothing but sand. Super Donald bought all three of them Yamahas. He's having a ball."

"You're not with Super Donald now, are you?" she asked, an edge of concern in her voice.

"Hell no. He and Paula are at work and Davie's on fall break. I'm using her bike, she never rides it. It's just Davie and me for the next three days."

"How are things between you and Donald?"

"I haven't killed him, if that's what you're wondering, but that's only because I promised you I wouldn't."

"Good. I'm glad you're a man of your word."

"Of course, maiming is still on the table."

"Well, progress, not perfection. Isn't that what you guys say?"

"Very good, Flowers. Stick with me and I'll have you levitating in a lotus position."

"I could use a little good Karma, I kind of hit a roadblock."

"What's up?"

"That tip I told you about, with the warehouse? I'm out here now and there's nothing. No activity, no signs, no vehicles, just looks like an empty business. I'm going to sit on it for a while and see if someone shows up."

"Sounds like a good place to set up a surveillance camera."

"That's exactly what I was thinking. I was going to call Frosty and see if he's up for a road trip."

Jessup laughed. "I guarantee you he'd do it. If you decide to go that route, let me know. We can head that way when I get back in Memphis on Saturday."

"That's a deal. Café au lait and beignets on me."

"Sounds good. Watch your butt out there, Flowers. Just because you're not in DC anymore doesn't mean they've forgotten about you."

"Will do, and don't you break your neck."

He laughed and hung up.

Flowers sat back. She felt better after talking to Jessup. He sounded more upbeat and confident, and she prayed his reclaimed sobriety would stick for good this time.

In DC she had floated the idea of paying Jessup as a private contractor since there were no other agents available to help her, but her boss had literally laughed her out of his office. Now that she was in New Orleans, she'd run it by her new supervisor. But she'd pay him out of her own pocket if she had to.

Vehicles came and went, and by 2:30 she was feeling the effects of the coffee and Diet Coke. She was about to head to a gas station she had passed earlier when a white panel van pulled in and drove past the row of businesses.

Her heart rate kicked up when the truck stopped in front of number eleven and two people got out. She grabbed her binoculars, focused, and her heart rate jumped again. She recognized them. It was the man and woman she and Jessup had seen leaving PIT City.

4

The Bell 206 helicopter came in low over the trees, flared, then landed on the concrete pad, facing west into a light wind. The passenger, in tan cargo pants, a blue, long-sleeved North Face hiking shirt, and a red ball cap with Arkansas Razorbacks on it, jumped out and strode over to two men standing by a four-seat ATV.

Derrick Flattner stepped from the four-wheeler and extended a hand. "Senator Blanton, nice to see you again, sir."

"Derrick, always good to see you," he replied, his campaign smile firmly in place. Then he nodded to the driver. "Dotson."

The short, musclebound man returned a snarl-smile that always reminded Flattner of a grinning alligator. "Senator."

Flattner chuckled at the congressman's discomfort.

Dotson retrieved Blanton's bags and the helicopter lifted off.

"I'll tell you boys what, that's the only way to travel. Beats the hell out of sitting in traffic. You can't just call up a police escort whenever you want, not in an election year, anyway. Bad optics."

"I didn't know we had any green Bells in our inventory," Flattner said as they headed down a gravel road.

"Don't know if we do or not, but that's a buddy of mine, Earl Tanner. Owns Tanner Chicken. You've heard of him, hell everyone has, unless you're a fuckin' vegan. Great guy. Big campaign contributor. In fact, he's going to join us for the hunt with the German ambassador. He's excited."

Flattner lifted an eyebrow. "*Us?* I didn't know you hunted, senator?"

"Hell no, I don't hunt. My cook does all my huntin' at the meat department of the Piggly Wiggly. But I'll be there in spirit. Now," he said, slapping his hands together, "what have you got for me?"

"Gus is waiting for us at the lodge. He's promised to give you a memorable experience."

"Ole Gus is a hoot. You know that man was born and raised on this very property? Been in his family for generations. It was farmland, but he always hunted hogs on it. Turned it into a hunt club when he took over."

"He's an interesting guy," Flattner said. "And he's very appreciative. Getting that additional 300 acres doubled his land, and it didn't cost him a thing."

"Ah, just a useless chunk of Arkansas swamp land."

"Useless' is in the eye of the beholder, Senator. Backs up to his property, perfect environment for raising hogs, and for us, perfect cover."

"Yep, a win-win for everyone." Blanton said, chuckling. "Went from begging, borrowing, and stealing to keeping things going, to having some of the most powerful people in the country begging to hunt his property."

The gravel road opened into a large clearing sprinkled with magnolia trees and massive pin oaks draped with Spanish moss. Tucked between the ancient trees was a two-story lodge constructed of golden oak-colored logs and topped with a hunter green metal roof. A wrap-around porch with half a dozen rocking chairs and a couple of swinging benches framed massive stained-glass double doors.

"Very nice, very nice," Blanton said. "I've seen photos."

Fifty yards to the right was a large barn with a matching roof, and siding stained to match the house. The doors were open and two people were working with ropes and a pulley.

"There's Gus," Flattner said, and they drove over.

As they approached, the two men pulled on the ropes and slowly lifted a large object into the air.

"What the hell is that?" Blanton said.

"*That* is a wild boar, Senator," Flattner said.

"Hmm, it's big."

Flattner chuckled. "No, sir, that's a small one."

"Senator," came a booming voice. "Welcome to the Rebel Yell Hunt Club. I'm glad you finally got to come down and see the place."

Gus Erickson stuck out a beefy hand, then paused and yanked off the bloody glove. He was a stocky, red-haired man with a full beard and a perpetually wind-burned red face. He would have resembled Santa Claus if his hair was white and he wasn't wearing bloodstained camouflage overalls.

"Gus, great to see you," Blanton said, giving the man his special big-donor smile. "Thank you for inviting me. You've got a beautiful spread."

"Well, I have you to thank for it. I'm just glad I can do my part to help keep our country safe."

And your bank account full, Flattner thought.

"What the hell are you doin' back here?" the senator asked.

"Dressing a hog one of our clients shot last night." Flattner and Dotson looked at him, and Erickson held up a hand. "He left this morning. We're going to send it to him on dry ice. The place is all yours until tomorrow. Got the CEO of First One Bank flying in after that."

Erickson motioned toward a lanky boy who was sliding a skinning knife across a large sharpening stone. "You remember my son, Gary?"

"Of course. Good to see you again, son."

The teen nodded, then went back to his chore.

"Man, that thing is huge," Blanton said, examining the dead animal.

Gus huffed. "Nah, this was only 175 pounds before we dressed it. Probably send the customer 120 pounds of meat, mostly ground up into sausage."

"That can't be cheap to ship," Flattner said.

Erickson waved a hand. "That's nothing to these guys. Besides, I'm sure they'll write it all off on their taxes, right, Senator?"

"I would, and I told you before, call me Dirk."

Blanton reached over and touched a wicked-looking curved incisor jutting up from the dead animal's muzzle. "Look at those teeth."

"Those things will ruin your day if you're not careful." Erickson jerked up the pant on his right leg revealing an ugly, foot-long scar running at an angle across his calf. "This is what happened when I wasn't paying attention. Got the video of the hunt on the website to remind myself."

Flattner shook his head. Dotson smiled.

"Looks like you're putting a good edge on that blade, son," Blanton said.

"Gary already cut the skin back from the hind legs before we hung it up. It's easier that way. He's about to pull the entire pelt off in one piece. It's important to have a knife with a good edge. Besides being easier to work with, it's safer. That way you don't have to force it, so you're less likely to slip and cut yourself."

The boy took the newly sharpened knife and cut the skin away from the meat while slowly working it away from the carcass. He cut a couple of slits for handles, then used them to pull the entire pelt down to the head, like a sock. After cutting the meat down to the neck bone, the teen grabbed the head and twisted it in a circle until the spine snapped and the head and pelt dropped away. Then, starting at the groin, he reached inside and used his fingers to push the guts back as he worked the tip of the knife down the belly, opening the chest cavity so the intestines spilled out. That done, he reached in with the knife, separated the internal organs from the cavity, and let them fall to the ground with a *plop*.

Blanton winced a little. "This is not your son's first rodeo,"

Erickson chuckled. "No. Gary's been skinning hogs since he was old enough to hold a knife without cutting himself."

"I'm impressed, Gus," Blanton said as they walked back to the four-wheeler, "but you said this was a small one."

"Over here on the huntin' club side, we got pigs upwards of four, five hundred pounds, Dirk."

"Wow, I didn't know they came that big."

Erickson looked over at Flattner. "You haven't told him about the north side, have you?"

5

Flowers' heart pounded as she snatched up her phone and hit redial. The phone rang six times, then went to voicemail. *"This is Jake. I can't come to the phone right now. Please leave a message."*

Crud, she thought, *he's probably on that motorcycle.*

"Jake, the two people we saw leaving PIT Industries just showed up in a white van. Call me back when you get this message." She clicked off.

They went inside the business, and Flowers read the tag number on the van. "Mississippi?"

She wrote the number down, then snapped a few photos with her phone, holding it up to the lens of the binoculars. She thought about driving past, but she knew they'd recognize her, so she waited and watched.

Ten minutes later, a UPS panel truck pulled in through the lot's other entrance and drove down the loading bay side of the building. She panicked, not sure whether she should watch the van, or see where the UPS truck went. Her gut told her it wasn't a coincidence that the PIT people had showed up just before the delivery truck, so she started up the car and pulled to the other side of the parking lot.

"Yes!" she hissed as the delivery truck backed up to the now-open garage door of number eleven. The driver jumped out and jogged inside. Flowers backed into an empty slot and waited. Five minutes later, the driver got back in and drove off.

Her heart drumming with excitement, Flowers pulled back to her previous spot just as the female suspect came out and walked to the van. At the door she paused and looked toward Flowers.

Though a hundred yards away, in the shade, and slumped down in the front seat of a tiny car, Flowers swore she could feel the woman's eyes lock on hers. She held her breath. A second later, the suspect climbed into the van and drove around to the back of the building.

Flowers fought her panic. Her first solid lead and here she was, conducting a surveillance by herself in an unfamiliar city, following people who knew what she looked like. It was a recipe for disaster, but what else could she do?

Again, she crossed the parking lot, but stopped before the corner of the building. She got out on foot and peeked around the corner in time to see the white van back into the loading bay. She let out a sigh of relief, then wondered what she looked like skulking around. She got back in her car, parked, and waited.

Fifteen minutes later, the male suspect jumped into the driver's seat and pulled the van clear of the building. The garaged door closed. The woman came out, locked the doors, then walked toward the van. As she reached the passenger door, she paused, and once again peered toward the entrance.

"Get a grip, she can't see you," Flowers hissed as she sank further into her seat until she could barely see the van. Her heart slammed in her chest as the vehicle came toward her, and she was glad for the near limo-dark tint on the compact.

She sensed more than saw the vehicle stop next to hers, just feet away. When it didn't immediately pull onto the street, she was sure that the driver and passenger were peering down at her through the window. She stopped breathing. Then she heard the engine accelerate and the tires crunch as it pulled onto the street. Flowers sucked in a breath, sat up and watched the vehicle turn at the corner. She threw her car into drive and went after it.

Surveillance with one car was tough, especially when that one car was a bright red compact that screamed "Look at me!" but she had no choice.

Her heart lurched when she didn't see the van at the main intersection, then she saw it heading up the southbound I-49 on-ramp. She jammed the accelerator, ran a red light, and shot after it. What the little car lacked in stealth, it made up for in peppiness, and seconds later, she was speeding up the on-ramp in pursuit.

Murphy's First Law of Surveillance states that half the cars on the road will look exactly like the one you're trying to follow. Flowers had never seen so many white vans in her life. They were everywhere. She weaved in and out of traffic as she searched for hers.

There it is!

She whipped over two lanes and pulled close, but she saw a magnetic carpenter sign on the passenger door. She passed three more until she finally glimpsed the male suspect in the side-view mirror of one. He seemed as oblivious as he had that day he had driven past Flowers and Jessup while they hunkered down in her old Taurus outside the guard dog training facility. The woman, on the other hand, was sharp, so Flowers backed off and tried to stay away from the passenger side.

They continued south on I-49 for an hour, and Flowers became uncomfortably aware of her need to use the bathroom—another one of Murphy's Laws of Surveillance. She tried not to think about it and was considering some disgusting options when the right turn signal on the van came on.

She backed off, got into the far-right lane, then followed the vehicle down the ramp, keeping a flatbed wrecker between them. The van turned right, then immediately entered a huge truck stop. After working their way through the parking lot, the suspects parked in the fourth slot down from the front door.

Flowers hung back and watched as both the man and woman exited the van and walked inside. They entered the restaurant, and through the window, she saw the hostess seat them at a booth near the back.

She couldn't believe her luck. She parked on the opposite side of the building, went in the side door, then made a beeline to the woman's bathroom, praying the female wouldn't pick that moment to use the facilities. Flowers could see the van through a bank of windows as she entered the bathroom.

As she exited the stall the bathroom door swung open, and Flowers cringed. She relaxed when a woman came in with a little girl. She hurried past them and out the door, then froze. The van was gone.

She ran to the restaurant entrance. The booth was empty.

"No!"

Flowers ran out the side door and sprinted to her car, which was sitting at an odd angle. "No, no, no!" she said as she ran to the passenger side and saw the two flat tires.

6

"What's this all about, Derrick?" Blanton said, sounding annoyed. "Sounds like everybody's in on the secret but me."

The government operative smiled. "Not everybody, just a handful, sir. I think you'll agree it was worth the wait. I'll even throw in a video afterward."

His eyes narrowed. "Will there be night vision?"

"Yes, sir."

Blanton's face lit up. "I love that shit. Let's do it." He started towards the four-wheeler.

"We're not taking that unless you've got a death wish," Erickson said.

Just then, the rumble of a powerful motor filled the late afternoon air as a large tan vehicle pulled around the side of the barn.

"An armored Humvee?" the senator said. "We going to war?"

The driver's door flew open, and Dotson said, "You ready?"

The big vehicle growled as it rolled north along the gravel road, its super suspension transmitting every imperfection in the surface.

"I've bought a hundred thousand of these things through appropriations bills," Blanton said, "but I've never been in one." He glanced at the gun port built into the front passenger side window and the roof opening for a machine gun turret. "What the hell are you growing down here, fuckin' tyrannosauruses?"

"It may seem a little extreme," Erickson said, "but these surplus Hummers are cheaper in the long run. So far, the worst thing that's happened to them is a couple of ripped tires, but they're run-flat, so the guys were able to hobble back to the compound."

"What *were* you using?"

"Pickups and Jeeps. That didn't last long. The first week, we sent two guys to the hospital. Rolled one Jeep completely over."

Blanton stared at him.

The road cut through thick woods, and ten minutes later they stopped at the edge of a narrow clearing.

"Holy cow," Blanton said as he looked left to right. "That's a huge ditch."

Erickson nodded. "Ten feet deep, ten feet wide, dug in a square. Encompasses most of the 300 acres."

"I don't think I've ever seen a cattle guard that big before," the congressman said, noticing the huge, ladder-like device that spanned the opening.

"Custom made. The space between the bars is usually four inches to keep cows and horses from crossing. These are eight inches apart. Bumpy as shit to drive over, but it keeps the things inside." They bounced across, got back onto the gravel road, then entered the tree line.

A few minutes later, they came to a large gravel clearing, a hundred yards in diameter. It was surrounded by shoulder-high brush and grass. At the far side sat a second Humvee.

Blanton leaned forward, squinted, then pointed. "Why are those soldiers standing out there at attention?"

"Those are our volunteers," Flattner said.

"What!" Blanton said.

They pulled closer and he could see that the "volunteers" were actually metal effigies with scraps of uniforms attached to them.

"One inch rebar welded into stick figures and embedded in concrete," Erickson explained. The metal men were lined up about three feet from each other. Some of the thick bars were twisted out of shape. Six-inch pieces of sharpened rebar protruded from around the neck and arms, making them look like porcupine people.

As they watched, two men exited the other Hummer carrying cardboard boxes. They pulled out slabs of meat and speared them onto the pointed protrusions. A third man stood in the gun turret holding an M-16 and watching the tree line.

Dotson caught Flattner's attention and nodded toward the tall grass behind the pretend soldiers. Flattner watched for a second, then saw the brush move in two different locations. The guard was looking in the other direction. Flattner chuckled and shook his head knowing the two men had no idea how close they were to dying.

"I know what that is," Blanton said, nodding at the dripping meat.

"That's regular meat, Senator," Flattner said. "These things eat too much to feed them the special diet. But we've discovered a cost-effective way to deal with that."

Blanton looked puzzled, then said, "What's that black tube near the speaker on the telephone pole behind them?"

"A thumper," Flattner said. "We'll activate it in a second."

"Are we getting out?"

"Uh, I don't think that would be wise," Flattner said.

The senator scowled.

The sight of the fake soldiers standing in a Louisiana swamp in the wanning daylight with slabs of raw meat sticking out at different angles was more bizarre than anything a horror writer could have come up with. It became even stranger when one of the workers took a garden pump sprayer and began coating the statues with a red liquid.

"Is that what I think it is?" Blanton asked.

Flattner nodded. "Yes, sir. Just as effective at a fraction of the cost."

The workers got back in their vehicle, then it backed away, and stopped near the middle of the clearing.

"Why metal figures? Why not just use mannequins like—"

Flattner interrupted the senator before he could say more in front of Erickson. "They tried mannequins, senator, but the animals ripped the plastic to pieces."

"And ate them," Erickson added.

A radio on the dash crackled. *"They're ready to go, Mr. Erickson."*

"Okay, thanks," he replied. He turned to Blanton and held up a small remote control. "Want to do the honors, Dirk? Just flip that switch and twist the dial."

"Open that gun port so you can hear, Senator, and watch the thumper," Flattner said.

Blanton opened his window six inches, then activated the remote. A loud, fast, thumping noise sounded as a green light atop the black tube flashed in sync.

"So, what—"

Three massive animals, each as large as the Hummers, exploded from the brush line and raced toward the metal men. The first one slammed its head against the other vehicle and jerked up. The side of the Hummer lifted a foot off the ground, then crashed back down. Over the radio, the occupants whooped and laughed as the armored car rocked back and forth.

Erickson held up another remote and hit the button. The sound of gunshots and screaming erupted over the speaker, and more of the creatures burst from the tree line.

One ran past their Hummer, its massive, humped body level with the window. Blanton caught the flash of white tusks sticking up from a long, narrow face and slammed the gun port closed.

"Jesus Christ, Jesus Christ," he muttered, his eyes locked on the things.

They ripped the meat from the metal figures like starving men tearing chicken from a skewer. They snapped at each other as they quickly devoured the morsels. Squealing, grunting, growling filled the clearing, and the sounds were as frightening as the creatures themselves.

"They look like frickin' buffalo!" Blanton said in awe.

Erickson barked a laugh. "Yeah, but buffalo don't have twelve-inch butcher knives for teeth."

"How many are there?"

"Twelve," Flattner said.

"A couple of them are smaller," Blanton said, pointing at two animals trying to crowd in from the sides.

"Those are our 'runts,'" Erickson said. "Just eight hundred pounds."

He jerked his head around. "*Just* eight hundred pounds?"

"It happens sometimes," the Rebel Yell owner said. "We remove them to make room for new ones." He smiled. "Makes a hell of a barbeque, I'll tell you that."

"How much do the big ones weigh?"

"Twelve, thirteen hundred minimum. We've got a couple that break fifteen."

"My God."

"You get domestic pigs bigger than that on a farm, but these are killers. Pure-blood Russian wild boars, only three times bigger, four times stronger and five times meaner. The only thing that will stop them is a bullet to the brain."

The creatures made quick work of the meat, rooted around, then whipped their heads through the air, searching for more scent as the thumper continued to pulse. Finding none, they squealed in annoyance. A big brown one trotted to the senator's vehicle and sniffed. It brought its face to the window, locked eyes with the congressman, then slammed its head against the glass, its saber-like tooth scraping the surface and smearing it with the residue of raw flesh and blood.

Suddenly, Erickson smashed his hand onto the steering wheel and the horn blared. Enraged, the giant pig repeatedly slammed its head and body against the Hummer, rocking it on its springs.

"Hang on," he said, laughing.

"Jesus Christ!" Blanton yelped as he clung to the overhead grip.

After a few more seconds, Erickson switched off the thumper and speaker. The animals grew bored and ambled back into the grass.

Blanton took a couple of deep breaths. His hands were trembling.

"What do you think, Senator?" Flattner asked.

Blanton glared at him. "The next time I say I want to tour a project, just shoot me in the head."

7

— • —

Flowers sat in her car, the seat laid back, staring at the ceiling while she waited for the wrecker. Her phone rang.

"Flowers, ya gotta stop stalking me like this. People are beginning to talk," Jessup said. "Hello...? April?"

"Yeah, I'm here," she sighed.

"Uh oh, what happened?"

She told him the story and he said, "Wow, slick move. Do you think they saw you at the warehouse?"

"They must have. I mean, how else do you explain it?"

"Unless they had somebody following the van," he said.

"I don't think that was it. I think she noticed my clown car and kept an eye out for it."

"Well, don't beat yourself up. A one-vehicle surveillance is almost impossible to pull off with just one bad guy driving, let alone with a noisy passenger keeping an eye out. At least you got the tag. That's huge."

"Not so much. It's a rental listed under the company name. Backstopped. A dead end. No traffic tickets, nothing."

Jessup grunted. "Think there's anything at the warehouse?"

"I'm going to check once my car gets fixed, but I'm not hopeful. I have my lock pick with me."

"Man, I wish I was there to go with you. You need to be careful. You said they have cameras?"

"I'll be careful. I'll put on one of these stupid surgical masks."

"Trust me, Flowers, that mask ain't gonna disguise you."

Not sure how to take that, she flushed and said nothing.

"But I agree. If they showed up just before the UPS truck, it's probably just a drop location. I'd wager the place is empty."

"And now they'll stop using it."

"More than likely," he said. "I imagine they have other warehouses they can use. That would be a minimal expense for them."

She heard the rumble of a diesel motor behind her and let out a sigh of resignation. "Here's my wrecker."

"All right," Jessup said. "Do me a favor, call me after you check out the warehouse. Let me know what you find."

She smiled. "Will do. And don't break you neck."

She heard a dirt bike rev high, and Jessup shouted, "Who, me?"

Two hours and four new tires later, Flowers drove back to the Ivanhoe Industrial Complex. The tire salesman had pointed out the low tread on the two remaining tires, so she opted to change them all. She could claim routine maintenance and not have to explain the vandalism when she got back to the office.

It was almost six by the time she got to the warehouse. There was only one car, parked near the front of the building. She drove around the back, past the secured bay door for number eleven, then stopped at the front door. She had thought about pulling off her license plate but figured whoever had flattened her tires had already gotten a good look at her car.

After donning her dust mask, she walked to the door as if she owned the place, inserted the lock pick gun, and clicked the lever until all the tumblers slid into position. She pulled the door open, flipped on the lights, and illuminated an empty facility. There wasn't even a scrap of paper inside. She dropped her head and wondered if she would ever get a break in the case.

Just then, she heard what sounded like a heavy vehicle roll to a stop by the garage door. She listened, then a half minute later it moved on. She flipped off the lights and went to the front window. She looked out in time to see headlights coming from around the back of the building. A large SUV slowed almost to a stop next to her car. She peered out the side of the window but couldn't make out any details as it continued towards the street. After a minute, she cautiously stuck her head out the door. The SUV was gone, and the parking lot was empty.

She thumbed the lock on the door handle and pulled it shut.

As she walked to her car the hairs on her neck suddenly lifted and she felt as if she had a target on her back. She forced herself not to run. She slid behind the wheel, cranked the motor, and pulled to the lot entrance.

The street was empty. She sighed with relief and rolled forward.

Headlights came on in the parking lot two businesses down, and a large black SUV bumped onto the street and turned toward her. Flowers hit the gas, and the little car shot forward with a chirp of its new tires. She ran the stop sign at the corner and floored the accelerator.

In the mirror, she saw the big vehicle slide through the corner and turn in her direction. Heart pounding, she swerved around a car slowing for a yellow traffic light and cut through the intersection as it turned red. She shot up the interstate on-ramp, tires squealing.

She pushed the little car to ninety, then kept one eye glued on the rearview mirror until she was sure she'd lost the SUV. Only then did she slow down and release the breath she'd been holding since she got in her car.

8

After dinner, they went to the conference room. Flattner powered up a laptop and linked it to the sixty-inch monitor on the back wall.

"I'll tell you what," Blanton said as he poured himself a glass of scotch. "I've got a whole new respect for the mascot of my alma mater after seeing that. Stick football helmets on a couple of those bad boys and we'd never lose a game. They ain't nothing like the hogs my buddy raises."

"The smooth pink domesticated pig is just a couple of generations away from feral pigs," Flattner said. "Most people don't know that pigs are not native to the United States. Early settlers brought them over as a food source and later for sport hunting. When domestic pigs escape, they mate with wild pigs and become feral, and since each female can have up to ten piglets, the population has grown to epidemic proportions. It's open season on the animals."

He clicked the mouse and a side view of a large pig appeared on the screen next to a silhouette of a man. The animal came to mid-thigh and was covered with coarse brown and black fur.

"This is an average-size feral pig, Senator," Flattner said. "This one is about two hundred and fifty pounds. They're found in all the southern states, from Florida to California." *Click.*

"This is a wild Russian boar." This pig, positioned behind the first one, was a foot taller and a half a foot longer. A dark brown, almost black, ridge-like tuft of thick fur ran between its shoulders, and white tusks protruded from its elongated snout.

"As you can see, it's stockier and has thicker fur. They are fast, mean, and all muscle. It takes a large bullet, properly placed, to bring one down."

"That looks like the ones we just saw," Blanton said, "only pint-sized."

Flattner nodded. "Yes, sir. This one is only four hundred pounds, but they can grow as big as seven-hundred pounds. As you know, the name razorback comes from the ridge of fur that runs down their backs, like a mohawk."

"Damn right. Go U of A," Blanton said, and took a sip of his drink.

"This is a Tall Grass boar." Another *click* and a third hog appeared behind the first two, dwarfing them.

"Holy shit," Blanton said.

It came to the shoulder of the human silhouette and was two feet longer than the Russian boar. The 250-pound feral hog looked like a baby next to it.

Muscles bulged from beneath its thick fur, and the tusks that jutted up from its narrow snout looked like curved machetes.

"My God, it's enormous," Blanton said, even though he'd just seen them up close an hour earlier. "How big are they?"

"They average five feet tall, ten feet long, and weigh over twelve-hundred pounds."

The senator sat back, then looked at Flattner. "Is this like the pit bulls? You only alter them a little, but the growth is exponential?"

"Yes, sir. Like the others, we genetically tweaked these by twenty-five percent. The growth rate doubles throughout the cycle."

"Jesus," he muttered. "How about the aggression? They seemed pretty pissed off."

"Off the charts. They are literally fearless. Unlike a normal wild boar who will run from humans unless cornered, these animals will charge and attack anything that moves once they're triggered by the thumpers. We think a lot of it has to do with their appetites, they can't seem to get enough to eat. Normal pigs will grow from four pounds at birth to 250 pounds in five to six months. With their increased metabolism, these mutants reach max weight in four months. We bring in feed corn by the truckload and use a front-end loader to distribute it."

"Corn? I thought you used meat, flesh."

"It would take too much meat to keep these things fed. We've stopped using human flesh, even with the baboons and pit bulls. Turns out we don't need it. Regular beef or pork works just fine—if we coat it with human blood, which we can get by the bucket from mortuaries. All that matters is that they associate their food with human scent. In fact, for the hogs, the meat doesn't even have to be fresh. They don't mind if the 'use by' date has expired."

"Huh. That must save a lot of money."

"It wasn't the money, per se; we have the funding. It was becoming difficult to get enough human product, even with the supply chain we had developed. But you are right, it saves a lot of money."

"How do you control them?"

"You don't, you direct them with the thumpers. Just like Pavlov's dog, only instead of a bell, they produce a tone which the pigs associate with food. When we first started the program we moved the thumpers around to train the hogs to find the food, to hunt. Once we established that pattern, we set up the permanent feeding location you saw today. Pigs are social animals, so the new ones quickly learn from the others to associate the thumping with food."

"And the screams over the loudspeaker?"

"We stole that idea from a serial killer movie and added the gun shots. Works great. Gets them excited. Occasionally, we'll dump a load of corn mixed with meat into a remote location, then drop a thumper nearby to make them hunt for it. It only takes them a few minutes. But let me show you a video so you get a better idea."

"Now you're talking," the senator said slapping the table.

Flattner hit the mouse and a night vision video appeared on the television.

"This is drone video footage of an insert."

In the greenish night vision glow, two Blackhawks stopped above the tree-tops and operatives fast-roped down. Body-cam videos populated the screen and seconds later the soldiers assaulted a jungle camp, cutting down their surprised opponents with suppressed weapons fire. After a short, one-sided fight the operatives gathered a large group of young girls from several huts and escorted them through the trees to waiting helicopters.

"That's the Delta rescue of those kidnapped schoolgirls from the Boko Harum site in Cameroon a couple of weeks ago," Blanton said. "Hell of a good op."

"Yes, sir. What you didn't see is what happened to the rest of the terrorists."

He gave him a puzzled look. "I thought they were all killed during the raid, including Jengtang Yusef. I hope that's true. You know how many innocent people that worthless piece of dirt has killed over the last five years? Thousands."

"Yusef's dead, but he wasn't at the site where the girls were being held. He was at his main camp five miles away, along with thirty-five other soldiers. We hit it at dawn."

"Any casualties?"

Flattner gave a tight smile. "Yes, sir, thirty-six."

New drone video appeared showing a large open area surrounded by dozens of huts constructed of thatch, wood, and tin. A couple dozen uniformed soldiers stood around cooking fires. The time stamp read 0607.

"This is Yusef's camp a few hours after the raid on the hostage location," Flattner explained.

A second later, a technical—a small pickup truck with a machine gun mounted in the bed—jerked to a stop in front of a large hut. The passenger jumped out and stormed inside the building.

"Who was that?" Blanton asked, his eyes locked on the screen.

"Yusef."

Nothing happened for about two minutes, then the front door flew open, and a man ran out. Yusef came out behind him, raised a pistol, and fired. The man went down. He attempted to crawl away, but Yusef killed him with a machete.

The rebel leader turned back toward the hut, stopped, and looked in the sky.

A second video appeared on the screen, and in a strange juxtaposition, showed the rebel leader peering up while the other showed an object skimming across the treetops, heading toward the camp.

Soldiers ran for cover as a large quad-rotor drone appeared and zipped across the clearing. In rapid succession, four projectiles shot from beneath it and slammed into the ground, kicking up puffs of dust, then it was gone.

"Those are the thumpers," Blanton guessed, observing the four black tubes staggered across the field, twenty feet apart.

"Yes, sir," Flattner said.

Yusef, hiding behind a technical, barked some orders. A man slowly approached the nearest tube and picked it up. He examined it for a few seconds, then jerked his hand back and dropped it.

"They just activated them," Flattner said.

The man said something and Yusef approached, accompanied by two soldiers.

Three new video boxes appeared on the screen. These were at ground level, with brush and grass rushing by.

"Pig-cams," Flattner said.

Blanton looked at him, incredulous.

The images shifted back and forth as the animals wove through trees and brush. One animal broke through the foliage and smashed into a hut.

On the overhead camera, the building beside Yusef blew apart and a massive boar slammed into the men, knocking the leader to the ground. It flipped one guard into the air, then turned on the other, trampling him.

Blanton jerked back in his chair. "Jesus, look at the size of it!"

Yusef scrambled backward as soldiers ran up and shot at the creature, but it kept attacking.

Two more burst from between the huts and attacked, running the rebels over, throwing them aside, or flipping them through the air like rag dolls.

The pig-cam feeds took on a red hue as everyone still on their feet fired at the creatures. From overhead video, several more soldiers fell, victims of friendly fire as 7.62 slugs flew in a deadly crossfire.

Two technicals appeared from the corner of the screen. The machine-gunners sprayed the animals with .50 caliber round, and seconds later the battle was over.

"My God, they wouldn't stop," Blanton said, as he took in the bodies scattered around the blood-covered clearing.

Suddenly, a pig jerked its head up and sliced open a soldier.

He chuckled. "Guess I spoke too soon."

He pointed at a figure on the screen. "Very impressive, Derrick, but Yusef's still standing. And it looks like he found the cameras."

"We're not done yet, Senator."

Blanton turned back in time to see someone straddling a hog. The man reached down, grabbed the harness holding the camera, and cut it.

Blanton fell back in his seat as three explosions rocked the clearing, blasting red mist into the air.

"Jesus Christ, Derrick, you put explosives in their heads?"

Flattner smiled. "We knew they'd cut off the camera harnesses, so we rigged them with det cord to explode."

Yusef, now splattered with blood, stood over one of the decapitated animals while he and his remaining fighters fired their weapons into the air.

Still watching the screen, Blanton said, "NF-13?"

"Yes. The new strain. Sprayed it on with a pump sprayer en route to the mission. Yusef and the others were dead within two hours."

"Good," the senator growled. "A bullet's too quick for that son of a bitch."

"And there were no friendlies at the base, so no unintended deaths."

"That's a plus, I suppose, but anyone who supports animals who kidnap little girls deserves the same fate."

"Speeding up the efficacy of the bacteria means it's less likely to spread. On the other hand, if you want it to spread..." He shrugged. "It's a trade-off."

"Hmm, I suppose," Blanton said. "Good job, Derrick. Another successful project." Then he chuckled. "I like the irony of using pigs to kill a bunch of Muslim extremists."

"All part of the PSYOPS," the operative said, speaking of the psychological operations aspect used in covert warfare. "Like with Operation PIT, when the Cuban villagers thought Costa Norte was cursed and refused to help the rebels overthrow the government."

"Those mutant dogs were big enough. How did you get these things to the camp?"

"Moving the boars into the theater of action—in this case, Africa—was the biggest obstacle. We crated them up, knocked them out, then flew them in on a C-130. A Blackhawk helicopter has just enough payload capacity to get them into position. Once the quad-drone delivered the thumpers we opened the gates and the pigs headed to dinner."

Blanton shook his head.

"There's no finesse with these things," Flattner said. "They are point and shoot, so-to-speak. But with complete deniability. Anybody coming to the camp will see dead soldiers, the carcasses of dead animals, and a lot of enemy brass, and no sign of foreign involvement."

"What about the thumpers?"

"They're made of cardboard. Each has a small C4 charge woven into them, set to explode fifteen minutes after deployment. All that's left are bits of paper and some unrecognizable electronic components available anywhere."

"Looks like you've thought of everything. Did you get our, uh, New Mexico supply problem worked out?"

"Yes, Senator, Dotson took care of it."

Blanton gave him a smile. "Good job, Dotson."

Dotson returned a snarl-smile but said nothing.

"And we have a couple other projects coming out that will knock your socks off, senator," Flattner said.

Blanton huffed. "Yeah, well, I just had my socks knocked off, literally. I'll stick with the video presentations from now on. Keep up the good work and I'll keep the bean counters off your backs. Now, if you gentlemen will excuse me, I'm beat. But before I fly out in the morning, let's meet for coffee. I want to talk to you about some business-related issues."

9

Later that evening, Dotson knocked on Flattner's door.

"Hey, what's up?" he said, motioning for Dotson to sit.

"April Flowers showed up at our transfer warehouse in Alexandria."

Flattner said nothing for several seconds, then, "Go on."

Dotson explained what had happened, and Flattner said, "She gets transferred to New Orleans and suddenly shows up at one of our warehouses? She didn't waste any time. She saw nothing, but the drop location is burned?"

"Correct."

"This trainer has spotted her twice now. Maybe we need to move her to covert ops."

"Cathy Patton. She's pretty sharp," Dotson said, "But she's too good a trainer. It would be nice to clone *her*. Smart, tough, and almost as good with the animals as Bradley."

"That's saying something. So, back to Flowers. How did she find out about it?"

"There has to be an informant somewhere," Dotson said.

"Who knew about the transfer site?"

"Just the people working at PIT and Tall Grass, and whoever ships out the animals from the lab in New Mexico."

"I think we can rule out the training sites. If it was someone there, they'd just tell Flowers the location of the facility, not tip her off about an incoming delivery. Must be someone at Duogen."

"That would be my guess. Someone with knowledge of delivery locations and schedules."

"Someone in the shipping department, or a computer guy."

"Not a lab tech? They were the ones who complained about producing the animals to begin with," Dotson said.

"They'd be the logical suspects, but they wouldn't know delivery locations and times unless they were working with someone else."

"So, I'll start with shipping or IT."

Flattner nodded. "I'll have Hampton send you the personnel files. Now, what about Flowers?"

"She's leery from getting her tires slashed. A team followed her back to the FDA office in New Orleans."

"What about her phone?"

"We've been monitoring her work cell, but she hasn't said anything about Section 17 on it; she hardly uses it. I'm pretty sure she's using a pre-paid."

"I'd be disappointed if she wasn't. Do we need to put a surveillance team on her?"

"Between site security, putting out fires, and the side projects, we're a little tight on operatives."

Flattner grunted. "All right. Losing the Memphis site was a hit. I don't want any more surprises. Let's make sure we have cameras on all the other pickup sites. We can monitor those from Fort Hood. If she shows up at another warehouse, we'll *have* to take action. A lot of bad things happen in New Orleans. People fall victim to random violence there all the time."

"Some good came out of the move. Bradley's been working with the new animals for a month and he's already doing better with them than our military trainers were after six months."

"So, he's not just a dog whisperer? He's able to work with them *and* the pit bulls at the same time?"

"Yeah. He put Patton in charge of the dogs while he oversees training for both operations."

"What about the other guy? He have problems taking orders from his female partner?"

"Trey Douglas? He's a yes man—no problem taking orders. And he's good with the dogs. Besides, they're all making more money than they ever hoped to make as trainers, so they're happy."

"Okay," Flattner said. "Do we have another place to deliver the animals?"

"We have a warehouse in Lafayette and one in Baton Rouge. That one's closer to the PIT site, but an extra hour's drive for Tall Grass. But all those animals do is eat and sleep, anyway."

Flattner nodded. "Priority number one is finding out where Flowers is getting her information. He or she is undoubtably the one who's been feeding her the information for the last year. In the meantime, I'll try to convince our friend the senator to free up a few million for more manpower."

"A few weeks' worth of toilet paper?" Dotson quipped.

Flattner chuckled. "A million dollars' worth of toilet paper wouldn't touch DC And speaking of the senator, you think he'll bother us about going into the field after today?"

"I think the closest he'll ever want to get to the field will be the lawn and garden department at Home Depot."

10

The following morning, Flowers pulled into one of the FDA slots in the parking garage. She grabbed her computer bag, got out, and looked at the little compact. It was so red it seemed to shimmer in the early morning light. Maybe if she never washed it, the dirt would tone it down, but the thought made her shiver. She was too much of a neat freak to go more than two weeks without hitting the carwash.

As usual, she was the first one in, despite getting back late from her adventure. She hated rush-hour traffic, which, though not nearly as bad as in DC, backed up quickly on the Lake Pontchartrain Causeway Bridge coming into the city. Besides, getting in early she could do her lunch time workout without feeling too guilty.

She flipped on the lights in her new office and looked around. She'd never had an actual office before, just a cubicle. It had been a pleasant surprise, especially since she hadn't known what to expect when she got there. Since she was assigned to a special project, they didn't expect her to help with the division's enormous workload, so she felt like a burden. But her new boss, Special Agent Jamie Reynolds, was cool. She said she didn't care as long as she didn't lose an agent.

Flowers looked from the bare walls to the unopened boxes filled with certificates, photos, and other memorabilia she'd brought from DC. She sighed and opened her laptop. She'd get to the boxes when she got to them.

She brought up the SAAR program Greg Crandall had created, then moaned as dozens of animal-related complaints populated the screen. The Suspicious Animal Activity Report was basically a gigantic database of information gathered from every legally available source on the internet—at least, that's what Crandall had said when she asked where he got the information. The first time she'd asked, he said, "don't ask," but when she got upset and said she wouldn't use it, Crandall told her he was joking and that all the databases he accessed were authorized.

Flowers assumed that meant search engines and social sites, along with law enforcement databases such as NIBRS, the FBI's National Incident-Based Reporting System, along with all the state databases connected to it. She knew he accessed local, state, and federal emergency communications systems. That was how he'd found out about the mutant pit bull attacks in Memphis. What concerned her was that a lot of the information she was looking at appeared to be from private communications, emails, texts, and other computer entries.

She knew nothing on the internet was completely secure. PRISM, the National Security Agency's web crawler, was old news. After that came XKEYSCORE. Now, who knew? The agencies claimed they obtained their information only by court order, but she didn't believe that for a second. They captured everything, then sought a court order only when they needed to use it. And she had never heard of an FISA court denying a request.

Those same three-letter agencies had all courted Crandall for his computer prowess, but he had turned them down. He told Flowers he had ethical problems with spying on the world. Now, however, she wondered if he was using SAAR to tap into those same sources, using data gathered by one secret government organization to track down another—a payback of sorts. It was the sort of challenge that would interest Crandall, but would his ethical misgivings keep him from doing that? And if not, what would happen when they caught him?

She was a third of the way through the 732 entries for the past week when her phone rang. She looked at the screen and smiled.

"Hello."

"You're still alive," Jessup said.

"Check with me in four hours after I've gone through these computer records. How about you? You in a full body cast from your motorcycle adventure, Evel?"

"Nah, I'm good. It's Mesa, Arizona, Flowers. How can you get hurt? The whole damn state's a sand pit. Besides, to break something, you have to fall off."

"Ha! Famous last words. You guys having fun?"

"Yep, we're having a great time. He's doing well; likes his new school, lots of kids to play with in the neighborhood."

"How's he doing as far as the... you know..."

"We actually talked about the kayak trip and why I wasn't a cop anymore."

A twinge of sadness hit her.

"I explained about the government operation and the attempts to cover it up. But I mainly wanted him to understand that there aren't supernatural boogie men in the shadows waiting to get him, that it was just normal animals bad people had trained to be mean. That it wasn't the animal's fault. I'd hate for the kid to be so traumatized he never wants to set foot in a zoo."

"Did you tell him they fired you for trying to tell the truth about what really happened on the Pyatt? That they set you up? That you hadn't been drinking?"

"I did. I also told him that after that happened, I messed up and did start drinking again. And I told him it was my fault, no one else's."

"Was he glad to hear you weren't drinking anymore?"

Jessup chuckled. "I love the way you slid the question in, Flowers. Very slick."

"No, I—" she stammered, turning red. She was glad she was on the phone.

He burst out laughing. "I can read you like a book, Flowers. That's okay. I'm glad to say that I'm still not drinking and that he's glad I stopped. In fact, I've found some great meetings here."

"Good. Speaking of that, any word on getting reinstated?"

"Last I heard, my attorney had taken depositions from Mutt and Jeff about Forester telling them he rigged my urinalysis. He gave the depositions to the Civil Service Commission and is waiting to hear back."

Flowers shivered at the memory of how the two detectives planted drugs on her and Jessup at the direction of their supervisor, Lieutenant Leon Forester, and then charged them both with felony trafficking.

"What did the attorney say about that?"

"Honestly, he's not optimistic. It's hearsay, and he's never seen a firing get overturned based on second-hand information."

"But Forester is dead."

"Like Frosty said, for them to admit that illegal activity took place would open the city up to a lawsuit."

"Is he a good attorney?"

"Yeah, he's really good. I could never afford him. I still can't believe the guys started that fundraising page. It's embarrassing."

"No, it's not. Just smile and be grateful for the help. Besides, all this attention might prevent some other supervisor from trying this again."

"That's a good point," Jessup said.

"How's *Tortuga*, and EZ and Stella?"

"*Tortuga's* still afloat, and EZ and Stella are good, far as I know. When I get back, I'm going to have them over for burgers."

"I didn't know you cooked."

"I microwave, but I do have a hibachi grill attached to the transom. It's big enough for two or three hamburger patties. Besides, anything's edible if you put enough catsup on it."

"Just check the expiration date on the bottle first."

"Spoken like a true FDA special agent," he said. "Speaking of... what's up in secret agent land?"

"Like I said, I'm going through these SAAR records, looking for something that jumps out. You'd be amazed at the number of Big Foot sightings, by the way."

"Not me. I believe."

She snorted. "The business in Alexandria was a bust, like I expected. So, I'm waiting to hear from my source on the next delivery date and location, and I'm submitting another proposal to use you as a paid advisor."

"Tough to justify paying someone when you've got no leads, don't you think?"

"I have plenty of leads," she said, trying not to sound defensive. "I need help sorting them out, that's all."

"Hmm. Well, if it works out, great, just don't put yourself in a trick bag. I'm in good shape here."

Flowers felt guilty. She knew he was strapped for cash and had turned down job offers, hoping to work for GENIT as a contractor. But it was hard getting approval for anything from DC when you worked there, let alone when you were in another state.

"It's going to happen, Jake," she said, trying to convince herself, too. "But nothing happens fast in the federal government."

"Unless they want it to," he added.

"That's true."

"Well, do this, send me some data and I'll go through it on my laptop. That should save you some time."

"I hate to ask you to do that until the funding is in place."

"Hey, Flowers, it's not like it's going to interfere with my busy social life. Send it to me. It'll give me something to do."

"Okay, but remember, it was your idea. This is some boring stuff."

"I'm a boring guy. Send it on."

"Okay. Thanks. Talk to you later."

She clicked off and fell back into her chair. She was torn. She wanted—no, she *needed*—Jessup's help, but what did she have to justify it? Her only physical evidence for the existence of genetically altered animals was a grainy video of what appeared to be giant dogs barking in cages, and there was nothing illegal about that.

The clock was ticking. If she didn't find something soon, she wouldn't have to worry about getting funding for GENIT.

11

Across the field, the distant trees floated on a veil of fog that thinned as dawn broke and slowly warmed the brisk Louisiana air. Flattner had counted twelve deer, three wild turkeys, and a 'possum, but no boars. He knew the highly intelligent, crafty animals spooked easily, which was one reason their population was exploding.

Senator Blanton pushed through the door onto the front porch.

"God damn it!" he said as he sloshed coffee on his pants. "Don't you ever sleep? Next time I tell you to call me when you get up, just shoot me in the head."

"Actually, I slept very well, Senator," Flattner said as the man sat in a rocking chair next to him. "Getting up early is an old habit. Besides"—he gestured towards the forest—"you sleep in, you miss all this."

Blanton grumbled something, then said, "Hell, even Dotson isn't up yet."

"Actually, he was up before me. Just finished his run. He's taking a shower."

Just then, the operative came out wearing combat boots, camo pants, and a black T-shirt that clung to his muscular body like a coat of paint. He looked like a compact Mr. Clean on steroids, minus the earring.

"Senator," he said as he trotted down the stairs and headed toward a black Yukon.

"Jesus, the guy's a goddam machine."

"No arguments there," Flattner said.

"Where is he off to?"

"The new PIT facility. They're finishing up construction on a containment area for a new animal. He wants to do a security check."

"Is that the new animal that's going to knock my socks off?" Blanton asked.

"One of them."

"I've been wondering about that. Why don't you run these projects on military bases? They have built-in security and they rarely get shut down."

"As you know, we use Fort Hood for research, basic training, and viability studies for the animals, but for the actual application—the covert side—civilian sites give us deniability. If one of our operations goes south and they try to trace it back it's easier for us to deny knowledge if they can't tie it directly to the military."

The senator nodded.

"Also, remote locations work much better for the commercial side."

"How so?"

"The people who buy our animals prefer to stay under the radar. It's hard enough to get them into the country, let alone onto a military base."

"Just show them the videos," Blanton snapped. "Hell, they have the word of the U.S. Government backing this up."

"Senator, we're charging these people an ungodly amount of money for something that didn't even exist until we produced it in a lab. You saw the videos of Operation Night Terror and Operation PIT."

"That's my point," he said, slamming a fist on the table and spilling more coffee. "It was damned impressive. If it was good enough for me, it should be good enough for them."

"With all due respect, sir, that was government money. If you had to purchase these animals with your personal money, would a video have sufficed?"

Blanton squinted.

"If I told you we had giant pigs trained to attack the enemy, you'd laugh me out of your office. But if I put you in an armored vehicle and give you a closeup, real-time demonstration of the animals attacking, how many would you buy?"

"I see your point."

"The demonstration we held for that buyer at the new PIT facility last week?"

"That Bolivian plantation owner?"

Flattner nodded. "He didn't blink. Didn't argue about the price. He ordered four dogs on the spot, half a million each, with a fifty percent cash deposit. I don't think he'd have done that based solely on videos and photographs."

Blanton sat back. "Two million dollars?"

"Half of which will go to your off-shore campaign account as soon as we make delivery."

The congressman beamed a smile.

"Plus, we've already gotten two referrals from the deal. That's just the tip of the iceberg—as long as we can keep it off the radar. And that means remote training locations. But, having said all that, I'm arranging for a live demonstration video to show prospective buyers of the Tall Grass animals."

"I?" Blanton said, lifting an eyebrow.

"Dotson's not completely onboard with the commercialization of the projects, so I'm going to handle that myself. That will free him up to take care of the military operations, which are, of course, our primary focus."

"Yes, of course. No question."

"After all, it's the basis for continued federal funding," Flattner said.

"The sole purpose of this project is to reduce military combat casualties," Blanton said, repeating his favorite line, the one he used during closed-door sessions of the Senate.

The senator's phone buzzed. He looked at the text, cursed, then punched in a number.

He put it on speaker and said, "What the fuck do you mean, he's got the votes, James?"

"Berryman took advantage of you being out of town. He tied the project to a border security bill and picked up two more votes from our side. He's ready to send it up to the Senate for approval," his aide said.

"God damn it! That sneaky little bastard. I'll cut his fucking balls off when I get back!" Blanton said, his face red, his hands shaking.

"I'm trying to keep a lid on it and get our people back, but it's not looking good."

"Not with it tied to that funding bill! You were supposed to handle this, James." Blanton stared into the distance, his face a mask of rage. Then he said, "I'll be back in Little Rock in a couple hours. Have the jet waiting. I'm gonna chop some fuckin' heads off for this." He stabbed the screen and threw the phone onto the side table.

"Bad news I take it?" Flattner said.

"Neil Berryman, the Libertarian prick, pushed a bill through the House funding the expansion of the Okaloosa National Wildlife Refuge, turning the surrounding swampland into a no-go zone. He waited until I was out of town to talk some fence sitters in the Senate into supporting it when it comes up. You know what's sitting under that land? About a quarter of all the oil reserves in Louisiana, that's what. And do you have any idea how much money I stand to lose if we can't drill there?"

Blanton's face was beet red, and Flattner wondered if the lodge had a defibrillator.

"They've got twenty-three federal wildlife refuges in this damn state already, every one of them swamp-land full of snakes and alligators. Why do they need another one? The answer is, they don't. This is a political move meant to embarrass me and let the environmental pussies shaft big oil again."

Flattner shook his head. "We actually considered setting up an operation in that area. I'm glad we didn't."

"That fuckin' little prick," the senator snarled. "He needs to walk in front of a bus."

12

Enos Norton threw an old Igloo cooler into the bed of his truck, then grabbed his rifle and a flashlight from the garage. He had two full magazines of .223 rounds for the AR, plus a couple extra boxes of ball ammo. The .223 wasn't as powerful as the 5.56, but if you aimed right, it didn't matter. He stowed the weapon on the gun rack over the back seat and headed out.

Overcast, no moon or stars, he thought glancing at the sky. *Should be perfect.*

He felt confident. There was little chance of running into the fish and game police where they were going. In fact, he couldn't remember ever seeing a Louisiana Department of Wildlife and Fisheries agent outside of Marion. And the ones he had seen were checking fishing licenses, not looking for poachers.

He pulled up in front of Pizza King and tapped his horn. A minute later, a girl ran out wearing jeans and a green polo shirt bearing the store logo. A matching head visor covered the half inch of brown roots in her blonde bob-cut and a jade-colored stone sparkled from the right side of her nose, which was dusted with pizza flour.

She climbed up into the cab and gave Norton a quick peck.

"Hi, baby," he said.

"Hey back," said Georgina Clacker as she crawled in beside him.

He eyed her flour- and pizza sauce-stained shirt. "Tough night?"

"I'm so glad to be out of there," she said snatching the shirt hem and pulling it over her head in one quick move, leaving her sitting on the seat in a lacy pink bra.

"Woohoo! Keep going," crowed Norton.

"Oh, hush," she said. "It's nothing you haven't seen already."

"I haven't seen it enough," he protested as she slipped a black Pearl Jam T-shirt on in its place.

She smiled and tipped the rearview mirror down to check her hair.

"Good thing you did that now. No tellin' what Owen would have done if he'd seen you like that."

"Stay at home and play on his computer, knowing Owen."

"He'd play with something," Norton snickered.

"So, what are we doing? Or should I say, what are you guys doing?"

"I got a line on a place just across the state line where there's supposed to be some huge wild pigs that walk right up to your truck."

"We're going to Arkansas?"

He rolled his eyes. "The state line's only five miles away, Georgina."

"I know," she said. "It just sounds... sketchy. How did you hear about it?"

"Uh, just some guy."

She looked at him. "Some guy, who?"

Norton huffed. "Cleve Pike."

"Cleve Pike? What are you doing messing with him, Enos? He's nothing but trouble."

"I wasn't *messin'* with him. He came into the shop for a new set of tires. I told Dave I knew him and he gave Cleve ten percent off, enough to pay for the spin balancing."

"I thought everybody was getting ten percent off this week?"

Norton grinned. "They are, but he didn't know that."

She rolled her eyes. "And he says it's okay for you to go onto private property and start shooting their hogs?"

"Not exactly. We have to sneak in, but nobody lives there and there's never anyone there at night."

She shook her head. "Still sounds sketchy."

"I can drop you off at your house."

She gave an exaggerated sigh, then she said, "No, I'll go."

Norton smiled.

As they approached Owen's house, she laughed. "Is that a tree standing at the curb?"

Norton pulled up and rolled down the window. "What the fuck, dude? Why don't you just scream 'look at us, we're going to go do some illegal hunting'?"

"What do you mean? There's no season on wild pigs," said his best friend, Owen Boswell. The teen was dressed all in camo and carrying a tricked-out AR-15.

"Uh, do you have a license to hunt them?"

"Well... no."

Norton shook his head. "Get in."

"Hey, Georgina," Boswell said as he crawled past her and into the back seat. After he hung up his rifle, he held up her shirt.

Norton grinned. "Should'a been here, dude."

Boswell fell back into the seat with a grunt. Clacker smiled.

"So, where are we going?" he asked.

"Highway 27 past Clements to the power lines. We follow them five miles to the state line, then cut east for one mile."

"Isn't that Rebel Yell property?"

"Yeah, on the south side, but this place is on the north side."

"We're going into Arkansas?"

Norton just grinned.

"Cool," Boswell said. "That power line trail is pretty rough."

"Whatever. It'll give me a chance to try out my new mud tires."

"Before we do anything else," Clacker said, "let's stop and get some beer."

Norton looked in the mirror at Boswell. "This woman has her priorities straight."

They loaded the cooler with beer and ice at Clements Quik Stop. Norton strapped it in place at the rear vent window, then headed down the highway. At the power lines, they turned north and followed the access road toward Arkansas. It was a rough run, but even in high gear, the twenty-year-old Dodge four-wheel-drive diesel took it in stride.

The state line was a different matter.

"Where is it?" Boswell asked, staring through the windshield, his arms draped over the front seat.

"Right there," Norton said, pointing to where the trees were slightly smaller than the surrounding ones.

"That ain't a fuckin' road," he protested.

Clacker laughed.

"It was...a while back."

"How long's a while?"

"I think the state bushhogs the dividing line a couple times a year," Norton said.

Boswell looked again, then shook his head. "I don't think I'd try it with this puny Dodge." He was a die-hard Chevy man and he loved to tweak his friend.

Norton growled, threw the lever on the transfer case into low, and the truck lurched forward.

The first twenty feet were touch-and-go, but away from the power line clearing where the sun didn't reach, the vegetation thinned out and they were able to make out a trail. Still, Clacker squealed, and shouted "Woo-hoo! Ride 'em cowboy!" as the cab of the truck rocked back and forth through decades-old tire ruts.

After a mile of bone-jarring action, they came to a gravel road that cut north and south.

"So, this side is Rebel Yell property, right?" Boswell said, looking south.

"Hey, dude..."

Boswell turned and Norton flipped the spotlight on in his face.

"Argh, you motherfucker! You blinded me!" Boswell yelped throwing up his hands in front of his eyes.

Clacker barked out a laugh, then turned away in case she was next.

"That's what you get for doubting the power of MOPAR."

"Yeah, well," Boswell said, rubbing his eyes, "we'd have gotten here twice as quick in my truck."

"Whatever," Norton said. He turned left and entered the forest.

13

The headlights lit up the woods for twenty-five feet, but beyond that everything was a black void.

"It's creepy," Clacker said. "I can't see anything except trees and bushes."

"Want to see creepy?" Norton reached down and flipped off the headlights. Complete darkness enveloped them.

"Man, it is dark as a tomb out there," Boswell said.

"You've never been in a tomb," Norton said, unable to see even the mirror to look back at his friend.

"I've seen 'em in movies and this is how dark they are."

"Give it a second and our eyes will adjust," Norton said.

They waited, and sure enough, impressions of the gravel road and the surrounding vegetation soon took shape.

"Georgina, trade places with Owen so he can shoot from the side window when we get to the hogs."

With a grumble, Clacker started crawling over the seat.

"You could just open the door and get out," he said.

"I'm not opening that door! Who knows what's out there?"

"We got rifles, Georgina," Boswell said as he slid the two weapons, muzzle first, onto the front seat.

"Yeah, well, I've seen plenty of movies, too," she snapped. "Where stupid people park in the middle of the stupid woods in the middle of the stupid night then open their stupid door and get snatched by some stupid monster!"

The two boys burst out laughing.

Norton pulled forward and said, "Cleve said you go down this road for a half mile to another road, then turn left. He said the hogs are another half mile from there, in the low area, after you cross a cattle guard."

"A cattle guard?" Boswell said. "What good is that gonna do? You can't keep hogs fenced in."

Norton shrugged. "There's the crossroad."

He turned left and followed it until they came to the cattle guard.

"Holy shit," Boswell said, stabbing his flashlight out the passenger window. "Look at that ditch."

Norton grabbed his spotlight and lit up the excavation. "That's why they don't need a fence. You ever seen anything like this?"

"Hell, I've never *heard* of anything like this. They must have some prime pigs in here."

"This is getting sketchier and sketchier," Clacker said. "I don't like it. I mean, why would someone *raise* wild pigs? It's not like there's not enough of them already."

"Yeah, but these are big pigs. Cleave said some of them are four or five hundred pounds."

"Cleave Pike is full of shit," she said. "I wouldn't trust him as far as I can throw him. And why would he tell you? Why wouldn't he keep it to himself?"

"Cause we're neighbors. We grew up together."

Clacker snorted. "Cleave is two years older than you and bullied you your entire life."

"At least until you hit him with that chair in the cafeteria," Boswell said. "That was awesome."

"I don't know why he told me," Norton said. "But he did and we're here now. I'm going in." He turned to Clacker. "You can wait here, and we'll pick you up on the way out."

"There's no way I'm waiting out here by myself!"

"Then here we go."

As they rumbled across the bridge, Boswell said, "I've seen plenty of cattle gates, but I've never seen one this big."

They went up a slight rise, then the road began to slope down. "The further down we go, the swampier it will get. That's where they'll be," Norton said.

"You just keep it between the trees, and I'll watch for the hogs," Boswell said.

Norton looked in the rearview mirror. "Awful quiet back there, Georgina."

She was huddled in the back seat and she peered into the gloom, her eyes narrow, arms wrapped around her knees. "I've got a bad feeling about this place, Enos. I think we should turn around."

"Come on, baby, we're here," he said.

She glared at him.

"Ok, we'll go another hundred yards down the trail and if it doesn't open up, I'll turn around and we'll go home, okay?"

She nodded, then turned away.

· · · ● · ● · · · ·

Corporal Albert Randal heard a chirp, looked up from his cell phone, and saw a light flashing for the Tall Grass facility. Suddenly his phone announced, *"Waah, waah, waah!"* He held it up and saw a leering green goblin dance across the screen.

"Damn it," he said, tossing the phone down. "Fuckin' pigs. Almost had level 132."

He tapped his keyboard and brought up the game camera that covered the cattle guard leading into the preserve. A green-tinted night vision scene appeared, showing the metal bridge and the gravel road leading into the trees, but nothing else.

"Nothing, as usual," he mumbled. The boars rarely went into that part of the compound, preferring to stay in the swampy area to the west unless they were scavenging. Not that it mattered, where would they go? They couldn't cross the moat and they wouldn't make it five feet across the cattle guard before they broke a leg. They weren't going anywhere. As far as he was concerned, this whole setup, with its twenty-five solar-powered game cameras, was a waste of money.

It only got interesting at feeding time, and every time he saw that, he was glad he worked in the comm center four hundred miles away. Let the civilians deal with those things. Those Louisiana rednecks grew up hunting hogs. It was just another day in the woods for them.

He entered the alert in the log. He'd already made one entry, after a branch fell and blocked the camera at the back entrance. It happened occasionally, and when it did, he emailed the hunt club, advising them so they could clear it. It always took them a day or two, though. They were on civilian speed, not military, that was for sure.

He moved the cursor to the column marked "Animal ID Number" and hesitated. He could just pick one. He had a list of all the numbers next to the embedded trackers codes. *No, do it right*, he thought. *Bring up the tracker program and see which one it was. You're not some fuckin' civilian.* He glanced at his phone. *But first, level 132.*

14

— · —

Around the next bend the trees thinned, and they came to a large clearing.

"See, I told you."

The expanse was about a hundred yards across, surrounded by a sea of chest-high grass and shrubs.

Boswell shone his light out the window. "I don't see anything. Your old-ass backfiring truck must have scared them off."

"Diesel motors can't backfire, dick wad. We'll just sit for a minute, they'll come back out, then, *ka-pow!* We won't even have to get out of the truck except to toss it into the back."

Boswell held his flashlight out the window and moved it across the clearing. "What's that?"

· · · ● ● · ● · · · ·

"Whoo hoo," Corporal Randal yelled as a lightning bolt flew down and blasted the green goblin from his phone screen. "Level 133, you're next. But first, pig patrol."

He punched up the animal tracker program and waited for it to populate.

Randal liked working for the Special Projects Animal Assets Division—once you got past the selection process. The baboons were scary, but they were nothing compared to the pigs. With the monkeys, at least you had a padded suit to protect you. Nothing would protect you against these things. He was glad they had put him in communications.

It had surprised him to learn that Tall Grass, as well as two other animal assets, was an all-civilian project, and SPAAD was only involved in the logistics. It didn't make sense to him, but if it kept him from having to deal with the creatures directly, he was good with it.

He wondered what they paid the guys to work with the hogs. It had better be a lot. You could somewhat control the other animals with shock collars and water hoses, but those things? Once they started feeding, they didn't stop until they're full—or until they ran out of food.

He remembered when, six months back, one of the big ones ran out as a couple guys were loading meat onto the metal men. It sliced one open and impaled the other onto a piece of rebar. The guy who got cut made it back to the Humvee, but the other guy hung from the metal spike like a screaming scarecrow while the hog ate him alive. The screams acted like a thumper, and within seconds half a dozen of the monsters were fighting for a piece of the guy.

The tracking program showed all the pigs were in the western quadrant, a quarter mile from the cattle guard.

"Huh, that's weird. What set you off?" *Probably a deer,* he thought. Besides the pigs, they were the only things tall enough to trip the beam. He brought up the cattle gate camera, rewound it to just before the alarm tripped, then pushed play.

"Oh, crap!" He snatched up the phone. "Lieutenant, get to the control room quick!"

· · ● ● ● ● ● ● ● · ·

"They look like statues or something," Norton said edging the truck forward. "Weird rebar stick men painted red."

Boswell chuckled. "Whoever owns this place must think he's an artist."

"Well, I hate to tell him," Clacker said, "but that's some ugly shit."

"Dude, shine your light on the ground," Norton said.

Boswell lit up his side and whistled. "Those are some monster pig tracks."

"I told you," Norton said excitedly. "We are going to be in pork heaven. All we have to do is sit and wait for them to come into the open."

"I need another beer if we're gonna wait," Boswell said. "Hey, Georgina, can you reach out the window and grab me one from the cooler?"

"Enos, you said we were going to leave," she replied, staring at his reflection in the rearview mirror.

"Come on, baby, we drove all this way. Just ten minutes, okay?"

She blew out a sigh.

He grinned at her in the mirror, and said, "Can I get a beer, too?"

Clacker rose to her knees and stuck her head through the back hatch. She fell back into the seat and crossed her arms. "I can't reach the cooler. The bungee came loose. It slid to the back of the bed."

Norton turned to Boswell. "Guess you're up, Kemosabe."

"Me? You wanted one, too."

"Yeah, but you wanted one first, and it's my truck, so my rules."

Boswell shook his head, leaned his rifle against the dash, and stepped outside. He walked around to the back and a second later the cooler latch opened with a loud *snap*. Norton winced at the noise.

Boswell stuck his head back in the cab, tossed Norton a beer and said, "I'm going to check out the artwork."

• • • ●•● ● • • •

"What's up, Randal?" Lieutenant Walter Culligan said as he entered the communications room.

The corporal pointed at the screen.

"Shit." Culligan watched the truck enter the restricted area. "How old is this?"

The kid hesitated, then said, "Twenty minutes."

Culligan's eyes widened. "Bring up all the cameras, live feed," he barked, then he pushed a speed dial button on the phone. It rang twice.

"Dotson."

"This is Lieutenant Culligan. We have an intrusion at Tall Grass."

"What do you have?"

"Pickup occupied three times. Looks like kids. There in the feeding area."

"Hang on, I'm bringing it up," the government man said. "Any idea who they are?"

"No, none."

"Why am I just now getting a call? It would take them twenty minutes to get that far in."

"Uh, we're looking into it. Maybe an equipment malfunction," the supervisor said, trying to cover for his man.

"Yeah, well, we'll talk about that later," Dotson said.

"Should I call the hunt club so they can send someone?"

"No. By the time they get a Hummer, it'll be too late."

"Well... what do we do?" Culligan said.

"Watch... and make sure all the cameras are recording."

• • • • ●•● ● • • •

"Just get back in the truck, man," Norton said, but his friend was already gone. Maybe it was Clacker's paranoia rubbing off, but he was starting to get the creeps, too. He'd give it five more minutes, then they were out of there.

When you're out in the woods, the cacophony of noise from the insects and frogs quickly blends into the background and doesn't register—until it stops. Just as Boswell reached the metal men, the forest went silent.

The hairs on the back of Norton's neck rose.

Boswell paused and looked around, then he shrugged and examined the figures.

The grass on the far side of the clearing shifted, as if something were moving through it. Norton felt a quiver of fear and excitement. He slowly lifted his AR15 and pulled the charging handle back an inch to make sure a round was chambered.

He tracked the movement, which was barely a shifting of lighter and darker shadows. Boswell was in front of the truck, so he couldn't hit him, but if Norton fired without warning, it would scare the crap out of him. Norton thought that might be kind of funny. He stuck the barrel out the window.

"Hey, Enos," Clacker whispered from the back seat. "There's something out there."

"Yeah, I know. I'm about to kill it."

"No, not over there. Behind you."

He turned and followed her gaze. On the other side of the clearing, the grass and brush were moving in several places. He shifted back to his side and spotted even more movement.

He went to jab the truck's horn when Boswell jerked his head up and shouted, "Hey man, this ain't paint, it's blood."

15

On his laptop, Dotson watched the pickup pull into the clearing. He grabbed his phone and sent a text. GET ME A HELICOPTER TO TG.

The response said, CHECK. ETA TWENTY MINUTES.

Over the speaker, Culligan muttered, "Oh, shit. One of them's getting out."

Dotson watched the passenger exit and retrieve something from the bed of the pickup.

"Looks like beer," he said.

After tossing a can to someone inside, the passenger walked over to the metal soldiers.

Get back in the truck, you little asshole, Dotson thought, shaking his head.

The brush and grass bordering the clearing shook like a wheat field in a windstorm and a gigantic brown head lifted from the tall grass.

"Shoulda got back in the truck," Dotson said.

• • • ● • ● ● • • ·

The head of a huge boar rose above the brush. Clacker screamed and Norton dropped his beer. Boswell followed the spotlight, and his eyes went wide. Norton jammed down on the horn and lit his friend up with the headlights.

The monster boar burst from the foliage and charged Boswell, snorting and squealing with excitement. The young man sprinted for the truck, but his seven miles per hour was no match for the animal's thirty. Just as he touched the door handle, the pig caught him with a ten-inch tusk and flipped him through the air like a dishrag.

Boswell crashed onto the windshield, cracking it and splattering blood from a gash across his thigh and buttocks. The dying teen looked through the windshield at his friend, his eyes wide from shock, his mouth open in a silent scream.

Clacker's scream was not silent and competed with the blare of the truck's horn. Three more of the gigantic creatures ran from the tree line and charged the truck, lured by the cries.

Like a magician jerking away a tablecloth, a boar snatched Boswell by the foot and yanked him off the hood. The boy found his voice, but his scream lasted only a second as the other animals trampled him.

Two charged the driver's side. Norton jammed the truck into drive, stomped the gas, and the mud tires dug grooves into the gravel pad. One pig hit the bed of the truck and slammed it sideways against the metal men, which kept the vehicle from flipping over. The cooler flew across the bed, hit the other side, and slung beers and ice through the air.

Norton jerked the wheel to the right to avoid hitting a pig, but another crashed into the passenger side, spinning the truck a hundred and eighty degrees, and pointing them toward the gravel road. He yelped with glee, hit the accelerator, and fishtailed away. Clacker was still screaming.

They left the clearing and hit the gravel road at break-neck speed, the headlights strobing off trees as they slewed from side to side. Clacker suddenly stopped screaming and Norton jumped in surprise. He glanced in the mirror and saw her bolt upright in the seat. Her eyes were wide with horror and staring straight ahead.

"We're going to make it, baby," he shouted above the roar of the big Cummins diesel. *357,000 miles and still going strong.* All they needed was one more mile.

He looked in the mirror and saw several of the hogs chasing them. They were fast, but he was pulling away. Suddenly, a huge shape appeared on his right and slammed into the bed, knocking the big truck sideways into the trees. Unable to brace himself, he felt like a pinball hitting a double flipper.

Norton shook his head to clear it, heard the old engine still running, and stabbed the gas pedal, praying the transmission and gearbox would hold. He got back up to speed, and once again watched the hogs recede in the mirror.

The cattle guard came into view and he grinned.

· · • ●•● ● • • ·

"We have to do something!" Culligan said panicking.

"A little late for that, Lieutenant," Dotson replied.

They watched the old Dodge pickup tear away from the clearing, pursued by the enraged animals.

A boar slammed the truck into a tree, but the driver kept going.

"Damn, kid, are you any relation to Jake Jessup?" Dotson muttered.

"They're gonna make it!" Culligan said as the vehicle approached the cattle gate.

Dotson shook his head. He knew that one way or the other, those kids were not going to live through the night, not after seeing the animals.

· · · · ●·●· · ·

"We're gonna make it, Georgina!" Norton said looking in the rearview mirror. When he turned back, he saw a boar the size of the truck blocking the road.

Enos Norton never paid attention to physics during high school science, it just wasn't cool. So, he never really understood the forces involved when a mass traveling at a particular speed stopped instantaneously. If he had, he might have been wearing a seat belt, which also wasn't cool. And though his vision was obscured for the 1/25 of a second it took for the airbag to deploy and deflate, he got another physics lesson as he watched his girlfriend fly past him and smash into the windshield.

When he came to, Norton was on his back on the roof of the overturned truck, unable to move. He panicked, thinking he was paralyzed, before he realized he could move his arms and legs. He pushed away the obstruction, and Clacker's pretty, blood-streaked face flopped onto his chest, her head canted at a strange angle.

Norton screamed and scrambled from beneath her. A chorus of grunts and squeals rose from outside, and the truck shook and rocked violently as the hogs tore at the dirt trying to get to him.

He pushed the deflated airbag out of his way and stared into a giant eyeball. With a squeal of excitement, the giant boar jammed its snout through the driver's window. Norton jerked his legs back as enormous jaws snapped shut on empty air. He kicked and scrambled over his girlfriend's body as the metal frame groaned. The pig lunged again, grabbed the woman's foot and jerked back.

"No!" he screamed and grabbed her arms. In a mismatched tug-of-war, the thing yanked Clacker halfway out of the cab. Norton slammed a boot into its snout, but it was like kicking a tree stump. He wedged himself against the steering wheel and gave a mighty heave. Her foot broke free of the creature's grasp, but the momentum drove him back into the passenger door. The truck rocked again as another pig drove its snout into that window, knocking Norton off balance and making him drop Clacker. He screamed in horror as the first pig reached back in, grabbed her leg again, and jerked the teen through the driver's window in one quick motion.

"Georgina!"

"Oh, shit!" he said as another hog jammed its face into the opening. As he scrambled for the rear access window, his hand fell on the stock of a rifle. He snatched it up and crawled into the space under the bed of the overturned truck.

The pigs continued to squeal, grunt and root at the cab as they searched for him. He wondered if he remained still if they would forget about him and move on. His question was answered when one of them slammed into the truck and knocked it sideways several feet. Norton yelped, and that was all they needed to home in on him.

They came at him from both sides, digging frantically, trying to burrow under the truck bed. Norton flipped the AR15 to fire and shot at snouts as they appeared. The creatures squealed and screamed in pain and outrage and slammed their massive bodies against the truck. Norton was pummeled as the chassis swung back and forth like a tetherball. He dropped the rifle, and it disappeared in the dirt as the truck pivoted around.

The pigs came at him from three sides. Norton crawled back into the cab as quietly as he could and pushed through the broken windshield as the animals continued to burrow under, unaware that their evening snack was crawling away.

He crawled forward for several feet, looking for something to climb, but the pine trees rose twenty feet before the first limbs appeared. He was close to the road and the cattle gate wasn't too much further. With a little luck...

He stood, took three steps, then his foot fell on a dry branch.

Crack!

The pig's heads jerked up like a dog hearing the mailman.

"Fuck!" He hissed.

The porcine pack scrambled after him, grunting, snorting, and squealing with excitement. The sound spurred Norton on with newfound energy. He crashed through the brush, hit the gravel road running and saw the bridge, ten feet away. He was going to make it.

He lunged forward, then his eyes registered the oversized gap between the bars. In a split second, his brain involuntarily calculated the chances of successfully running, panic-stricken and at full speed across a ladder in the pitch black and it told him he wouldn't make it.

He tried to slow, but his feet slid on the gravel. Just as he got to the barrier, he picked a rung and sprang forward. His foot landed true, but he was thrown off balance. On his next step, his boot slipped on the rounded surface and fell through the eight-inch gap. Physics once again came into play as momentum drove his body forward, but the steel bars kept his left foot in place. There was a *crack!* as the bone snapped, and he slammed face first into the bridge.

Norton's screams excited the drift of pigs as they gathered at the edge of the cattle guard, snorting and squealing and growling, their evening meal sitting just out of reach. A couple ventured forward, then yelped and jerked back as their hooves slid through an opening.

Then the largest of them slapped a massive hoof onto the second rung. The rusted surface provided friction, and it leaned forward with its long, narrow snout.

Norton, in shock from pain, fatigue, and the horror of the night, could do nothing but watch as the animal latched onto his shattered foot and jerked him back into the compound.

· · · · ●·●· · · ·

Dotson watched the big pig run in front of the speeding vehicle. The camera was perfectly positioned, and while there was no sound, he could imagine the impact as the boar was knocked off its feet and the back of the truck lifted from the ground, its forward progress stopped almost instantaneously.

Airbags exploded and what looked like blond hair smacked the inside of the windshield. The hog was flipped to one side, while the truck flipped to the other.

The hog would be sore, but he didn't think it would die. The things were like organic tanks. He once asked Gus Erickson what he thought it would take to put one down. Almost reverently, the man said, "One of the big ones? Besides a .458 Winchester Magnum, I don't know. And even then, you better hope he's standing still and you're right with your maker."

The overturned truck was out of camera range, but Dotson assumed the occupants were dead from impact or had been eaten. A minute later, however, he saw a young man dart from the tree line and sprint for the bridge.

"Go, kid, run!" he heard Culligan shout over the speaker.

When the kid slipped, smashed against the cattle guard, and threw back his head, Dotson thought he could almost hear the scream though he was a hundred and twenty-five miles away.

"Get up, kid!" came the other voice.

When the pig grabbed the boy's foot, Dotson shook his head in pity.

"Goddamn it," Culligan said, "we should've done something."

"If your people had been doing their job, Lieutenant, we might have gotten there in time to run them off. Their deaths are on you," Dotson growled. "Now,

I'm going to go there and clean up this mess. Then after that, you and I are going to have a face-to-face and I expect a full account of what happened." He hung up without waiting for a reply.

16

— • —

"What happened, Mr. Erickson?" Dotson said over the prop wash pushing them toward the waiting Humvee.

"The kids lucked up on the spot is all we can figure," Erickson said as they climbed in.

Montel Ruderman, Erickson's foreman, was in the back seat. "Dotson," he said, as the government man jumped in the front passenger seat.

Dotson glanced at him, then said, "Which way did they come in?"

"The state line," Ruderman said.

"How'd they get past the cable?"

"They cut the lock." Erickson held up a padlock with a cut hasp. "Found it on the ground."

"And the camera and alarm?"

"Just bad luck there. We had some rough weather yesterday. Must have knocked down a branch; it was covering the game camera. We got an email from your communications center telling us about it. We were going to fix it when we did the feeding tomorrow, or... well, I guess, today, now."

Dotson peered at him. "Show me."

Erickson drove to the access road that led from Rebel Yell to the Tall Grass facility.

Dotson looked at the cable lying across the gravel road, then at the now exposed game camera. "What was blocking it?"

"Just a leafy branch," Ruderman said. "I tossed it into the woods back there. Why? Did you need it?"

Dotson ignored his question and got out with a flashlight. He studied the trees surrounding the camera. "I don't see any breaks from a branch coming off."

"I don't know what to tell you. It was pretty windy. It could have blown in from further away, or fallen from high up in the tree," the foreman said.

Dotson looked further, then noticed a clean stub where a branch had recently been cut from a small oak tree. He got back into the vehicle but said nothing about it.

They drove to the ditch and stopped in front of the cattle guard. The gravel on the opposite side was stained red and churned up as if someone had gone over it with a tiller. The blood looked black in the headlights.

"Get someone in here tomorrow and smooth that out, then drop some more gravel on it."

"I'll take care of that," Ruderman said from the back seat.

They pulled even with the overturned truck and Erickson lit it up with a spotlight mounted on the roof of the massive four-wheeler. Here, too, the ground was churned up and stained red.

Dotson got out with his flashlight. Erickson and Ruderman looked at each other but said nothing. While the government man searched, the foreman pointed his rifle out the gun port but remained inside.

Dotson picked up a rifle from the ground and sniffed the breech. The barrel was bent. He tossed it on top of the truck then got back into the Hummer.

"Whoever they were, one of them got off some shots. When we're done, check the tracker software for any animals that haven't moved for an extended period."

Ruderman huffed. "An AR won't do much damage, not to these things."

"It will if he was under the truck shooting them point blank in the face," Dotson said. He flicked his fingers straight ahead. "Let's go."

They continued down the gravel road until the trees opened up. They came around the edge of the tall grass and the headlights lit up half a dozen giant pigs gathered around a large object in the middle of the clearing.

"Holy shit," Erickson said. "Would you look at that? They're eating one of their own."

As they watched, the hogs grunted and snorted and jostled each other as they ripped chunks from a dead boar. Half of the animal was already gone, stripped to the bone in some places.

"Jesus," Ruderman muttered.

"Do you have any idea what each one of those animals is worth?" Dotson asked.

When neither man answered, he said, "That had better be the only one."

He looked at Erickson. "Get me back to the helicopter. At first light, bury that truck."

• • • ● • ● • ● • •

Dotson pushed through the front door of the SPAAD Communications Center, leaving behind a shaken Lieutenant Walter Culligan and a soon-to-be Lance Corporal Albert Randal. Culligan had started to argue about his soldier's demotion until Dotson told them he had considered charging them both with involuntary manslaughter and neglect of duty.

His primary concern, though, was determining whether they were a part of the conspiracy to lure the trespassers onto the property. Dotson had run the license plate and done a background on the driver. A seventeen-year-old senior in high school, decent grades, no problems with the law other than a runaway complaint when he and two friends went to New Orleans to watch a concert. He was sure those two friends were the other victims. They weren't professional poachers; they were kids. And he seriously doubted they cut the lock on the cable to gain entry into the compound.

The state line entrance camera was blocked an hour before they showed up. He reviewed the footage just prior to when the branch covered the lens. There had been no bad weather, just a flicker of a light coming from the direction of the hunting camp. Someone had orchestrated this entire incident, he was sure, but why?

Then it hit him. It was a demonstration. They had the Boko Harum operation to prove the concept worked, but that was classified. They couldn't show it to civilians, to their commercial customers.

Dotson knew Flattner was pushing hard to monetize the programs, reaching out for potential buyers outside the US government. He didn't like the idea, but he understood the reasoning. Washington DC was like a spoiled, vindictive child. One day rational and eager to please, and the next throwing a tantrum and breaking all his toys. To keep Section 17 up and running, they might one day need alternative funding.

But it had to be done with care and reason, with the main goal of protecting the lives of military personnel—not turning a profit. And though Flattner professed that same goal, Dotson was beginning to have his doubts.

· · · · ●·· ● · · · ·

Derrick Flattner rubbed his eyes and turned away from his computer monitor to watch a rower slice through the flat surface of the Anacostia River. A year ago, it would have been him sculling past multi-million-dollar office buildings at dawn instead of sitting inside an office wading through files. Running Section 17 came with a loss of freedom, and while it had its perks, it wasn't nearly as much fun. But such was the war on terror.

His phone buzzed. It was a video attachment. He clicked on it.

Fifteen minutes later, he called a number.

"Is your phone secure?" he asked when the person picked up.

"Yep."

"Very impressive. Exactly what I was looking for. Who are—or were—they?"

"Just some kids who won't be missed. They ran away last year, so everybody will think they did the same thing this time."

"And the vehicle?" Flattner asked.

"In the ditch, back where nobody ever goes. We'll bury it after we get the backhoe repaired."

"And the bodies?"

"What bodies?"

"Excellent work," Flattner said. "Who else knows about this?"

"On my end, just me, Gus, and his foreman, Montel Ruderman. I don't know about your people. I know they had to be watching it unfold. It would have been nice if there had been a way to disable the server and kill all the feeds."

"I'll look into that, and don't worry about my people," Flattner said. "What about the one who set it up, this Pike guy?"

"He just told them where to sneak in to get some big hogs. He doesn't even know if they actually showed up."

"He's going to know something happened when they're reported missing."

"Pike won't be a problem. He's a very eager employee. They ran away once, he'll buy that they did it again. But if it becomes a problem, I'll take care of it."

"Very good. I'm impressed. I'll make sure Gus gets you that bonus we discussed."

"Thank you, Mr. Perkins."

"I'll be in touch."

Flattner hung up, then replayed the video of the three teens being attacked and killed. The operation had turned out well, and this would be a great advertisement for their private buyers.

He smiled. It felt good getting his hands wet again. Maybe the next time he would take a more direct role.

17

April Flowers was a third of the way through the latest SAAR entries when her phone chimed with a video call. She looked at the screen, sagged in her chair, then pushed the button.

A stern face with a strange nose and long black eyebrows flashed onto the screen.

"Greetings, Earthling," said the voice behind the nose.

"Hi, Greg," Flowers said, forcing a smile. "What's that on your face?"

"Cool, huh?" he said, pulling off the fake nose. It had attached eyebrows that jutted out like angel wings. "Just got them today. Silicone tinted to my skin tone. Got a pair of ears, too." He held up long flaps of rubber that folded over like limp pasta. "Big Star Trek convention this weekend. Several of the original cast are going to be there."

"Sounds like fun. I hate that I'm going to miss it," Flowers said.

"Just say the word and I'll send in a fake request from headquarters for an emergency meeting. I can have you on the next flight out of Orleans."

She started to speak, then peered at the screen. "Greg! What happened to your eyebrows?"

His pupils swiveled upward. "Oh, heh, heh. Shaved 'em off. I would look kind of stupid walking around with two sets of eyebrows, wouldn't I?"

Flowers had no words.

"Anyway, say the word and I'll get you here." He gave her a hopeful smile.

She took in the dyed black hair, bangs cut straight across his forehead, mirroring the famous space alien, then said, "I would if it were any other weekend, but there are a couple of leads I have to follow up on from the SAAR reports." She hoped the lie sounded sincere.

"Oh?" He leaned toward the screen and whispered, "More mutant pit bulls?"

She gave a nervous chuckle and looked over her shoulder. "You never know with this stuff."

"Well, I found something. It's not directly animal related, but it's interesting." She sat up.

"Three teenagers went missing in northern Louisiana a few days ago."

"What's so strange about that?"

"According to one parent, they left about ten o'clock at night to go hunting and never came back. Last year, the three of them went to a concert in New Orleans without telling anyone, and the cops figure the same thing happened this time. So, they're treating it as a runaway. Two guys and a girl. All seventeen."

"Girlfriend, boyfriend, and a buddy?" Flowers asked.

"Yep. From reading the reports, the girl's mothers not too concerned, but one boy's mom isn't convinced."

"Why is that?"

"He took his rifle with him and left all his money and clothes behind. She said he got the rifle from his deceased father and wouldn't take the chance of losing it or getting it taken by the police."

"Can you hunt at night?" Flowers asked. "I thought that was illegal."

"It's Louisiana for God's sake. Ya'll got a whole nuther way a doin' thangs down thar," he said in a really bad hillbilly accent. "Anyway, could be nothing, but it just feels off to me. And it's not too far from that transfer site in Alexandria. I figure while you're out snooping around..."

"Like I said, you never know. Send me the info, Greg, and thanks."

"Yep. You sure you don't want me to beam you up to DC for the convention? It's not too late."

Her smile tightened. "I wish I could, but duty calls."

"Okay," Crandall said. He gave a split-finger salute. "Live long and prosper."

"Bye!" she chirped, then stabbed the end-call button. She dropped her head and closed her eyes. She always felt so guilty after talking to him. Crandall was a god within the Food and Drug Administration because of his computer abilities. When she'd asked him for help, he'd jumped onboard. But ever since, he'd been asking her out to dinner or drinks after work or to some strange sci-fi fan gathering.

She'd gone out with him a couple times, to be sociable, usually with coworkers, but she had never given Crandall any sign she wanted a more personal relationship with him. He was a nice enough guy, but they had zero in common. She knew she should tell him she wasn't interested, but what if he got angry and shut down SAAR?

It was one reason the transfer to New Orleans had been a godsend—he couldn't blame her, and it took away some of the pressure of turning him down all the time. Then again, out of sight, out of mind. What if he lost interest in the project because she wasn't around? She needed it. Other than her mystery, once-in-a-while informant, it was the only source of leads she had for GENIT.

She just wished she didn't feel like she was using him, leading him on. She moaned and laid her head down on her desk.

She took a minute to feel sorry for herself, then sat up and continued scrolling through reports. After a while, she opened the email Crandall had sent about the missing kids and read through it. He was right, something was off. It didn't sound like a normal runaway case. But you never knew.

She nodded. "First thing in the morning, road trip."

She looked back at the spreadsheet on her screen but decided she just couldn't do it, so she grabbed one of her shipping boxes and went through it. An hour later, she felt better, having set out most of her memorabilia and photographs. She'd bring a hammer and nails from home to hang stuff up.

In the last box, she found an expired Tennessee license plate. She pulled it out and smiled. It was the tag Jake Jessup had put on her work car when they were hunting the mutant pit bulls in Memphis. He'd thought it would draw less attention from the Section 17 operatives.

It had helped once, she thought. *Maybe it will work again.*

18

At six the following morning, Flowers was on the road. She brought up the GPS, then frowned. She grabbed her phone.

"What's up, earthling?" Greg Crandall said.

"What did you say was the name of that town?"

"Rutland. Looking on the map, it's about seven miles southeast of Spearsville, on Highway 27."

Flowers peered at the tiny screen and enlarged it until Spearsville appeared.

"Okay, I got Spearsville, but I still don't see Rutland."

"I'm not surprised. The population's only 117. There are more people than that in my apartment building. When you get up there, just stay on Highway 27 and don't blink."

She expanded the view until the tiny town appeared. "Gotcha. Hopefully, the mom will be at home."

"Well, don't blame me if it turns out to be a big goose egg. The more I think about it, a girlfriend and boyfriend running away from home isn't unusual, especially if they're in their late teens."

"Yeah, but with the kid's best friend missing, too, it doesn't feel right."

"Maybe it's one of those ménage á trois things," he said in a very bad French accent.

Flowers turned red and clamped her eyes shut, imagining the computer geek lifting his eyebrows like Groucho Marx. Then she remembered, he no longer had eyebrows.

"Okay, thanks, Greg," she said, chuckling nervously. "Guess I'd better keep my eyes on the road, so I don't miss it. Talk to you later."

"Live long and prosper."

Thirty miles from her destination, she plugged the mother's address into the GPS and followed the red line to Rutland.

The navigation system took her through the five blocks that comprised the town, then another quarter mile to a street that ran north off the highway.

Like most small communities, the neighborhood homes were either well maintained, run-down wrecks, or somewhere in the middle. Three blocks and two turns later, she pulled up to Clara Norton's house. It was somewhere in the middle, with some peeling paint and a couple broken slats on the front porch railing, but well kept, the grass cut and edged.

Flowers guessed it had three bedrooms. A drooping detached garage sat at the end of the empty driveway.

No dogs barked as she stepped onto the porch and knocked.

"She ain't at home," came a voice.

Flowers looked towards the house on her left and saw an older woman wearing a robe and fuzzy slippers standing partway out her front door. She leaned with both arms against the doorjamb and the screen door, a lit cigarette dangling from the fingers of her right hand. Her house was in the run-down-wreck category with an overgrown lawn littered with empty beer cans and an ancient Dodge Dart in the driveway on four flats.

"Oh, hi. Do you know where she is?"

"Who's askin'?" the woman snapped in a scratchy voice which Flowers suspected came from a lifetime of smoking.

"My name's April Flowers. I wanted to ask her about her son."

She waved a hand, knocking ash from the cigarette onto the front of her robe. "Ah, him. He's out gettin' drunk, as usual."

"What makes you say that?"

"Cause he's always out drinking, him and that damn fool friend a his and his slut girlfriend." She squinted at Flowers. "You some kinda investigator or something'?"

"Yes," Flowers replied, feeling a growing dislike for the woman.

"Hmm. Well, you ain't gonna find 'em around here. I guarantee they're down in New Orleans gettin' trashed. That's where they went last time they run away."

"When was that?"

"Bout a year back. Came back when they run outta money."

Just then, a Chevrolet pickup pulled into the driveway and parked next to the Dart. Music thumped loudly from behind the limo-tinted windows. Splotches of black paint showed through a thick layer of dirt, probably kicked up by the huge mud tires that lifted the chassis two feet off the ground.

The music died with the motor, and the truck door opened with a *clunk*. Mud-caked boots slapped the driveway, and a second later, a tall, stocky guy came around the front. He was in his early twenties, with patchy facial hair and a black... mullet? Flowers stared at him and shook her head.

"Can you tell me where Mrs. Norton works?"

"Hell, you're the investigator, ain't ya?" she cackled.

Flowers gave her a plastic smile. "Yes, ma'am, and that's how we find out stuff, by asking questions. So, can you tell me where she works?"

"Well, ya don't have to be snippy about it," the woman said, wrinkling her nose. The guy from the truck slipped behind her and into the house, but not before looking hard at Flowers. "The Wooden Nickel on the main drag." Then she stepped back inside and slammed the door.

"Good ole Southern hospitality, huh?" Flowers said.

19

The Wooden Nickel wasn't hard to find, it was the only restaurant in town, and despite being almost noon there were only three cars in the parking lot. Flowers noticed the neon beer signs in the windows and wondered if that was the main attraction.

Inside, the place was nicer than she'd expected. Deco-style red padded chairs, Formica tables, and matching booths filled the bright interior, while in the background, a country music song played unobtrusively from the jukebox. One guy sat at the diner bar, drinking a beer, while two groups of people sat at tables.

A stocky blonde in a white waitress uniform slid dirty dishes into a plastic tub.

"Sit anywhere you want," she said, glancing over her shoulder.

Flowers took the booth by the door, farthest from the jukebox. Everything was clean and neat. She optimistically grabbed the menu wedged behind the napkin dispenser. After a quick glance, ruling out everything fried or otherwise cooked in grease, she was left with salad or grilled cheese sandwich.

"Here you go. Sorry for the wait," the waitress said, setting down a glass of ice water. She had a tired smile and bloodshot eyes, as if she had been crying. Her nametag read "Clara."

"Oh, no problem," Flowers said. "You by yourself?"

"Yeah, the other gal called in... again," she said, shaking her head. "What can I get you to drink?"

"Diet Coke, please."

"Okay. Do you know what you want to eat?" Clara asked.

"I boiled it down to the salad or grilled cheese."

Clara nodded knowingly, then scribbled on her pad. "One grilled cheese coming up." She leaned over and whispered conspiratorially, "Salad's turning brown."

"Thank you," Flowers whispered back. She liked her instantly.

The woman brought the soda, then saw to the other tables. Five minutes later, she brought out the sandwich and the check.

"There's nothing wrong with the tomato slices, so I put some on the side, no charge. And you don't look like a dessert eater, so I brought the check," she said with a wink. "Anything else I can get you?"

"Actually, yes. I wanted to talk to you about your son."

The smile vanished and her eyes tightened. "What do you know about my son?"

"Only that you reported him missing and that two of his friends are gone, too."

"Who are you?"

"My name's April Flowers. I'm a special agent. I work for the federal government," she said, handing her a business card.

Norton's eyes went wide as she stared at the card. "The fed... the federal government. What's the federal government got to do with my boy?"

"Nothing that I'm aware of. I'm investigating unusual incidents involving animals. I heard about the kids going missing and I wanted to rule out any connection. I went by your house. Your neighbor seems convinced they all ran off to New Orleans."

"That bitch..." She held up a hand. "I apologize for my language."

Flowers smiled. "No problem."

"Celia Pike puts her nose into everyone's business except her own. She's held a grudge ever since Enos stopped mowing her lawn for ten bucks—when he was eleven." She shook her head. "Hang on."

After checking on the other customers and pouring coffee, she came back and sat down across from Flowers.

"My son did not run away. He's missing." Her words were firm, her glassy red eyes locked on Flowers.

"What makes you so sure? After what happened last year..."

Norton grabbed a napkin from the dispenser and began tearing pieces from the edge. "He didn't run away last year. He and his girlfriend and Owen, Owen Boswell, his best friend, went to a Widespread Panic concert—*after* I told him he couldn't go, mind you. He said he was going to spend the night with Owen, but instead they snuck down to New Orleans. I never would have found out about it if his truck hadn't gotten towed for illegal parking. They called me because my name is on the registration." A slight smile ghosted her lips as she shook her head. "He paid for that one, though. I put him under house arrest for two months."

"But you don't think that's the case this time?"

"I know it's not because his rifle's gone. He loves that rifle. It was a gift from his dad before he died in a truck crash two years ago. Enos wouldn't take the chance of it getting stolen. Plus, all his money's in his dresser drawer. Are you going to go to the Big Easy without cash?"

"What about his girlfriend and Owen?"

"Georgina's a sweet girl. Enos thinks he loves her. Maybe he does, but her mom didn't even realize she was gone until the deputies talked to her. Her deadbeat father is long gone; working the oil rigs last I heard. Owen's folks are worried, but they suspect he's off with Enos on another adventure."

"But you don't think so."

"Something's happened to them, Agent Flowers. I can feel it. Owen's rifle is gone too, and all the kid's cell phones go straight to voicemail. What are the chances of all three of them not answering their phones, even if they did run off?"

"Not likely," Flowers agreed, watching the small pieces of napkin pile up. "So, what do you think has happened?"

"I think they went hunting somewhere they shouldn't have and got into trouble. That's all those two boys live for, all they talk about, and it's the only thing that would explain why their rifles are missing and nothing else."

"I don't know much about hunting," Flowers said. "What would they be hunting for? What's in season?"

"Yeah, I figured you're not from around here from the accent," she said, smiling. "Hogs."

Flower's eyes went wide. "Pigs? You mean like on a farm?"

Norton chuckled. "No, sweetie, even though some of them might have started out on a farm. Wild hogs, boar, Arkansas razorbacks. They're everywhere, and there's an open season on hunting them. Enos loves hunting pigs. It's big business up here, though. You get in the wrong area, step on the wrong toes..."

"And you think that's what happened to the kids?"

"I don't know, Agent Flowers," she replied, her eyes tearing up again. "I just know they didn't run away."

"Any idea where they might have gone hunting?"

She held up her hands. "Take your pick. You saw the land comin' in, this area is nothing but forest and swamp, with farmland and a couple of small towns sprinkled in. There are pigs everywhere, but the closest hunting camp I know of is the Rebel Yell, up by the state line."

Norton saw her confused expression and pointed out the window. "It's not far. Arkansas' only five miles from here. Enos always talked about working there as a hunting guide. Got the fool notion from the kid next door. He works there."

"Big black truck, mullet?" Flowers said.

Norton frowned. "Cleve Pike. Nothing but trouble. Had Enos thinking he could get him a job there. I knew that wouldn't happen. Before his daddy died, we talked Enos into going to diesel mechanic school. Money's way better and you don't have to worry about a pig ripping your leg open. He starts after he graduates from high school."

"Hey, Clara," someone yelled from the kitchen.

Norton's shoulders sagged, then she reached across the table and gripped Flowers' arm.

"Please find my son."

20

As Flowers walked to her car, she peered into the shadowy areas around the buildings and shrubs, half expecting something to come running out at her. She could understand alligators and snakes, the state was mostly swamp, after all. But pigs?

She noticed a truck with large tires parked halfway down the block. It was the same one that had pulled in next door to Norton's house. What was that guy's name? Steve? No, Cleve, Cleve Pike. *This could be a lucky break,* she thought. Maybe he knew something about Enos and his friends.

She pulled off the lot and turned toward it, but as she neared, the truck did a U-turn and drove down the next street.

That was weird.

She pulled over and took out her laptop, linked it to her cell phone, then searched for the Rebel Yell Hunt Club. Their website was impressive, professionally built. The club itself was equally impressive, complete with a hunting lodge that looked like something you'd find on a ski slope in Aspen.

She clicked the drop-down menus and found the prices for the various hunt packages. They ranged from $2,500 for two hunts, with two nights room and board in a cabin and went up to $9,500 for five hunts with meals and a bed inside the main lodge. Additional fees and expenses added several hundred dollars to the tab.

"Geez, all that to shoot a pig?"

There was a photo of a wild boar's head at the top of the page, and below it, "Live hunt." She clicked on the link.

A loud squealing-grunting noise erupted over the speakers as a massive, hairy brown face rushed the computer screen. Flowers jumped in her seat as the person recording the video lurched backwards and ran. The image shook violently like a found-video scene in a horror movie as the person ran from the charging animal. A second later, there was a yelp and the camera tumbled through the air. Someone screamed, "Get it off me! Get it off me! Kill it!" There was a gunshot and Flowers jumped again, then louder squeals and grunts, a second gunshot, and everything went quiet.

Someone picked up the video camera and panned it around to show a man moaning and holding his right leg. Blood was seeping from between his fingers. Someone else yanked off his belt and cinched it around the wounded leg to stanch the blood flow.

The camera panned to a creature lying just feet from the injured hunter. Three-inch-long tusks covered in blood curled up from the animal's jaws. It was covered in coarse brown and gray hair, with a hump between its shoulders. It was huge. The caption below the video box showed "Weight, 343 pounds."

"Holy cow," she said, letting out the breath she didn't realize she had been holding. The next shot was a closeup of the wound and Flowers quickly clicked off the video.

She brought up a "Trophies" page with Rebel Yell customers posing proudly behind their kills. A couple of the animals were about as big as the one on the video, but most were smaller.

From the website and photos, the hunt club looked reputable, not the sort of place that might disappear some kids caught hunting on their land. But they might have seen them or run them off. According to the GPS, it was seventeen miles away.

"I'm here, so I might as well check the place out."

Flowers started to pull off, then thought about the Tennessee license plate she'd brought with her. *Better safe than sorry*, she thought, so she switched them, then headed east.

A mile outside of town, she saw a sign for the Clements Quik Stop convenience store. She saw Cleve Pike's truck parked out front, along with four other cars. She parked next to him, got out, and peered up at the vehicle. The huge tires brought the bottom of the truck even with the door glass on the Focus.

"How the heck do you get up in it?" she said, looking around for a retractable ladder, a knotted rope, or something. "It would be easy to change the oil, though."

She walked to the rear of the mud-splattered vehicle and saw about twenty bumper stickers covering the tailgate: Hogzilla Killer, Boar Removal Technician, I'd Rather Be Hog Hunting. All had cartoon pigs with giant tusks. There was even a Hog Life sticker on the back window that mimicked the popular Salt Life sticker.

"This guy is obsessed," Flowers said, shaking her head. She noticed a sticky red substance leaking under the tailgate. Mixed in were tufts of coarse brown hair. *Hog blood?* She went to step onto the bumper hitch to look, but thought she'd better try to talk to Pike first.

An overhead bell clanged as she pushed through the front door. The clerk looked up, nodded, then went back to whatever it was she was reading on her phone. Across from the register, at an eating area, four men stopped talking and looked up. After making a quick assessment, they resumed their conversation. Pike was not with them.

Pans of deep-fried food sat under heat lamps behind a display case and Flowers wagered there wasn't a single leaf of lettuce to be found in the place. Stacked in front of the food counter were fifty-pound burlap bags of feed corn. The label showed a cow and a sheep, but the handwritten sign taped to the front read "Hog feed special, $20 per bag."

Across from the feed was a bulletin board with trophy photos. Most of them displayed dead hogs.

The men's bathroom door at the back of the store opened and out walked Mr. Mullet. When he saw Flowers, Pike hesitated, then he put on a cocky grin and walked up to her.

"I know you. You were over at Enos's house earlier. My mom said you're some kind of investigator or something."

"Yeah, I remember," Flowers said. "And I saw you down the street from the diner a little while ago."

He frowned and his eyes looked down and to the left. "Nah, wasn't me. I've been here for the last half hour, haven't I, Deloris?"

The store clerk gave him a whatever shrug and went back to her phone.

"Hmm. I wanted to ask if you know anything about Enos and his friends. Where they might be, where they might have gone—"

"They're down in New Orleans. I thought my mom told you that."

"She said they went there last year."

"Yeah, well, that's where they went," Pike said.

"How do you know that?"

He again looked down and to the left. "I mean, they didn't tell me outright that's where they was headin', but they'd been talkin' about going there for the last few weeks."

"You tell the sheriff that?"

He shrugged. "They never asked."

"You know anything about them going hunting?"

"Nah," he said a little too quickly, glancing toward the eating area. "I don't know anything about any of that. Like I said, far as I know, they're drinkin' beer on Bourbon Street."

He peered at her. "Who'd you say you were again?"

"Just a friend of Mrs. Norton's, trying to find out the truth about her son. You work at Rebel Yell?"

His eyes widened a little, and he shot another glance at the group of men. He leaned toward her and hissed, "Look lady, I ain't got time for any more of your questions."

"What's the big deal? I just asked you where you worked."

"I ain't gonna tell you shit, and if you know what's good for you, you'll take your ass back to wherever it is you came from."

Flowers pulled her head back a fraction, then she smiled and said in a loud voice, "Okay. Well, thanks for the info, Cleve."

"Wh—what are you talkin' about, lady? I ain't told you shit," he said as he followed her to the door.

She felt his eyes on her as she crossed the parking lot. He was scared and nervous. And he was lying. He knew something.

Just to tweak him, Flowers pulled herself up on the tow ball of his truck and peered into the bed, which was covered with blood and hair.

Somebody's been doing some hunting, she thought. Then she noticed a small wooden crate with a skull and crossbones stenciled on the outside.

"Hey! Get off my fuckin' truck!" Pike shouted from the doorway.

She gave him another grin, got into her car, and drove off.

21

Flattner was sucking air by the time they reached the junction of the La Luz Trail and Spur Trail 84. Though only nine miles long, the La Luz Trail in the Sandia Mountains climbed from seven thousand feet to almost eleven thousand, compared to DC's relatively flat four hundred feet.

"Whew," he said, leaning against a rock and pulling out the second quart of water from his daypack. "I'm not used to this altitude."

"Poor baby," Janice Hampton said as she stood at the edge of the trail looking down at the Sandia Peak Tramway. Her tight-fitting hiking outfit followed every curve of her trim, rock-hard body, and her long red hair, tied in a ponytail, fed through the back of a green ball cap that shaded her hazel eyes. Flattner wondered what the new CEO and lead scientist for the Duogen Corporation was thinking behind the dark lenses of her Ray-Ban sunglasses.

"What are you, some kind of cyborg? You're not even sweating."

She flipped a hand through the air. "The La Luz is just a warm-up trail for me."

"Smart ass. Comments like that can be very damaging to the male ego."

"Ah," she cooed, walking over and grabbing his crotch. "When we get back, mommy will get you in the shower and massage your male ego."

"Hmm, I feel a second wind coming on."

She chuckled. "That's not the wind, but that's good, because we have another three hundred feet to go."

He stuck the water back into his pack and pushed off from the rock. "I run five miles nearly every day, and this is kickin' my ass."

"I'm not surprised. At ten thousand feet you have about thirty percent less oxygen than at sea level. I'm used to it. If we do this trail again in a couple of days you'll feel much better."

"I wish I could, but I have to head back tomorrow. Got any ideas on our leak?" he asked as they started up the trail.

"I gave Dotson all the personnel files he requested. That guy is a strange one."

Flattner smiled. "How so?"

"I don't know. Not too many people make me nervous, but he's one of them. Not that he said or did anything. There's just something... unsettling about him."

"He's handy to have around. People underestimate him, to their peril."

"As for our leak, it has to be from one of three sources: a scientist or lab tech, our computer people, or our logistics team."

"Dotson and I came to that same conclusion."

"A scientist or lab tech wouldn't have access to delivery information unless he or she was working with someone else. The logistics department would know when something was being shipped out and where it was going, but they wouldn't know what it contained because we use codes to describe the contents."

"Which leaves..."

"The computer people. That's where I would look first."

Flattner nodded. "Dotson's already going through their phones and emails."

She glanced over. "Don't underestimate him, indeed. You have the manpower for that?"

"It's automated. A computer sifts through the calls and information looking for certain words or phrases. If it picks up something, we listen to that conversation or read that email to put it into context. If it sounds promising, we go live on them."

"So, there's a lag."

"Yeah," Flattner said. "But, despite what you see on TV, we only have so many resources. And it's not like we're preparing for an imminent attack, though I need to get this son of a bitch."

"Or daughter of a bitch. Don't be sexist."

"What's your thoughts on motivation? Is he—or she—doing it for money? Revenge? Self-righteousness? That seemed to be your former boss's problem—until he ceased to be a problem."

"I never believed he was anti-military," Hampton said as she pushed off a ponderosa pine to climb a rock. "I think he was afraid the project would be exposed and that he would get in trouble. Some of the scientists are definitely anti-military, or anti-government, however you want to describe it, but after I fired the two most vocal ones, word got around, and things settled down."

He grinned. "I knew getting rid of Felix would reap benefits. How's the new office, by the way?"

"Very nice, thank you. It took the painters a gallon of spackle to fill all the nail holes from the shit he had hanging on the walls."

"I understand the Albuquerque natural science museum was quite pleased with the donation of Rosen's bug collection."

"Yes. They're actually talking about renaming the street in front of the museum to 'Felix Rosen Boulevard.'"

"Got a nice ring to it."

"Whatever," she said rolling her eyes. "You give any more thought to a lab dedicated to the Section 17 projects?"

"Trying to get rid of me?"

She laughed. "Hardly. I don't see enough of you as it is. Besides, I would run them both."

"Oh, you would?" Flattner said chuckling.

"Yes. And it would alleviate a lot of our security problems."

"How so?"

"Fewer employees, plus they would work exclusively on the SPAAD animals. At Duogen, most of the time the scientists and techs are working on civilian cloning projects. When we isolate a portion of the lab to work on your animals, they get very curious. And you know how people talk."

"But the civilian projects are what provides cover for the military side," Flattner said. "Besides, we haven't monetized the SPAAD animals enough to pay for a separate site. You know how much it costs to get a lab like yours up and running, all the government red tape, which, despite my connections, I have no control over."

"It doesn't have to be in the United States. Go offshore, or across the border into Mexico. Little to no government interference, at a fraction of the cost."

"Where would you find enough qualified scientists?"

"Wouldn't need them. This stuff isn't rocket science. The process is established, basically cut and paste. All you'd need are a dozen decent techs. The science would still come out of Duogen. The biggest problem at our plant is birthing the animals. With rats, mice, and family pets, it's not that big a deal, though even that takes up a lot of room. You throw in oversized pit bulls and monster hogs, and that attracts attention."

Flattner stopped in the shade of an ancient juniper, sucked in a breath, and took another drink of water.

Hampton turned toward him and placed her hands on her hips. "Plus, if there is a problem, if word gets out or something gets loose, it's a lot easier—and cheaper—to pay off a Federale in Juarez than a bureaucrat in Santa Fe."

Flattner nodded. "I like the idea. A lot. Work up some specs on it. And speaking of running out of space, we need to stick to smaller animals. The giant hogs are lethal and inexpensive to maintain, but you can't control them and they're tough to transport."

"What did you have in mind? I'm always up for a new challenge."

"We'll discuss it over dinner—if I live that long."

She laughed. "Only fifty more feet and then it's all downhill."

22

Flowers continued east on Highway 27 from Clements and saw power line pylons in the distance running north and south. She knew power companies co-opted electricity and assumed they continued north into Arkansas.

As she got closer, she saw a pair of ATVs come out of the weeds and stop at the edge of the highway to check for traffic. They were big, mud-covered machines, with rifles strapped horizontally across the handlebars. They crossed the highway and headed north along the power lines. The whine of the engines reminded her of the operatives pursuing the mutant pit bull across Memphis.

A fifty-foot-wide swath of land had been cleared away beneath the huge steel structures and several muddy trails cut along it. Judging from the map, the hunt club would be east of the power lines and south of the state line. A gravel access road led toward the first pylon, then disappeared into the weeds. If it continued the length of the grid, it would provide a miles long playground—and hunting ground—for four-wheel enthusiasts.

Curious, she pulled onto the gravel road and stopped under the tower. She gawked up at it. The thing was massive, and from the ground it looked a mile high, with a dozen power lines running in each direction to the horizon. The gravel road continued past it and disappeared into a large mud puddle. Pike's truck wouldn't even notice the hole, but the compact would probably sink to the windows. She smiled at the thought of Jessup and his son blasting off down the trail on their dirt bikes.

She got back on the highway, continued east, then turned north onto State Road 112. A solid green wall of impenetrable jungle crowded in from both sides of the road, the sunlight allowing the smaller plants to grow and fill in the voids. She wondered if behind those thick green walls, where the trees blocked the sun's rays, if the forest thinned out and became more navigable.

The website said the club was three hundred acres, but she had no idea how big that was. She saw purple swatches painted on the trees denoting private property like she'd seen in the Ozarks.

Maybe this is where the hunt club property begins, she thought.

Driving her usual speed, she shot past the turn-in for the Rebel Yell.

"Dang it," she said, and slowed to the posted speed limit of fifty-five miles per hour. As she looked for a place to turn around on the narrow road, a southbound semi blew past her, rocking the little car.

"Not a good idea, April," she muttered.

A minute later, she saw a small blue and white sign that said "Welcome to Arkansas." She flew past it and felt the light bump as her tires rolled over the change in paving surface from one state to the next. In her rear-view mirror she saw a blue sign with a gold fleur-de-lis that said "Welcome to Louisiana." They were the only indications that she'd gone from one state to another, other than an old, overgrown swath cut through the tree line, running arrow straight, east to west.

She grew eager for a turnoff and almost missed a break in the foliage to her left. Braking hard, she turned onto the gravel drive, digging ruts into the surface as the car skidded to a stop. She started to back out, but then she noted the condition of the trail.

Just like the access road leading to the PIT City facility in Memphis, the gravel looked almost new, well-graded, wide, and elevated from the forest floor. There was no mailbox or any sign of what the road was for, just a break in the wire fence that lined the highway. Purple swatches on the surrounding trees marked it as private property.

She brought up Google Earth and zoomed in on the area. The year-old image showed a solid green mass from the state line north several miles with no roads on either side. A half mile to the south, on the Louisiana side, she saw the buildings for the Rebel Yell Hunt Club, with several roads and trails cutting through it.

So, where does this gravel road lead to?

Someone had probably just purchased the land and put in a driveway to prepare to build a house, though the gravel road was almost wide enough for two vehicles, which was unusual for a country driveway.

Recalling the video of the pig attack, Flowers peered into the vegetation, watching for movement. Were they like deer? Could they be standing right in front of you, and you wouldn't see them?

She remembered a camping trip to the Sawtooth National Forest when she was seven. She and her dad were heading back to the campground from the visitor's center when he pulled over and pointed out the window.

"You see 'em?" he had asked.

"See what?" Flowers had replied, excitedly.

"The deer." He pointed at a spot twenty yards off the road.

She looked and saw only trees and brush... and then she saw them, a family of five deer. Three adults and two fawns were standing just inside the tree line, as obvious as the nose on her face.

"I see them!" she said, glancing at her father. But when she looked back, they were gone. She peered at the spot as they drove on. Suddenly, she could see them again, in the same spot, just like magic.

She assumed it was the same with the pigs, or with any wild animal that adapted and survived in the wild. Camouflage was key.

"You're here. Might as well check it out."

A hundred yards in, she came to a gate. It was nothing fancy, just a metal farm gate, but it had a heavy chain and lock and a large sign that said "Private Property, No Trespassing, Violators Will Be Prosecuted." Triple-strand barbed wire disappeared into the trees in both directions.

Flowers looked at the low, swampy land on either side of the gate and imagined all the things crawling around in the mud and muck. Though she had an extra pair of shoes in her luggage, sneakers probably weren't the best thing for exploring a swamp. Beyond the gate, the gravel road disappeared around a bend.

She could climb over and go on foot, but she didn't know how far the road went. More importantly, she didn't know if this property had anything to do with the missing kids, or, for that matter, if the missing kids had anything to do with a Section 17 case. This whole thing was a long shot, though Pike's reaction to her questions nibbled at her brain. What she needed to do was get to the Rebel Yell, ask about the kids, then move on.

23

Flowers crossed back into Louisiana and pulled onto the Rebel Yell Hunt Club driveway. Twenty feet in, fieldstone pillars stood on either side of the wide gravel road, spanned by a massive wooden sign bearing an intricately carved boar's head, along with the club's name.

"That sign alone would be a year's salary for me," she said, driving under it.

A side road cut to the left, with a sign that read "Maintenance area. All deliveries turn here." Recalling the PIT CITY incident, Flowers turned. If anyone stopped her, she'd say she got lost.

The gravel road opened onto a clearing, and fifty yards to her right, she saw the back of a massive two-story log building with a wrap-around porch. Several pickup trucks and a couple of sedans were parked nearby. The setting was picture-perfect, the impressive structure nestled among ancient pin oaks and cypress trees laced with Spanish moss.

She continued down the access drive and came to a pair of pole barns. A couple guys were working on a big four-wheel drive buggy inside the first one, so she waved. They paused and waved back. They watched as she drove past but didn't try to stop her.

Flowers passed the second barn and followed the road as it wound through the forest. She glanced up at the compass built into the rearview mirror. It indicated she was heading north, back toward the Arkansas border.

What's up here? she wondered and glanced down at her laptop. She didn't see any structures on the Google Earth map other than the hunt club buildings.

She looked up and yelped as a massive vehicle came at her. Flowers jammed on the brakes. The two vehicles skidded to a stop six inches apart.

She stared up at the thing, her eyes wide. She sucked in air and tried to get her heart rate down. It was a Humvee, but not the kind you can buy and drive on the street. This was what you saw on the evening news in war zones, with armor plates and gigantic tires.

It loomed over the tiny compact like a rogue elephant facing down a rabbit. She could feel the vibration of its massive engine through her steering wheel.

The dark tint on the flat, rectangular windshield gave no hint of who was inside and no one got out.

She heard a noise behind her and looked in the mirror. A large four-wheel-drive buggy skidded to a stop behind her. The driver and passenger jumped out and ran up to her car as she rolled down the window.

"Who are you and what are you doing back here?" demanded the driver, a big, thick-boned man wearing camo pants and shirt. The other, a teenager, had been one of the workers in the barn.

"I asked you a question, miss," said the older man.

"Well, uh, I'm trying to find the way out," Flowers stammered.

"What are you doing here in the first place?"

"I'm trying to get to... Ruston. I got lost, so I pulled in here to ask directions."

"Then why didn't you stop and ask?"

"I, uh, cause I figured it out and was trying to get back to the highway. I got turned around."

He looked at her hard for several seconds. "What's your name?"

"Gladys Kravitz." Flowers wasn't sure why, but her gut told her not to give them her real name, and not to mention the missing kids.

He continued to peer at her, then he took a step back and said, "I'm the owner, and the area back here is off limits to everyone except workers and registered guests. There are a lot of dangerous animals running around. Get yourself turned around and follow us. We'll lead you back to the highway. And I suggest that in the future you don't go onto private property without a proper invitation."

Flowers' shoulders sagged in relief as the man returned to the ATV. There was a rumble. She looked up and saw the Hummer pull down a side trail.

She followed the four-wheeler down the access road, past the pole barns and out onto the highway. Then it turned around and drove away, leaving her with more questions than when she had arrived.

•••••••••••

Montel Ruderman was waiting at the lodge. Erickson jumped out and told his son to return the vehicle to the pole barn.

"What's up, Montel?" he said, turning to his foreman.

"Who was that?"

Erickson looked at him for a second, then said, "Some woman that said she got turned around. Was looking for directions. Why?"

"Cause I saw her at Clements about an hour ago... talkin' to Cleve."

"What were they talking about?"

Ruderman shook his head. "Couldn't tell, but when she left, she told him thanks for the information."

Erickson stiffened. "That's not good."

"No, it's not."

"Thanks," Erickson said. "I gotta make a call."

· · • • •• • •• • ·

Derrick Flattner was returning from New Mexico when his phone vibrated. "Hi, Gus. Is your phone secure?"

"Yes," Erickson said. "So, what did you think of the demonstration?"

"It was exactly what I was looking for; something to show our private investors what the animals are capable of. In fact, we have a buyer with a private island who wants three pigs for hunting. The video should seal the contract."

Erickson chuckled. "Now, that's the kind of huntin' club I need to run. Beaches, palm trees, naked native women. What is he? A software developer, cartel leader?"

"It's strictly 'don't ask, don't tell' on the commercial side of things," Flattner said. "As long as they're not an enemy combatant of the United States when they place their order—and they're paying with cash or in Bitcoin—we don't care."

"Mind if I ask how much a pig?"

"A quarter million."

The Rebel Yell owner whistled. "So, this guy's gonna lay out three-quarters of a million dollars to go on a pig hunt?"

"Without even flinching. Everything go okay with Dotson?"

"He flew in and we took him over to look at the site. He barked a few orders, then he jumped back on the helicopter and took off. He was not happy about losing an animal. I think he suspects something's not right. You think it's a good idea to keep him out of the loop on this? He's no dummy."

"You let me worry about him," Flattner said.

"Okay, you're the boss. We're going to need a pig to take the place of the one that was killed. A couple of others got shot, but it doesn't seem to be bothering them."

"They won't be around long enough to worry about. We have an operation planned in two weeks."

"With that op and this pending purchase, we'll need another six pigs. Plus, we have the two runts. We've held off putting them down, hoping they'd fatten up, but they haven't."

"How big are they?"

"They're both around eight hundred pounds." Erickson chuckled. "Never thought I'd call an eight-hundred-pound boar small."

"Okay. I'm sure Dotson is on top of it, but I'll check. We had a slight logistics problem last week. Your guys are going to have to pick up the next shipment of pigs in Lafayette until we can arrange a new site in Alexandria."

"Anything I need to be concerned about?"

"No," Flattner said. "We're taking care of it. Anything else?"

"Yeah, one thing. Cleve Pike, that employee of mine who arranged for our test subjects? He was talking to some investigator about those three kids."

"What does he know?"

"Only that he told them where to find the pigs and now they're missing. I didn't think anything of it until she showed up at the hunt club snooping around."

Flattner gripped his phone tighter. "She?"

"Yeah. Said she was lost, so I ran her off. Then my foreman tells me she's the one Pike was talking to."

"What was her name?"

"Gladys Kravitz."

Flattner lowered his phone and rubbed a hand across his face. Then he said, "Hang on."

He tapped on his phone then said, "I just sent you a picture."

He heard a ping on the other end of the line. A few seconds later Erickson said, "Uh, yeah, that's her. How did you know?"

24

Cleve Pike had just unloaded bags of feed corn at one of the Rebel Yell hunting cabins when he got a text from Montel Ruderman.

SEE ME AT THE BARN WHEN YOU'RE DONE.

His heart lurched. Pike had been on edge ever since that woman confronted him inside the convenience store. Actually, he'd been worried ever since Enos Norton and his friends went missing.

Ruderman was waiting for him outside the big metal building when he got back.

"Get that feed taken care of, Cleve?" the foreman asked.

"Yes, sir, Mr. Ruderman," Pike said, trying to keep his voice steady.

"I wanted to talk to you about those kids."

His heart nearly stopped. He searched for words but froze under Ruderman's stare.

"I talked to Mr. Erickson about it..."

Here it comes, he thought, dropping his head.

"...and he was impressed."

Pike looked up.

"We got a good test of how the hogs react to vehicles and people they don't know. Your friends even killed one," he said, tipping his head to the side.

"Well, uh, I didn't..."

"When we pulled into the reserve, they shot past us, going about fifty down that gravel road. Busted right through the front gate. Last we saw 'em, they were heading north into Arkansas."

"They did what?" Pike said, his mouth dropping.

Ruderman chuckled. "I guess they thought we were gonna have 'em locked up for trespassing and poaching. Didn't want to get their truck and guns seized."

"I'm sorry, Mr. Ruderman," Pike stammered. "I'll pay..."

He waved a hand. "The gate's not a big deal. We've already fixed it. I just wanted to tell you good job, and that Mr. Erickson thinks you're ready for more responsibility. He wants to start you over at the breeding farm."

Pike's eyes went wide. There were only a handful of men allowed onto that property and working there meant a substantial pay increase.

"Thank you, Mr. Ruderman," he said grinning.

"You deserve it. Park the ATV then get in your truck and drive up there. Just stay on the main trail until you come to some buildings. A couple of the guys will be waiting for you. They'll show you what to do."

"Will do, Mr. Ruderman." Pike shook the man's hand. "I won't let you down."

Pike drove up the trail, almost a straight shot north from the hunt club. He couldn't believe his luck. The men who worked at the breeding farm had been at the Yell for years, and here he was, less than a year on and already getting promoted.

He'd heard rumors about five-hundred-pound hogs being bred for hunting, and at first he hadn't believed it. But when he thought about the lodge and what they charged for hunts, it made perfect sense. Now he was going to be a part of it. He snickered. Next time he saw Enos and crew, he'd have to thank them for the promotion.

He came to a clearing with four pole barns on a large gravel pad. The structures looked almost new.

"Wow," he muttered. "Talk about first class."

The doors were open on one barn. He pulled up but didn't see anyone. He looked inside and saw two Humvees. His heart raced with excitement.

He got out and called, "Hello?"

Gravel crunched behind him. He turned around and saw a man dressed in camo, wearing a balaclava, and pointing a strange-looking rifle at him.

"Hey! What—"

BANG!

It was near dark when Pike regained consciousness. He sat up, then moaned as a sharp pain shot through his head. He gagged at the stench of pig feces and rotten meat that permeated the air.

Flies were buzzing around his face and he lifted a hand to shoo them away.

Clank.

He looked down and saw the handcuff.

"What the fuck!" He scrambled to his knees, whipped his head from side to side, and was rewarded with another sharp pain in his skull. When he saw what he was attached to, his eyes widened: a row of rebar stick figures covered in bits of torn camouflage material.

Wedged along the top edge of the welded metal men were hunks of meat dripping with a red liquid. Pike looked down and saw that he, too, was coated in the red substance.

Headlights flared on, lighting up the grisly scene. He spun around and threw his free arm up to block his eyes.

"Hello? Help me!"

"Tsk, tsk, tsk," came a voice.

Pike squinted into the bright lights. "Who is that? Hey, man, help me. Can't you see I'm trapped?"

"You just couldn't keep your mouth shut, could you, Cleve?" came a familiar voice.

Pike stopped struggling and drew in a breath. "What? What are you talking about? Unhook me."

"Everything was going fine. Nobody suspected a thing until you started running your mouth."

"I didn't tell anybody anything," he said, his voice shrill. "I did exactly what you told me to do, that's all." He squinted at the figure sitting on the hood of the Hummer, even though he knew who it was.

"I wish I could believe you, Cleve, but loose lips sink ships. We've got too much at stake to risk losing it all because you got scared." The man stood and walked across the hood.

"No, wait, you got it all wrong!"

He slid through the turret opening, then paused. "Don't worry, it'll only hurt for a second."

The vehicle clunked into gear, backed up thirty yards, and the headlights went out.

Pike spun his head from side to side, and yanked at the handcuff, the pain forgotten. With the lights off, he could make out more detail. In the tall grass to his left, he saw something move. Something big. More shapes appeared and within seconds, the brush line was alive.

"No, no, no, no, no, no, no!" Pike said as he grabbed hold of the rebar figure he was cuffed to and tried to pull it from the ground.

Above him, a noise went *thump, thump, thump, thump.* He looked up and saw a green LED flashing on a pole behind him. Suddenly, screams and gunshots erupted from a speaker and four-legged nightmares exploded into the clearing.

Cleve Pike had time for one scream, but like the man said, it only hurt for a second.

25

Low, gray clouds kissed the tip of the Washington Monument as a cold, damp mist blanketed the Capital City. The weather matched Flattner's mood as he stared out the hotel window. There was a knock. He walked over, opened the door, and a man walked in.

"Derrick," Senator Dirk Blanton said.

Dressed in gray slacks, a burgundy polo shirt, and a darker gray jacket, he might have just left a country club were it not for the dark sunglasses and the ball cap pulled low, making him look more like an unfaithful husband heading to a rendezvous.

Flattner motioned at the couch. "I like the hat, but it's not very P.C."

"Fuck those politically correct pussies," Blanton said flopping on the couch and tossing the glasses and the Washington Redskins ball cap onto the table. "I haven't met the first fuckin' Indian who gave a shit about being called a redskin. With all the crap going on in this world, people are worried about the name of a football team?"

Flattner chuckled. "Sorry to call you on such short notice."

"No problem. Got me out of a shopping trip with my wife that I really did not want to go on. But why all the cloak and dagger? My aide could have brought me here. You didn't have to send a driver."

"I thought it best we keep this conversation confidential."

Blanton glanced around. "Where's Dotson?"

"He has his hands full with other projects. I'm going to handle this on my own."

Blanton rolled forward, rested his arms on his legs, and looked at Flattner, but said nothing.

"You remember Special Agent April Flowers?"

"Yes."

"Twice in the past two weeks she has come close to compromising operations. First at a drop off location during an animal delivery, and again a few days ago at Tall Grass." Flattner explained what had happened.

"Where's she getting her information?"

"Three ways. The first source is an informant at Duogen Industries, where the animals are created. That's the only way she could have known about the delivery location."

"Any idea who it is?" the senator asked.

"We're working on it. We suspect it's someone in IT."

"So, a computer geek?" Blanton said.

"That's what we're focusing on. Unfortunately, a computer expert would be savvy enough to cover their tracks. We're also listening to their phones and watching them online."

"Okay," Blanton said. "What are the other two sources?"

"Another computer geek."

He gave a puzzled look.

"Flowers is using a database of animal complaints from across the United States, searching for unusual incidents that might be related to a Section 17 project," Flattner explained.

"How is that even possible? There must be thousands of reports like that every day. And where would she get it? It's not like there's some animal emergency hotline."

"Ever heard of a guy named Greg Crandall?" Flattner asked.

Blanton shook his head.

"He's one of the top computer geniuses in the country, in the world, actually. A savant. All the agencies courted him, but he turned them down to run the computer system for the Food and Drug Administration."

Blanton sat back and understanding crept onto his face.

"Seems he's taken a liking to Ms. Flowers and developed a new software program to gather information on animal-related incidents. Once we found out about him, it was easy to figure out how he was doing it. He uses the FDA mainframe to search all the normal databases—as well as those of the three-letter agencies he refused to work for."

The color faded from Blanton's face. "You mean..."

"PRISM, XKEYSCORE..."

"My God," Blanton gasped. "If he can do that..."

"Then he's a major threat to national security."

Blanton blew out a breath, then asked, "And the third source?"

"Representative Neil Berryman."

Blanton's eyes narrowed. "What's that Libertarian piece of shit got to do with this?"

"He's one of Flowers' connections on Capitol Hill."

Blanton leaned forward again.

"A source inside the FDA told us Berryman's the one who arranged for Flowers' transfer to New Orleans."

"What's the connection? They sleeping together or something?" Blanton asked, a hopeful look in his eyes.

"Unfortunately, no. One of his sons has severe asthma. A few years back, he required a certain type of inhaler that tweakers apparently combine with some other drug to get this phenomenal high. They were so sought after that pharmacy workers were selling them for huge profits and replacing them with defective Mexican knock offs."

Blanton nodded. "I remember that. A couple of dozen people died across the country."

"Twenty-eight kids," Flattner said.

"My God."

"Flowers, fresh out of the FDA special agent school, ran with a lead everyone else ignored and busted the source of the Mexican inhalers. The guy had just delivered a box of the defective devices to a pharmacy in New Orleans, the same pharmacy the Berryman's used. She wanted to put out a news alert, but no one would listen to her. About that same time, a couple of kids ended up in the hospital in respiratory distress from using the things, so on her own, she got the pharmacy records and tracked down each customer prescribed one of the knock-off inhalers. Thirty-seven children."

"And one of them was Berryman's kid," Blanton said.

Flattner nodded. "She knocked on the front door of their house at the same time the kid's mother was handing him the bad inhaler. It was like a made-for-TV movie. After that, Flowers pretty much became untouchable."

"And Berryman, being a member of the House Committee of Armed Services..."

"Who's probably going to be the next chairman..." Flattner added.

"So, you think Berryman is feeding Flowers information about Section 17 projects?"

Flattner shrugged. "Not specifically, because even he doesn't know that much. Only a handful of people know about the covert use of the animals in the SPAAD program, and even fewer about the NF-13. While the Special Projects Animal Assets Division is no secret, most of the people on Capitol Hill only care about the sexy stuff, like invisibility and guided bullets. But thanks to Flowers, I think he knows about our 'alterations.' That's why he pulled strings and got her assigned to her own task force within the FDA."

Blanton pursed his lips. "Is it time to stop making the alterations?"

"Might as well cancel the entire program."

"What do you mean?"

"Without the NF-13 and the razor nails, all you have are very big, very mean, very expensive animals doing the same thing a platoon of Rangers can do. The animals can do a lot of damage and can kill a lot of the enemy, but the ceramic attachments—along with their teeth—do the real damage, and the flesh-eating bacteria keeps killing after the animals are dead. Without those, you leave half your enemy combatants alive to tell the tale. They, along with the carcasses of the dead animals, point right back at the US."

Blanton nodded. "I see your point."

"It would also mean fewer private sector sales."

The senator's head jerked up.

"Again, what would we have to offer them?" Flattner said, holding his arms out. "A bunch of very big, very mean, very expensive animals doing the same thing a platoon of their own people can do."

He knew this would get the man's attention. Blanton could spout all he wanted about patriotism and the welfare of the troops, but the bottom line was money flowing into his offshore account.

"So, what are you suggesting?"

"I'm suggesting we take care of all three of our problems once and for all. Flowers, Crandall... and Berryman."

Blanton's eyes went wide. "Kill a sitting congressman? Are you insane? Do you have any idea how much heat that would bring down?"

"None if it's done right. And if we do all three at the same time, Berryman's death will overshadow the others. When Mother Teresa died, the whole world was too busy talking about Princess Di."

The senator closed his eyes and wiped a hand across his face.

"Here's what we accomplish," Flattner said, holding up a hand and lifting a finger for each point. "One, we take care of a dangerous cyber security threat. Two, we stop a woman who has already disrupted two of your programs and come close to compromising two more. Three, we cut off a leak of sensitive military information from Capitol Hill."

Blanton looked at the floor and shook his head. Then Flattner lifted one more finger.

"Four, it takes care of your Okaloosa National Wildlife Refuge issue. With Berryman out of the picture, there's no one to strongarm the fence sitters, and oil exploration continues, unimpeded."

Blanton looked out the picture window. Then he shifted, lifted his shoulders, and sat upright in the sofa. "The safety of our nation and its people take precedence. If we do not make the tough choices now, future Americans will have to make even tougher ones."

"Well spoken, sir. Well spoken," Flattner said, fighting the urge to smile at another of Blanton's oft used phrases.

After several seconds, he said, "Shall we proceed?"

"I give you authorization to take whatever action you deem necessary to protect and defend the Constitution and the people of the United States as an agent of the Department of Homeland Security, subject to the laws of said Constitution."

Blanton grabbed his ball cap and glasses and stood. Then he shook Flattner's hand, gave a curt nod, and walked out.

Flattner smiled as he punched a button, turning off the video and audio recording equipment. *If that sly old bastard thinks adding that little phrase "subject to the laws of the Constitution," is going to protect him, he's sadly mistaken.*

26

Gus Erickson stood on the front porch of the lodge and pressed the button on the portable radio. "Montel, you read me?"

A second later, *"I got ya, Gus."*

"Come up to the lodge. I want to talk to you about the hunt."

"All right."

As Erickson waited, he admired his sprinkling of southern oaks, how their long limbs swooped towards the ground, blanketed with Spanish moss like tinsel on a Christmas tree. Quercus virginiana, the only species of oak native to Louisiana. *That's a stupid name,* he thought. *Who would name an oak tree queer Virginian?* He shook his head. Probably some fag from the east coast.

He'd be glad when this week was over, so he wouldn't have to worry about all those east coast idiots for a while. Blanton was an okay guy, a Razorback native, but he'd been in Washington too long as far as Erickson was concerned. All he worried about was money. Not that there was anything wrong with money. The club owner planned to make as much of it as he could once the new and improved Rebel Yell got established.

Erickson had built it from nothing and turned it into a decent hunting destination. He was paying the bills, even putting away a little money—during the good years. Then Blanton came along and promised to make him rich. All Erickson had to do was maintain a breeding farm for the military. The government would pay the bills and even double his land holdings. And, as the senator loved to point out, he'd be doing his patriotic duty.

And here he was, several months later he had three hundred acres of Arkansas swamp land with a moat and a million dollar hunting facility. To say he was star struck would have been an understatement, but the benefits did not come without cost. He'd already lost two men to the hogs, and it wasn't easy finding workers you could trust to keep their mouths shut. It was even harder to find men brave enough—or crazy enough—to work with the animals.

Though Blanton said that the land, the lodge, and all the equipment were now the property of the Rebel Yell, it hadn't come without expectations, some of which took the form of veiled threats. For instance, this hunt with the German ambassador to the United States. He'd already gotten a dozen calls from the senator or his aide during the past week alone, wanting to know if everything was ready. *Do you realize how important this trip is? Did you get the beer he likes? What kind of food are you going to serve? Can you guarantee he'll get a hog? How big will it be?*

Knowing Blanton, Erickson suspected there was more to this trip than simply international relations. There was likely a backdoor deal at stake, and the senator had put him square in the middle of it. Which meant the future of the Rebel Yell was at stake, so this hunt *had* to be a success.

"What's up, boss?" his foreman asked as he walked up. Montel Ruderman resembled a wild boar. Squat and barrel-chested, with coarse brown, black, and gray hair that tangled along his sun-browned arms and poked from the neckline of a blood-stained Rebel Yell T-shirt. A chaw of tobacco jammed inside his cheek poked out from under a shag-carpet growth of hair that covered most of his face and disappeared under an oily John Deere ball cap.

"How are things looking for the hunt?" Erickson asked.

"Not bad. There's a couple of three hundred pounders back there, several between two and two fifty. They should have a good hunt."

Erickson gave a grunt. Those were good-sized pigs, but not memorable. A lot of the clubs were boasting kills near that, at a fraction of what the Rebel Yell charged for a "wild boar hunting experience," and why was everything an "experience" anyway? It almost made him wish for the old days when he ran the hunts out of his garage. Then the sun glinted off his wife's Cadillac Escalade parked next to his Ford Super Duty F-250 Platinum pickup and he shook the thought from his head.

"Anything good coming in lately?" Erickson asked. For years, he had paid landowners for the biggest pigs they trapped while clearing their land of the invasive creatures, and over time, had increased the average size of their boars.

"That horse left the barn, Gus. All the hunt clubs are doing the same thing. We haven't gotten a call on a pig over 175 pounds in weeks."

Erickson shook his head.

"You know," Ruderman said, leaning over the railing and spitting a glob of tobacco juice onto the ground, "we got those couple of runts we have to get rid of on the other side."

"You know we can't touch those pigs," Erickson said.

"I know. But we're just going to put them down and let the other pigs eat 'em anyway. Seems like a big waste to me when we could bring them over here and let the German's kill 'em."

Erickson looked across the field and stared at the road that led to the breeding farm.

"Accomplish the same goal," Ruderman continued. "Plus, it'd be a big win for the hunt club."

Erickson shook his head and looked down, but when the foreman turned to leave, he asked, "How big are they?"

"One is eight hundred, and the other is just over that. Both well below the twelve hundred pound minimum for the military."

Erickson looked at him. "That would get some attention."

Ruderman gave a tobacco-stained grin. "It sure would."

"Let me make a call."

Erickson went to his office and poured himself a glass of Maker's Mark, then pulled up a phone number. He stared at it. Not that long ago he couldn't have imagined knowing someone at that level, let alone having their private cellphone number. He pushed send.

A second later, Senator Dirk Blanton said, "Gus, how's it going down there? You ready for our visitors?"

"Everything's going good, Dirk. Got all our supplies and special amenities. I think he's going to be impressed."

"Good, good, 'cause I really need this one. There will be some serious financial benefit for all of us if we can get this guy on our side."

"That's why I'm calling. We have a couple of three hundred pounders out here, but if you really want to wow this guy, we're gonna need to up our game."

"I'm not sure I follow," Blanton said. "I thought three hundred pounds was big."

"It's a good size for around here, but this guy is German, right?"

"Yeah."

"Over there, they'd walk hogs that big around on leashes. Hell, a four hundred fifty pounder is no big deal to them."

"No shit."

"Yes, sir," Erickson said. "But I have a solution. We got two runts ready to be put down over at the facility."

"Ah," Blanton said, "those animals are only to be used for Tall Grass-related activities."

"I know, Dirk, but this is a special situation. I'm afraid if we sent this guy back home with a three hundred pound pig, we may lose him."

Blanton hesitated, then asked. "How big are we talkin'?"

"You saw 'em during the tour. The two smaller ones. Both right at eight hundred pounds."

"Are you kidding me? Eight hundred pounds is a runt?"

"Yes sir. Well below Tall Grass requirements. But for a pig hunter, you ain't gonna top that. Your German bags one of them, I can guarantee he'll sign whatever papers you put in front of him."

"But is it safe? They're trained to attack, aren't they?"

"Only when the thumper is activated. Without that, they forage around just like any other wild hog. We'll make sure they're well fed before our guests arrive. The good thing is, they both have tracking devices in them, so we'll know where they are at all times; we can take the Germans right to them. Plus, me and my son will be there with our rifles to keep everyone safe."

"You sure you can pull this off?"

"Yes, sir, I guarantee it. We'll give that German a hunt he'll never forget."

27

Seated inside the desert camo Hummer, Montel Ruderman watched as the men affixed the separator to a trailer at the end of an eight-foot-deep trench. Welded from thick gauge angle iron, the separator was simply a funnel the pigs ran through with a trap door to divert the selected pigs into the back of the forty-foot container trailer. The massive triple-axle trailer was attached to an M915 Army transport truck, both of which had been green camo, but were now royal blue.

One benefit of working on a military project was that you got to use their toys. Not that they had a choice. It was that or foot the bill for repairs when an animal the size of a rhinoceros tried to mate with your Jeep Wrangler.

On a dash-mounted laptop, Ruderman monitored nine red dots and two green dots, each representing a wild pig inside the Tall Grass facility. Earlier, he'd changed the icon color for the two runts to make them easier to harvest.

They'd be down to nine animals after today, and he hoped they'd get replacement animals soon.

"Okay, boss," came a voice over the handheld radio. *"We're set."*

"Check, Bo" the foreman replied. "Okay, Tommie, start the first thumper."

The man stuck his head out of the turret opening of the armored Hummer and flipped a switch. Fifty feet away, suspended above the trench, the tubular device pulsed its ninety beats per minute.

Through the windshield, Ruderman watched the tall grass at the edge of the clearing. Thirty seconds later, a gigantic pig shot into the clearing followed closely by three more. He felt a surge of adrenaline as the monsters ran directly at the Humvee. They closed the gap in seconds, then veered at the last instant and headed toward the ditch, drawn by the thumping beat. He released his breath, wondering if he'd ever be crazy enough to face the charging animals.

That nut-job Dotson claimed they wouldn't attack you until they first went to the thumper. He'd verified his claim by standing twenty feet from his vehicle during a feeding. When they activated the thumper by the metal men, Meatloaf, a 1,450-pound Russian boar, burst from the overgrowth and ran past Dotson close enough to brush his clothing.

The lesson didn't reduce Ruderman's fear of the animals, but it had increased his fear of the bald-headed government man. But that was six months ago, not long after the start of the program. Since then, the animals had been treated to six live meals and he wondered how that experiment would go now.

The first animals crowded into the ditch, digging at the side walls, trying to reach the thumper hanging over their heads. Fifty feet beyond the trench was a second thumper attached to a large trough filled with feed corn.

Four more of the beasts appeared, one of them much smaller than the others, and made for the cut.

"Okay," Ruderman said into the radio, his excitement building. "Here comes the first runt. Bo, you got it on your screen?"

"Yep, we see her," came the reply.

Two more of the creatures charged from different directions and stormed toward their dinner bell.

"Where is that second pig?" he said, scanning the laptop.

Over the radio, a tense voice said, *"They're piling up in the ditch!"*

In the background, he could hear the loud squeals and grunts as the monsters fought with each other to reach the pulsing tube, kicking up mud and dirt and slinging their powerful heads from side to side.

"Want me to hit the feeder thumper?" Tommie shouted.

"No," he snapped. "We need the other runt in position first." Just then, the smaller pig crashed through the underbrush.

"There it is!" Ruderman shouted into the radio. "As soon as it hits the ditch start the other thumper."

The new arrivals slammed into the grinding porcine mass and struggled to get closer.

The second runt found an opening, lunged forward, and wedged itself between the dirt wall and another creature.

"Start the second thumper, Tommie!" Ruderman shouted. Then he yelled into the radio, "Open the gate!"

Tommie pressed another button and the thumper at the corn trough started up.

The first pigs in the ditch, hearing this new tone, started forward, then hesitated and looked up at the first thumper, unsure which one to follow. The others pushed them forward, and slowly, one after another, they ran through the cage and to the feeder.

"The first runt's coming out," Ruderman said over the radio.

"Got it, boss," the man said. He was watching from behind a heavy metal screen, an electronic switch in his hand. The switch activated a fast hydraulic pump that threw the open trap door in front of the pig selected for harvest. The animal ran through the opening and into the trailer, then the door slammed shut behind it. Hydraulics ensured there was enough power to contain an angry animal weighing upward of fifteen hundred pounds.

The first runt ran up the slope of the ditch behind a monster twice its size. As soon as the larger hog entered the funnel, Bo pushed a button and the trap door flipped open, smacking the large boar on the butt, and blocking the exit. The runt veered left and ran into the trailer. He pushed the button again and the gate closed.

"One down!" he shouted above the din.

"Turn off the first thumper, Tommie," Ruderman said.

He did and the remaining hogs stampeded from the ditch towards the active thumper.

"Here it comes," Ruderman said over the radio.

The second eight-hundred-pound pig entered the funnel and Bo flipped the switch. The trap door sprang open, and it ran inside the trailer, but as Bo clicked the button again, another boar, right on its tail, ran in behind it. The big metal gate slammed shut on its head and the giant pig squealed and screeched, twisting and shaking the metal cage as if it were plastic. Bo snatched up a cattle prod, stuck it through the bars, and zapped the hog in the face. The creature bellowed in pain and wrenched itself backward, allowing the trapdoor to slam shut.

"Got it!" he yelled as the remaining monsters tore past.

"Good job," Ruderman said, sinking back into the driver's seat. He blew out a breath. "Get them to the hunting grounds and let 'em out."

28

April Flowers grabbed the lat bar, did her last set of pull-downs, then crawled onto the mat for one more set of crunches. That done, she plugged in her headphones, jumped on the treadmill, and started her twenty-minute run-walk program. The gym in the office building was awesome, not only because it was well equipped, but because hardly anyone used it, especially at lunchtime. It was like having her own private gym.

Most people thought all the government agencies were housed in one big federal building in the middle of downtown. In reality, they were scattered, often sharing space with other businesses. The FDA, for instance, was the only federal agency in her building. A lot of the people who worked there weren't even aware of it.

Her workout finished, she took a quick shower and returned to her office. After logging on to her computer, she brought up a report she had been working on, then reached for her lunch bag.

"Rats," she said. "Left it in the car."

She pushed through the parking garage doors and cringed when she saw the cherry-red Focus. It practically glowed in the dark.

"At least it's easy to find," she grumbled.

She grabbed her lunch and as she was walking back noticed a sedan parked at the very end of the row. It was an old Ford Taurus, like the one she'd driven in DC, only gray instead of dark blue. It was covered with a thick layer of dust. She peered in the windows and saw a plain cloth bench seat, power windows, and air conditioning. A standard, no-frills government package. She walked around and noted the plain white and black government license plate. She went back inside.

"Hey, Jamie," she said, peeking around an office door.

"Hi, April. How's it going? Getting settled in?" asked Jamie Reynolds, her supervisor.

"Yep, everything's great, thanks. Uh, had a question. There's a gray Ford Taurus in our vehicle row downstairs. What's up with that?"

"That old thing? It's one of our extra cars. We use it when someone's vehicle is in the shop, or if someone comes in from out of town and needs something to drive. Why?"

"Does it run okay?"

Reynolds shrugged. "I've never driven it, but nobody's ever complained, other than its old and has a lot of miles."

"How many miles?"

She grabbed a sheet of paper from a drawer and ran a finger down a row of figures. "Uh, 87,332."

Flowers felt a rush of excitement. "Can I switch?"

Reynolds' forehead creased. "Why would you want to? Yours is almost brand new."

"Too flashy for me," Flowers said. "My car is DC was an old Taurus. Guess I'm just used to them."

The woman shrugged. "Fine with me." She reached into a metal box and pulled out a set of keys. "Just bring me the keys to the Focus after you swap out."

Grinning like a teenager getting her first car, Flowers returned to the garage.

The Taurus felt like slipping on an old pair of slippers. It could use an oil change and maybe some new tires in the next few months, but it was in good shape for its age. It even had a gun box in the trunk, just like her old one. After filling it with gas and running it through a car wash, she headed back to the office.

A couple hours later, she glanced at the clock. Four-thirty. Greg would be getting ready for his Star Trek convention. She thought about the video call earlier in the week when he showed off his Vulcan ears and nose. She felt a twinge of guilt for turning down his invitation but was glad for the thousand miles of distance between them. She would call him later.

There was a knock on her door.

"Come on in."

Carolyn Richardson peeked around the doorjamb. She was the newest of the five FDA agents assigned to the New Orleans Field Office, having graduated from the academy eight months earlier.

"Do you have a second, Agent Flowers?"

She smiled and pointed at a chair. "Only if you promise never to call me Agent Flowers again. It's April. Come in, sit down."

Flowers was a bit of an item at the office, a mini legend within the small cadre of FDA special agents. They had all heard about the inhaler case in the academy, how she had single-handedly solved it during her rookie year and had saved the lives of several children. They also knew about her connections on Capitol Hill.

Everyone assumed she'd be a supervisor by now, but she had passed up several promotions to remain in the field. Now she was assigned to a "special project," which only added to the mystery. All the attention made Flowers uncomfortable.

"I don't want to bother you," the younger woman said. "I know you're super busy."

"No, not at all. What's up, Carolyn?" The woman reminded Flowers of herself when she was a rookie, full of energy and wanting to save the world but scared to death of messing up. They even looked a little alike, with slim builds and shorter black hair.

"Well, um, I wanted to ask you about your car."

"My car?"

"Yeah," she said fidgeting. "I just dropped mine off at the shop. The transmission went out, and they said it'll take three weeks before they can even get to it. Jamie said you had the keys to the spare car, and I—"

"You need a car?" Flowers said, cutting her off with a smile.

"Uh, yes," she said, looking as if she'd just been called back to the dentist's chair.

Flowers yanked open her desk drawer and pulled out the keys to the red Ford Focus. "You mind driving a fire truck?"

Richardson stammered, "Oh, no, I can't take your new car, I just—"

Flowers laughed. "Trust me, you'll be doing me a favor. I feel kind of guilty not driving it, but as long as someone is..." She handed the fob to the younger agent.

"Thank you so much. I'll take very good care of it," she said, turning red.

"Glad to help. So, how do you like the job so far?"

"I love it, but there's so much to learn."

"And no shortage of work," Flowers added.

"Boy, that's for sure. Seems like there are a hundred new drugs coming onto the market every day, and that's not counting the stuff coming in from other countries. If we had a thousand more agents, we'd still have more work than we could handle."

"I know," Flowers said, feeling a twinge of guilt for not being able to help with the caseload. "But until we have our own TV show and they start writing thrillers about us like the FBI, it ain't gonna happen."

"If we did," Richardson said, "the lead character would be named after you."

"Ha! I stay as far away from the cameras as I can. You need help with anything, just let me know."

The young woman beamed, then stood. "Thanks again, Agen—April."

As she walked out, Flowers wondered how long it would take for the drudgery, paperwork, and bureaucracy that was the United States government to knock the glimmer from her eyes.

29

Greg Crandall rode his motorized skateboard to the East Falls Church Metro Station for his ride to Crystal City. Tall and slender with new silicone ears and nose and clad in a blue and black Star Fleet uniform, he was a dead ringer for the famous alien. He ignored the stares from the other riders, playing up his Vulcan aloofness to a tee.

A few seats over, he caught a young boy watching him and he gave him the split-finger Vulcan greeting. The boy's eyes went wide, then he lifted his right hand and returned the greeting, using the fingers of his left hand to spread the middle fingers apart. Crandall nodded, maintaining his stern look. The boy grinned and whispered something to his mother, who looked over at Crandall and smiled.

As he rode, he thought about the intrusion alerts he'd gotten a couple days earlier. His SAAR program was always being challenged; he would have been concerned if it wasn't. After all, he was tapping into some of the most secure data-mining programs in the world, designed by some of the best computer programmers alive. Their job was to make sure no one did what Crandall had been doing for the past ten months.

These recent attempts had been of a magnitude higher in sophistication than those in the past, but once again his program dodged them. They were good, but he was better. He didn't simply install a firewall or an intrusion prevention system that would terminate the connection when probed, he used what he called a honeypot to attract their attention. When they came at him, his firewall directed them to a mildly sophisticated but benign program which only appeared threatening. This made the computer engineers at the three-letter agencies think they had blocked something important when, in reality, all they had intercepted was a paper tiger. They could claim victory and move on. Then, once a month, he tweaked the bogus program to give them something new to find—and stop—and once again stroke their egos.

In critical moments, men sometimes see exactly what they wish to see. Crandall found the Spock quote to be very true and he wouldn't have been surprised to learn that he'd gotten his computer abilities from a previous life as a Vulcan.

At each stop more Trekkie's piled in, and by the time they reached Crystal City, the tram held three Captain Kirks, a Scotty, a Worf, and a very attractive Deanna Troi. There were even a couple other Spocks, neither of whom came close to capturing the essence of the character like Crandall did.

His excitement grew when he saw costumed characters of every shape, color, and description milling around beneath a model of the USS *Enterprise* suspended above the entrance to the hotel. The mild mid-October night was perfect weather for the convention. The only thing that would have made it better would be if April were with him.

"She doesn't know what she's missing," he said as he put on a stern look, furrowed his brow, and walked inside.

· · · · ●· ● ● · · ·

April Flowers brought up the SAAR spreadsheet, looked at it, and moaned. She hadn't always been so negative. Her first few years, she had been excited, eager to get to work, looking forward to the next battle. While straight enforcement cases could be boring, she got an occasional victory which helped keep her charged up. But the newness soon wore off.

The Genetics Investigation Team had kick started her enthusiasm, and she once again woke up every day looking forward to the next challenge. But all she'd encountered so far were brick walls. It made it hard to maintain her optimism.

Geez, aren't you a Debbie Downer?

One good thing that had resulted from the investigation was getting to know Jake Jessup. If it hadn't been for his support, both physical and emotional, these last couple of months she didn't know if she would, or could, have stuck to it. They made a good team.

That it might turn into something more flitted through her mind occasionally, but when it did, she remembered something he had said on several occasions that he didn't have a problem using animals in combat if it would save the lives of soldiers.

She was concerned with the mistreatment of animals in laboratory environments, and she viewed the creatures in the Army's SPAAD program as lab animals. That was, in fact, her only real venue for investigating, so she had never looked beyond that point—had not wanted to look.

She tried to avoid the "greater good" argument, preferring to see the trees for the forest. Someone had to stand up for these animals. Besides, it was her job to make sure people followed the rules, not to make life easier for the military. *But is it my job to make things more difficult?*

"Ahhh." She laid her head back and stared at the ceiling. "Life was so much easier before I realized how little I knew."

She tilted her head and looked at her phone. Then she grabbed it and punched in a number. It rang twice.

"Joe's Morgue, you stab 'em, we slab 'em."

"That something you picked up in seventh grade?" Flowers said.

"Kindergarten, actually," Jessup said. "I always ran with the fast crowd."

"You sound like you're in a wind tunnel."

"Driving. Got my windows down. Hang on... That better?"

"Yep, much."

"So, what's up? Got a wild weekend planned in the Big Easy?"

"Oh, yeah. Just me and seventy-five pages of SAAR spread sheets. I'm still in the office, slogging through them."

"You're a wild woman. Send me another batch. I finished up the last."

"Anything interesting?"

"Not really. The most unusual one I came across was 25,000 angry bees in a six-foot-wide honeycomb in some guy's attic."

"That doesn't sound like a Section 17 operation to me. Any Big Foot sightings?"

"No, but I did see Elvis in the frozen food section at the Piggly Wiggly the other night," he said.

She chuckled. "Well, you do live in Memphis."

"Got any road trips planned? You had me a little worried after your last excursion."

Her stomach fluttered. "Really? Why's that?"

"It's one thing to go solo in the middle of a decent size city like Alexandria, but to go off in the woods by yourself..."

Her heart sped up and she smiled into the phone.

Then he said, "There's gotta be somebody in your office you can take with you the next time. One of the guys?"

The flutter turned to nausea, then anger.

"What's the matter, Jake?" she said, a knife edge in her voice. "Don't think I can handle myself?"

"No, I didn't say—"

"I handled things just fine this past year, thank you very much. If I need a babysitter, I'll let you know."

"Hey, wait—"
She hung up.

30

— • —

"Congressman, can you step a little more to your left, please? I want to get that sign in the photo."

Congressman Neil Berryman and his wife, Rebeca, dutifully shifted over to reveal more of the information panel, which detailed the animals that could be found along the swamp boardwalk. It had been a day full of photo shoots, meet and greets, and news conferences, and they were tired. But the pictures would look good in the papers, which might keep the environmentalists off his back for a change.

As usual in politics, you traded one set of enemies for a new set. He had stepped on a lot of toes when he pushed through the land acquisition. Though the landowners would get a fair price, they wouldn't get as much as they could have from the oil companies. But the state had enough oil rigs creating sink holes and other environmental messes, which they left behind after they sucked the land dry.

Stopping big oil wasn't the only reason he supported the expansion of the Okaloosa National Wildlife Refuge. He really cared about the park and remembered camping there as a boy scout, back when the area was wild and undeveloped. Besides, the landowners could visit whenever they wanted. They'd just have to do it with everyone else.

The swamp boardwalk hadn't been his idea, but he liked it and had pushed for it. As a result, the four million dollar project, half from federal funding and half from private donations, had been named after him. Thus, the photo op.

At just over two miles, it wasn't the longest boardwalk in the federal park system, but it was close. It was definitely the most scenic. It circled Wood Stork Lake, twenty feet offshore, weaving in and out of the bald cypress and the water tupelo trees. It was designed so that you couldn't see more than twenty-five percent of the structure from any given point, giving people a sense of solitude as they enjoyed nature.

There were four entry points along the route, each connected to different hiking trails. Berryman knew the swamp walkway would be the focal point for the nature preserve and would draw enthusiasts from across the country, and every time one of those thousands of visitors stepped onto the structure, they'd see "Congressman Neil Berryman" blazoned at each entrance.

What he liked best about the boardwalk, though, was that it got you up off the ground, away from the snakes and the ticks. He hated snakes and ticks. Ticks worse than snakes. A snake will stay away from you if you leave it alone. Not a tick. A tick'll crawl up and latch onto you, and you'll never even know it.

He remembered one scout trip, to this very park, when one got him in the crotch. He didn't notice it until it filled with blood and got huge. He freaked out. He didn't know what to do and it was only day three of a week-long campout. He couldn't call his mom, not that he would have anyway, and he sure as hell wasn't going to light it with a match—not down there, so he yanked it off... and it exploded. Blood spattered all over like something out of a slasher movie. But even after he got it cleaned up, the damn spot itched like crazy the rest of the week and for another three days once he got home. No, he did not like ticks.

"I think we've got all the pictures we need, Congressman Berryman," said his chief aide, Phil Joyner, as the photographers returned to their cars. "We ought to get some good writeups from it."

"I just hope it brings in enough votes to balance out the ones I lost when I pushed this thing through."

"The construction brought in a lot of jobs, and the increase in visitors to the park will help fill the restaurants and motels in Yancey City. That'll help offset it," the aide said.

"I hope so. What time is the opening ceremony again tomorrow morning?"

"The two-mile fun run starts at nine as soon as you cut the ribbon. More than two-hundred people signed up for it. That's two hundred potential voters," Joyner said with a wink.

Berryman turned to his wife. "Maybe I should tell them my tick story."

"Oh, Lord," Rebecca said. "Don't let him tell that story, Phil. It'll gross everybody out and he'll never get reelected."

"Yeah," the aide said, nodding. "Better save that one for the cocktail parties."

"Look at that sunset, the way it reflects off the surface of the lake," she said, gazing at the pink and purple clouds that painted the western horizon.

Berryman nodded admiringly.

"It sure grows dark quickly when you're away from all the lights," Joyner said. "You guys sure you want to do this? You gotta be beat."

"Rebecca and I have been looking forward to being the first ones to take an official walk around the lake at night all week. This will be our last chance to have it all to ourselves. Besides, after *The Times Picayune* heard about it and branded us hopeless romantics, we have to do it."

"Thanks a lot," his wife said.

"You sure it's a good idea?" Joyner said, looking at the black surface of the water. "There could be anything waiting in there."

"We're not going swimming, Phil," Berryman said rolling his eyes. "You sound like Rebecca. Everyone thinks if you come to a Louisiana swamp, the alligators will eat you, but they won't bother you unless you wade into the water with them. They avoid humans as much as we avoid them. Probably more. And trust me, we kill a lot more gators than gators kill people. Plus, we'll be four feet above the water, safe, sound, and dry. And if that's not high enough, we'll climb one of the four observation towers."

Unconvinced, Joyner watched the structure slowly disappear into the shadows and said, "It's going to be really dark out there."

Berryman held up a couple of headlamps. "Got it covered, and if you shine it just right, you can see the gator's eyes glow, so you see them before they can get you. Besides, it's a circular trail. As long as we stay on the boards, we can't get lost."

"All right, have fun. I'll be waiting for you."

"No, you won't, Phil," Berryman said. "You look like you're about to fall asleep on your feet. Go back to the hotel and get some rest. We'll see you in the morning for breakfast."

"You sure?"

"Yep, that's an order." Then he turned to his wife and held out his arm. "Ready?"

31

Two hours after he got to the convention, Crandall was exiting the hotel, disappointment and a real scowl etched across his face. He was scratching at his ears and wondering why his mother never told him he was allergic to silicone. The itching had started a half hour after he had arrived. At first it was just annoying, but within an hour, he was clawing at his ears and nose, and drawing strange looks. He even had to cancel a photo-shoot with the hot Deanna Troi he'd seen on the Metro so he could run into the restroom and yank off his body parts. When he came out, his human ears and nose were so red and swollen that someone asked him what character he was impersonating because they didn't remember it from the series.

He thought about stopping at a pharmacy on the way home for some Benadryl but didn't want anyone to see him like this. He even untucked his pants legs from his boots and rolled up the sleeves on his shirt to hide the Star Trek rank insignia. He was miserable and he wondered how long it would take for the swelling to go down.

At least tomorrow is Saturday, he thought.

Frustrated, he rode the escalator down to the train platform and waited for the next northbound car. Fortunately, the station was quiet for a Friday night. There were a couple young women off to his right and a couple of guys to his left. The two girls, probably in their early twenties, seemed pretty tuned up, giggling and laughing, while the two men stared out at the tracks.

The women were very attractive. Students, he figured, judging from their jeans, T-shirts, and light jackets. He eased closer to a Metro map display to avoid their attention.

Crandall thought about Flowers. He had planned to call her from the convention, maybe do a video call so she could see him in his costume. That would not happen now. He was just glad he got some shots for his Facebook page before his wardrobe malfunction. He'd send her one of those tomorrow.

The runway lights on the platform flashed, signaling the approaching train. It pulled efficiently to a stop, the doors swished open, and three people got off. The two young women rushed on, laughing as they went. Crandall waited by the sign for the two men to get on, but they didn't move. He shrugged and boarded.

Just as the doors were about to close, the two men got on, then sat on opposite sides of the car. They stared out the windows, almost as if trying not to look around.

That's weird, Crandall thought.

He glanced over at the two girls and caught them staring at him from the far end of the compartment. When their eyes met, one woman put a hand to her mouth and snorted a laugh, then they both turned away. Crandall's ruby-colored ears turned a deeper shade of red as he summoned a look of Vulcan disregard.

Nobody got off at the next two stations. Crandall watched the men in the reflection of the windows. Though they had been standing together on the platform, they didn't talk or even acknowledge the other's presence. At least it seemed like they had been together earlier. Now they acted like total strangers. And why weren't they looking at him?

If someone walked onto the train doing a Dumbo imitation, I would probably look at them, Crandall thought.

The call for Rosslyn Station came over the speakers, his transfer stop to the Orange Line for the second half of his trip. The doors opened. One girl jumped up, grabbed her companion's arm, and said, "Come on, I gotta pee!" They ran off the train, laughing.

Crandall stood, fighting the urge to scratch his ears. The two men remained seated and kept staring straight ahead. He walked to the exit and a voice at the back of his mind told him to wait. When the lights flashed to signal that the doors were about to close, he stepped off. Behind him, he heard the hiss of the doors closing and felt a wave of relief. Then he frowned and thought, *Vulcans don't get paranoid. It's not logical.*

He took a step, then heard a pop and hiss. He looked back and saw an arm sticking from between the doors. They hissed open, and the two men stepped out.

Crandall's heart rate rocketed as the train pulled away, leaving him alone on the platform with the two strangers.

His skateboard held at port arms to use as a weapon, he shot towards the escalator. He ran to the top and looked back to see the two men coming up behind him, taking the steps two at a time.

To his right were doors leading to the street.

More people, and maybe a cop, Crandall thought.

He heard voices and turned to see the two young women staring at a Metro map on the walkway over the tracks leading to the connecting station. The brunette, wearing a green jean jacket, bounced on her toes and squealed, "Find the bathroom! Hurry!"

Heart pounding, his itchy ears and nose forgotten, Crandall rushed toward the women, hoping his pursuers wouldn't try anything in front of witnesses. He glanced back. The two men had reached the top of the escalator. They stopped and watched him.

Then he remembered, *My phone!* In his panic, he hadn't thought about calling the police. He jammed his skateboard between his legs and fumbled with the keypad.

His eyes went wide with panic. *What's my password!?*

Then he remembered he didn't need it and jabbed the Emergency Call button. When he looked up, he saw the two men walk out the exit doors and into the street.

His skateboard clanked to the ground as his body relaxed and his shoulders drooped.

"911, what's your emergency?" came a voice over the speaker.

"What? Oh, crap." He jerked the phone up. "Sorry, misdial." He clicked off, then shook his head and chuckled. "Dude, you are losing it."

He heard the rumble of an approaching train, snatched up his board and ran for the stairs. As he got to the overpass, he looked to his right and saw the glow of the headlight in the westbound tunnel.

Perfect timing, he thought.

Just then, the brunette stepped in front of him. He skidded to a stop.

"Excuse me," she said, "Do you know where the bathroom—"

A jolt of white-hot pain hit Crandall's neck and his body seized up. The walls of the train station tilted and the train tracks appeared overhead. He suddenly shot upwards towards the tracks and a bright white light.

Katra! Crandall thought just before the Metro Blue Line train number 2047 slammed into him.

32

— ● —

"What the heck?" Jake Jessup looked down at his phone. He was just teasing her. He figured the comment would get her riled up, but he didn't think she'd get that angry.

His phone rang and he smiled. *She's calling back to apologize.* But he saw it wasn't her.

"Good evening, Obi-Wan," he said.

"How's the drive so far?" Frosty Williams said. Williams was Jessup's old partner from the Memphis Police Department and his AA sponsor.

"Making good time. I'm driving past Lake Pontchartrain now. About to get onto I-10."

"You're only a half hour from New Orleans, then. I'm sure she'll be surprised and glad to see you."

"I'm not so sure about that. I just called and was messing with her a little, told her she should be more careful, and take someone with her next time, and she got mad and hung up," Jessup said, shaking his head. "She's so competitive. Thinks she can handle everything herself and won't admit when she needs help."

"I can't imagine anyone being that stubborn," Williams said dryly.

"All right, I get your point, but I'm getting better. After what happened in Memphis, you'd think she'd realize how quickly things can go south. What if they had grabbed her when she was in the woods? Nobody even knew where she was."

"The guy running the SAAR database knew she was heading there to check on the missing kids."

"Yeah, but he's in DC, and from what I understand, he's not exactly field operative material."

"So, who did you say she should take along next time?"

"Somebody," Jessup replied. "One of the guys."

"Ah," Williams said.

"What's 'ah' mean? And don't go throwing that sexism stuff at me. I know women are just as capable of handling themselves as men. I was just thinking that being in the backwaters of Louisiana up against guys with guns... things could turn ugly fast."

"Why are you heading down there if she can just grab one of the guys from the office to go with her?"

"Well..." He hesitated. "I'm bored, for one thing. I don't have anything else going on, so why not go and get a good cup of café au lait? Besides, you told me the AA meetings down here are awesome."

"Hmm."

"Don't 'hmm' me. Why else would I go?"

"It's okay to say you care about someone and are worried about them, Jake."

"She's a friend. Of course, I care about her, just like I care about you and EZ. I mean, she can take care of herself. She doesn't need *my* help in particular."

Williams laughed. "Then why are you about to pull up at her doorstep?"

"I don't know. Maybe I'm as big a control freak as she is."

"I'm sure that's part of the reason," his sponsor said. "When you see her, give her a hug for me and EZ, and check your six. She's been stirring up the hornets' nest again. I don't want either of you getting stung."

"Will do, Frosty. Thanks for the call."

Jessup wondered what Williams was trying to say. It sounded like he was implying there was more than simple friendship involved. But that was ridiculous. Flowers was obviously attractive enough, but they say opposites attract, and they were too much alike. They were definitely more like brother and sister. He pulled into the New Orleans city limits and pushed the thought from his mind.

His timing was not good. The interstate had ground to a stop in the Friday night rush-hour traffic, and his phone app had several red crosses showing traffic slowdowns or accidents between him and 6600 Plaza Drive. This was going to take a while.

He had planned to surprise her at work but hadn't planned on the traffic. Unless she stayed late, she'd be long gone by the time he got there.

He tried calling her and listened to it ring six times before it clicked over to voicemail. He shook his head.

Forty-five minutes later, he finally reached her exit. He had always prided himself on his map reading ability, but he was glad for the GPS on his phone, which took him right to the front door of the office building.

The visitor's lot was across the street. Jessup found a spot, got out, stretched his legs, then headed for the front door. He was halfway across the street when a red Ford Focus shot out of the parking garage and onto the main street. The side tint was dark, but through the windshield, he glimpsed the driver. It was Flowers.

He grabbed his phone and punched in her number as he walked back to his truck, stepping out of the way as a large black truck hurried from the visitor's lot. Again the phone rang six times before rolling to voicemail.

"Ah, come on, April."

By the time he got into his truck and back onto the street, her car was gone. He craned his head around and saw it flash through an intersection and onto the I-10 on-ramp. She lived across the lake in Madisonville, so he headed that way, hoping to catch her.

· · · ● · ● ● · · · ·

Flowers fumed as she skimmed the spreadsheets. She didn't know what made her angrier; him thinking she couldn't take care of herself or her thinking for a second that he actually cared about her.

Why had she thought that, anyway? He had always given her the impression that he was just putting up with her. He hadn't sought her out in Memphis, she had gone looking for him. Even then he'd shot her down, until his friend got hurt and he needed *her* help. Why was she acting like a schoolgirl chasing a boy who didn't even know she existed?

Sure, he showed up at PIT Industries after she'd run him off, but that was only because he wanted to get those responsible for releasing the mutant dogs. He wasn't there for her. She meant nothing to him. Who was she kidding? Well, she wouldn't make that mistake again.

Her phone buzzed with an incoming call. She looked down and saw Jessup's face on the screen. She wanted to be angry but felt an emptiness instead. She turned the phone off, turned back to the computer screen, and hung her head.

Forget this, she thought, *I'm going home.*

33

Berryman and his wife doused themselves with bug spray, then stepped onto the six-foot-wide pressure-treated timbers. They followed the finger pier twenty feet to where it connected with the circular boardwalk, then turned right. The structure wove through a stand of cypress trees and was lit by solar lights attached to the bottom of the guard rails every fifty feet. They gave off just enough light to keep you going in the right direction without being obtrusive or spoiling the mood.

"This really is beautiful, Neil. Your constituents will be very proud of you," Rebeca said.

"It turned out nice, didn't it?" he replied, as the sun dropped below the horizon, turning the lake surface from blood red to black. "I think there's something magical about a boardwalk over the water."

She smiled and gripped his hand tighter.

They walked through a stand of tupelo gums and they found themselves in a bend that was unilluminated.

"Turn off your headlight," he said.

She did, and they were thrown into total darkness.

"Oh, my," Rebecca said. "I can't even see my hand in front of my face!"

"You won't see darkness like this in DC unless you're in the Metro during a power failure. Look at those stars. Come on, let's find some alligators."

Rebecca laughed. "You're as bad as the boys. Next thing you know, you're going to want to bring a frog home."

"Too bad they couldn't come on this trip. They'd love this."

"If they went on every trip you had to take, they'd never graduate from high school. But you're right, they would. We'll have to bring them here on their next break."

They continued around the boardwalk and came to the first of the four observation towers. Berryman climbed to the top of the eight foot by eight foot platform and shined his headlamp around the swampy water. He stabbed a finger at a spot to their right and said, "There!"

Rebeca looked and saw a pair of red orbs glowing just above the duckweed. "Is that an alligator?"

"Yep," the congressman said, smiling. "Very cool. This light's not strong enough to tell how long it is, could be a monster though. They get big around here. We're probably safe up here. They can only jump three or four feet out of the water."

She slapped him on the shoulder. "Stop trying to scare me."

"We'll have to be careful when we're back down on the boardwalk."

"Shut up," she said, trying to sound serious.

He chuckled. They climbed down and continued their walk.

A quarter of the way around, they came to the next finger pier that led to dry land. According to the legend posted at the intersection, it led to the Eagle Peak Creek Trail. The map showed where it connected to other hiking trails and listed the fauna and animals common to the area.

Rebeca looked down it toward the woods. The walkway seemed to vanish into the darkness. "That's creepy." Her husband started to reply, but she threw up a hand. "And don't tell me what might eat me if I walk down there."

His eyes went wide. "Who, me?"

A little further along was a marker for the halfway point. All around them, a million bugs and frogs sang out, each with its own rhythm and cadence.

"It's such a contrast," Rebecca said. "The total darkness combined with all the sounds. It's not quiet, like in your house when all the lights are out, and it's pitch black. I think that's spookier than this is."

"Yeah, but at least in your house, you can hear what's sneaking up on you." He leaned toward her and whispered, "Out here, you'll never hear it coming."

She stopped and placed her fists on her hips. "Neil Berryman, I'm going to throw you over that rail and feed you to the alligators if you keep trying to scare me!"

He barked a laugh and held up his hands in surrender. "Okay, okay, I'm sorry. No more teasing."

"Hmm," she said, her eyes narrow and her lips tight.

A hundred feet later, they came to an area thick with cypress and tupelo trees, two of the most common species in southern deep-water swamps. The canopy grew together and blocked out the star light, making it feel even more closed in. Berryman knew this had been the most difficult and expensive portion of the project to complete because of the dense forest. He was glad he had his headlamp.

Hidden among the trees was the next connecting pier, called Gator Bay Access Point, which led to the Moccasin Point Trail. The Moccasin Point Trail reached the most remote portions of the federal park, and according to the sign, the animals one might see included bobcats, lynx, black bear, alligators, and wild boars.

"I'd love to see a black bear," Berryman said, reading the legend. "But you sure wouldn't see one tonight. Unless it was wearing a headlamp."

Rebecca peered at the walk leading to the woods, the darkness so complete it seemed to suck the illumination from the two tiny solar lights. She shivered.

"No way in the world I'd walk down there, even with this headlamp."

He chuckled. "Trust me, honey, the animals out here are much more afraid of you than you are of them."

"Uh, you would be wrong about that," she said.

The cacophony of insect noise cut off, the sudden silence as startling as a shotgun blast.

"Why did the bugs stop?" she asked, moving close to her husband.

"Curfew," he said laughing as he wrapped his arm around her.

They took a couple of steps, and Rebeca said, "What's that noise?"

Berryman heard it, too. A rapid knocking sound, like someone hitting a log with a stick.

"I don't—"

He paused and looked back at the finger pier. He let go of her, stepped over to it, and looked into the woods.

"What is that?"

"Neil," she said in a warning tone.

"No, no, I'm not trying to scare you. I thought I saw something." He flipped on his headlight, but the feeble beam failed to penetrate the darkness. He relaxed and turned back toward her.

"I guess it was—"

He slowly turned. He peered into the darkness, cocked his head to listen, leaned around a cypress tree, and sucked in a breath.

There was something on the pier.

As he watched, a shape moved into the glow of the furthest footlight.

"Ooooo," he said, blowing out air as if he'd been punched in the stomach, then in a harsh whisper, "Let's go, let's go, let's go." He walked backwards using the handrail to guide himself.

Rebecca's eyes grew wide.

He grabbed her arm and jogged side-stepped, keeping his eyes locked on the access pier. "Come on, come on," he said, as clattering footsteps sounded against the boards.

She threw a terrified look over her shoulder. "What is it? What did you see?"

"There's something on the pier; some kind of animal. I'm not sure what it is, but it's big."

She jerked to a stop and looked at him.

He tightened his grip on her. "Baby, I'm not kidding, I promise. Now let's go!"

The clacking grew louder and faster. Rebeca must have believed him because she was now pulling him.

Berryman saw a huge shadow turn from the finger pier onto the main walkway, its body almost touching the side rails.

How big is it? he wondered in horrified amazement.

It paused by a deck light and he saw the pointed snout and long white sickle-like teeth.

"Run!"

34

Westbound traffic was no better on the interstate, and Jessup was quickly bogged down. He tried the phone again, then sighed when it went directly to voicemail.

I just don't get women, he thought, shaking his head.

He worked his way through traffic and a few minutes later spotted a red compact several car lengths ahead. He maneuvered closer and saw a Tennessee license plate.

I guess that's not her. He looked again and saw the expired sticker. It was the tag they'd used on her car back in Memphis. She must have kept it and put it on her new car.

Jessup chuckled. Then it hit him—the hunt club; if they *were* connected to Section 17 and they ran the tag... He suddenly recalled the warning from the mystery man in PIT City.

He snagged his phone and called April again, and it went to voicemail. He threw it down and jockeyed his way up the fast lane, cutting off a couple of cars. Just when he was about to pull next to her, the tiny Focus shot two lanes to the right.

Jessup cranked the wheel, then jerked it back as the blast of an air horn rattled his windows. A semi blew past him, missing his passenger mirror by inches.

"Shit!" he yelped, his heart pounding.

This time he looked before he eased across into the next lane and saw the compact on the North Causeway Boulevard exit ramp, twenty cars ahead, in front of a large black truck.

He gritted his teeth, threw on his blinker, and bullied the big Tundra across traffic, ignoring the blaring horns and hoping New Orleans drivers weren't as gun happy as Memphians. By the time he got to the exit, the red Focus was on North Causeway Boulevard and committed to the Lake Pontchartrain Causeway Bridge.

· · · ● · ● · · · ·

Flowers pulled out of the parking garage and worked her way to the I-10 on-ramp. Traffic was heavier than she expected, and the old Ford Taurus was not quite as nimble as the Focus.

If she had any sense, she'd get off, head to Bourbon Street and drink a Hurricane at Pat O'Brien's until the traffic died down. The thought of going home to an empty apartment didn't thrill her, but Bourbon Street made her think about her promise to take Jessup to Café du Monde for coffee and beignets, and that depressed her even more. So, she passed the exit for the French Quarter and merged onto the Causeway Bridge exit.

· · · ● · ● · · · ·

Jessup tried to catch up, but everyone around him seemed to have the same idea. Traffic remained tight and the best he could do was use the big black truck as an indicator of where the red car was. He felt anxious and wondered why. Nothing had happened, and other than being irritated at him, Flowers had sounded fine on the phone. He just needed to relax and enjoy the drive.

A minute later, he was on the bridge. Jessup loved crossing it. The lake was so wide it was like driving over the ocean. He'd read about its construction at the Lake Pontchartrain Basin Maritime Museum during an earlier trip to the city.

At just under twenty-four miles, the structure, which was actually two separate bridges, was the world's longest continuous bridge over water. The first bridge, just two lanes wide, was built in 1956 and carried traffic in both directions until its sister bridge opened in 1969, allowing for two lanes of traffic to flow in each direction. The LPCB had never sustained major damage from storms—a rarity among causeways. Even after Hurricane Katrina, they were able to use them as a route for emergency services into the city.

Traffic started to spread out, and Jessup was finally able to jockey closer to Flower's vehicle. The bright red compact came in and out of view in front of the truck.

Whoever was driving the big Chevy was keeping it tight and Jessup was surprised Flowers hadn't left it in the dust, considering how she drove.

I'd hate to have his gas mileage, he thought listening to the rumble of its massive mud tires against the pavement. The Tundra's was bad enough.

He inched closer and noticed the stickers on the back bumper and tailgate. Most of them were cartoon pigs. Boar hunting, he knew, was big in the south, which explained the mud tires and the dirt that seemed to cover every surface.

He pulled up next to it and looked up at the cab. The tint was as black as the paint, and Jessup wondered how anybody could see out. The older he got, the worse his eyes got, and the less he like window tint, especially at night.

Damn, you're only forty-three, but you're bellyaching like you're seventy.

He tried to pull next to Flowers, but a woman in the car ahead of him kept pace with the Focus as she talked on her phone. Jessup looked again. Yep, the same old Tennessee license plate they'd taken off that abandoned car in the marina parking lot. *It was a good thought, April, but now you're just a spotlight for the bad guys.*

The lady in front of him slowed down, forcing him to fall back. As he did, he looked again at the rear of the truck and noticed that the license plate was clean. At first, he assumed it was new, but then he noticed the six-month-old registration sticker.

Now why is that plate not splattered with mud like the rest of the truck?

Jessup's spidey senses tingled. He picked up his phone and called Williams.

"What's up, Jake? How's April?" the man said.

"Don't know yet, Frosty. I'm still trying to catch up to her."

"What?" he said, laughing.

"I'll explain in a minute. You got someone who can run a Louisiana tag real quick?"

"Of course; give it to me."

"1X7FW4. It's on a black Chevy Silverado."

"All right, give me a minute and I'll call you back." Williams hung up, asking no questions. Using official databases for unofficial purposes could get you fired, but Williams had friends in the department who trusted him. And he knew Jessup wouldn't ask if it wasn't important.

A half minute later, his phone rang.

"Yep," Jessup said.

"It comes back on a 2001 Dodge pickup registered to Clara and Enos Norton in Rutland, Louisiana."

His radar cranked up a notch. "Somethin' ain't right, Frosty."

"What do you have?"

Jessup gave him a twenty-second sketch of the situation.

"You're right, something's not right."

"And I know that name from somewhere," Jessup said. Then he said, "Oh shit, that's the name of one of the missing kids April went searching for. I gotta go, Frosty."

He hung up and pushed redial for Flowers. Again, it went straight to voice-mail.

"Damn it!"

He had to catch up to her, but the woman in front of him was blissfully ignorant of the world around her.

"What is wrong with you, April? You don't drive this slow in the McDonalds drive thru!" Jessup shouted at the windshield. "Speed up!"

He jammed down on his horn and flashed his lights, trying to get the woman to move, but she only slowed down.

"Damn it!" Jessup cursed in frustration, and for a split second he considered bumping the woman to get her to move. Then he saw blue lights flashing at one of the thousand-foot-long emergency turnouts installed every two miles along the bridge. A causeway police car was stopped behind a disabled car, its emergency lights flashing. Jessup hit his horn again and waved his arm at the officer as they shot by, hoping to get his attention, but all he saw in his rearview mirror was a solid block of traffic and the emergency lights fading into the distance.

35

They gasped for air as they ran, weaving through the trees, while across the lake the dim glow of the ranger's station came in and out of view. Spanish moss brushed against Rebeca's face and she screeched. Behind her, the monster squealed and snorted excitedly.

"What is it, Neil?" she gasped, terror in her voice.

"Hog!"

She slowed. "A pig? Are they dangerous?"

"Keep running!" he barked, yanking her forward. "I don't know, and I don't want to find out, 'cause this one's big. Real big."

The wood structure trembled as the creature gained on them. For a second, Berryman thought he should stop and try to scare it, but it was so big, he didn't think it would be able to turn around within the confines of the walkway.

His wife slowed to a fast stumble, looked over her shoulder, and screamed, "Oh, my God! Oh, my God!"

"There!" he shouted as an elevated deck came into view. "Maybe it will run past us."

They hit the platform and Berryman practically threw his wife onto it. He was clawing his way up the steps when the giant hog slid to a stop, turned, and lunged at his feet. Its snout slapped the riser where his shoe had been a split second earlier, and the impact shook the structure. Rebeca screeched as Berryman yanked his knees up and rolled across the wood.

He looked over and saw a black tube duct taped to a support. It was knocking loudly, and a green light was flashing at one end. It was the noise they'd heard earlier

What the hell?

The huge boar slammed its hooves onto the second set of stairs, looked up at them, and squealed in protest. It swung its massive head back and forth, grunting and snarling, seemingly confused by the obstruction it now faced.

Impossibly big, covered in brown and black hair, the boar filled the four-foot-wide staircase. Twin foot-long tusks jutted up from its lower jaw, backed by six-inch upper incisors; they swung through the air like razor sharp scythes. Nothing grew that big in the wild, at least not in Louisiana.

"Get out of here!" he shouted as he charged the edge of the stairway, trying to scare it off. The thing squealed louder and lunged forward, placing a front paw on the next step.

"Oh, shit!" he yelped as he jumped back.

The pig climbed to the third step, locked its black eyes on Rebeca, and squealed a challenge. She screamed and dug at the guardrail, her terror exciting the animal as it scraped a hoof across the wood.

My phone! Berryman suddenly remembered. He yanked it from his pocket and punched the emergency call button—nothing. He looked at it. No service. How could that be? They'd had three bars at the ranger station.

Bang! The pig slammed a foot onto the platform and rocked its massive head and shoulders back and forth like Ray Charles singing "Shake a Tail Feather." The deck groaned and Berryman wondered if it would support them.

He pulled his wife to her feet. Her eyes were wide, her face ghost white. She shook her head as if denying what she was seeing would make it go away.

"Jump!" he barked.

She looked at the water, then back at him, her eyes even wider. "No, no, no, no, no."

He grabbed her arm and pushed.

"Alligators!" she screamed.

"They won't bother you," he screamed back, trying to convince himself as he grabbed her arm to force her over the rail.

"No!"

She ripped away from his grasp just as the razorback stomped onto the platform.

Berryman shouted and charged the beast.

With a flip of its head, the creature hooked the congressman in his inner left thigh. The foot long tusk cut through his flesh like a hot knife through butter, slicing tendons and muscle, and severing his femoral artery. It hit bone and propelled Berryman through the air, over the railing and into the lake. He landed with a loud splash but was dead from blood loss before the first alligator reached him.

Splattered by her husband's blood and screaming at the top of her lungs, Rebeca ran past the animal and down the stairs.

By the time the boar got turned around, she was a hundred yards down the boardwalk, and running faster than she thought possible.

The structure shuddered when the pig slammed down onto the walkway. When she looked back, it was coming after her at a full run. She couldn't believe something so big could run so fast. She sobbed for her husband. She couldn't make herself jump into the swamp. The thought of being ripped apart by one of those reptiles was more frightening than what was coming after her.

It was almost on her.

Rebeca stumbled forward, her breath coming in great, jagged gasps. She could almost feel its breath on her neck as massive hooves slammed into the wood and rattled the structure.

She saw the next walkway leading to shore. If she could get there, she could climb a tree. She hit the intersection, grabbed the handrail, and swung herself around, losing no speed.

The giant pig had to slow to make the turn, and it snorted and squealed in protest as its prey started to slip away.

Hope rose in her as she ran past the first deck light. Halfway to the second, a huge shape lumbered onto the walkway. Rebeca skidded to a stop as a second hog bellowed a challenge and charged. She looked back and saw the first pig running at her. The pier shook as if caught in an earthquake.

She looked into the inky black water, lifted a foot onto the cross rail, and hoisted herself up. Her eyes locked on the shining surface, she pushed herself off. Just as she cleared the guardrail, the second hog jumped, clamped onto her foot, and snatched her back.

Her last thought as she was crushed under their weight was, *I'm glad the kids aren't here.*

36

—·—

April Flowers snarled in frustration as she crept along, going just under the speed limit. Why people drove in the passing lane when they weren't passing was a mystery to her. A basic rule of driver etiquette was if you're in that lane, never go slower than the person behind you.

Of course, she didn't know why she was in a hurry, the only thing waiting for her was an empty apartment. She glanced again at her phone sitting on the passenger seat. She should turn it back on, but the phone not ringing was easier than ignoring it when it did ring—but not by much.

Had he even tried to call back? she wondered, then she shook her head. *Stop it, April. He doesn't care about you, so just accept it and move on. If he offers to help, take it, or don't, but don't make yourself crazy trying to see something that's not there.*

A sea of red lights appeared as a causeway police car worked its way into traffic from an emergency lane, its lights and siren blaring.

"Great, probably heading to an accident."

She turned on a Pandora folk music station, settled back, and resigned herself to a long slow commute home.

• • • ● • ● • • •

Jessup saw the flashing emergency lights in his rearview mirror, but they were a quarter mile back. Around him, cars had backed off a couple of lengths, no doubt from his honking and erratic driving. He whipped in behind the black truck, hoping the woman blocking him would slow enough for him to get past. But she maintained her speed and kept watching him in her mirror.

Just then, her brake lights flashed. Behind her, horns blared, but Jessup didn't hesitate. He whipped into the passing lane, but the Chevy beat him to it and pulled alongside the red Focus, the subcompact looking like a toy car next to it.

The truck's brake lights flared and Jessup instinctively locked up his brakes. The nose of the Tundra pitched forward as the tires squealed in protest and everything on the seats flew forward.

"You motherfucker!" Jessup shouted as he hit the gas, but the Silverado had already shot ahead. It pulled alongside the car just as the next emergency lane came into view. When the red compact drew even with the turnoff, the big truck eased to the right, forcing it over. Then it jumped behind the Focus and accelerated, ramming into the little car, pushing it toward the barrier at the end of the breakdown lane. When the car tried to get back into traffic, the truck slammed into it, pushing it sideways. Smoke poured from the Ford's tires. At the last minute, the truck jerked back to the left and the little car hit the barrier.

Jessup watched in horror as the red Ford Focus flipped over the guardrail and disappeared into the darkness.

He jammed on the brakes and the Tundra slid sideways to a stop, two feet from the guardrail. A second later, Jessup was at the concrete railing looking into a black abyss and kicking off his sneakers, oblivious to the sounds of screeching tires, crashing cars, and blaring horns.

He had a foot on the rail and was ready to go over when a strong pair of hands grabbed him and jerked him back.

"Get off me! I gotta get her!" he screamed as he fought to pull away.

"Someone help me!" said the cop. Two more sets of hands latched onto Jessup and they pulled him down as he kicked and cursed and screamed.

"Let me go. We have to help her! Get some divers out here!"

"It's too late," the officer said. "You can't get to her, dude. The water's sixty-five feet deep. The car's gone."

Jessup pressed his face into the concrete and moaned.

"That's him, officer. He's the one who pushed that car over the railing," said a woman as she climbed out of a brown Jeep Cherokee. It was the one who had blocked Jessup in traffic.

"What?" Jessup said, still struggling to get free. "It wasn't me. It was another black truck. I was trying to stop it."

The woman, who wore a blue baseball cap and sunglasses, said, "He's crazy. He was honking and flashing his lights. I thought he was going to ram *me* with that truck."

Jessup felt handcuffs tighten around his wrists.

"Hey!" he shouted. "It wasn't me. There was another black truck. I have the tag number, damn it. That was my friend that got pushed in."

The cop jerked Jessup to his feet, and with the help of a couple of bystanders, dragged him over to a squad car. As they went to put him in the back seat,

Jessup saw the woman in the brown Jeep pull off her hat and sunglasses and look straight at him. His mouth dropped open.

It was the trainer from PIT Industries.

· · · · ●· ● · · · ·

Flowers saw another wave of brake lights, started to complain, but caught herself.

At least I didn't get in a wreck, she thought. *I should be grateful.*

She tried to concentrate on the music, but it was hopeless. All she could think about was how Jessup had risked his life for her; had gotten thrown in jail for drug trafficking while helping her. He was a good friend and she had no right to expect anything more from him.

Feeling guilty for getting angry and hanging up on him, she grabbed her phone and turned it back on. It lit up, then chirped three times with missed calls, all from Jessup. She quickly pushed the redial button. The phone rang six times, then: *"This is Jake, please leave a message at the tone."*

She cringed, then said, "Hey, it's me. Just wanted to say hi, and I shouldn't have hung up on you like that. I know you're just concerned and I appreciate it. Call me back when you get this message."

She put the phone down, then looked at it, wondering if he was busy, or if, like her, he was angry and had turned his off.

She sat in traffic for ten minutes thinking about it. Then the left-hand lane slowly moved forward. She tried him again and got his voicemail. She shook her head. *He's mad at me.*

Traffic crept toward flashing blue lights a half mile up. Behind her, several more sets of emergency lights approached.

Wow, it must be a bad one, she thought. She started to pull over, but the other lane was bumper to bumper. Better to just keep going, get past it and get out of the way.

As she drew near, she saw the blockage was in the breakdown lane.

Convenient, she thought.

But instead of a mass of crushed vehicles, all she saw was a squad car and a single black truck, turned sideways near the abutment, with a dozen people at the guardrail looking into the water.

Oh my God, she thought. *Did somebody jump?*

Then she saw the Tennessee license plate with the thin blue line sticker and her heart froze. "Jake? No!" she jerked to a stop at the side of the bridge, jumped out and ran back, chanting, "No, no, no, no!"

37

Horns blared and sirens screamed as emergency vehicles pulled up, lighting the bridge like the noon sun. Below, powerful engines roared, and the red, white, and blue emergency lights of a Coast Guard Zodiak and a Sheriff's Department Rescue boat painted the bridge supports and the water's surface.

"Stop right there," a cop shouted, holding up a hand. "Get back in your car."

"I know that truck. I know the owner," Flowers said in a panicked voice.

"I don't care. You gonna have to—"

She yanked out her credentials. "Federal agent, let me through."

The officer hesitated, not sure what to say. She pushed past him and glanced inside the truck. It was definitely Jessup's. She ran to the railing where first responders were shouting instructions to a fishing boat idling below.

"Depth finder says fifty-seven feet," one of the fishermen said. "Don't see any shapes on sonar, but with the current, it probably floated off as it sank."

"What floated off?" Flowers asked.

A fireman looked at her. "Who are you?"

"Federal agent. What floated off?"

"A car. The guy in that truck pushed it into the lake," the fireman said, jerking a thumb toward Jessup's Toyota.

Her eyes went wide. "What?"

He shrugged. "According to a witness, the driver of that truck pushed a red car over the guardrail. He's in the back of the squad car."

Flowers spun around and ran for the police car, but before she got there, a beefy hand grabbed her arm.

"Whoa, hold up, young lady."

"I'm a federal agent," she said to the police officer. "I'm looking for Jake Jessup."

He peered at her. "What's your name?"

"April Flowers."

His eyes went wide. "Show me some ID."

She did. He looked at it, shook his head, blew out a breath, then keyed his mike. "This is Unit 2117. Continue searching for an unknown victim but cancel the broadcast on April Flowers. I've got her right here."

"What? What are you talking about? Why did you think it was me?"

"Because of him," the cop said, pointing at the police car.

She looked over and saw Jake looking at her as if he'd seen a ghost.

"Let him out," she demanded.

"We have a witness who said he pushed a car over the railing, Agent Flowers."

"That's ridiculous. Look" —she jabbed a finger at the front of the Tundra— "there's no damage."

The cop nodded. "I realize that. We're checking on someth—" His phone rang. He listened for a second, asked a couple of questions, then hung up. "That was my dispatcher. They just reviewed the bridge cameras and verified that it was not Mr. Jessup's truck that caused the accident."

"Good. Let him out," Flowers repeated.

The officer opened the back door and removed the handcuffs. Jessup pushed past him and grabbed Flowers in a bearhug.

Eyes wide with amazement and bloodshot from crying, he held onto her and stammered, "What—how—who..."

"What happened, Jake? Why are you here?" she asked, tears now streaming down her own face.

"I came down to surprise you and to help you with your investigation. You scared me to death when you told me what happened in the woods."

She looked up at him, not sure how to respond. "But how did you end up here? And what's this about a truck running someone off the bridge?"

"I was heading to your office when you hung up on me. When I called back and you didn't answer, I drove there to talk to you."

Her face flushed.

"I saw you come out—well, I thought it was you—in a red Ford Focus. I caught up to it on the bridge and saw the expired Tennessee tags, so I knew it was your car."

Flowers paled. "What?"

"Yeah, there was a big black Silverado following it. The license plate said it belonged to one of the kids you were looking for."

She suddenly grabbed Jessup's shirt, her eyes filled with terror. "What happened to the red car, Jake?"

"That's what I've been trying to tell the cops. The Chevy truck rammed it and pushed it into the lake."

• • • ● • ● • ● • • •

Flowers waited in the lobby of the New Orleans Police Department Headquarters, staring out the window, her eyes raw from crying, praying she would wake up from this horrible nightmare. Carolyn Richardson, twenty-five years old, nine months on the job, was dead. Dead because of her.

A door slammed open and Jessup stormed out. "These bozos were trying to call it an accidental hit and run. Now they're putting out a BOLO on the missing kids and saying Enos Norton is wanted for homicide." He shook his head. "The only good thing is that somebody will actually look for them now."

He sat beside her; concern etched on his face. "How are you doin', kiddo?"

She looked down and said nothing.

He put his arm around her shoulders. "This is not your fault, April."

"It *is* my fault. If I had given her the keys to the old Taurus, she'd still be alive."

"Yeah, and you'd be dead."

"But this wasn't her fight, Jake. She had nothing to do with any of this. At least I knew the stakes. Heck, it was because I went into the woods that brought all this about."

"No, rogue agents conducting illegal operations killed Carolyn, not you. You were just doing your job, which is to investigate their activities. You've gotta focus all that anger on the people who are responsible."

Flowers tipped her head back, closed her eyes and took in a deep breath. "Are you sure the woman in the Jeep was the trainer from PIT?"

"Yeah," he said, nodding. "I'm sure. It's only been a couple months, and when she drove past at PIT Industries she was twenty feet away and looked straight at us."

"I talked to the officer on the bridge. The tag on the Jeep was stolen off a car in Slidell yesterday and he didn't get a chance to get her name before she drove off," Flowers said.

"So, what now?" Jessup asked.

"My supervisor, Jamie Reynolds, is on her way over here."

A television next to the desk sergeant was tuned to a 24-hour news station, which was showing scenes from the bridge incident. A helicopter news crew had filmed the scene not long after the calls went out. On the replay, Jessup's truck was sitting sideways on the bridge near the railing while emergency vessels lit up the lake's surface and divers prepared their gear.

The automatic doors swooshed open and in walked Reynolds. An attractive black woman in her mid-forties, she wore tan slacks, a dark blue blouse, and a black windbreaker with "FDA Special Agent" stenciled across the back. Her red-rimmed eyes belied her stern look.

Flowers shook her head and wept. Reynolds pulled her close as she, too, teared up. After a second, she said, "Sit down, April." She turned. "You must be Jake Jessup."

He nodded.

"I heard what you did out on the bridge. I want to thank you for trying to save her."

"I just wish I could have."

"Me, too." Then she turned to Flowers. "Tell me what happened."

Flowers told her about Richardson's car being in the shop, asking to borrow the keys to the extra car, and how Flowers had convinced the woman to take the red Ford Focus.

"Sounds like if it hadn't been Carolyn it would have been you."

"It should have been me," Flowers said staring at the floor.

Reynolds scowled. "That's bull. This is not your fault, so don't blame yourself. The son of a bitch who rammed her car into the lake is one who's responsible."

Flowers said nothing.

"Now, I'd like to know why they came after you, but I also know you are working a highly classified case; need to kn—"

"You know James Costa at headquarters?" Flowers asked in a quiet voice.

Reynolds chuckled. "Ole Jimmy C? Yeah, he was one of my instructors at the academy a thousand years ago."

"Jimmy's one of a handful of people who knows what my assignment is. When I told him I was heading to New Orleans, he said if there was one person in the FDA I could trust, it was you. So, I'm going to tell you everything."

Just then an announcement came over the television at the front desk.

"This just in. The bodies of Louisiana Representative Neil Berryman and his wife Rebeca were found at a federal wildlife refuge in northern Louisiana, the apparent victims of an animal attack."

38

— • —

"Oh, my God, no!" Flowers said running over to the counter. She stared at the stock photos of the congressman and his wife as the anchor read from notes someone had placed in front of him.

"Details are still coming in, but reports say that Congressman Berryman and his wife were at the Okaloosa National Wildlife Refuge for tomorrow's grand opening of a boardwalk bearing the representative's name. The couple went for an early evening walk around the boardwalk. When they didn't return, park rangers investigated and found their remains on a trail, several feet from the water. Unnamed sources say the bodies appear to have been mutilated by some type of animal."

Jessup looked at Flowers as the color drained from her face. She leaned against the counter to steady herself.

Reynolds stared at Jessup and Flowers. "What the hell is going on?"

Tears rolled down Flowers cheeks and she drew in a deep breath. "Let's go back to the office and I'll tell you everything."

As they headed for their vehicles, two men got out of a dark blue Chevrolet Suburban and approached them. Jessup stepped in front of Flowers, while Reynolds pulled back her jacket, exposing her service pistol and badge.

The two strangers stopped and held out their hands. "FBI," said a husky black agent. "I'm Agent Preston Robbins, and this is Agent Richard Crispen." They held out their IDs.

Robbins looked at Flowers and asked, "Agent Flowers, do you know Greg Crandall?"

She felt her chest tighten. "Yes."

"He was killed tonight in Washington."

Flowers staggered and Jessup grabbed her arm.

Reynolds asked, "Isn't he the FDA's computer expert at headquarters?"

"Yes, ma'am," Crispen replied. "And you are...?"

"FDA Supervisory Special Agent Jamie Reynolds. Agent Flowers works for me."

"But—what—how?" Flowers said, trying to focus, but unable to breathe.

"All we've been told is that he committed suicide. Jumped in front of a Metro train," Robbins said.

"That's bull! Greg would never kill himself!"

"It happened right after we learned he had hacked into several government databases. Have you ever heard of something called SAAR?"

This time Flowers did collapse. Jessup and Reynolds grabbed her to keep her from falling, then Robbins said, "Why don't you have a seat in our vehicle, Agent Flowers? You'll be coming with us, anyway."

· · · · ●· ● · · ·

It took until six the following morning for Flowers to convince the agents she did not know where Crandell was getting his information. She deflected some of the questions concerning GENIT, saying it concerned the abuse of laboratory animals and civilian casualties related to that activity.

Physically and emotionally numb, she walked through the lobby of the FBI office where Jessup waited. As he gave her a hug, Agents Robbins and Crispen rushed out the front door wearing their FBI windbreakers and carrying duffle bags.

"Let me guess, Congressman Berryman," Jessup said. "Since we got here, I've seen at least twenty agents arrive then run out with their gear."

She nodded. "Yeah, the whole time they were talking to me, they kept checking their phones for updates. I bet every FBI agent within a five-state area is up there."

"I learned a while back that the most dangerous place to stand is between an FBI agent and a TV camera," Jessup said, hoping for a smile, but her lips just tightened.

"So, now what?" she said.

"Your boss is waiting for us at her office. She had someone pick up your car, so you can ride with me."

· · · · ●· ● · · ·

Reynolds had the television on when Flowers and Jessup came in. On the screen were news crews standing outside the entrance to the Okaloosa National Wildlife Refuge. Two state police cars blocked the entrance behind them.

She grabbed the remote, hit mute, and motioned them to a pair of chairs. After they sat, she lifted her hands. "Well?"

Forty-five minutes later, Reynolds stared disbelievingly at Flowers. "My God, all those people killed?"

"That's just in the states," Flowers said. "Most of them were innocent. That doesn't count the hundreds killed overseas in military operations using the animals. While most of them were enemy combatants, not all of them were."

"And they died from a bacterial infection caused by this NF-13?"

"In combat situations, the animals kill the enemy almost exclusively because that's who they encounter first. Civilian deaths occur when people come in to tend to the wounded and bury the dead," Flowers said.

"The mutant pit bulls in Memphis weren't infected with the bacteria," Jessup said. "That was pure animal rage."

"And these kids that went missing, what caused you to look into that?" Reynold asked.

Flowers voice caught. She swallowed and said, "That was Greg. He ran across it while searching police reports. It was just a hunch he had because it was close to the delivery warehouse in Alexandria. And we know Section 17 moved Operation PIT somewhere down here."

"They made a mistake using the tags off the missing kid's truck and that trainer to block traffic for the killer," Jessup said. "Now we know without a doubt their disappearance is tied to Section 17."

"But what does a wild boar hunting club have to do with giant pit bulls?" Reynolds asked.

"I have no idea," Flowers said.

"And you're sure Greg didn't kill himself?"

"I *know* Greg didn't kill himself," Flowers said, her voice rising. "They killed him, just like they killed Carolyn, and just like they killed Congressman Berryman and his wife."

"Are you suggesting these giant pit bulls killed them?"

"It's the only thing that makes sense," Jessup said.

"But why? What did he have to do with any of this?"

Flowers looked at the floor. "The congressman was one of my backers on Capitol Hill. He and a senator pulled the strings at the FDA that got GENIT started."

Reynolds fell back in her chair. "The inhaler investigation."

Jessup looked confused.

Flowers said, "A couple of years after that, he heard federal funds were being used to genetically alter animals. He thought it might fall under the purview of the Food and Drug Administration and asked me to look into it. I followed the trail to the military's Special Projects Animal Assets Department Project. While investigating them, I heard rumors about the genetically altered necrotizing fasciitis."

"Basically, germ warfare," Reynolds said.

"Yes."

"But why now? Surely checking on three missing kids didn't set all this off. I mean, at that point, all you had were some suspicions."

"Exactly," Jessup said. "There's more to this than April stumbling onto that hunt club. But whatever it is, it all points back to them protecting Section 17. Taking out Greg shut down SAAR. Taking out Berryman removed half her support in Congress. And if they had been successful in killing April, we wouldn't even be having this conversation. Operation GENIT would cease to exist. In the meantime, the congressman's death would overshadow the other two murders."

"And you seriously think these people would go to these lengths to protect their operation?"

"Yes," they said at the same time.

There was a knock at the door.

"Come in," Reynolds said.

When the door opened, she stood. "Director Dillon."

39

Walter Dillon was a big man in an expensive suit. He was accompanied by a shorter man in a cheaper suit. They both wore the same arrogant look.

He glanced from Flowers to Jessup and his lip curled. Then he turned to Reynolds. "We need to talk to you... alone."

In the hallway, Jessup asked, "Who's the suit?"

"The director of the FDA. The big kahuna."

"He didn't look happy."

"Well, he's got two dead employees."

"Who's the other guy?" Jessup said.

"No clue."

"You ever met Dillon?"

"No," Flowers said. "He's the third new FDA director we've had since I've been here; they're all political appointees. I try to stay away from them if I can."

Five minutes later, the door opened, and Reynolds stuck her head out. Flowers' stomach tightened at the look on her face.

"April, can you come back in, please?"

The two men were sitting in the chairs, so Flowers stood.

"Agent Flowers, I'm Director Walter Dillon and this is Special Agent Downey with OPR."

Her stomach clenched again at the mention of the Office of Professional Responsibility, the equivalent of internal affairs at a police department.

"I won't ask you any questions now. We'll have plenty of those at your official hearing back in DC when you're accompanied by a union rep, or preferably a lawyer."

Her eyes narrowed. "I don't see why I would need either, Director."

Dillon drew back in surprise. "Oh, you don't? How about the improper and unauthorized use of government equipment for that little database program Greg Crandall was handling for you? You did know it was tied into the FDA mainframe, didn't you? Potentially exposing sensitive data to the outside world?

Or how about possible charges of espionage? Are you saying you didn't know about the secret programs he accessed to get that information?"

"No," Flowers said, her lips curling into a snarl. "I did not."

"Oh, okay," he said condescendingly. "I'll try an easy one then. They just pulled Agent Richardson's car—your car—out of the lake. She was still in it, by the way."

She sucked in a breath and leaned against the door.

"Can you at least tell me why a government vehicle came to have an expired Tennessee license plate on it?"

She dropped her head.

"No?" But before she could reply, Dillon said, "No, don't say anything. The hearing will be at headquarters a week from Monday. Until then, you're suspended. Give your gun and your shield to Agent Downey."

Downey held out a hand, but Flowers slapped her credentials and pistol onto Reynolds' desk.

Downey smirked. "Your rifle and shotgun?"

She pulled the keys to the Taurus from her pocket, tossed them onto the desk, and walked out.

• • • ● • ● • • • •

Her body trembling, she walked up to Jessup. "Did you..."

"Yeah, I listened at the window."

He followed her back to her office. She pointed at the empty chair. He sat and looked around, then said, "I didn't know you were a *Star Trek* fan." He nodded toward a photograph on a filing cabinet.

Her shoulders drooped and she fell into her chair. "That's Greg. He's a—*was*—a huge fan. Got himself professionally made up as Spock and had that picture made, then gave it out for Christmas last year."

There was another photo of Flowers and Crandall in a restaurant.

Jessup gave a small smile. "I'm really sorry about your friend, April. I wish I could have met him."

She grabbed a tissue and dabbed at her eyes.

He looked at the floor. "Were you two... close?"

"Huh?" she said, lifting her head, a confused look on her face. "Close? You mean, like... close-close?"

Jessup flushed, then stammered, "I—I don't know."

A sad smile crossed her face and she shook her head. "He wanted there to be something, but no. He was a nice guy, a little weird, but nice. And he didn't kill himself—and he didn't deserve to be killed."

"After everything that's happened tonight, there's no doubt in my mind he was murdered."

"There are surveillance cameras covering every inch of the Metro, but I'm sure that's already been destroyed." She pointed at Jessup's left arm. "What's that on your wrist?"

Jessup smiled and unclipped it. "It's a survival bracelet. Davie gave it to me during my visit." He handed her the black strap. "It's woven from parachute cord. I can use it in emergencies to build a raft or rappel down a mountain. That kind of stuff."

"That's very cool," she said, studying it. "Just the thing for a MacGyverite."

Just then her door opened, and Reynolds walked in carrying a long, black duffle bag. She sat in the other chair and rubbed her face.

"You're having almost as bad a day as me," Flowers said. "Sorry I brought all this down on you."

Her supervisor shook her head. "It's not your fault. And don't be fooled, Dillon isn't as outraged as he makes out. Berryman was one of a handful of congressmen who voted against him getting the head FDA slot. Besides, with him and his wife getting killed, Carolyn's and Greg's deaths will be ancient history by the time everything dies down. He won't feel any heat from it."

She reached down and opened the duffle. "In the meantime, I'll do what I can from here."

Flowers looked puzzled.

"What kind of weapons do you have at home?" Reynolds asked.

"Uh, a five-shot Chief and a Glock 40. Why?"

"Here." Reynolds lifted a lethal looking black rifle equipped with a reflex sight, from the bag. "This is my personal Colt M5. There's also a Remington 870, plus plenty of spare ammo."

Flowers and Jessup looked at each other, then back at Reynolds.

"If you need anything run, anything checked, or if you get in a serious jam, you call me on my personal cell phone. Here's the number." She handed Flowers a business card.

"Wait, I don't understand," Flowers said.

"You can't go after these sons of bitches with just a couple of pistols," Reynolds said. "Better get going. You only have a week to figure out who killed my agent, your friend, and a decent politician and his wife."

40

"What should we do first?" Flowers asked as they walked out to Jessup's truck.

"Stop by your place, get you a change of clothes and your guns, then head to the scene of the crime. Maybe shake something loose. It worked in Memphis."

She huffed. "Which crime?"

"Good point," he said. He thought for a moment. "The federal park. It's in the same area as the missing kids and the hunt club." He looked at her glassy eyes. "You sure you don't need to get some sleep first?"

"I don't want to close my eyes. When I do, I see their faces. Let's go do this."

After stopping at Flowers' apartment, they worked their way to I-55, where Jessup turned north.

"What's up?" Flowers asked. "We're heading toward Mississippi."

He pointed to the GPS map on his phone screen. "If we take 55 north to Jackson, then cut west on I-20, it's all interstate. Should save us some time. Either way, it's a long drive."

American flags were flying at half-staff along the route. Flowers turned to a news station out of New Orleans which had non-stop coverage about the Berryman's death. There was no mention of Richardson's death.

"It'll be even bigger in DC," she said, turning it off. "Greg won't even rate a footnote to a footnote."

"Especially if they claim it was suicide."

"But how can they say that? Anyone who knew Greg knows he would be the last one in the world to kill himself."

"Remember who we're dealing with. They'll come up with someone who will say he'd been depressed lately, that he was always kind of moody. Add to that an overworked and understaffed coroner's office and police department, and no video to prove otherwise? It won't take much."

Flowers stared out the windshield, her jaw set.

"And they'll say a hit-and-run driver caused Carolyn's accident."

She spun toward him. "But you saw it happen! And it's on video."

"What's on video is a drunk runaway kid in a big truck, rear-ending a car and knocking it over the guardrail. They'll say he got scared and drove off. I'd wager there are a couple dozen hit and runs in New Orleans every day, and hundreds of people driving drunk at any given time."

She shook her head and turned away.

A while later, they passed a Cadillac sedan with rubber monster hands sticking out of its closed trunk lid. The driver wore torn, blood-splattered clothing and had a long scar that cut across his face. He smiled at Flowers as they went by, displaying hideously twisted teeth. His female passenger looked like the clown from *It*.

"People are so bizarre."

"One more week until Halloween," Jessup said. "I'm going to go as an undercover cop."

"Already in costume, huh?"

"Yes ma'am. Ready to protect and serve."

"Speaking of that, what's the status of your reinstatement request?"

Jessup took a deep breath, then blew it out. "Not going to happen. The civil service board shut my attorney down. Said that without a sworn deposition from Forester, they won't even consider it."

"That's BS," Flowers said.

"I always knew it was a long shot. Of course, being this close to Halloween, if I got a Ouija board..."

She shook her head. "How big a leap is it to think that the guy who planted drugs to set us up would doctor a urinalysis to get you fired?"

"Obviously, I agree with you, but it's not going to happen. I gave up expecting the city to do the right thing."

"But if the federal government had done the right thing to begin with and admitted the baboon attacks, none of this would have happened!"

"Yep. Congressmen riding into Capitol Hill on unicorns promising to vote in term limits."

Flowers growled, then leaned her head against the window. After a few minutes, her eyes closed. Jessup grabbed a pillow from the back seat and put it in her lap. Without opening her eyes, she grabbed it, stuck it behind her head, and went to sleep.

Jessup took the westbound exit for I-20. Flowers stirred, but he told her to go back to sleep and she didn't argue. An hour later, he slowed and exited.

"What's up?" she asked, opening her eyes.

"Pit stop and gas."

"Hmm," she grunted, then laid her head back against the pillow.

A few minutes later, she looked up. Now they were heading down a two-lane road.

"I thought we were stopping for gas."

"We are."

"Why didn't we stop by the exit?"

"I want to check out a place," he said, looking straight ahead.

"What place?"

He glanced over and grinned. "You'll see."

After driving another ten minutes, she said, "They must have really cheap gas."

"We're almost there."

They went around a slight curve and Flowers saw the sign.

"Transylvania?"

Jessup grinned. "Cool, huh? Transylvania, Louisiana. They built the town over an ancient Indian burial ground that dates back to the 1400s. Legend is that the grounds are protected by a half-dog, half-gargoyle ghost." He glanced around, as if hoping to catch sight of it.

"That's cute," she said, pointing at a water tower with the town's name painted above a giant black bat.

"Be a shame to drive all the way to northern Louisiana and miss the chance to say you've been to Transylvania."

She rolled her eyes, then said, "It's kinda small."

"Yeah, don't blink." He nodded toward a convenience store. "I'll stop there."

Spiderwebs and plastic bats covered the building and its entrance was guarded by a dozen skeletons. Orange light glowed through the windows from between the lottery and beer signs, and spooky music and screams poured from a speaker by the gas pumps.

She read the name. "The Castle. Clever. I'll get this tank while you go in and look around. While you're in there, see if they have a little ghoul's room."

"I'll be back," he replied in his best Bela Lugosi accent.

"Heh, heh, heh, heh, heh," went a mechanized witch's head as Jessup entered. The young female clerk, dressed as a goth, didn't look up from her phone screen as she chewed gum, her face half-hidden behind bright green hair. Jessup wondered if it was a seasonal thing, or her year-round look. The counter was covered with plastic body parts, from vampire fangs to monster hands to a surprising variety of eyeballs.

Jessup spotted a coffee machine and headed back. A bulletin board caught his attention. Amid the thumb-tacked business cards and handwritten ads for home repair was a missing person's notice with the faces of three teenagers:

two boys and a girl. It was a copy of the one Flowers had gotten from Clara Norton, Enos Norton's mother.

Something tickled the back of his mind.

He heard the witch laugh and saw Flowers enter the store. He caught the eye roll as she glanced at the assorted anatomy for sale on the countertop.

"You want a cup?" he yelled, holding up the carafe.

"No, thanks. I'm going to grab a bottle of water."

He motioned with his head as he poured himself a cup. "Check out the bulletin board."

"It's them. Poor Clara Norton, I can't imagine what she's going through."

"What if there's more to all this than Operation PIT?"

"What do you mean?"

"Four homicides, two of them about as high profile as you can get, just because you stumble onto a transfer site in Alexandria that turns out to be a dead end? Why take such a huge risk?"

She thought about it for a second, then looked back to the photos of the kids. "You think this has something to do with the hunt club?"

He shrugged. "I think maybe we shouldn't get tunnel visioned on pit bulls. What if there's something else going on that we don't know about?"

"Like what? More baboons?"

"Whew, I hope not," he said, shaking his head at the memory. "But remember who we're dealing with; the resources they have available. Who knows what else they might have created in their mad scientist lab?"

He saw her shiver.

"Anyway, food for thought. Give me your water. I'll get it while you go to the "ghoul's room."

A few minutes later, Flowers came out and got in the truck.

Jessup held up a plastic bag and grinned. "Here."

She pulled out a set of plastic vampire fangs, a green eyeball, and a gray T-shirt that said, "TRANSYLVANIA LOUISIANA, EST 1830." She put in the plastic teeth, then said in her own vampire accent, "How nice, thank you."

"You're welcome. It was that shirt, or a pink one that said 'I was impaled in Transylvania, LA.' The blue one for guys said 'I got sucked in Transylvania, LA.' I figure this was the better choice."

"It is if you ever expect me to wear it," she said drolly.

"I got the same one," he said, holding up another bag. "But we can't wear them at the same time."

"Huh?"

"The Jake Jessup T-shirt rule."

"What's wrong with two people wearing the same T-shirt?"

He shrugged. "I don't know, it's just... weird."

"Well, I think it's cute."

"Hmm."

She looked at the shirt again. "Established in 1830. Been around a while. Where did the name come from?"

"Believe it or not, some guy named it after his school, Transylvania University, in Lexington, Kentucky. A liberal arts college, still in operation."

"Well, I'm glad we stopped," Flowers said. "You were right. It would have been a tragedy to be this close and miss it."

He winked at her, then turned the truck around and headed back to the interstate.

41

—·—

Derrick Flattner arrived at the Rebel Yell Hunt Club in a black Ford Expedition along with three of his Section 17 operatives.

"Derrick," Gus Erickson said as he exited the lodge.

Flattner shook the man's hand. "Gus, how's it going?"

"Everything's good. We're all set for our VIPs and the hunt."

"Excellent."

"Where's Dotson?"

"He's working on another project," Flattner said.

The club owner looked at the two men and the woman standing near the SUV. They were wearing tan BDUs, blue polo shirts, and dark sunglasses to mask where they were focusing their attention.

"You're lighter on security than I thought you would be."

"We're stretched a little thin, but everyone will be focused on the Berryman thing and not on a diplomat flying in for a two-day excursion. I'm confident the hunt will be over long before anyone even knows the ambassador was here. Plus, we'll have a state trooper parked at the entrance to keep people out."

Erickson looked at the government man. "Terrible thing what happened to the congressman and his wife. If a five-hundred-pound hog can do something like that, I hate to think what *your* hogs are capable of."

Flattner gave a smile that did not reach his eyes. "No one was more shocked than I was."

"I'm surprised the ambassador didn't cancel after word got out."

"If anything, he's more eager. A German machismo thing, I suppose. I'm sure it hasn't hurt the hog hunting industry."

"You kiddin'?" Erickson said, smiling. "Our phone hasn't stopped ringing. We're booked up 'til next summer. Everybody wants to kill a hog. Is the senator still flying in with him?"

"Yes. They should be here in a half hour."

"Is he going to take part?"

Flattner chuckled. "Come on, Gus. You know the senator's idea of roughing it is staying at a hotel where the soap is wrapped in paper. He's flying back to Little Rock tomorrow morning, then heading to DC to give his condolences. Berryman's death disrupted some pending legislation, and he needs to attend to it."

"So, we're still looking at three hunters?"

"Yes. The ambassador, his son, and an aide." He looked at his watch. "I guess we should head to the pad."

They jumped in a four-seater ATV and headed to the heliport, followed by his son, Gary, and his foreman. They arrived at the concrete slab just as the Bell 206 helicopter broke the tree line, flared, and set down.

Senator Dirk Blanton jumped out. He was wearing his signature outdoor attire of tan cargo pants, long-sleeved North Face hiking shirt, and a red Arkansas Razorbacks ball cap. He turned and waited as another man exited the bird.

In his forties, short, stocky, and balding, the man was unshaven, unsmiling, and wearing thick camo hunting gear despite the hot, humid day. He barked orders in German to another passenger, who was pulling bags and rifle cases from the helicopter.

From around the front of the chopper came a miniature version of the ambassador, obviously his son. The boy's eyes were glued to a cellphone screen.

Blanton led them to the edge of the helipad, beaming with his best campaign smile. "I'd like you all to meet German Ambassador Otto Kohl and his son Lars. Otto, this is Gus Erickson, our host, his son, Gary, his foreman, and my associate, Derrick Flattner."

After shaking hands, Blanton gestured to the third man who had just marched up. "And this is the ambassador's assistant, Armin Joost."

Joost, tall and lean, stood at attention and gave a quick nod. Flattner could almost hear the man's heels click together. Everything about him was precise, from his pressed hiking shirt down to his unblemished hunting boots.

After they stowed the gear, Erickson asked Blanton, "Senator, when are you going to get the guy who owns that helicopter to come hunt with us? The chicken guy."

"Ah," Blanton said, waving a hand, "he was supposed to come on this one, but he said something came up. I think it was the Berryman thing. I understand his wife had a meltdown when she found out he was going on a pig hunt."

The ambassador huffed. "In Germany, our wives do not dictate what we will and will not do. I see this a lot in your country."

"Boy, you got that right, Otto," the congressman said. "This fuckin' metrosexual generation is going to be the death of us unless something changes. Spare the rod, spoil the child; that's what I say."

"*Das stimmt,*" the German agreed.

In his heavy Louisiana accent, Erickson said, "Of course, if your friend makes his wife too angry, he might end up choking his chickens as well as cooking them."

Blanton barked a laugh, and the German demanded, "What is this? What is this 'choking your chickens' thing?"

Blanton whispered in his ear, then Kohl burst out laughing.

"Ambassador let's get back to the lodge and wash some of this dust out of our throats," Erickson said. "I've got Becks, Krombacher and Warsteiner to choose from."

The German, whose red nose and cheeks told of more time spent in bars than outdoors, smiled, and Blanton gave the hunt club owner a wink.

"Hey Dad," Gary Erickson called out, "I'm gonna take Lars for a tour on the four-wheeler."

Erickson turned to the ambassador, who nodded and said, "*Ja, ja.*"

"Okay but stay on the trails."

Gary threw up a hand as they drove off.

Back at the lodge, while Flattner went to check on his people, Blanton pulled Erickson aside.

"Is it safe for those kids to be out there with those two Tall Grass pigs running loose?"

"Oh, yeah. Like I told you, without the thumpers they feed like regular wild pigs and avoid human contact. Besides, Gary's one of the best shots at the farm. As long as they stay on the trails, they won't have any problems."

"Okay, but remember, Derrick doesn't know about them. So, keep it to yourself."

Erickson nodded. "I'm just glad Dotson's not here. That guy seems to have a sixth sense."

"Yeah, he's special," the senator said. "Makes me nervous as hell. But you don't have to worry about him. Just make sure the ambassador is happy."

· · · ●·●·●··· ·

Gary hooked his cellphone to the buggy's sound system and was soon blasting out sets of Zydeco and outlaw country music as they ran through mud puddles and jumped deer.

They stopped in a clearing and Gary pulled out a baggie containing a couple of joints. He lit one, took a deep drag, then held it up and raised his eyebrows.

"Hell, yeah, dude," the teen said in a strong German accent that made Gary laugh.

"You get Wi-Fi out here?" Lars asked. "Got some killer beat music on my iPod, but I left it back at the hotel."

"Nah, not out here, but there's a good signal at the lodge. You can download some stuff onto your phone and we can play it later."

"Cool."

"You want to drive?" Gary asked.

The teen's eyes lit up and they switched placed. Then, after taking another deep drag, he popped the gearshift into drive, pushed the peddle and shouted "Cowabunga!" as they disappeared down the trail.

42

As they neared the interstate, Jessup said, "I've been noticing a lot of weird bumper stickers with cartoon pigs and stuff. You always see Salt Life stickers, but out here it's Hog Life.

"Yeah, according to Clara Norton, boar hunting is huge down here. It's big business."

"There was even a big red Hog Life sticker in the back window of that truck that ran Carolyn off the bridge."

Flowers spun toward him. "What?"

He looked at her. "What, what?"

"The sticker. You said the truck on the bridge had a big red Hog Life on the window?"

"Yeah."

"Cleve Pike has a big red Hog Life sticker on the back window of his jacked-up Chevy truck!"

"Holy shit," Jessup said. "You think...?"

"It makes sense. He was awfully nervous about Enos and them disappearing. And he was really upset when I confronted him in that store."

Jessup's eyes narrowed. "Upset enough to try and kill you?"

"I didn't think so. Like you said, maybe there's something else going on."

"Like what?"

She threw her hands in the air.

"Well, that's the best lead we've got so far," Jessup said as they pulled back onto I-20.

"According to the GPS we're forty-five minutes from the Okaloosa National Wildlife Refuge," Flowers said.

"It's already four. Going to be late by the time we get there."

"Don't most parks stay open until sunset?"

"Yeah, and they have campsites, so people come and go, but with them investigating the killings, I'm not sure what we'll find."

The question was answered as they pulled up to the entrance of the federal reserve and saw dozens of news vans lined up outside the main road leading into the park. They slowly drove past and saw two Louisiana State Patrol cars still blocking the entrance.

"There goes that," he said.

Most of the news crews were inside their vehicles to avoid the late October heat and mosquitos. A few stood outside, huddled in groups; T-shirts and ball cap logos announced their affiliation.

Jessup pulled up next to two men and a woman. Like minnows darting toward a crumb in the water, they turned toward them, but after spying the cracked windshield and worn paint on the old black truck, they resumed their conversation.

"Hey, now," Jessup said, cranking up his Southern accent. "What's going on? My wife and I have a campsite reserved."

One man rolled his eyes while the woman said, "You guys must have been listening to Pandora for the last twenty-four hours. The refuge is closed."

"Closed?" Jessup said, putting on a confused look.

"Yeah. Congressman Berryman and his wife were killed here last night."

"Tarnation," Jessup said, looking at Flowers for effect. "We heard about that. That happened here?"

"Tarnation?" she whispered, trying not to laugh. "What is that your Jed Clampett impersonation?"

"You're not getting in today," said a cameraman, with a face not meant for TV. "The Feds shut the park down for the investigation."

"And they evicted everyone who was already there," the woman said.

"I bet they were some unhappy campers," Jessup said.

The three newsies stared at him.

There was a commotion at the front gate as two black Suburban's pulled out of the park and stopped at the highway.

"That's Lemont. Something's happened," one of them said.

They ran back to their vehicles and slapped the sides to alert their coworkers. Soon a wave of cameramen and reporters were surging toward the park's driveway.

Agents in tan cargo pants and blue windbreakers bearing the FBI logo piled out of the two SUVs and stood in front of the highway patrol cars. News crews turned on bright camera lights, illuminating their sweaty faces. A female agent stepped to the front.

"That's Claire Lamont," Flowers said. "She runs the FBI New Orleans field division. Very political, very powerful. Park the truck."

He squeezed between a CBS van and a compact SUV wrapped with the insignia of a station from Texarkana, and they got out.

Lamont scanned the crowd and locked her gaze on the NBC news camera out of New Orleans, which currently held the highest ratings.

"Ladies and gentlemen, thank you for your patience. Our investigation into the tragic death of Congressman Neil Berryman and his wife, Rebeca, is now complete. With the help of trackers from the US Forestry Department, we identified, located, and destroyed the animals responsible."

"That was quick," Jessup said as the crowd erupted with questions.

Lamont held up a hand. "Please, let me give you the information I have, then I'll take your questions. Wild hogs killed Congressman Berryman and his wife."

"As most of you know, pigs were brought to this country as a food source hundreds of years ago. Since that time, many have escaped or were released to the wild. They eventually developed into an invasive species. These animals can grow to enormous sizes, and pigs weighing several hundred pounds are not unusual in this part of the country. Hunters have killed rogue animals weighing over eight hundred pounds.

"Using dogs, the trackers followed two large boars to a swampy area in the northeast part of the reserve. After they killed the animals, they recovered human remains that were positively identified through DNA as Congressman Berryman and his wife."

Like a horde of zombies, the news crews surged forward, jockeying for position. Several reporters dragged camera crews to the side and began broadcasting.

"The two pigs were unusually large, a male weighing 573 pounds and a 487-pound female."

There were gasps from the crowd.

"Wild pigs usually avoid contact with humans, so unprovoked attacks are uncommon. However, the females are fiercely protective of their young, and the trackers found baby pigs nearby. They speculate the couple exited the boardwalk, inadvertently stumbled upon the babies, and were attacked by the mother. The male pig then joined in.

"As I said, the animals responsible for this tragic accident are dead and we plan to reopen the park tomorrow."

"Shouldn't be any problem getting a campsite here for the next few years," Jessup said.

"I will now take your questions," Lamont said.

Flowers and Jessup returned to his truck amid a frenzied eruption of questions.

"Wild pigs?" Jessup said. "I never would have seen that coming."

"I would have bet money it was the giant pit bulls."

He shook his head. "Something's off. I can feel it."

"Your spidey senses?"

"Yeah. It's all a little too convenient, and too fast. Have you ever known the United States government to work that quickly? Berryman and his wife are killed less than twenty-four hours ago, and they not only figure out what killed them, but they bring in trackers, find the animals responsible, kill them, and then verify it through DNA?"

"To believe the story, you have to believe that what happened to Greg and Carolyn was just a coincidence."

"And we don't do coincidence."

"So, you think it was murder?" Flowers asked.

"Yeah, and it could still be the pit bulls. Maybe they're using the hog story to cover it up."

"And the trackers?"

"You saw those teams chasing the dogs on four-wheelers in Memphis. It could have been any of them."

"Another giant coverup," Flowers said, rubbing her face. "So, what now?"

"I'd love to get in there and look around, but unless you have a couple of FBI windbreakers stashed away somewhere, that ain't happening."

She pulled out her laptop, brought up Google Earth and zoomed in on the refuge. "I don't see any service roads leading into the park, but this road circles the perimeter," she said, pointing at the screen. "Can't hurt to drive around it. Maybe we'll find something that's not on the map."

"Tarnation. That's a great idea, April."

She rolled her eyes as Jessup put the truck into gear.

43

The road surrounding the reserve was remote, with an unbroken wall of vegetation on both sides. They were about to give up when Flowers stabbed a finger at a dark cut in the tree line.

"There!"

Jessup hit the brakes and peered into the dark recess. In the rapidly dimming light, he could see an old gravel trail, grown over with weeds.

"That's an access road of some type." He cranked the wheel and started down it.

Overhead, the vegetation crowded in and blocked the sky, forming a tunnel and creating a false dusk. Brush and tree limbs clawed at the sides of the old Tundra and screeched like fingernails on a chalkboard.

"Creepy," Flowers said.

"Definitely not used much." Jessup stopped and reset his odometer to zero. "That'll give us an idea how far we've gone."

"According to the laptop, we're heading due south."

They drove about a hundred yards and came to a swinging metal gate secured with a chain and padlock.

"We go on foot?"

Jessup looked at the laptop. "We're at least two miles from the lake. I say we keep driving for as long as we can."

She raised an eyebrow and nodded toward the lock.

Jessup smiled and grabbed a black backpack off the rear seat.

"Those look familiar," she said as he pulled out a set of bolt cutters.

"Never leave home without your bag of tricks. When I open it, pull forward so I can close it up. No use advertising that we're here."

She pulled through, then rolled down the window and said, "Remember in Memphis when you said we just went from misdemeanor to felony? Well, we just went from federal misdemeanor to federal felony."

He chuckled. "Hand me that padlock in the bag. That should throw them off if they come by and check."

Jessup crowded one side of the trail and then the other, dodging mud holes as they worked their way along. A tense fifteen minutes later, the vehicle jerked to a stop in front of a huge water hole.

He sat up in his seat, scanning the obstacle. "Ooh. This should be fun."

"Uh, why don't we get out and walk now?"

Jessup was quiet and stared at the big mud hole. He backed the truck up twenty feet and threw it into drive.

Flowers' eyes went wide. "No, don't—"

He hit the gas.

The Tundra plunged into the pit and water flew up over the hood and out from either side. They were okay for the first fifteen feet; the big truck had a lot of weight and good tread on the tires, but it didn't have four-wheel drive, and he felt the backend drift as the tires spun and fought for traction. He floored the gas and the tires spun like a roulette wheel on a Saturday night. His grin turned to a grimace as he fought to keep the vehicle going straight. The old truck slowed almost to a stop—but not quite. Then, little by little, it edged forward until Jessup felt the tires hit gravel. He blew out a breath as the Tundra slowly pushed itself out of the hole and onto dry ground.

He leaned his head back against the rest, then looked over at Flowers with a big grin. His smile wilted when he saw her face.

"And what," she asked, her eyebrows arched skywards, "were we going to do if we got stuck here, in the middle of nowhere?"

"Yeah, well, it was a little deeper than I thought it was going to be," he said, sheepishly.

She shook her head and looked out through the mud-streaked windshield. Jessup put the dripping truck back into drive, ran the wipers, and continued.

The surrounding forest was pitch black, and the muddy water had left a film on the glass. Flowers rolled down her window and mosquitos swarmed in.

"Yikes," she said, rolling it back up.

"Grab that bug spray from the bag and spray down."

After they coated themselves, Jessup rolled down all the windows. "We're in it now. I'd rather keep them down so we can hear what's going on."

Just then, something darted past the headlight beam.

Flowers yelped. "What was that?"

"Probably just a deer."

She peered out. "The growth is so thick it's like staring at a wall. A rabbit couldn't get through there, let alone a deer."

"It does make you wonder what's out there."

She gave an involuntary shudder, and Jessup chuckled when she clicked the door lock button.

A few minutes later, they came to a clearing filled with construction debris. "Civilization, at last," he said.

"Looks like old pressure-treated boards and pilings. I bet it's from the boat dock they tore down to build the walkway," Flowers said.

"That means we're getting close." He pointed across the clearing and she saw where the trail continued. "That part of the road is well worn. I bet it leads to the lake. This was probably a staging area during construction."

He turned off the headlights, pulled through the clearing and back onto the trail. Fifty yards later, the path veered to the left.

"According to the GPS, the lake is just past that copse of trees," Jessup said, pointing straight ahead. Through the branches, they could make out the distant glow of lights.

"That glow is probably the visitor's center. This section of the service trail is on the map. It leads back to the main entrance," Flowers said. "So, what now?"

"Now we're on foot." He pulled a couple of headlights from the backpack, handed her one, then reached for the door handle.

"You sure it's safe out there?" she asked, looking into the shadows.

"With all the armed people combing this area for the last twenty-four hours, it's probably the safest place in the country. Any big animal with half a brain is ten miles from here."

"How big a brain does a wild pig have?"

Jessup looked at her for a second, then reached back and grabbed the two handguns. He handed one to Flowers and stuck the other into the small of his back.

44

— • —

They walked slowly, letting their eyes adjust to the darkness. Jessup could easily hear their footfalls on the gravel despite the cacophony of insects, birds, and reptiles sounds, which quickly became background noise. The sounds grew louder as they neared the water.

"You'd think there would be dead silence in the middle of nowhere, but this place is more alive than downtown New Orleans," Flowers said.

The gravel road intersected a walking path that led in either direction.

"This must be Lake Trail that circles the lake," she said.

"Supposedly Berryman and his wife left the boardwalk, got on this trail, then were attacked and killed."

"That didn't happen," Flowers said. "Rebeca was scared to death of alligators. She never would have gotten off that boardwalk in the dark."

Jessup looked at her.

"She used to joke about it. How strange it was that a girl born and raised in Louisiana would be so afraid of them. Said she didn't know where it came from. I guess it's like some people being afraid of snakes even though they've never seen one in real life."

Jessup nodded, then said, "Which way?"

"If we turn left, we're not too far from the visitor's center. I'd say our best bet is to go right."

After a few minutes, they came to the first entrance onto the walkway. A sign with a grinning cartoon alligator pointed toward the water and said Gator Bay Access Point.

"She definitely wouldn't have gotten off at a place called Gator Bay," Flowers said.

"Those things are everywhere down here. But as long as you stay away from the edge of the water, you're fine. Heck, they come as far north as Memphis."

"Great. And you live on a boat."

"Very nice," Jessup said, as they stepped onto the finger pier leading to the boardwalk. "Six-foot-wide walkways, six-inch-by-six-inch support posts, full-dimensional lumber railings. Lumber alone must have cost a couple million dollars."

"Our tax dollars at work. Though I have to admit, I'd rather they spend it on something like this than on some of the stuff they come up with."

"Ain't that the truth. You want to stay on land or try the boardwalk?"

"They started on the boardwalk," Flowers said. "Let's check out a section."

"I love the way it weaves in and out of the trees," she said as they walked.

"Hey, check it out," Jessup said, leaning over the railing and shining his headlamp into the water.

She started to lean over the railing, and he grabbed her arm. "Watch the bird poop."

She moved over a foot, then leaned out and flipped on her light. "What are those red things?"

"Alligator eyes."

"What?" She lurched back and stood in the middle of the deck.

"Relax, Flowers. They can't get you up here. Check the other side."

"There are dozens of them," she said, awed.

"I guess that's where the name came from."

"This is absolutely cool—as long as I'm up here and they're down there."

They turned right at the boardwalk. Through breaks in the foliage, they caught glimpses of the star-filled night sky.

"The architect couldn't have done a better job. This is like something out of a fairy tale," she said. "Neil must have been very happy with it."

They continued walking through tight clusters of trees, shining their headlamps from time-to-time on the boards and into the water, looking for anything out of place. They came to an elevated platform that rose five feet above the walkway and overlooked the lake.

They climbed it and gazed around.

"Look at those stars," she said.

Jessup didn't reply.

"Still admiring the construction?" she asked.

"Huh?" He looked up. "Oh, yeah, something like that. Come on, let's get going."

They continued around to the next exit, which read, Armadillo Landing.

"I haven't seen anything that looked out of place so far," Flowers said. "What about you?"

"If this construction wasn't brand new, I'd almost say it looked too clean."

"What do you mean?"

"There are no bird droppings on the boards, no dust or pollen. I checked the weather before we got here. It hasn't rained for days."

"There are no trees here, like back at the alligator place."

"No, but there should still be something. It's almost as if it's been cleaned off."

"Why would they do that?"

He shrugged. "Let's check this exit."

When they got to the end of the connecting pier, they found yellow plastic crime scene tape stretched across the opening.

"We found our crime scene," he said.

They stooped under the tape. The trail leading into the woods showed heavy foot traffic. They followed it around a curve and stopped in their tracks. The intersection of Armadillo Landing and the Lake Trail looked as if someone had taken a five-gallon bucket of red paint and splashed it around. Boot prints and animal tracks cut back and forth across the trampled grass, and disappearing into the brush was a two-foot-wide blood trail where someone or something had been dragged away.

Flowers felt her knees weaken and she clutched Jessup's shoulder.

"Whoa, you okay?" he asked, grabbing her elbow.

She sucked in a breath, then nodded. "Yeah, I'm good."

He watched her for a second, then crouched. "These hoof prints look pretty big." He took photos of the indentations.

She pulled out a quarter. "Lay this by the print to give it a reference."

He nodded and took a few more pictures.

"What do you think?" she asked.

Jessup shrugged. "I just don't know. I mean, this certainly looks like the scene of an animal attack, and those are not dog prints. Maybe that part's true."

"But Greg and Carolyn."

"No," Jessup said, shaking his head, "those definitely were not accidents. They were killed. But killing Greg because of the SAAR program and trying to kill you is the only thing that makes sense. The Berryman's just don't fit. What if this part was just a horrible coincidence?"

"What if, like you suggested, they used the pits to kill them then covered it up using hogs?"

"I mean, it's a possibility, but how would we ever prove it? They'll have stacked all the evidence."

She deflated. He put his arm around her shoulders and led her back to Armadillo Landing.

They turned off their headlamps, ducked under the crime scene tape, and stepped onto the finger pier. They took two steps and were blinded by a brilliant light.

45

"Don't move!" a voice commanded.

Jessup and Flowers jerked to a stop. Jessup raised a hand to block the beam from his eyes.

"Put your hands down and don't move!" the man barked

Jessup held his hands out to his sides, then noticed a red laser dot bounce from his chest, over to Flowers.

"Hey, you don't need to paint us with that red dot. We're not going to do anyth—"

"What you're going to do is put your guns down on the deck, then back away. You first, young lady."

She looked at Jessup, then reached behind her, removed the pistol, and laid it down.

"You next." The red dot hovered on Jessup's chest.

He pulled the revolver out with two fingers, laid it down, then stepped back. Blinded by the light, Jessup couldn't see who was holding them hostage, or even how many there were. For all he knew, there were a half dozen guns aimed at them.

"Okay, we're unarmed. Can you turn the light off?" he asked.

"Who are you and what are you doing out here?" the stranger asked, the light remaining steady.

Flowers started to speak, but Jessup cut her off. "We're lost. We were supposed to camp here, but they wouldn't let us in, so we snuck in. I know we shouldn't have, but if you'll let us go, we'll leave."

"Campers, huh? Where's your gear?"

"In our truck, down the trail a-ways," Jessup said.

"You mean that tired mud-splattered Tundra?"

"Hey," Jessup said, his eyes narrowing.

"I'm amazed you made it through that mud hole."

"She made it just fine," he snarled.

The mystery man laughed. "Didn't see any camping gear in it, either. Saw a sweet TK and a shotgun. Hope your hunting license is up to date."

Jessup remained silent.

"I'm going to ask you again. Who are you and what are you doing out here?"

"I'm Special Agent April Flowers and this is Investigator Jake Jessup," she said loudly.

"A special agent, huh? Who are you with?"

She lifted her chin. "The FDA."

The man remained silent for a second, then said, "The what?"

"The Food and Drug Administration."

Another pause. "O—kay. You got some identification?"

Her mouth opened.

"Well...?"

She sucked in a breath. "It's complicated."

"Humor me."

"I've been suspended."

"Ah. And Investigator Jessup?"

She lifted her chin again. "He's suspended too."

"Of course, he is," the man said with a chuckle. "And you are here because..."

"We're investigating the death of Congressman Berryman."

"Well, Agent Flowers, you're a day late and about seventy-five agents short. The FBI already came through and declared victory."

"I don't believe the FBI," she said, peering into the light, her fists clenched. "I think—no, I know—that Congressman Berryman and his wife were murdered, along with two of my friends. And I intend to prove it!"

For a full five seconds, nothing happened. Then the laser and the flashlight clicked off. Footsteps sounded against the deck boards and a slender man in a dark green uniform appeared from the shadows. He extended a hand.

"Agent Houston Windler, Louisiana Department of Wildlife and Fisheries."

Jessup grabbed the hand. It was boney, but strong.

"Nice to meet you," Flowers said.

"Mind if I turn my light back on?" Jessup said.

"Of course. It's a cauldron out here," Windler said, flipping his back on, but aiming it at the deck boards.

Jessup's eyes narrowed. "Where's your rifle? Your pistol?"

He nodded toward the woods. "Back in my Jeep. That rifle's heavy and my gun belt hurts my back."

"But the laser sight..."

Windler pulled a small silver tube from his shirt pocket and turned it on. "Laser pointer. Got it for ten bucks at Walmart. I get the same reaction from people that I do from racking a shotgun, only it's a lot lighter."

Jessup shook his head. "It got my attention."

"Why do you think the congressman and his wife were killed?" Windler asked.

"Wait a minute," she said. "Who are you and why should we trust you? The FBI closed the park, but you're still out here."

He drew back. "Who am *I*? *I* have a uniform and a badge. I even have a shiny gold plate with my name on it," he said, pointing at his chest. "What do *you* have?"

Flowers lifted her chin defiantly. "Like I said, it's complicated."

"If you're not working with the Feds, why are you here?" Jessup asked.

"Because I believe they were murdered, too."

They both stared at him.

"Grab your guns and let's head back to the trail. A pair of agents have been walking the loop every hour and they're about due. We can talk in my Jeep."

"How long have you been watching us?" Jessup asked as he stuffed the .38 back in his belt.

"I heard you coming down the trail in your truck. You walked right by me when you got out."

"You followed us down the boardwalk?" Flowers asked.

Windler shrugged. "Wasn't that hard. Where else were you going to go? I assumed you wouldn't go for a swim."

She shivered.

They crossed under the crime scene tape and skirted the bloody scene.

"Keep your headlights off," Windler said as they started down Lake Trail. "In this dark, they're like a beacon to anyone on the boardwalk."

Jessup's eyes adjusted quickly to the darkness. To his right, he could occasionally make out the dim glow of the solar lights under the boardwalk rails. Then he heard voices and saw the flash of a light: the agents on patrol. Suspended above the water, their lights seemed to float in the air like giant fireflies.

They stood still while the sentries walked past. The patrol would undoubtably have intercepted them had they not encountered Windler, and Jessup had the slightest hope that their luck was changing.

46

— • —

Ten minutes later, they were standing in front of a dark green four-door Jeep Wrangler tucked back in the foliage twenty feet from where Jessup had parked his truck.

"How did we not see this?" Jessup said, as he climbed into the back seat.

"It's hard enough to see things in the woods during daylight, let alone at night," the ranger said.

"Unless you have the right equipment," Flowers said, lifting a set of night vision binoculars from the front seat. "Like these."

"Those definitely help," Windler said. "Seized them from a poacher last year. High dollar. Very good technology."

"Why are you doing this? Why do you believe us?" Flowers asked.

He put on a crooked smile. "Who would make up a story about being a Food and Drug Administration special agent?"

Jessup laughed, and Flowers threw him a scathing look. Then she said, "Why do you think they were killed? And why are you out here if you're not working with them?"

"When I got word about the attack yesterday, I, along with every other state agent north of I-10, came to help. We were some of the first people here, but we weren't *the* first people."

"What do you mean?" Jessup said.

"There were already a dozen FBI agents in place. They had the park locked down. Booted all the campers out, all the employees. They wouldn't let us in."

"How did you find out about it?" Flowers asked.

"Friend of mine, Genni, works at the gift shop. She was just about to leave when a half dozen SUVs stormed in. People in FBI windbreakers piled out and start running everyone out of the park. Then she sees an ambulance arrive, so she called me at home. I hightailed it over here, but they had the entrance blocked. I found out later an animal had killed Berryman and his wife."

"Shutting out the locals is pretty much standard operating procedure for the Feds," Jessup said.

"Yeah, but I'm one of the best trackers in the park service," he said without a trace of ego. "When I heard it was an animal attack, I called my boss and told him I was sitting outside the front gate, ready to help. He said to stand down, governor's orders; the Feds would handle it." Windler shook his head. "That made no sense to me, so I decided to check things out."

"How did you get in?" Jessup asked.

"I've been a game warden for fifteen years. This park was my first duty station back when it was called the Okaloosa State Wildlife Preserve. I know it like the back of my hand, so getting in wasn't a problem. The problem was not being seen once I got here."

Flowers looked puzzled.

"By the time I got back here the bodies were gone and a dozen guys were swarming the boardwalk and the entrance to Armadillo Landing."

"Why were they on the boardwalk?" Jessup said. "The crime scene was on the dirt trail."

"Because that's where they had the pressure washer."

Jessup's eyes went wide.

Windler nodded. "I heard what you said about the boardwalk looking too clean."

"Why would you wash down a brand-new boardwalk?" Flowers said.

"Right," Windler said. "And at ten o'clock at night."

"To get rid of evidence," Jessup said. "To get rid of blood."

"But why say they were killed on the trail if they were killed on the boardwalk?" Flowers asked.

"Because wild pigs avoid humans. They only attack if they or their young are being bothered. And they would never come onto a boardwalk and attack someone like that. And since you won't stumble onto baby pigs on a boat dock..."

"They had to get them into the woods," Jessup said.

"Exactly."

"So," Flowers said, "they get killed on the dock, then they move the bodies to the trail to make it look like it happened there. Then they pressure wash the deck boards to remove the paw prints and other evidence."

"Yes, but they don't call them paws. More accurately, they're described as hooves," the game warden said.

"They weren't killed by pigs, they were killed by giant pit bulls," she said.

Windler actually shook his head as if to clear it. Then he looked at her. "What?"

She glanced at Jessup, then said, "It's a long story."

The game warden held up his hands. "We've got all night."

Flowers told him the story but left out the deaths of Greg Crandall and Carolyn Richardson. When she finished, he looked at her and said, "You're serious?"

She nodded.

He turned to Jessup. "So, you're the baboon guy?"

Jessup looked up and sighed. "I'm the baboon guy."

"I read about it. You know, I never bought the whole wild dog story. I'm glad you made it out. Sorry about your friends."

Jessup nodded. "I wouldn't have made it out if it hadn't been for April."

She gave a small smile.

"Well, I hate to break it to you," Windler said. "It wasn't giant pit bulls that killed the Berrymans. It was giant pigs."

47

"Wait a minute," Jessup said. "You just said wild pigs wouldn't go onto a board-walk and attack people."

"Normal hogs won't," he said. "But these hogs aren't normal."

"Yeah, we heard all about the six-hundred-pound monsters at the front gate," she said.

"No, April," the state agent said, shaking his head. "The animals that did this were more than twice that size. As big as this Jeep."

"You saw them?" Jessup said.

"No, thank God, but I found this in the sand after they left." He clicked some buttons on his phone and brought up a photo of an indentation on the ground. It was tinged with red and as wide as the dollar bill the ranger had placed next to it for reference. "They missed this hoof print when they were cleaning up."

Flowers' mouth dropped open. Her mind flashed to the photo of the giant paw print Sergeant Betty Davis had found in Memphis.

"Here." Jessup brought up the hoofprint-photos he had taken at the crime scene and compared them. They were less than half the size. "This is like déjà vu all over again."

"Is that blood?" she asked.

"Yep. I got a sample. And I even made a plaster cast of this print."

Flowers sat up. "You what?"

He grinned. "Even us back-woods yokels know a little about police work."

"So, a new animal," Flowers said as she sipped her tea inside the truck stop café.

"Still, why kill the congressman, and why use a pig?" Jessup said.

"If you wanted to make it look like an animal attack, a wild boar makes sense. That or an alligator," Windler said.

"No, an alligator wouldn't have worked," Flowers said. "Rebeca was scared to death of them. I'm surprised Neil even got her out on the boardwalk."

Windler tilted his head. "Sounds like you knew them."

She smiled sadly. "That's another reason I didn't buy the animal attack story. She might have walked that trail during daylight, but she never would have left that dock at night."

"Again, we're back to what precipitated all this," Jessup said.

"It all started after I checked on those missing kids."

"Missing kids?" Windler asked.

"Yeah, I got word about three kids that went missing a couple of weeks ago in Rutland and came here to check on it."

"You talking about Enos Norton and his two friends?"

She looked up. "You know about that?"

"All the agents do. We've been keeping an eye out for them. He's a good kid. Supposed to start training on diesel repair next fall."

"Yeah, his mom is going crazy."

"Clara's a good woman. Been working at the Wooden Nickel ever since I can remember. How did you hear about it?"

She glanced at Jessup, then said, "I do web searches for animal related stuff and saw a post on Facebook about three teenage hunters who went missing. I had nothing else going on, so I came up to talk to Mrs. Norton about it."

Windler grunted. "Yeah, we hoped they would show up by now, that they just took another field trip to New Orleans, but it's been too long. I'm not hopeful for a happy outcome."

"Checking on them led me to that hunt club, but that turned out to be a dead end."

"What club was that?" Windler asked, taking a bite of his eggs.

"Some place called the Rebel Yell."

"I know the place. What brought you there?"

"Clara Norton said Enos talked about wanting to work there. Cleve Pike, the neighbor kid, works there and said he could get him a job. I talked to Pike about Enos and he got real nervous, like he was trying to hide something. I was curious, so I drove up to the club and looked around, but I didn't see anything."

"Cleve Pike is a lying little piece of shit, pardon my language. Caught him poaching a couple of times when he was a teenager. He's a thief and he likes to poison animals with cyanide bombs."

"What?" Jessup said.

"Poison packets some people use to kill wild boars. The problem is that other animals, like foxes and dogs, eat the bait and die. Kids have almost died from them. I keep hoping to catch him doing something now that he's 'of age.' I'm kind of surprised he works at Rebel Yell. That's high dollar, very exclusive. They even have their own helipad."

Flowers glanced at Jessup, then said. "Well, we'd like to talk to him again."

"Tell you what," Windler said. "I'll put out the word that I'm looking for him. When I get him in hand, I'll call you."

"Thanks, Houston," she said.

"You guys look beat. How about I show you the best inexpensive motel in the area?"

"That sounds great," Jessup said, yawning. "I am the walking dead."

They followed the ranger to a motel near Farmerville. It was packed with news crews and displaced campers, but Windler knew the owner and wrangled them a couple of rooms.

"Why are you doing this?" Jessup asked, grabbing their bags from his truck. "You were told to steer clear. This won't be good for your career if they catch wind of it."

"I liked Berryman. I didn't vote for him, too liberal on the social stuff, but I think he was as honest a politician as you can be in DC. I think he tried to do the right thing on environmental issues, and I appreciated what he was doing to protect the park. He didn't deserve to die like that, and his wife certainly didn't. Besides, it's a homicide that occurred in the state of Louisiana, so I'm assuming jurisdiction."

Jessup chuckled, then held out a hand. "Thanks again."

"And thanks for pushing us through the mudhole on the way out," Flowers added, giving Jessup a withering look.

Windler laughed. "My pleasure. Hey, what do you guys know about wild hogs?"

"About as much as I know about nuclear physics," Jessup said.

"How about a crash course in boar hunting tomorrow? I have a friend who traps them for farmers. He's forgotten more about feral pigs than I'll ever know."

Jessup looked at Flowers, who nodded.

"Yeah. That sounds good," she said.

"Okay," Windler said as he climbed into his Jeep. "Call me once you're up."

48

"So, what's the game plan, Gus?" Senator Dirk Blanton said as they gathered outside after breakfast.

"This morning we're going to take a tour and show everyone the layout, the swamp, and where we'll be hunting tonight. I'd like everyone to get a good idea in the daylight where they are and which direction to shoot. That way, when we go back out this afternoon, we won't have to mess around. We'll get the boys in the deer stands and go straight to the hunting blind and settle in. That'll give the hogs a couple hours to calm down and forget about us being there."

Erickson turned to the German. "You all set weapon-wise, Otto?"

Kohl nodded and pulled a rifle from its case. He opened the bolt and thrust it towards the club owner. "See what a real weapon looks like."

Erickson gave a low whistle. "A Blaser R8 Ultimate. I've heard of these, but I've never seen one." He sighted through the scope. "Hmm, very nice, Otto."

The man beamed. "The best hunting rifles in the world. True German quality and precision. What the Swiss do with watches, we do with weapons."

"I've priced these things. They ain't cheap."

"No, not cheap," Kohl said, shaking his head. He slid an eye toward Blanton. "A gift from a grateful benefactor."

The senator gave him a lopsided smile and said, "That's what makes the world go round, Otto."

Erickson offered the weapon to Blanton, who waved him off. "I save the rugged outdoors stuff for photo-ops during campaign season. My cook does all my hunting at the Winn Dixie. Speaking of, I've got a helicopter to catch. Duty calls. Derrick will give me a ride; you guys get going. And, Otto"—he shook hands with the German—"by this time tomorrow I expect photos of a cooler loaded with wild pig."

"Ha," the German said, his eyes bloodshot from a valiant attempt to damage Erickson's beer supply. "Two coolers! And find out if your friend's wife made him choke his chicken." He laughed loudly at his own joke as they headed towards the ATVs.

• • • ● • ● • • • •

"Okay, Otto," Erickson said. "You and I will take one machine. We'll put Montel and Arman in one, and let the boys take the third buggy. That way we'll have plenty of room and a spare machine if one breaks down."

Kohl nodded, and they headed down the trails toward the west end of the property, weaving their way through old growth oak and cypress trees. The powerful four-wheel-drive Mules easily negotiated the rough terrain. They drove into a low, marshy area where Erickson pointed out red maples, black willows and cypress-tupelo trees; water-loving species common to southern deep-water swamps, where the land dried out only during the most severe droughts.

The early morning light filtered through the thick vegetation, revealing a landscape that looked primitive and untouched—until the shadows fell away.

"This land, it's so torn up," the German said, clinging to the handhold as they rocked back and forth.

"This is what wild pigs do to the land. It's part of the reason there's an open season on them. No limit. They're considered an invasive species," the hunt club owner said. "A lot of their ancestors came from your country. Brought over for hunting."

"*Ja,*" Kohl said, nodding. "We have the same problem in Germany with the raccoon dogs."

Erickson spun his head towards him, his eyes narrowing. "Raccoon dog? You're makin' that up."

"No, it's true. They are a big problem. They spread rabies and other diseases, and they drive away the foxes."

"Raccoon dog?" Erickson said.

"*Ja.* A dog that looks just like a raccoon."

Erickson watched Kohl from the corner of his eye, waiting for a hint of a smile, but the politician stared straight ahead, his expression never changing.

"Your man looks a little seasick," he said, peering in the rearview mirror.

Kohl looked over his shoulder and scowled. "Arman is a good man, but he is not used to being outside. He prefers, like the senator said, to do his hunting in the store."

Erickson chuckled. "Huntin's not for everybody. Takes a special person to look an animal in the eye knowin' it's you or them. Gets you back to basics. Man versus beast. Life or death."

The ambassador nodded knowingly. "Yes, that is what I want Lars to experience. All he wants to do is stay in his room and play video games or text with his friends on the phone."

Erickson waved a hand. "They're all like that, Otto. An entire generation of wimps—no offense meant."

"Augh," he said shaking his head. "What is the term? Snowflakes? German men used to be so strong, so tough. Now our women run everything, including our country."

"Don't get me started. But you don't have to worry about that at the Rebel Yell. Out here, it's all men."

"Good," Kohl said. "I hope Lars will get something from it."

"Don't you worry, your son is about to learn a few things."

• • • • • • • • • •

"Holy crap, man," Gary Erickson said, jerking away from a small tsunami of water that erupted on his side of the ATV. "This ain't a submarine."

Lars's eyes went wide as all four tires spun and they lost momentum in the giant mud hole.

"Put it in low gear!" Gary shouted, stabbing a finger at the gearbox lever by the driver's seat.

The boy slapped it back and with a *chunk*, the spinning ATV tires slowed and dug in. The machine jerked and slowly crept out of the pit.

Lars stopped on dry ground, his eyes wide. "Man, that was close."

"Yeah, you were pushing it, dude. Didn't think we'd get out of that one." Gary pulled a joint from his shirt pocket. "Time to celebrate." He lit it, took a drag, then handed it to Lars, who inhaled deeply.

"You have it made out here," Lars said, handing it back. "Run around on four-wheelers all day and hunt. All I do is ride in a limo from the embassy to school and back."

Gary huffed. "Yeah, sounds tough. But trust me, this isn't what I do all day. Mostly when I'm not in school, I'm cutting up pigs or checking for breaks in the fence line. It gets old."

"I've got it," Lars said. "We can do an exchange student thing. I'll come hang out here for a couple of months, and you can go to DC"

"Now you're talkin'," Gary said as he passed him the joint. "I bet the chiquitas in your school are fine."

"Dude, you have no idea. But they're all rich, wear fancy clothes, drive to school in BMW convertibles; they've got their noses in the air."

Gary laughed. "You're going to have to work on your sob story if you want me to feel sorry for you." He threw his hand forward. "In the meantime, tally ho! Or whatever it is you guys say over there."

49

— • —

The next morning, Jessup and Flowers met Windler at the truck stop, then followed the game warden fifteen miles to a white farmhouse set a couple hundred yards off the highway. A gravel driveway led to a large pole barn, where a shower of sparks flew from the open doorway.

They parked and got out, and a tall, lanky man standing inside a tubed cage flipped up his welding helmet and yelled, "Houston! Come over here and hold this gate in place so I can finish up this hinge."

"Damn, my timing has always sucked," Houston said as he tromped over.

Jessup and Flowers stood by the truck and watched as the LDWF agent wrestled a heavy metal door onto two bricks while the other man flipped the face guard down and activated the MIG welder.

"Hey, watch those sparks!" Windler yelped as a shower of yellow embers flew into the air. "This is a brand-new shirt."

The man flipped the helmet up, gazed at the joint, then smacked the slag loose with a pointed hammer. "Damn good job, if I do say so myself."

"Well, NASA won't be calling you to work on rockets," Windler said as he leaned in to inspect his friend's work. "But it's not bad. Should keep a pig or two in,"

The man huffed. "Pigzilla himself couldn't break out of this jail."

Windler waved the pair over. "Ernest, meet April Flowers and Jake Jessup. They're the two investigators I told you were looking into the Berryman killing. Jake, April, Ernest Perrin, rocket scientist, YouTube rock star, and pig-catcher extraordinaire."

Perrin grinned, pulled off a heavy canvas welding glove, and stuck out his hand. "Nice to meet you folks." About forty years old, tall, and lean, he had dark, sun-wrinkled skin and short salt and pepper hair that peeked out from under a green baseball cap embroidered with ears of corn. The front of his tan T-shirt had a massive boar's head with giant teeth, circled by the words, "Rut 'n Root Logistics."

"Nice to meet you, Mr. Perrin. Houston speaks highly of you," Flowers said.

"It's Ernest," he said, then he glanced at the fish and wildlife man. "And the last time Houston said anything nice about me, I ended up being chased through Morgan City by a four-hundred-pound hog."

Jessup's eyes lit up. "That is a story I'd like to hear."

Houston cleared his throat. "Take everything Ernest says with a grain of salt. When he tells a story he tends to—what's the word—embellish?"

"I resemble that remark, thank you very much," Perrin replied, lifting his chin as if offended. "My stories don't need salt. They are perfectly seasoned, and grow better with age, like a fine wine."

Flowers smiled. "YouTube star?"

"Rut 'n Root. Forty-five thousand subscribers," he said, pointing proudly at the logo on his T-shirt.

"Uh, that's good, I guess?" Jessup said.

"Gets me a couple of thousand a month from advertisers. But when I come out with my pig rub next spring, things are really going to take off." He leaned toward Flowers. "It's my wife's recipe, but she doesn't have the name recognition." He winked, and she laughed.

"So, what can I do for you folks?" he said, in his twangy Southern accent.

"The closest April and Jake ever got to a wild pig is on a computer screen. They were hoping you could share some of your vast knowledge about the creatures," Windler said.

"You're in luck. It just so happens we have a wild pig or two in this very area. We'll start by showing you how we catch them."

He led them to the steel cage he had been welding and slapped a hand against it.

"This one is constructed of six-foot-long metal farmyard gates attached end-to-end with a piece of rebar stuck through tabs. I use panels because you can add or remove them to make the pen bigger or smaller. It's simple, fast, strong, and portable. You can also do something as simple as drive t-posts into the ground in a circle, then fasten goat wire panels to them, but the farm gates are stronger."

"How do you catch them?" Flowers asked, examining the steel frame poised above the three-foot opening like a guillotine. Attached to the side was a small black box with a glowing green LED.

"Stand back." Perrin pulled out his cell phone and clicked some buttons on the screen. The black box clicked, the LED turned red, and the metal panel dropped to the ground.

"Remote triggering device," he explained. "We set up the cage and install a trail camera nearby with motion sensors. The camera sends a message to your phone to alert you when there's movement. You check your phone, see what's inside. When you're satisfied, you trigger the gate and lock them in."

"Very high tech," Jessup said.

"Of course, for those of us who need our beauty sleep and don't want to get woken up a half dozen times in the middle of the night, there are passive traps. Got one over here."

He led them to a smaller cage that looked like a giant dog kennel.

"How do they get in?" Jessup asked.

Perrin reached down and pushed on the front panel. It swung inward. "It's like a lobster trap. Hogs root at the ground with their snouts when they eat. We put feed leading into the pen and more inside. The pigs follow the trail of feed into the cage and push through the gate. Simple but effective. You usually only catch the younger hogs and ones new to the area, though."

"Why is that?" she asked.

"The older boars and sows shy away from them," the trapper said. "Pigs are smart. Depending on which list you're looking at, they range from the second to the seventh smartest animals on the planet."

"Nah," Jessup said, a grin forming on his lips.

"Google it," Perrin said. "They learn fast, and unless you catch them the first time, you might not get a second chance. That's why I like to use large cages; you can catch a bunch of them at one time. You have to be patient, though. Just a few will go in at first. You leave food outside and inside. Let them come and go without anything happening to them, so they get used to it. Eventually, they'll congregate. Then, if you're watching live, you can trigger the cage and catch the entire sounder, instead of five or six individuals."

"Sounder?" Flowers asked.

"A group of feral—wild—female pigs and their offspring."

"What about the males?" Jessup asked.

"Boars are solitary animals except during mating season, that's why it's so hard to trap them. They'll stay outside the traps and watch to see what happens to the sows. The older females are hard to catch, too. That's one reason it's so tough to get rid of the darn things. They're skittish and they breed fast. If you don't eliminate at least ninety percent of the animals in your area, they'll keep coming back."

"How many can you catch at one time?" Jessup asked.

"I think I still hold the record," Perrin said, looking over at Windler.

"I haven't heard otherwise," the game agent replied. "Fifty-seven in one catch."

"Fifty-seven?" Flowers said, her mouth dropping open.

"That was in that one catch," Perrin said proudly. "I emptied the trap and put in more feed. Caught another thirty-five the next night, then sixty-two more the following two nights. The farmer didn't have any more trouble for a while after that."

"Holy crap, how many was that?" Jessup asked.

"A hundred and fifty-four," Flowers said.

They all turned to look at her.

"I'm good with numbers," she said, blushing.

"How many are there?" Jessup asked.

Windler said, "There's roughly nine-million feral hogs in thirty-nine states, about 700,000 here in Louisiana, which is one of the largest percentages by state. According to the experts, we would need to cull seventy-five percent of the population every year just to keep it under control, and we're not killing half that number."

"What's so bad about them?" Flowers asked.

"I'll tell you what," Perrin said. "I'm going to set up this flap gate trap on my neighbor's land. Give me a hand with it and I'll show you."

50

— • —

They wrestled the large steel trap onto a flatbed trailer, then piled into Perrin's truck. He drove a quarter mile, then went through a stand of trees, before stopping next to a large field that looked like an artillery barrage had hit it. Muddy depressions, some five feet wide and three feet deep, peppered the field, and all around the clearing, the roots of trees had been dug out and were now exposed.

"Wild pigs did this?" Jessup asked.

"Yep, this was a thirty-acre soybean field last season. Now the owner can't even run his tractor across it," Perrin said. "They dig into the ground looking for grain and grubs and other insects."

"They also carry a bunch of diseases that humans are susceptible to," Windler said.

Perrin circled the field, the sixteen-foot trailer and its load rattling and clanking as it rolled across the rough terrain. He cut through the trees and came to another clearing, this one a third the size of the destroyed field.

"We'll set it up here."

They helped him yank the large metal cage from the back of the trailer. He pulled two long metal bars and a small ram from the bed of the truck and drove the bars a couple of feet into the ground. Then he fastened them to the cage with wire.

"These bars will keep the pigs from tipping over the cage enough to crawl out," he explained.

"They can tip it over?" Flowers said. "This thing is awfully heavy."

Perrin chuckled. "You get three or four pigs weighing five or six hundred pounds total trapped inside a pen and they decide they want out... it'll surprise you what they can do."

"And don't get between them and the exit. You won't stop them," Windler said.

Flowers' mind flashed back to the Rebel Yell video of the boar attacking the hunter.

The trapper pulled a bag of corn from the bed of the truck. It was the same kind Flowers had seen at the convenience store the day she ran into Cleve Pike. Perrin sliced it open, then said to Jessup, "Scatter this about five feet from the cage entrance and put a good bit at the doorway."

As Jessup did that, Perrin slid a five-gallon plastic bucket onto the tailgate.

"You can help me with this, April," Perrin said. He shifted his eyes to Windler, who chuckled and shook his head.

Flowers stood next to him and watched as he carefully pulled off the lid. As soon as he got it off, she recoiled.

"Ugh, what is that?" she asked, scrunching her nose. "It stinks."

He let out a deep laugh. "Sour corn. The pigs love it, but the other animals, not so much. Helps keep them out of the cages."

"It's called non-target bait consumption," Windler explained. "A lot of animals like the same food that attracts the hogs, so you try to find something the hogs like that the others don't."

"It's disgusting," she said. "What is it?"

"Fermented corn with some goodies added in. You fill a bucket with corn, add water, yeast, maybe some milk, and gelatin powder or a liter of soda to sweeten it up. Molasses works real good. Then you put the lid on it and let it sit in the sun until it's ready."

Perrin balanced the bucket on the edge of the trap, then tipped it forward, letting the feed fall inside. Flowers shook her head. She looked in the truck bed and pulled out a dull, white object.

"Is this what I think it is?"

"That is the skull from a four-hundred-pound boar. Biggest one I ever trapped. Kept it for a souvenir."

Five-inch-long tusks curved up from the bottom of its long, narrow jaws. A smaller set of teeth on the upper jaw sat alongside the large incisors.

"Some people call the teeth 'tushes.' The longer bottom tusks are called cutters because the tips are very sharp. They use them to cut up a rival or their prey—or a hunter. Those upper tusks are called 'whetters,' as in a whetstone for sharpening knives. Their primary function is to sharpen the lower tusks."

Flowers shook her head and replaced the skull.

As they headed back to Perrin's house, Jessup reached down and picked up a mason jar filled with red-stained bits of gray metal from the floor of the truck.

"What's this?"

"Bullet fragments and shotgun pellets," Perrin said. "I find them in the pigs I catch."

"You must have a lot of rifles and shotguns," Jessup said. "There are a couple of dozen calibers in here."

"Oh, no," he said. "All I ever use is a .22 rifle. Those are the rounds that didn't stop the hogs when hunters shot them."

Jessup and Flowers looked at each other.

"Think of boars as tanks with thick skin and very dense muscles," Windler said. "They are loud, aggressive, and vengeful. They remember faces and smells and recognize individuals. They won't hesitate to run you down on sight if they feel threatened, so shot placement is very important. Every year we get a dozen slash injuries where a hunter thought he knocked an animal down, but merely wounded it. And trust me, you do not want to be the focal point of a pissed off pig."

"That's why people like to shoot them from helicopters," Perrin said.

"Helicopters?" Jessup said.

"Oh, yeah. Hunters pay big money for two hours of shooting pigs from the air."

"That doesn't sound very sporting," Flowers said.

Perrin laughed. "You ever try to hit a small running object on the ground from a large flying object? It ain't as easy as you'd think."

"One man's feast is another man's famine," Jessup said. "It sounds like contractors who get rich after a hurricane. The wild pigs are hurting the farmers and the land, but they create a boon for another group of people."

"Yep," Windler said. "As much as people complain about the damage they cause, many people have turned feral hog hunting and eradication to their advantage by opening pig hunting businesses and selling everything from specialized hunting and trapping equipment to pork seasonings."

"What do you charge to trap pigs, Ernest?" Flowers asked.

"I don't charge anything for that," he said. "I make my money selling and renting traps."

"Seems like a lot of work for nothing," Jessup said.

"I get most of my business through word of mouth, plus I get to help my neighbors."

"Ernest is just being humble," Windler said. "All those pigs he catches, he donates to churches and the poor. He's filled a lot of stomachs over the years."

Flowers sat up. "You don't just take them somewhere else and let them go?"

"No, ma'am," Perrin said. "That would kind of defeat the purpose."

"Either of you scuba dive?" Windler asked.

Jessup and Flowers both nodded, then looked at each other, surprised.

"You know about lionfish?"

"Oh, yeah," she said. "People buy them for their aquariums then dump them in the ocean when they get tired of cleaning out the tanks. Over the last twenty years, they've migrated from the Atlantic over to the Gulf Coast and have pretty much taken over."

"They have no natural predators, and they eat up the baby game fish and other species," Jessup said.

"You ever hunt them?"

Again, they both nodded.

"Why not catch them, drive the boat to another section of the water, and let them out?"

Flowers started to speak but stopped. Jessup smiled.

"Feral hogs are lionfish on land," Windler said. "Brought here hundreds of years ago from Europe and Asia, with no natural predators other than man. They eat all the resources the indigenous species consume and prey on reptiles, amphibians, bird eggs, and small mammals. They're also a huge predator of baby turtles along the coastal areas. That's in addition to the crop damage and erosion issues. Wild pigs cause an estimated two and a half billion dollars in damage to the US economy every year."

Flowers pursed her lips and looked out the window.

51

Back at the barn, Perrin asked, "Well, what did you think?"

"Very interesting," Flowers said, "but we didn't get to see any. With so many of them around, I would have thought we'd see them everywhere."

"Like a lot of animals, they usually come out to feed at dawn and at dusk, to avoid predators, in their case, hunters. Besides being very smart, they blend in well. Their hair varies from black to brown to red. It makes them hard to see in the shadows," Windler explained. "That's one reason they're such popular game animals.

"If you want to see some, I'm fixin' to go empty a trap over at Elmer Raynor's place if you'd like to go along."

"Sounds good," Flowers said. "But how do you know if you have any?"

Perrin took out his cell phone, clicked the screen, then held it up. A night vision video appeared. It showed a large round structure suspended above the ground on four poles. Beneath it, several pigs were eating from a pile of corn.

"What is that?" she asked.

"It's a drop trap," Perrin said. "The legs hold it up until you send a signal from your phone to release it."

"There's a trail camera with night vision attached to a nearby tree," Windler explained.

"What are you waiting for?" Jessup asked. "There's a bunch of them under it."

"Look off to the right, in the shadows. See that shape? That's a big sow, and just behind her is a good size boar. You can see it better on a computer screen. I was hoping one or both would make their way under the cage."

They watched as pigs came and went, unaware of the danger suspended above them. Flowers felt the tension grow as a minute later, the sow walked over, pushed aside the smaller animals, and began eating from the pile of corn.

"When are you going to push the button?" she asked, her eyes locked on the screen.

Perrin laughed. "I pushed it last night. This is a recording."

She shook her head. "Oh, yeah, right."

"A few more seconds..." he said.

At the edge of the video, a large hog came toward the cage, then stopped.

"Holy cow, that's a big one," Jessup said.

"That's the boar. Probably two fifty, three hundred pounds. I really wanted to catch him." The trapper's eyes locked on the phone.

A second later, the boar moved closer. He hesitated at the outer edge, then stepped inside. As soon as he crossed the perimeter, the big metal cage shuddered. The steel structure dropped like a stone, but in the split second it took to hit the ground, the pigs reacted. As if shocked by the same electrical wire, they leaped up, spun around and tried to escape, but they were too late: their metal prison had slammed closed. Repeatedly, the animals ran from one side of the cage to the other, slamming their faces against it.

"Damn," Jessup said.

"They'll do that until their faces are bloody. It's like they don't feel pain," Windler said. "What you don't hear is the racket they're making. The squealing and grunting. A pig's squeal can top a hundred and ten decibels; loud as a motorcycle."

"How many are in there?" Flowers asked.

"Let's go find out," Perrin said.

"You need to unhook your trailer?" she asked.

"No, gonna need it," he replied.

Flowers nodded and walked toward Perrin's truck, but Windler stopped her.

"Let's follow him in Jake's truck," Windler said. "Then I'll ride back with Ernest."

Flowers shrugged and got in the Tundra.

"This is a lot more complicated than I would have thought," she said as they followed Perrin down the highway.

"There's a science to it," the game warden said. "It's a game. Man against pig, and right now, the pigs are winning."

Ten minutes later, they pulled off the highway and onto a gravel road that led south, with a drainage ditch on one side and recently harvested soybean fields on the other.

"Big spread," Jessup said.

"Yeah, about six hundred acres," Windler said. "Raynor had a good crop but lost about fifty acres of beans to the pigs."

"Ouch," Jessup replied. "That had to hurt."

"Yep, and if he doesn't get on top of them now, it'll only get worse. That's why he called Ernest."

They came to a large area where the ground was riddled with ruts and holes.

"Is that from the wild pigs?" Flowers asked.

"Yeah. He's going to have a heck of a time straightening it out enough to plant again. But today should help."

They drove around some trees, and near the back edge of a large clearing stood the circular cage. Inside it, several shapes huddled together. As soon as the vehicles came into view, the group exploded like a flock of panicked birds. The pigs squealed and screamed and ran around the trap, searching for a way out. With nowhere to go, they threw themselves against the metal bars. There were several small pigs, but most were the size of large dogs. A couple of them were much larger.

Perrin pulled up and the mass of hogs surged to the other side of the cage, crawling on top of one another, clawing toward the top edge of the four-foot walls.

"They're piling up," Windler said. "Drive to the other side. That'll scatter them."

They parked, then got out and approached the cage. A huge pig rammed the cage with its head, rattling the entire structure.

Jessup stepped back as it smashed into it again.

"Holy crap, he's pissed." The creature had black fur and a thick tuft of hair that ran down its back like a shaggy mohawk. Its legs were longer than a farm pig, and its snout was longer and narrower. Three-inch tusks swept up from its jaws.

"That's the boar," Perrin said, as it hit the metal barrier again at a full run. Blood ran from several cuts on the animal's face, but it didn't seem to notice or care as it repeatedly tried to get at its captors.

"It's huge," Flowers said.

"It's a good size one," Perrin agreed. "Like I said, two fifty, three hundred pounds."

"They get bigger," Windler said. "Ole boy over in Acadia Parish a few months back shot one that weighed out at 544 pounds. A monster. Said it looked like a rhinoceros."

"Twice as big as that?" Jessup said, pointing at the boar as it rammed the enclosure again.

"Yep. Hunted it for six weeks. Kept seeing it on his trail cameras, but never saw it in person. Soon as he'd climb down from the deer stand and drive off, it would show up. That's how smart these things are," Windler said. "Finally, its stomach overruled its instincts and he got it. Like I said, they can be very hard to hunt."

"I count twenty-seven," Flowers said, standing near Perrin. "Eight babies and the two big ones. The rest are medium size."

"That's a good catch," he said. "It pays to be patient."

"So, this will help the farmer," Flowers said.

"It's a good start," the trapper said. "I'll set it up a couple more times. Catch another twenty or thirty. I might drop off a flap trap for Elmer to use for a couple of months. Catch the occasional stray."

Perrin turned and walked back to his truck. He grabbed the .22 rifle from the rack in the back window.

"What's that for?" Flowers asked, though she already knew.

Windler gave her a sad smile. "If we don't stop them, they'll disrupt the whole ecological balance. Just like the lionfish are doing off the coast."

She looked at the baby pigs scrambling around the pen and tried to picture them as an invading horde rather than the cute little farm animals of her childhood memories.

"I get it," she said, and turned toward Jessup's truck. "But I don't need to watch."

52

Erickson stopped in front of two small cabins tucked into the trees at the edge of a large clearing.

"This will be our home for tonight," he said to Kohl as they climbed out of the machine. "This way we can get up at first light and be in place for another hunt."

"Ah, good," the ambassador said. "Better than sleeping in tents."

"We like roughing it the easy way, but don't get too excited. There's a wood burning stove, which we shouldn't need, and no electricity, but it's off the ground, it helps keep the Arkansas Travelers off you."

"Arkansas Travelers?"

"Ticks. Woods are covered up with them. That's why we brought plenty of this." Erickson held up a can of bug spray. "Hose down good around your ankles and your beltline. You'll still get a couple of the bastards on you, but it'll help."

Kohl gave the can a dubious look, then sprayed on the insect repellent.

"What the heck were you boys doing on the way here?" Erickson said when Gary and Lars finally pulled up, mud dripping from the ATV.

Gary started to speak but said nothing. Lars turned his head and snickered.

Erickson nodded. "Yeah, okay. Guess what you'll be pressure washing when you get back?"

"Otto, you, your son, and Armin can take that cabin," he said, pointing. "Me, Gary and Montel will take the other one."

The aide immediately began transferring Kohl and Lars's gear into the first cabin.

"Montel," Erickson said, "stick a bucket of that sour corn on the boys' ATV for them to sprinkle near the deer stands."

Ruderman nodded. "Will do."

"What is sour corn?" Lars asked.

"Here, I'll show you," Ruderman said, pulling a five-gallon bucket to the edge of the four-wheeler. He peeled off the lid and motioned for the boy to come closer.

Lars leaned in and immediately pulled his head back and gagged. Kohl and his aide looked alarmed, but Erickson and Gary just laughed.

"Sour corn," Erickson said, "Spoiled corn, basically. You dump different ingredients into it to get it to ferment. After a week or so, when it's good and smelly, you spread it out. Nasty stuff, but the pigs love it. It's like caviar to them."

"Yeah, well, it doesn't smell like caviar," Lars said, a snarl on his face.

"Okay," Erickson said, standing on the trail, "we have two shooting areas. The first is behind that stand of trees over there. There are a couple of deer stands twenty feet up facing south, toward a corn field. We seed the field every year to attract deer and pigs and to help control the erosion. It's a mess come spring, but it pulls in the hogs. At about four o'clock, we'll put Lars and Gary in the deer stands. Sun goes down around six-thirty. By seven, they should have six or seven pigs to shoot at."

"We sit up there for three hours?" Lars said.

"Gotta give the animals time to settle down," Ruderman said. "Let them forget you're there. Hunting is all about patience."

"Gary, run Lars over there and show him the deer stands. And don't forget to spread out that sour corn."

"Okay, Dad."

After the boys headed off, Kohl asked, "Where are we going to be?"

"Couple hundred yards that way," Erickson said, pointing in the opposite direction. "I'll show you."

The four men got into an ATV and headed north from the campsite.

"Got a good feed plot out there," Erickson said as he drove. "Gary has kept corn rollers filled up the past week to make sure there's plenty to pull them in."

He saw the confusion on the German's face.

"A corn roller is a five-foot length of PVC pipe with holes big enough for kernels of corn to fall through. You fill it with dried corn, plug the ends, then chain it down at one end. The pigs roll the tube around while they root, and corn falls out."

About a quarter mile from the cabins, they stopped and got out.

"Here's where we shoot."

Kohl and Joost looked around.

"I see no deer stands," Kohl said. "Nothing but trees and scrub brush."

Erickson nodded toward some bushes on his right. "We're shooting from right there."

The ambassador's eyes widened. "From the bushes?"

Erickson smiled, walked over, reached down, and pulled his hand back. An opening appeared.

"Mein Gott!" Kohl muttered.

Erickson grinned. "The Accutech 7000 six-man hunting blind, gentlemen. The latest and greatest camouflage tent on the market. Custom made, by season, for the northern Louisiana woods." He held the flap open for them.

"We will hunt on the ground?" Joost said. "Is that safe?"

"Absolutely safe," Erickson said. "The hogs will never see us."

They followed him inside and found a table, chairs, and a cooler.

"All the comforts of home... some of them, anyway." He pointed toward a wall of trees at the back of the clearing. "The feed plot is at the end of that clearing. You can sit down, rest your rifle on the table, and take aim. Shoot right through the screen. We have replacements."

"It's so clear. Surely the pigs can see us," Kohl said.

Erickson smiled again. "Would you gentlemen mind walking out there for a second?"

The ambassador and his aide went around, stood in front of the blind, and looked in.

The club owner said, "I'm waving my arms. Can you see that?"

"We can't even see you," Kohl said, shaking his head. "Amazing."

Erickson came out and pointed at the far end of the clearing where two white feed tubes were barely visible.

"That's where they'll come in. The big ones like this spot. There's a lot of brush around, gives them a sense of security. At this distance, there's no problem knocking them down, especially with the rifle you have," he said, playing to the German's ego.

The German sniffed. "Big? I have looked at the websites of the hunting outfits in this part of the country. Here big is three hundred pounds. Just last week in the Baden-Wurttemberg area, a hunter took down a Russian boar that weighed four hundred seventy-five pounds."

Erickson gave Kohl a crooked smile. "That's pretty big, Otto, but this is the Rebel Yell. We have our own breed here. Ever see that movie *Jaws?*"

Kohl nodded.

"Well, let's just say that after tonight, you're gonna need a bigger cooler."

53

When they returned to the lodge for lunch, Erickson met with Montel Ruderman in the main barn.

"Where are the pigs, Montel?"

His foreman pulled a computer tablet from a cabinet and clicked on the tracking program that showed an overlay of the combined six hundred acres of property. The Arkansas side showed a cluster of red dots at the Tall Grass compound, while at the Rebel Yell, two green dots hovered near the western border.

"Right where they should be," Ruderman said stabbing at the screen. "About halfway between the deer stands and the blind, back near the fence."

"How can we make sure they come north and not go back toward the deer stands?"

He shrugged. "The big ones almost always come to the blind field, but they're animals, they'll do what they want."

"Almost always ain't gonna cut it. This is important. We need to send this guy back to DC with a big smile on his face." Erickson stared at the barn floor. "We'll use a thumper."

Ruderman's eyes widened. "Are you serious? They go crazy when they hear that thing. Ain't no tellin' what they'll do."

"I'm not talking about turning it on and leaving it on. I'm talking about hitting it for a few seconds to get them moving in the right direction. Once they get to the blind field, we'll turn it off."

"We've never done that before. We've always left it on until all the meat's gone."

"Right. And what happens after we turn it off?"

"Well, they wander back into the tall grass."

"Exactly. They lose interest; they go back to their natural state. All we need to do is get them close enough to smell the corn."

Ruderman thought about it, then nodded. "Yeah, that'd probably work."

"It'll work," Erickson said. "Run out there and put a thumper in the grass by the clearing, then come on back. And while you're at it, dump out a bucket of sour corn, just to make sure."

"You got it, boss."

· • • ●•●• ● • · ·

After Jessup and Flowers thanked Perrin for the tour, Windler met them at the truck.

"I'm going to stay here and help Ernest load the pigs. How about after that, we do a little multi-tasking?"

"Multi-tasking?" Jessup asked.

"We can head to the Wooden Nickel to eat and pay Clara Norton a visit at the same time."

"That's a great idea," Flowers said. "Maybe she'll have some good news about the kids." She glanced hopefully at Jessup. He gave her a small smile.

"Okay," Windler said. "Let's meet there at one. The lunch crowd should be thinning out by then."

Just then they heard the crack of the .22 rifle, followed by a riot of squeals and grunts. Flowers drew in a breath, then climbed into Jessup's truck.

As they drove through the destroyed soybean field, she imagined the damage hundreds of thousands of wild pigs could cause. She tried to reconcile in her mind the killing of these animals with spearing lionfish that were devastating the Gulf Coast environment. She had no qualms about killing and eating them. And they were beautiful. It was no more their fault that unthinking aquarium owners dumped their ancestors into the ocean thirty years ago than it was the pigs' fault that their ancestors had been brought to this country three hundred years before.

And what about the indigenous animals whose populations were being decimated and, in some instances, eliminated by the introduction of foreign species by man? Didn't they have a right to live and to thrive? Was it still considered survival of the fittest, natural selection, when someone brought in outside players? When man unwittingly—or purposefully—played God?

She pushed the thoughts away and said, "You seem less than optimistic about the kids showing up safe."

"I want to be, but the realist in me says different."

"Because Enos's license plate was on that truck."

He nodded. "I can't come up with a reasonable explanation for that other than the kids are dead and someone is using them to cover up Carolyn's murder."

"You think it was Cleve Pike?"

"If it was, he's not a very bright killer. Using a stolen tag but putting it on his own truck which sticks out like a sore thumb."

Flowers raised her eyebrows. "I met him."

"So, you're saying he's not the sharpest knife in the drawer?"

"About as sharp as a marble," she countered.

"A few peas short of a casserole?"

"His driveway doesn't quite reach the road."

Jessup barked a laugh. "Hadn't heard that one."

"Why didn't you want to tell Houston about Pike's truck and the tags?"

"I don't know," he said. "Probably just the cop in me. Keep some stuff close to the vest, see what shakes out. I think our best bet, though, is to find Pike."

She nodded. "Makes sense. We've got an hour and a half to kill. I'd love a shower."

"Sounds like a plan."

At the motel, Flowers said, "Come knock when you're done."

A half hour later, he tapped on her door. Flowers answered, her head and body wrapped in towels.

"Come in and sit down. I'll be done in a minute," she said heading back to the bathroom.

Surprised at her lack of modesty, Jessup couldn't help but notice her firm calf muscles.

He called out, "Take your time. I'm gonna use your computer to look for AA meetings in the area."

She popped her head around the doorjamb. Both towels now gone. Her black hair drifted over her freshly scrubbed face, and a hint of flesh peeked from beneath her left shoulder. "Excellent idea."

A few minutes later, she emerged from the bathroom fluffing her hair with a towel and wearing her new Transylvania T-shirt.

"It fits," he said with a grin.

"Go put yours on."

"Not a chance," he said, and turned back to the computer.

"Any luck?"

"Believe it or not, there's one that starts at two on the east side of town. If we get done in time with lunch I think I'll hit it and get my mind right."

She threw him a thumbs up, then said, "Let's go eat. I think you'll like this place. It's nice and quiet."

54

Carl Dotson strapped himself into the C-130 jump seat as the Lockheed Hercules started up. The plane took a quick turn onto the runway and the four engines roared as the pilots jammed the throttles forward. Vibrations rocked the fuselage, which turned into a constant rattle a few seconds later as the old transport plane lifted off.

He looked at the four cloth-covered kennels and thought about the baboons lying unconscious inside them. Four hours from now, two Huey helicopters would release them outside a Sendero Espada base camp in the foothills of the Andes Mountains. Six hours after that a detachment of Peruvian army special forces operatives would go in and verify the remains of Jose Montero, the commander of the terrorist organization, and whoever else happened to be present when the animals arrived.

Almost seventy thousand people died in the conflict between the Shining Sword and the Peruvian government since Alejandro Perez established the Maoist guerrilla group in 1969. Although Perez had died in a prison hospital the year before, a few of his believers remained active in coca-producing areas of the country. After the group claimed credit for two recent bombings in the capital city of Lima, the government, fearing a resurgence, reached out for help.

"You assholes should've kept your heads down and stuck with terrorizing the locals," Dotson said, chuckling. He didn't know if the four-baboon Night Terror unit would completely destroy the radical group, but he knew it would cripple it.

He wasn't sure why he'd been tasked with handling this operation. His plate was full and there were two other operatives at Fort Hood who had conducted successful insertions. But he didn't mind. He was enjoying the break. Overseeing the different projects was becoming a challenge.

Operation Night Terror was proven and Operation PIT was running smoothly. And now that the latest creation had passed the beta stage, they'd soon put it into service. Next would be the PIT betas. He still cringed at the thought of a five hundred pound pit bull coming at you at forty-miles-per-hour.

The jury was still out on Tall Grass. The animals were certainly lethal enough, but they were hard to transport and impossible to control. That restricted their use to remote areas where the targets were isolated.

Dotson also didn't like that they were totally under civilian control. After the animals left the lab, Rebel Yell workers raised, tagged, selected, and delivered them to the military. So far, they had done an acceptable job, but their motivation was more monetary than military.

And though he couldn't prove it, he was convinced the incident with the kids had been intentional. He would have shut down Tall Grass if Flattner hadn't intervened. His boss wanted to monetize the hogs and some of the other animals. Dotson understood the reasoning. If they could self-fund Section 17, they wouldn't have to worry about inevitable spending cuts.

But at what cost? Some of the "customers" were as sketchy as the terrorists the animals were sent to dispatch. It had all come down to the age-old argument of the ends justifying the means.

Well, there was nothing he could do about it until he got back. He would just enjoy his mini vacation in the Peruvian jungle while his boss wined and dined Blanton and the German ambassador.

He gave a snarl-smile. *Just avoiding that shit makes this trip worthwhile.*

He wondered how the hunt was going. He had surveyed the shooting sites before he left. Two deer stands and a hunting blind hidden in the woods, both overlooking baited fields. It wasn't exactly his idea of a fair fight. He would have preferred being in the woods an hour before dawn, then stalking the creatures on foot, maybe with a spear to keep it fair, but to each their own.

The operative pulled out his phone and saw he had an internet connection for the first time in two days. That was one of the nice things about military planes, the Wi-Fi connections were as strong as land-based cable.

He had put out word he'd be incommunicado, but he still had three texts from the communications center at Fort Hood.

The first one said that the cameras system at the Tall Grass facility had gone offline.

Dotson pulled out his laptop, brought up the surveillance program and clicked on the Tall Grass icon. "Server offline."

The next text was sent fifteen minutes after the first, advising that the system was still offline and that the comm center had emailed the Rebel Yell asking them to reboot the system.

The third text went out a half hour after the first one. It said the system was still down, that they had again emailed the hunt club, and that the system operator had personally called the Rebel Yell to advise them of the problem but did not get an answer. Dotson looked at the sender and smiled. *Lance* Corporal Albert Randal.

"I guess I got his attention."

He grabbed his phone and called Flattner.

"Hey, Carl," his boss said. "Is your phone secure?"

"Yes. Just me and four monkeys in the back of a C-130."

Flattner chuckled. "Enjoy your well-earned break. What's up?"

"Did you know the surveillance system at Tall Grass was down?"

"Yeah. Gus said he got an email from the comm center. He had a guy check and supposedly there's an issue with the power lines up in Arkansas. The power company is working on it. I guess we need to get a generator at the site in case it ever happens again."

"Okay. How's the hunt?"

"They're taking a tour of the shooting sites now. They'll come back for lunch, then head back out for the night. The German ambassador seems excited."

"Good," Dotson said. "I'll let you know how this goes."

55

All thoughts of a quiet lunch were dashed as they pulled up to the Wooden Nickel. Almost every parking space was filled with four-wheel-drive vehicles and TV news vans.

Jessup found a space around back. Windler arrived in his Jeep as they were getting out.

"The food must be really good," Jessup said as the game warden walked up.

"I didn't think about the reserve being only twenty miles away," he said. "But you gotta admit, with wild hogs being public enemy number one, what better place to get sound bites for the evening news than at a restaurant called the Wooden Nickel in a town called Rutland?"

As they headed to the front door, they passed several reporters interviewing camo-clad hunters.

"So, what exactly is a wild pig, and how are they different from regular pigs?" a reporter asked a man with an orange ball cap cocked back on his head. Juice from the tobacco plug bulging in his left cheek stained the front of the forest-pattern T-shirt that was stretched to its limit over the man's ample stomach.

"Comparin' a feral hog to a farm pig is like comparin' a poodle to a Doberman Pincher. They're meaner, faster, and smarter than a regular pig. They got teeth like hook knives and they'll slice you open like a watermelon and keep on going—that is, if they don't turn around and eat you."

The reporter's eyes lit up like a slot machine hitting a row of cherries.

Flowers glanced around at all the pickups and Jeeps, some carrying ATVs, all with full gun racks hanging in their rear windows.

"This reminds me of that scene from *Jaws* where all the fisherman head out to catch the shark and crash into each other," she said.

Windler chuckled. "This might actually put a dent in the wild boar population for a little while—if they don't kill each other first."

"Can pigs see the color orange?" Jessup asked as they worked their way into the crowded restaurant. "Because if I was going into the woods right now, I'd spray-paint my whole body."

"Hogs have dichromate vision. While they can't see blaze orange, they are very sensitive to tone. If something contrasts sharply with its surroundings, they'll notice it. If it moves, they'll take off. That's why camo-patterned orange material is popular here, though it's not legal in every state, for some reason."

Flowers saw a couple of the hunters give Windler a hard look. "Some of these guys don't seem happy to see you, Houston."

He shrugged. "A lot of sportsmen think I'm here to ruin their day, give them a hard time. But as long as you follow the rules, I've got no problem with you. For some reason though, a handful of these guys would rather look over their shoulders all the time than spend the equivalent of a couple of twelve-packs of beer to get a license. It baffles me."

Jessup huffed. "You must feel like you have a target on your back."

"Ah, it's not so bad. No worse, I would think, than being a cop in Memphis. Wasn't it ranked the most dangerous city in America recently? Record homicides?"

"Yeah, but I had a radio and help close by if things turned bad. You're out there by yourself walking up on people armed with rifles, and ammo that will cut through Kevlar like butter."

"Now you know why I became such a good tracker," he said, smiling. "I sneak up on 'em before they know I'm there."

"And aim a laser pointer at them," Flower said.

He laughed. "Well, if it works..."

"Oh, it works," Jessup said with a shudder.

Just then, Clara Norton walked up to the register carrying menus and silverware. When she saw Flowers, her eyes went wide. Then she saw Windler, clutched the items to her chest and rushed up.

"What is it, April? Did you find them?" she asked. Her pleading eyes shifted from Flowers to the game warden.

"No, no, Clara, we haven't found them yet. We came to talk to you... and to eat," she said, flushing a little.

"Oh... oh, of course. Okay, well," Norton said. "Let me seat these folks, then I'll be right back for you."

Norton led the other group to a table and Flowers dropped her head and mentally kicked herself for not calling first.

The woman returned a minute later and led them to a table at the back of the restaurant.

"I'm sorry," Flowers said. "I should have called first to let you know we were coming."

"That's all right." Norton said, waving her off, but her wet eyes said differently. "It's just that when I saw Houston with you, I thought..."

"No, we don't have any news yet, Clara," Windler said.

She sniffed, then put on a smile. "No news is good news, right?"

The smiles turned awkward.

"Sit, sit. Who wants coffee?"

"I'll take coffee," Windler said.

"Same here, Mrs. Norton. I'm Jake Jessup, by the way. I'm working with Agent Flowers." He held out his hand.

"Nice to meet you. Please call me Clara." Then to Flowers, "Diet Coke, right?"

Flowers grinned and nodded.

After she left to get the drinks, Flowers said, "That poor woman. I want to cry."

"I can't imagine," Jessup said. "I don't know what I'd do if Davie disappeared."

"It's been tough for her. Her husband passed a couple years back, and now this," Windler said.

"Truck crash, right?" Flowers said.

"Yep. On his way back from a run to Texas. Ice storm. Hit an overpass."

"Okay, here you go," Norton said, setting down the drinks. "Know what you want?"

"I'll take a burger with fries," said Houston.

"Same here," said Jessup.

To Flowers Norton said, "Salad's still crummy. Grilled cheese with a side of tomatoes?"

She smiled. "Perfect."

"I'll put your orders in, then come back and sit. Julie can handle things for a few minutes."

"It's like you're a regular here," Jessup said as she walked off.

"Just that once. I guess I'm memorable."

"That's for sure," Jessup replied.

"Who's that guy at the bar? The one in jeans and a black T-shirt," Flowers asked, taking another quick look.

Jessup looked over. He locked eyes with him for several seconds before the man slowly turned away and took another sip of his coffee. A jagged scar ran from his left jaw to his temple.

"You mean Scarface?" Jessup asked.

"Geo Palmer," Windler said.

56

"He's a tough customer. Got that scar in a knife fight in a bar. The other guy fared much worse. Palmer did three years in the Elayn Hunt Correctional Center. After that, I put him away for six months for poaching gators. He's been working at the Rebel Yell Hunt Club for the last year. I'm kind of surprised to see him here."

"Why is that?" Jessup asked.

"From what I hear, some VIP flew in yesterday for a hunt. Figured it'd be all hands on deck."

"Still gotta eat, I guess."

"He was inside the convenience store the day I talked to Cleve Pike," Flowers said. "There were three other guys, all wearing matching T-shirts."

Jessup threw her a look, and she rolled her eyes.

Norton returned, and Jessup stood and slid a chair over for her.

"So, there's no news?" she said.

"Not yet, I'm afraid," Windler said.

She shook her head and looked around the restaurant. "For the last two days, all anybody's been talking about is the killin' at the reserve. Before that, people would at least ask if I'd heard anything about Enos."

"It'll die down, Clara," Windler said, laying a hand across hers. "In the meantime, we aren't giving up."

She gave him a weak smile.

"I guess *you* haven't heard anything?" Flowers said.

"Nothing."

"What about Cleve Pike? Have you asked him?"

"Funny you should ask. I haven't seen him or his truck for the past four days. His mother even asked if I've seen him. Then she made some comment about Enos being the reason he ran off." She shook her head. "If I didn't know how bad it hurts for your son to go missing, I'd have dotted her eye."

Flowers held a hand to her mouth to stifle a laugh.

"I just don't know anymore," she said, lifting a tissue to her eye. "First Enos and the kids, then Cleve, and now the congressman and his wife. It's like the whole world is falling apart.

"Have you asked anyone from Rebel Yell about the kids?" Jessup said.

"I did the last time they were in here. They all got quiet, as if I'd just told them we ran out of beer."

She stood. "I'm gonna get your food."

Jessup turned to Windler. "So, who's the VIP?"

"I don't know. All I know is my boss got a call from headquarters telling us all to steer clear for the next two days. They don't want anybody interfering with the hunt."

Both Jessup and Flowers gawked at him.

Windler held up his hands. "What can I say? Nothing puts a chill in the air like a game warden showing up at a pig hunt."

"They have that kind of power?" Flowers asked.

"In the state of Louisiana, it's all about money, politics, and power. And you can't get one without the others."

"Who's the hook for the Rebel Yell?" Jessup asked.

"George Rathburn."

"*Congressman* Rathburn?" Flowers asked.

Windler nodded. "The Rebel Yell owner supposedly knows a senator, too, but I'm not sure who that is."

"Neil hated Rathburn," she said looking at her glass.

Windler lifted an eyebrow.

She waved a hand dismissively. "Long story."

"Here you go," Norton said. She set down their food then wiped her hands on her apron. "I want you to know I appreciate what you're doing, trying to help find my boy, April."

Flowers gave her a hopeful smile. "We won't give up, Clara."

The woman nodded, then walked off.

Windler blew out a breath. "I hope to God those three ran away, 'cause if not, they're probably dead."

In the parking lot Windler said, "Don't mind my sayin', you seem as interested in those kids as you are in finding out who killed the Berryman's."

They exchanged a glance, then Jessup said, "All this started after April began looking into the missing kids, and Cleve Pike is the only common link we have."

"Who nobody's seen in several days," the game warden said. "I put the word out on him, by the way."

"We know the kids supposedly went hunting the night they came up missing and Pike works at a hunting club," Flowers said.

"Is there anybody in DC or back in New Orleans you can call to get an update on the Berryman investigation? Maybe someone who knows what you guys are doing? Who might have a line on the people involved?"

She gave a tired smile. "I'm suspended. Nobody's going to tell me what time it is let alone give me details about a congressman getting killed."

"Our best lead is Cleve Pike and the Rebel Yell," Jessup said.

"Well, as far as the Yell goes, I doubt you'll get within a mile of that place until their guest leaves," Windler said. "I'll tell you what, you guys hang loose for today. Meanwhile, I'll dig around on my end, see what I can find out. Then tomorrow, after this VIP heads home, I'll go with you to the Rebel Yell and see if I can scare some information out of them. At least find out if they know where Pike got to."

"That sounds good, Houston. Thank you," Flowers said.

He turned back. "Oh, I'll be out of pocket tonight. They're letting campers back into the reserve, so they're sending me and a couple of other game wardens to patrol the area so that they'll feel safe."

"All right," Jessup said. "Be careful."

As they walked back to Jessup's truck, Flowers said, "That might help, having him along tomorrow."

"Yeah, I'll be interested to see what kind of reception we get at the Rebel Yell."

Just then, a car pulled from a nearby parking space, and the driver stared hard at them as he drove past.

It was Geo Palmer.

57

Jessup found the church and pulled around back. He saw a half dozen cars parked near the door leading to a community center. He walked in as they were finishing the Serenity Prayer, grabbed a cup of coffee and sat along the side wall where he could see the room.

Old habits die hard.

By the time the meeting started, there were twenty participants.

Not a bad crowd, he thought.

After the usual announcements and readings, the chairperson asked if there were any visitors. Several eyes turned toward him, but Jessup remained quiet, though he wasn't sure why. After the chairman read a topic, she opened the meeting to whoever wanted to share.

A few minutes later, the back door opened and a large figure walked in, his face hidden in the shadows. He sat in the last row, and when Jessup looked over he saw the scar. His chest tightened. It was Geo Palmer.

Palmer nodded to a couple of the attendees, but when his eyes fell on Jessup, his lips parted, as if in surprise. He slowly blew out a breath, then faced the front of the room as if he hadn't noticed.

When it was his turn, Jessup shared but couldn't recall what he had said as he watched Palmer from the corner of his eye. Why was the man following him? Seeing somebody in the grocery store or walking down the sidewalk was one thing. You didn't just run into people at an AA meeting.

Palmer left before the meeting ended. Jessup considered following him but didn't. Ten minutes later, he walked outside, half expecting to be jumped by the scar-faced man and his friends, but nothing happened. The parking lot was empty except for the people leaving the meeting.

Jessup got to his truck, pulled out his keys and clicked the fob. As he reached for the door handle, he heard a menacing voice behind him.

"Why you followin' me?"

Jessup spun around as Palmer emerged from behind a large azalea bush.

He was bigger than Jessup had realized. Two hundred and fifty pounds of muscle slabbed up on a frame a couple of inches over six feet. His fists clenched and unclenched, making the tendons in his massive forearms roil like thick snakes beneath his skin. Jessup was glad to see they were empty. From ten feet away, he could clearly make out the jagged pink scar as it crawled across the big man's ebony skin and he shuddered to think what the other guy's face looked like.

"Following *you?*" Jessup snarled. "Why are you following *me?*"

"And why would I be following you?"

"You tell me. My friend sees you at a convenience store a week ago, then we see you at the restaurant this afternoon, now you show at an AA meeting of all places."

Palmer shrugged. "Seems like a good place for an alcoholic to go."

Jessup's eyes tightened. "You in the deal?"

"Yeah. Four years. You?"

"I had five. Took a year off for remedial training. Been back three months now."

The big man chuckled and nodded. Then he stuck out a hand. "Geo Palmer."

Jessup hesitated, then reached out and gripped it. It felt like a piece of steel. "Jake Jessup."

"What are you and your friend doing out here, Jake?"

Jessup shrugged. "Just enjoying the scenery."

Palmer smiled. "No, you're not. I remember when your girlfriend had her little run-in with Cleve Pike at the store. An hour later she showed up at the Rebel Yell snooping around." He leaned in and whispered, "I saw *her*, she didn't see me."

Then he turned and leaned against Jessup's truck. The big Toyota rocked a little on its springs.

"Now she shows up with you and Houston Windler a day after a congressman and his wife get eaten by pigs?"

Jessup lifted a hand. "What can I say? She's a curious girl."

"Friendly advice, one drunk to another," Palmer said, "stay away from the Rebel Yell."

"Sounds more like a warning."

He shrugged. "Take it as you like."

"Or you'll do what?" Jessup shifted his weight to his front foot, even though he was pretty sure a fight with this man would not end well for him.

Palmer pushed off the truck. Jessup tensed.

"*I'm* not going to do anything. I quit a few days ago."

"Right after Cleve Pike disappeared?"

"Yeah, as a matter of fact."

Jessup thought about the pistol sitting under the front seat. "Because you had something to do with it?"

The big man chuckled. "No. Because I *didn't* have anything to do with it."

"Seems kind of suspicious. A guy goes missing and the ex-con he works with quits right afterward."

His mouth twisted into a snarl. "What else did Windler tell you about me?"

"That you like to wrestle alligators, which in my book proves you're a fuckin' nut case."

Palmer looked at him, then threw his head back and barked out a laugh. "Yeah, I did time for almost killing a guy. He tell you it was self-defense? That the guy and his two buddies jumped me and cut me after they groped my girlfriend? Or that it was the guy's own knife I cut him with?"

Jessup shook his head.

"Old story. I was drunk and black in a white parish where I didn't belong. Mixed it up with the town favorite. For some reason, eyewitness accounts did not match my version of the story."

Jessup knew that story all too well.

"I didn't touch Pike, and I'm not sure what happened to him. But I know that if something *did* happen to him, I'll be the one they'll be looking at."

"You must suspect something, otherwise you wouldn't leave. Can't be that easy to find work with a record."

"No, it's not. But my sobriety is the main thing in my life now. Without it, I'll end up back behind bars, and working at the Yell ain't good for my sobriety."

Jessup tilted his head.

"There's some strange stuff going on there, and if you're smart, you'll stay away."

Palmer turned to leave, and Jessup made a decision.

"Neil Berryman and his wife, and at least two other innocent people, were murdered in the last forty-eight hours, and I think it has something to do with the Rebel Yell."

58

Palmer slowly turned back. "What do you mean, murdered?"

"They may have been killed by animals, but it wasn't an accident. And those same people killed two of my friend's coworkers and they tried to kill her to keep it quiet."

"What's that got to do with the Rebel Yell?"

"I don't know," Jessup said. "But I'm going to find out."

Palmer stared at him, then said, "You won't find anything at the Rebel Yell. Where you want to look is north of there."

"What's north of there?"

"Three hundred acres of Arkansas hunting land Gus Erickson recently acquired but could never have afforded."

"Maybe he hit the lotto."

He huffed. "I've known Gus my whole life. He was an insurance salesman. Became a school board member and thought himself some kind of politician. He slowly built connections. His grandpa died and left him three hundred acres of land too wet to farm, so he started a pig hunting business. When boar hunting got popular, he quit insurance and started doing it full-time."

"That just sounds like smart business to me."

Palmer chuckled. "You don't know much about runnin' a hunting business, do you?"

"Nothing."

"It's hit or miss. Depends on the weather, marketing. And even if all those things line up, you ain't gonna get rich. You're sure as hell not going to be able to afford a half million dollar log house to run it out of, along with another half mil in cabins and equipment, then double your land holdings on top of all that."

"I've seen the website. The hogs look pretty big."

"Big as any you'll find in Louisiana."

"That would explain the popularity. They can charge a lot, and they would need the extra hunting area."

"They don't hunt the Arkansas land."

"What do they do with it?"

"They say breed pigs."

"Breed them? I thought the things were overrunning the south. Why would you want to breed them?"

"According to them, to produce bigger hogs to hunt at the Yell. But only a handful of workers are allowed up there."

"Aren't you curious?"

"I was, until they told me to stop asking questions if I wanted to keep my job."

Jessup gave him a look and Palmer said, "Just because I'm an ex-con doesn't mean they trust me."

"They trust Pike?"

"Nobody trusted Pike. That kid was a weasel. But they liked having him around because he'd do whatever they told him."

Jessup caught Palmer's use of the past tense but let it go.

"Funny thing is, just before he disappeared, not long after his run in with your girlfriend, they told him he was going to start working the breeding farm. He was all excited."

"Run in?" Jessup said.

"Me and a couple of the other guys were eating lunch when she came into Clements Quik Stop and asked Pike about the missing kids. She thanked him for the information and the boy turned white as a ghost."

"What information?"

"I don't think he told her anything. I think she was just jacking with him for being a dick."

"Ahh," Jessup said, deciding he'd keep that piece of information to himself. "You know Enos Norton?"

Palmer hesitated, then said, "Yeah, I know Enos. Good kid."

"You know what happened to him and his friends?"

"I've heard rumors."

"What rumors?"

"That they stuck their noses where they didn't belong. I also heard they're sitting on a beach in Panama City. I prefer that rumor."

"But you don't really believe it."

"What I believe is that if you two keep sticking *your* noses into the Rebel Yell Hunt Club, they're liable to get bitten off."

"Would you tell Clara Norton the same thing? Imagine what she's going through."

He deflated a little. "Listen, I feel you. But if I get involved, there's a good chance I end up back inside."

"I'm not asking you to get involved. Just tell us how we can get into the breeding farm without being seen."

"What do you think you're going to find there?"

Jessup grinned and shrugged. "Don't know until we get there."

Palmer chuckled and shook his head. "Actually, tonight would be a good time to look. They got some VIP hunt going on, so all the workers will be at the Yell. There shouldn't be anyone at the Arkansas land.

"There's a main entrance off the highway, but I wouldn't use it. Go a half mile down the state line cut and you'll see a gravel road that connects the hunt club to the Arkansas land. Just go north. There may be a cable blocking it, so bring bolt cutters."

Jessup nodded and stuck out his hand. "Thank you, Geo."

Palmer grabbed it. "Don't thank me. Just forget we ever talked."

At the motel, Jessup told Flowers what Palmer had told him.

"Do you believe him?"

"I do."

"Does his being a 'friend of Bill' have anything to do with that?"

Jessup thought about that for a second, then nodded. "Yes, it does. He's got some AA time under his belt. That means something to me."

"Sounds like he wasn't a teetotaler before he went to prison," she said.

"We all have a past, and booze can make you lose your mind. But people change."

"So, what's the plan?" she asked.

"Nope," Jessup said. "You're the boss, you tell me."

She smiled. "I was going to say we sit in the motel room, eat popcorn, and binge-watch *Justified*, but now I think we break into a pig farm and look around."

Jessup shook his head. "Sit in bed eating popcorn with a beautiful woman and watching *Justified* or go on a pig hunt. I should have my head examined."

She blushed, then said, "Don't forget the bolt cutters."

59

"Hey, man, check it out," Lars said. He was sitting on a bed inside the lodge. He pulled off his headphones and handed them to Gary.

Gary smiled as he nodded to the heavy beat. "This is awesome. Never heard this before."

"It's a German group, Kul MC. They're hot. I downloaded some of their stuff."

"Gary!" his father called from downstairs. "Let's get going."

"Okay, be down in a second," he replied, then said to Lars, "Send me a copy before you leave."

"No problem, man."

• • • • •• • • • • ••

The group retraced their route from the morning and forty-five minutes later they were back at the hunting cabins.

Erickson said, "It's four. In a couple of hours, the hogs will start moving towards the feeding areas, so we have plenty of time to set up."

"I still don't see why we have to get here so early if they don't come out for two more hours," Lars said.

"Pigs are smart and they see, smell, and hear well," Erickson explained. "We may not see them, but believe me, they see us. We set up, stay quiet, and give them time to settle down and forget we're here."

Lars looked away, a bored look on his face.

"Otto, Montel will get you and Armin set up in the blind. I'll take Lars and Gary around to the tree stands."

Erickson caught his son's eyeroll. The boy had been climbing deer stands since he was seven. He didn't need help showing someone how it was done, but Erickson also didn't need the son of a VIP getting hurt. And while tree stands could be dangerous, twenty feet above the ground was the safest place to be when you were hunting hogs.

The two stands faced south and were twenty feet apart, attached to oak trees at the edge of a clearing.

Erickson jabbed a finger at the large, muddy field where broken corn stalks jutted up from the ground like splinters driven into someone's face by an explosion. "That's where the pigs will show up, Lars. You boys will be shooting toward the south, and we'll be north of you shooting north. As long as everybody's aiming in the right direction, there's no chance of anyone getting accidentally shot."

Another eyeroll from his son.

"Gary will show you how to climb the stand. He's way better at it than me," Erickson said, earning a smile.

"Okay, guys, good luck. Gary, hit me on the walkie-talkie if you have a problem."

"They're settled in," Ruderman said when his boss returned. "Kohl's kicking back sipping on a beer."

"How about Joost?"

He chuckled. "GQ all the way. He's wiped his boots clean five times since we've been here. That boy does not belong in the woods."

"I'm tellin' you, the whole world's goin' to hell, Montel. It's not like when we were growing up. I guess these new kids figure that when the shit hits the fan there'll still be a Walmart open somewhere."

The foreman pulled the tablet from a bag and powered it up.

Erickson's brow creased. "The hogs are near that same mudhole, maybe a little closer to the cornfield. I don't want them wandering down there. Let's activate the thumper for a few seconds and get them heading this way."

"Don't want the kid to kill a bigger hog than his daddy?" Ruderman said, reaching into the bag and pulling out the thumper activator, which resembled a small portable radio with a switch and a dial.

"That kid ain't gonna kill a pig. He's just like Joost. He's only here because his daddy wants him here."

Ruderman toggled the switch, then looked at Erickson, who nodded. He slowly twisted the dial.

Erickson stared at the two dots on the screen. "Nothing's happening."

Ruderman twisted the dial a little more, and the two green dots jittered about, like a cursor bouncing on a computer screen. He gave it another twist, and the dots started heading towards the northern hunt site.

They exchanged grins. When the creatures were halfway there, Erickson said, "Shut it off. We'll hit 'em again right at sunset and pull them in the rest of the way."

Ruderman flipped the switch. The green dots slowed, then stopped.

"You know, Montel, I don't know why we didn't think of this before. We cull the runts from Tall Grass and bring 'em over here. Word gets out we can guarantee a monster hog, and we'll get hunters from around the world."

"Think that government guy will be good with it?"

"All we have to worry about is Blanton, and when he sees how much money is involved, he'll be good with it."

· · · · ●·● ● · · ·

Gary Erickson sat in the deer stand, his feet on the guardrail and his rifle between his legs, sighting down the scope. He glanced at Lars who had his earbuds in, his rifle leaning against the tree.

"You don't want to be out here, do you?" he asked the young German as he tracked a squirrel through the scope.

"What was your first clue?" Lars said, laying his head back against the tree and closing his eyes. "I mean, it's cool riding around on four-wheelers and stuff, but dude, we've been sitting up here for an hour and a half. Don't you get bored just sitting around waiting for some dumb animals to walk out into a field so you can shoot it?"

Gary laughed. "It can get boring."

"We could be sitting in the four-wheeler listening to music and enjoying some of that fine Louisiana home-grown."

Gary nodded, still peering through the rifle scope. "We could do that, but won't your dad be disappointed if you don't get a pig?"

"Nah, he'll only be disappointed if *he* doesn't get a pig. Besides, who's to say we didn't shoot and miss?"

Gary looked at him and grinned. "What say we head to the buggy?"

60

Jessup turned the truck north onto Highway 112 and looked over at Flowers. "Looks like something's on your mind."

"Just thinking," she said, staring out the window.

"Take it from me. Thinking is overrated."

"Those FDA agents in DC who told me not to stick my nose where it doesn't belong are doing their jobs and people aren't dying. They're actually saving lives."

"First off, you're doing your job, it's just a different job. But let me ask you this: how would you feel if you stopped investigating Section 17 and an animal infected with NF-13 got loose in a city? How many people would die? Did you ever considered that you might already have saved dozens of lives by putting pressure on them?"

She blew out a breath.

"In the words of Obi-Wan Frosty, 'Woulda, coulda, shoulda are not your friends.'"

Though she didn't reply, a smile ghosted her face.

"We're coming up to the entrance," she said.

Jessup saw the break in the trees and slowed as they went by. "I see a state trooper vehicle."

"And a black SUV."

He drove on another half mile and saw the sign for Arkansas. He checked the mirror to make sure they weren't being watched, then slowed to a crawl.

"Looks like it's time to bushhog again," he said, looking west down the ten-foot-wide swath marking the state line.

"Can you make it?"

He nodded. "I think so. It looks drier than that mud hole. But I want to look at that access road you found first."

They crossed into Arkansas and the road sign changed to County Road 4317. A half mile later, she pointed. "There it is. It would be easier to go in that way."

"Yeah, but I think that's what they'd expect. Geo's probably right. The safest way in is the back entrance."

He started to turn around and she said, "Those purple paint splotches are on just about every other tree. Maybe if we follow them we can get an idea how long this place is."

He smiled. "You're brilliant."

A mile later, the paint spots stopped.

"I'd say that's the northern border. Three hundred acres is a big area," he said.

They returned to the state line. Jessup zeroed his odometer and turned west down the cut. It was bumpy, but manageable. At just under three-quarters of a mile, they came to a gravel road that ran north and south. He turned right, went ten yards, then stopped in front of a steel cable strung between the trees.

He grabbed the bolt cutters. "Why do I feel I just did this?"

"Here," she said, grabbing them. "You're getting much too comfortable with criminal life."

He huffed. "Says the girl with a mechanical lock pick."

A second later, she pulled the cable aside and held up a hooked end. "No padlock. I guess they're not too worried about this entrance."

Once he pulled through, she reconnected the cable.

"Glad we didn't have to cut anything. That's one less red flag," he said.

Trees and heavy foliage crowded in along the well-worn trail. It was in fair shape, but nothing like the access road at PIT City. This seemed more like an old logging road than an entrance to a government facility.

A few minutes later, they came to a crossroads. Jessup checked the odometer. "A half mile. Same as the distance from the state line to the entrance off the highway."

"So the highway should be three quarters of a mile that way," Flowers said, pointing out her window.

"Left, or straight?"

"Your turn," she said. "I picked last time."

Jessup cranked the wheel to the left and headed west.

He went a hundred yards then slammed on the brakes. He peered through the windshield and said, "What the hell?"

"That is the biggest ditch I've ever seen." Flowers looked in both directions for its end. "Look how deep it is."

He crept forward and stopped at a cattle guard spanning the crevice. "Gotta be ten feet wide and just as deep," he said, staring at it.

"What's that ladder going across it?"

"That is a big ass cattle guard." He saw her expression. "A device they use on farms to keep livestock in. See the gaps between the metal tubes? Horses and cows and things are afraid to cross because their hooves can fall through, but you can drive a tractor or a car over it. I've just never seen one that big."

"This is like a moat around a castle," Flowers said.

"Yeah, but moats are to keep things out. I got a feeling this is to keep something in."

Jessup gestured toward the opposite side of the ditch and gave her a questioning look. Flowers stared at where the trail disappeared into the dark forest, then nodded. He crossed the bridge.

The gravel road rose slightly, then leveled out. The trees, mostly pines, began to thin, replaced by brush and tall grass.

"The road's sloping down."

"Yeah, grounds getting wetter, too," Jessup said, looking off to the sides. "Probably heading toward a swampy area."

"Don't want to get stuck."

"We still have gravel."

Grass as tall as the windows, crowded in a foot from either side of the path. It felt like the plains of Africa.

"There are hoof prints everywhere," Flowers said, hanging halfway out the window. "And it's all torn up, like that soybean field."

"That would make sense if they're raising pigs. Breeding four or five-hundred-pound hogs is good business if you own a hunting company. It would definitely give you a leg up on your competition."

"I don't know. These look pretty big."

"It's getting muddier. There's a clearing up ahead. I'll park and we can get out on foot."

Flowers pointed over the grass. "There's a telephone pole back there."

"Hmm, maybe civilization."

He pulled the old Tundra around the corner of the clearing and slammed on the brakes.

"Who the hell is that?" he said, his hand ready to jam the gearshift into reverse.

Lined up at the far end of the field, a hundred yards away, were eight soldiers dressed in green camouflage uniforms.

61

Flowers peered at them through the windshield as she gripped her pistol. Then she relaxed. "Not who, what. They're statues of some kind."

Jessup edged forward, then stopped halfway across the clearing.

"What the hell is this?" Jessup said, gawking at the metal rods protruding from the shoulders, necks, and heads of the strange figures. "Some redneck Freddy Kruger's attempt at sculpture?"

He opened the door, started to get out, and froze. "Holy crap."

"Yeah, same here," Flowers said, looking down. "Some of these are bigger than the ones Houston showed us at the lake."

Flowers reached over the seat and grabbed the rifle and shotgun. She handed Jessup the twelve- gauge.

He looked at the rifle and then at her questioningly. "No qualms about shooting one?"

She checked to make sure there was a round in the chamber, then said, "Not when it's bigger than my car."

They approached the figures and swarms of flies buzzed around, annoyed at the intrusion.

"One-inch-thick reinforcement rod," he said. "That's heavy stuff."

"These uniforms are shredded, more like pieces of material zip-tied on."

Jessup nodded. "Made to look like soldiers." He fingered the ends of the protruding rebar. "They sharpened the tips."

"So they can attach something."

"Like slabs of meat? That would explain why they're sticky and red."

"I have a bad feeling about this," Flowers said as she scanned the tall grass.

Jessup approached the short telephone pole embedded in the ground ten feet behind the metal soldiers. "What is that?" he said, peering up at a foot-long tube attached to an L-bracket. Next to it was a speaker. "There's a solar battery to power it."

Flowers looked down, then squatted in front of a statue and dug around.

"What've you got?"

She held up a black lanyard with a metal object attached to it.

"It's a razorback necklace. I saw Pike wearing one just like this inside that convenience store."

Jessup peered at the chrome boar's head with its oversized teeth hanging from the leather strap. "That guy really is ate up with wild pigs."

She searched around, pushing aside some of the uniform fabric that had fallen to the ground, then gasped.

"Ooh, that's ominous," Jessup said, staring at the bloodstained set of hand-cuffs attached to a steel upright. "Especially since the other end is closed."

"You don't think... I mean, there's no body attached to it. They must have just closed it, right?"

"Remember what Ernest said. Pigs will eat anything and everything."

She suddenly stood and scanned the tree line.

They heard a loud snap in the grass across the clearing to their right. They spun toward it, weapons ready. They stared at the spot for several seconds but saw nothing.

"I think we're spooking ours—"

"There!" Flowers hissed, stabbing a finger. "Something moved."

"I see it. There's something to the left, moving this way. Ease back to the truck, nice and slow," he said in a low voice, wishing he had parked closer. They made it three steps when they heard a loud snort from the brush behind the metal men. They spun and saw the tops of the bushes shaking in three places.

Jessup turned in a circle and saw the grass moving in several spots all around them. Flowers took a quick step forward, but he grabbed her arm and held her as they slowly returned to the Toyota.

Five feet from the truck, a large, dark hump appeared in the grass to their left. It bellowed, then charged, knocking aside small trees and brush like a submarine cutting across the surface of the water.

"Shit!" Jessup let her go, sprinted around the truck, dove into the cab, and was cranking the ignition before he got the door shut. The old truck roared to life.

"Go! Go! Go!" Flowers said as she wrenched the rifle around, trying to point it out the window.

Jessup slammed the gearshift into reverse and floored the gas. The rear tires tore eight-inch grooves into the dirt as he spun the wheel to the left. Then he jammed the lever into drive and stomped the pedal again, rooster-tailing dirt and gravel into the air behind them.

He slewed left to right to left, then straightened it out just as something monstrous burst into the clearing behind him. He couldn't tell what it was through the dust and the dimming light, but it was big.

Big as this damn truck, he thought, his heart pounding.

Flowers knelt on the seat and jabbed the barrel of the M5 toward the rear window. "Open the vent window!" she said.

"You see it?" he asked.

Her eyes were saucer wide. "I saw something, but I don't think it's following us."

Jessup didn't let up on the gas until they were several hundred yards down the gravel road.

She looked over at him. "How did you stay so calm back there?"

He shot her a look. "You kiddin' me? I wanted to scream and run like a fat kid in dodgeball."

She kept watch through the back window, then said, "Giant boar?"

"No doubt. How big? No clue, but big."

"Big enough to kill a congressman and his wife?"

"Oh, yeah."

62

Ambassador Kohl and his aide sat in camp chairs and peered through the one-way fabric toward the baited ground as shadows stretched across the killing field. Erickson and Ruderman sat at either end, binoculars looped around their necks. Kohl was checking his watch for the tenth time when there came a gunshot, followed quickly by a second.

Erickson pulled out his walkie-talkie. "Talk to me, Gary. What you got?"

A second later, the boy replied, *"Lars got a bead on a big one, maybe two-fifty, but something spooked it as he shot and he missed. I took a shot as it was running off, but no luck."*

"Tell Lars not to feel bad. Happens to all of us," Erickson said over the radio. "They'll be back."

Kohl gave a tight smile. "At least he took a shot."

He suddenly set down his beer and looked through his rifle scope. "I think I see movement," he said excitedly.

Joost jerked upright and grabbed his weapon. "Where?" he almost shouted.

"Shhhh," Ruderman hissed. "A pig can hear a loud whisper at this distance."

Kohl looked at his aide disdainfully, then turned back and whispered, "I saw the grass move... yes, there."

Erickson looked through his binoculars and saw the grass part. Four pigs walked into the clearing, two larger ones and two piglets.

"Look how big they are!" Joost said, barely able to keep his voice down.

"Those are maybe a hundred seventy-five pounds. Good eatin', but nowhere near a trophy," Erickson said as the animals attacked the sour corn the foreman had spread out earlier.

"Calm yourself, Armin," his boss demanded. "We must be patient."

"That's the trick," Ruderman agreed.

Erickson caught his eye, held up a hand, and made a twisting motion. The foreman nodded and walked out.

At the Mule, he readied the tablet, then pulled out the thumper control. He switched it on and turned the dial. On the screen, the two green dots migrated towards the pulsing yellow light that represented the location of the thumper. He felt a strange twist of excitement and dread as the eight-hundred-pound behemoths approached.

Ruderman had set up the thumper in the grass on the far side of the clearing so the boars had to cross open ground to get to it. He kept his finger poised over the toggle switch. He would switch it off just as they emerged into the open area.

According to Dotson, the creatures only associated people with food when the thumper tone was active. After it was shut off, they avoided human contact like any other wild pig. Of course, that was after they had already eaten and were no longer hungry.

The two creatures were fifty yards from the clearing and moving fast. Ruderman's eyes flicked toward the blind. They were basically invisible. The boars wouldn't know they were there—unless someone attracted their attention. He felt a sudden urge to slap a piece of duct tape over Joost's mouth.

He heard a gasp and knew they had spotted the beasts. He flipped the switch off and the two green dots stopped just outside the clearing.

That should get them close enough to smell the corn and move in, he thought. He laid down the tablet and the controller and went back inside.

· • • ● • ● • • • ·

Lars and Gary kicked back in the ATV, putting their feet on the dash while they sipped the beers Gary had snuck out of the kitchen earlier that day. Outlaw country boomed from the overhead speakers.

"Now admit it," the young German said, "isn't this better than sitting up in that deer stand?"

Gary let a huge burp. "I'd be lyin' if I said it wasn't."

That started a burping war until Lars let out a massive belch and declared himself the victor. He nodded over his shoulder. "Can't they hear this music?"

"Nah, we're too far away."

"I bet they'll hear this." He lifted his rifle toward the clearing and fired off a round.

"Holy shit, dude!" Gary exclaimed. "A little heads-up next time?" Gary jacked a round into the chamber and fired it off.

"Hey, you talk about me."

"You'll see why in a second."

Just then, his walkie-talkie crackled, and his father said, *"Talk to me, Gary. What you got?"*

"Lars got a bead on a big one, maybe two fifty, but something spooked it as he shot and he missed. I took a shot as it was running off, but no luck," the teenager replied.

"Tell Lars not to feel bad. Happens to all of us. They'll be back," came the reply.

"Here's to Lars," the German said, lofting his beer bottle into the air. "The mighty hunter!"

"No more shooting, mighty hunter, unless you got something to shoot at," Gary said.

"Oh, you worry too much." He pulled a hand-rolled cigarette from his pocket. "Let's light this up, go for a ride, and listen to some real music."

Lars passed Gary the joint, then connected his cell phone to the ATV's Bluetooth. "Okay, my American friend, let's rock!"

He cranked the volume up and a strong bass beat vibrated the four-wheeler. *Whump, whump, whump, whump, whump,* went the heavy rhythm as the teens whooped and waved their arms overhead in time with the music. Lars tossed down his beer bottle, threw the ATV into drive, and tore down the trail.

· · ● ● ·● ● · ·

"Look at them!" Kohl said in a harsh whisper, peering through his scope at the two brown masses sticking above the grass. The telltale ridge of dark brown hair ran from their shoulders to the middle of their backs. They stood in the foliage at the edge of the clearing and milled about.

Erickson threw Ruderman a grin.

"Why don't they come out?" Joost said, a tremble in his voice.

The foreman was about to say "Because you're too fucking loud," when the monster hogs spun around and ran south.

Kohl glared at his aide, who looked stricken.

"We'll be right back, Ambassador," Erickson said. He and Ruderman ran from the tent.

· · ● ● ·● ● · ·

"Slow it down, dude, before we end up in a ditch," Gary shouted.

"You worry too much," the teen said as he punched the accelerator. The machine went faster, kicking up waves of mud as they slammed through waterholes.

Gary shook his head, then caught sight of something in the side-view mirror, but he lost it in a turn. When they hit a short straightaway, he glanced back at the mirror and sucked in a breath. "Holy fuck!"

He scrambled around in his seat to look.

"What?" Lars said, letting up on the accelerator.

"Don't slow down!" Gary shouted.

Lars stomped on the pedal and the buggy shot forward just as a gigantic boar appeared behind them.

"Mein Gott!" the German screamed.

"Faster!" Gary said, his eyes as wide as grapefruits.

It was bigger than the ATV and closing fast. A Russian boar, bigger than any he'd ever seen. He knew where it came from, but how had it gotten here?

Lars hit the next corner and almost lost control but straightened it out.

"Down that trail!" Gary shouted, jabbing a finger to the right.

The teen cranked the wheel. The rear end slid into a small tree, and they jerked to a stop. The pig shot past them, then slid in the mud as it tried to turn. Lars punched the accelerator, and the machine shot forward just as the creature lunged for them.

They crashed through the overgrown trail at thirty miles per hour, branches and briars ripping at their exposed arms and faces as the heavy beat music echoed through the forest. Gary heard their pursuer but couldn't see it and didn't know if that was better or worse.

The monster pig suddenly appeared and slammed its massive head against the roll cage, hooking a fearsome eight-inch tusk around the metal bars. Gary almost screamed as the pig jerked its head and the Mule lurched to the left. Lars *did* scream as he fought for control. Then, with a thunderous crash, something exploded from the trees next to them and collided with the first pig, knocking it off the trail.

"Oh, man!" Gary screamed. "It's another one! Go, go, go, go!"

63

Jessup crossed the cattle trap going thirty, then slowed down and sucked in a breath.

"Smoke everywhere, but no flames," he said.

"What about the handcuffs and this?" Flowers said, holding up the pig necklace.

"Where's the body?"

She shook her head. "This is heading in the same direction as the pit bulls. I can't let that happen. Not this time."

"Let's see what's at the other end of that gravel road."

They turned left at the intersection and headed north. It was dusk, but enough sunlight cut through the trees for him to make his way without head-lights.

A quarter mile on, they came to a clearing where four large metal buildings sat at the back of a freshly graveled rectangular lot. They looked new, and electric lines ran from a utility pole to each one.

"This is more like it. This has the feel of government money," Jessup said.

They watched for a few minutes from the tree line. Seeing no movement, they pulled forward.

All four were barn-style with swing-out double garage doors secured with padlocks and a walk-in door on the side. He parked behind the first building.

The side door was locked. Jessup held up the bolt cutters.

"Shall we?"

He clipped the padlock on the double doors, pulled them open, and yelped, "Holy shit!"

• • • • • • • • • •

"There's two of them?" Lars shouted punching the gas.

They broke into a clearing and Gary said, "There's the corn field! Turn right!"

The German teen cranked the wheel and spun through the turn, all four tires kicking dirt and grass into the air as the two boars burst from the trees behind them. Gary looked back and decided it was better not to see them.

"Faster!" he screamed as the pigs closed on them. *How can something that big be so fast?*

"I've got it floored!" Lars said.

"Turn right at the cornfield. Head for the deer stands."

The ATV made the turn on two wheels. Lars straightened it out and hit the gas again just as the creatures rounded the corner, their massive hooves ripping through the dirt, leaning into the turn like a motorcycle racer at Daytona.

Gary's eyes darted from the pigs to the deer stands then back to the pigs. Fifty yards... twenty-five... ten... Lars slammed on the brakes, and the ATV skidded sideways. The two boys were out of the machine before it stopped moving. Lars lunged forward, grabbed the ladder rungs and pulled himself up.

Gary jumped, but his foot came down on the empty beer bottle Lars had thrown out. He went down on a knee, but sprang up, grabbed the rungs, and jerked himself upward. His foot touched the fifth rung just as a boar got there. The massive beast, ten feet in length, scrabbled up the side of the oak tree like a dog chasing a squirrel. It latched onto Gary's left boot and tore the screaming teen from the ladder.

Lars watched the two animals devour his new friend while music blasted from the speakers.

· • • ●• ● • • ·

Jessup dropped the bolt cutters and danced in place.

Flowers saw the rat run past him and burst out laughing. "You keep your cool with killer pigs on our heels, but a little rat freaks you out?"

"*Little?* Did you see the size of that thing? It was huge!"

She kept laughing as she reached over and flipped on a light switch. There was a chorus of squeals as a dozen more rats scattered across the floor.

Jessup snatched up the bolt cutters and held them like a machete. "God, I hate rats."

"I see why they're in here," Flowers said, gazing at the pallets of feed stacked halfway to the ceiling. "That is a lot of corn."

"So far, everything points to a breeding farm for a large-scale pig hunting club," Jessup said, scanning the floor. She gave him a sour look and moved to the next building.

There they found several pieces of construction equipment.

"Military," Jessup said, walking up to a tan front-end loader equipped with a backhoe. "I bet they use this to move the pallets of corn and maintain that ditch."

Next to the loader was a blue semi-tractor and an enclosed trailer half the length of a normal one.

"This is a heavy, heavy-duty trailer," Jessup said, walking around it. "You could haul a big load with this."

"It's got vent holes along the top," Flowers said. She wrinkled her nose. "Smells like pigs."

"They've been painted over," he said, pulling open a side panel to reveal olive-drab paint. "Why would they do that?"

"To not attract attention?"

Jessup nodded. "Good guess."

"Military equipment. That's more smoke, right?" Flowers said.

"Not necessarily. Anybody can buy surplus military gear. There's a big market for it."

When they opened the third shed, Jessup whistled. "Now, this is smoke."

"One of these blocked me in at the Rebel Yell," Flowers said, stepping onto the running board of a Humvee.

"You didn't tell me about that."

"I didn't think about it. Didn't seem important at the time."

"These are armored. You can buy them," he said, "but why would you need them on a farm?"

"Look at this," Flowers said, reaching up and pulling off a tuft of brown fur wedged between the metal at the top of the windshield.

"That's six feet off the ground."

Flowers nodded. "About the right height for what I saw in the clearing."

"This would be a good vehicle to be in if you were being attacked by giant hogs."

"But Ernest said wild boars won't attack you unless they feel threatened. They run away from people."

Jessup nodded. "Unless they're trained to run toward them."

"Just like the baboons and the pit bulls."

Nearing the last building, Jessup said, "I hear something running in there."

They pulled the doors open to reveal two blue refrigerated semi-trailers.

"Painted over," Jessup said, scraping a bit to reveal tan paint underneath. He climbed onto the rear bumper. "Doors are unlocked." He grabbed a handle, then looked at Flowers, who was standing off to one side.

"What's up? Don't you want to see?"

She gave a quick shake of her head and pulled her arms around herself, as if chilled.

He nodded, switched on his headlamp and pulled open the door. He looked inside for several seconds, then reached in and picked something up. The insulated door blocked her view.

"It's human flesh, isn't it?" Flowers said, her face pale.

Jessup jumped down and turned to her. He was holding a rectangular object in his hand.

She took a step back.

"It's flesh... but not human flesh. Unless Winn Dixie has gotten into the undertaker business." He held it up.

Her mouth dropped open. She stepped forward and took the package. The sticker on the plastic-wrapped lump of tan meat said rump roast, four pounds, with a price stamp and an expiration date from two weeks earlier.

"Are they changing their program? Does this mean Section 17 is no longer targeting human beings?"

"No, April," Jessup said, shaking his head. "It means they're getting frugal."

Her brow creased. "What do you mean?"

He reached inside the cooler and pulled out a large plastic garden sprayer. He gave it a couple of pumps, aimed the nozzle at the side of the trailer, and pulled the trigger. Thick red fluid sprayed out.

He looked at her and said, "It's blood." Then his mouth opened, and his eyes went wide.

"Jake! Are you—"

He fell to his knees and slumped forward. Her mind registered the tranquilizer dart sticking from his back a split second before one hit her.

64

"What happened, Gus?" Erickson snapped.

"How should I know?" Ruderman said as he activated the tracking tablet. "They're pigs. You know how unpredictable they are."

"Where are they now?"

Ruderman's eyes narrowed as he peered at the screen. "That doesn't make sense. According to this they're heading for the cornfield."

"What?" Erickson looked at the screen. "They're moving fast, like they're running."

The foreman huffed. "Wouldn't it piss off the Kraut if his kid killed one and he didn't?"

"Don't say that word!" Erickson hissed, looking over his shoulder at the hunting blind. He jerked the walkie-talkie from his belt.

"What are you going to do?"

"I'm gonna tell Gary not to shoot our pigs." He clicked the receiver. "Gary, come in."

There was no response.

"Gary, answer your radio." Nothing.

"Think there's a problem?"

"No," Erickson said. "Probably has his earbuds in listening to music. Besides, they're up in the deer stands. That's the safest place to be."

"Well, they just ran past the cornfield and we didn't hear any gunshots. We would have heard something if there was a problem."

"They're not even paying attention," Erickson said, shaking his head. "Think the trackers are going bad?"

"Both of them at the same time? Look at the screen. Looks like they're running in zigzags. Maybe the tablet's bad."

Erickson snatched the thumper control. "Well, I don't give a shit what it is. We gotta get them back here." He flipped the toggle switch, cranked the dial up to a hundred percent, then tossed the device onto the front seat of the Mule.

He slapped the walkie-talkie into his foreman's hand, turned toward the blind, and snarled, "Yell when they get close."

Ruderman watched the two green dots drift apart, join back up, then separate south of the cornfield, and wondered at their bizarre behavior.

Suddenly, the computer blips came together again, then started moving in a straight line through the thirty-acre cornfield toward the deer stands. Though he knew the teens were safely off the ground, a jolt of fear hit him. He grabbed the radio.

"Gary, this is Montel. Come in."

There was no reply.

"Gary, answer your radio," he almost shouted.

The two dots closed on the deer stands and a chill shot up his spine. The chill turned to ice when they stopped beneath them.

"Oh, fuck!" he stammered. He clamped down on the transmit button and shouted, "Gary!"

• • • • • • • • • •

Lars Kohl looked into the black eyes of the two monsters as he hugged the trunk of the oak tree. The deer stand hung precariously by one strap after the pigs had torn away the ladder trying to get at him. Once they stripped the flesh from Gary's corpse, they turned their attention to him. He couldn't go down—like that was even a consideration—and the closest limb was five feet above his head, too far to reach, even if he had the nerve to stand on the guardrail.

"Go away!" he screamed, but his shouts only seemed to excite the animals.

Suddenly, over the music, he heard, *"Gary, this is Montel, come in."*

Frantically, he scanned the area and saw the walkie-talkie lying in the grass ten feet from Gary's corpse.

"Here! I'm here. Help me. Come help—"

"Gary, answer your radio," said the voice.

"Help! Help me! I'm in the tree. Can't you hear me?" the teen cried out. Then he remembered, it was not like a phone, you had to push the button on the side to talk. With a cry of anguish, he leaned his head against the tree. Then he thought, *Phone?*

He let loose with one arm and slapped his back pocket. *My phone!*

His hand hit the deer stand guard rail as he pulled it out. He fumbled with the device, but it slipped through his fingers. He watched in horror as it hit the deer stand floor, bounced, and fell to the ground.

"No! No! No!" he screamed, slamming his fist against the tree.

His shouts incensed the raging boars, and they renewed their assault, their huge hooves ripping the tree bark down to the moist cambium layer. One pig slipped on the slick surface and crashed downward and a hoof landed on the cellphone, obliterating it.

The music stopped.

The other hog dropped and joined its comrade, rooting around as if confused. Then one, and then the other, lifted its head and looked to the north.

· · · ● ● · ● · · · ·

Montel Ruderman jumped into a Mule and headed down the trail toward the cornfield, the computer tablet and thumper control bouncing in the seat beside him. He caught sight of his rifle slung in the overhead rack. As he reached for it, a massive shape exploded from the trees and slammed into the ATV, flipping it onto its side and pinning the man's legs.

He barely had time to scream before the monster bit him across the face.

65

Erickson spat a silent curse as Ambassador Kohl looked sullenly toward the empty soybean field. Even Joost appeared to have grown bored.

He stared at the tall grass, trying to will the animals back. He heard his foreman shout his son's name and an ATV started up and spun gravel as it took off.

Where the hell is he going?

Kohl suddenly sucked in a breath. Erickson looked over and saw the ambassador's eyes locked straight ahead. Beside him, Joost trembled in his seat. He followed their gaze and saw the monster boar standing in the middle of the clearing.

It was more massive than he remembered, and it chilled him to think it was considered a runt. A rhinoceros came to mind as he gazed upon it, only instead of a horn, this monster had shiny, eight-inch razor-sharp tusks.

The entire forest had gone quiet. Even the cicadas had given up their song in deference to the beast. It jerked its head about looking for a target, canines flashing like sickle blades in the dimming light.

A chill ran through Erickson as he thought about the thumper control sitting in the four-wheeler, while an innate fear, born from the primordial recesses of his mind, bubbled to the surface.

"Take the shot, Otto," he whispered to the ambassador, but the man was frozen. Joost whimpered and shifted in his chair.

"Don't move!" Erickson hissed as he grabbed for his rifle slung over his shoulder. He felt nothing. He snatched for it again, then remembered it was in the ATV.

Joost suddenly squealed and leaped to his feet, knocking his chair backward. In the quiet, it sounded like a metal trashcan bouncing down a driveway.

"Freeze, you idiot!" he whispered, but the terrified man emitted a keening moan, spun around, and ran out the rear flap.

Erickson looked up and saw the boar looking towards the blind, its dark eyes locked on them as if they were lit by a spotlight. Suddenly, dirt flew from its hooves as it charged.

"Shoot, Otto!" Erickson shouted. Kohl thrust the rifle out like a spear, closed his eyes, and jerked the trigger. The explosion lit up the enclosure like a camera flash, and in the glow he saw Kohl drop the rifle and run.

Erickson snatched up Joost's weapon. Muscle memory kicked in as he jerked it to his shoulder, thumbed off the safety and pulled the trigger.

Click.

The German had not chambered a round.

"You stupid fucker!"

He jerked back the bolt, slammed it forward and was pulling the trigger when eight hundred pounds of muscle and fury smashed into him.

· · • • · • • · · ·

Kohl stopped in the middle of the trail and whipped his head frantically from side to side. He heard a rifle shot, then a scream, then an ATV starting up.

Joost suddenly burst from the tree line and took off down the trail.

"Joost! Joost! Stop, wait for me!" the ambassador shouted as he ran after the man, waving his arms.

But Joost didn't stop. Joost didn't even slow down. Joost jammed the accelerator to the floorboard and left his employer, literally, in the dust. Half a minute later, the aide turned left into the woods, back toward the lodge, while Kohl ran after him, screaming vows to skin the man alive.

The ambassador saw an overturned four-wheeler and skidded to a stop. He came around it and lurched back when he saw Ruderman's bloody remains, one leg pinned under the vehicle.

The key was still in the ignition. He grabbed the rollbar and pushed. The huge machine rocked sideways a foot, then fell back. He tried again but got no further, it was just too heavy. He stood there for half a minute, listening, but heard nothing.

Kohl wondered how long it would take him to walk back to the camp, then realized he didn't have to. He only had to get to the deer stands. Lars and the other kid had the third ATV. He ran down the trail and was nearing the turnoff when he heard the whine of a gas motor. It grew louder and Kohl saw the jitter of a headlight bouncing down the trail toward him.

It's Joost, he thought, *coming to pick me up.*

"I'm still going to skin you alive," the ambassador growled as he ran toward the bobbing light.

A second later, an ATV appeared. It *was* Joost. The big machine fishtailed around the corner and headed straight for Kohl, who was standing in the middle of the trail waving his arms.

"Stop, Joost, stop!" Kohl shouted as the headlights lit him up. But Joost didn't stop, he didn't even slow down. The ambassador dove off the trail as the four-wheeler roared past him.

A second later, a monster pig tore around the corner. It ran past, and Kohl staggered wide-eyed to the center of the path. He watched as the creature caught the Mule, and with a quick snap of its neck, knocked the machine sideways. The ATV flipped twice, then came to a stop. The hog lunged forward and Kohl thought he heard a cry. He gave a sneer of satisfaction.

He walked backwards down the trail as he watched the carnage. He made it ten feet when he heard a snort. He slowly turned and screamed.

66

Jessup opened his eyes and saw only blackness.

I'm blind! his mind screamed as he jerked his head around. He felt material touching against his face and took a deep breath, trying to calm himself. He was on the ground, slumped forward, his arms secured behind his back. He listened but heard only the buzz of the cicadas. Then he heard a moan.

"April," he whispered, "is that you?"

"What happened? Where—"

He heard her thrash around, then there were footsteps, and someone ripped away the bags covering their heads.

Bright light stabbed him in the eyes and he turned his head to the side. They were both hooked to the rebar statues.

"Agent April Flowers and her trusty sidekick, Jake Jessup," came a familiar voice.

Jessup squinted, and tried to follow the source, but saw only the glare of headlights.

The man clicked his teeth. "We're going to have to change that old saying to 'more lives than Jessup and Flowers.'"

"I know you," Flowers growled. "Is it still 'Harry Perkins, CDC,' or are you using some other name today?"

Flattner chuckled. "That'll do for now."

"Thought you might change it after you killed Congressman Berryman and his wife, and then Greg and Carolyn," Jessup said. He twisted his fingers around, praying they weren't secured to the metal figures by zip-ties. He felt the cool, smooth surface of handcuffs. He twisted his right hand to his left wrist and felt for the parachute cord bracelet his son had given him as a gift. What he hadn't told Flowers was that the clasp had a built-in handcuff key.

"Those were just tragic accidents," he said. "Happens a hundred times a day across this country."

"Just like on the Pyatt and in Memphis?" Flowers said.

Jessup used two fingers to pinch the connector holding the ends of the bracelet together. It came apart with a click but slipped and fell to the ground.

"Yes, exactly," Flattner replied from the darkness. "Like what happens when trespassers enter the private property of a wild boar breeder, get their vehicle stuck in the mud, then fall prey to the very animals they seek to help. Tragic."

As he spoke, two camouflaged figures wearing balaclavas shoved slabs of meat onto the rebar spikes protruding from the metal statues. Jessup's stomach roiled from the smell of raw, semi-rotted meat.

"You won't get away with it," Flowers said. "We have people waiting for us and we haven't checked in. They're on their way now."

"Oh, you mean Agent Windler?"

She sucked in a breath. "What have you done to him?"

"Done to him?" Flattner said. "Why, he looks fine to me."

A headlamp flicked on and there, sitting on the hood of the Hummer, between the headlights, sat Houston Windler. He gave a chagrined smile and shrugged.

Flowers' eyes went wide. "You bastard!"

Jessup spun his head toward her.

Windler chuckled. "Hey, it's nothing personal. Like I told you, hog hunting is important to the local economy, and the Rebel Yell is important to *my* personal economy. Being a state game warden isn't exactly a lucrative profession."

"So, all that stuff about respecting Berryman and how he helped northern Louisiana was bullshit?" Jessup said.

"Pretty much. Everything was fine, but he wasn't content with his little boardwalk. He had to stick his nose into the oil business, and oil is *the most* important thing for the local economy. A lot of very important people stood to lose their financial fortunes when he moved to shut down the Okaloosa Reservoir Project."

Flowers looked confused. "The Okaloosa Reservoir Project? You mean this isn't about Section 17?"

"It's interconnected," Flattner said. "In politics, everything touches everything else."

"You mean money," Jessup growled, as he squirmed around searching for the fallen bracelet.

"Of course. Politics is all about power and money. You can't have one without the others, and it takes all three to keep our nation's enemies at bay."

Jessup barked a laugh. "You keep pushing that whole God and country theme, Harry, but we all know what this is really about."

"Does your hillbilly posse know your scheme includes germ warfare?" Flowers asked.

"Agent Windler," Flattner said. "How do you feel about using unconventional weapons against our nation's enemies?"

"I say nuke the bastards and be done with it," the state agent said. "And if anybody's got a problem with that, nuke them, too."

Jessup could feel the government operative smiling in the darkness.

One of the masked men jammed a piece of putrid meat onto a spike above Flowers. Drops of blood splattered onto her and she lashed out and kicked the man in the crotch. He yelped and went to one knee, his eyes flaring through the openings of the face cover, while his partner laughed.

Jessup waited for him to backhand her. Instead, he grabbed a sticky, smelly chunk of meat and slapped it into the crotch of her pants.

"Ooh," Windler said. "That'll be the first place those bastards go." He shook his head. "What a waste."

Flowers glared at him.

A radio crackled and a voice said, *"TG4 to TG1, can you return to base? We have a situation."*

From behind the glare of the headlights, Flattner replied, "TG1, what's the problem?"

"We can't reach anyone at the hunt. Nobody's responding to our calls."

"Well, send someone out there," Flattner said.

"We did, thirty minutes ago. Now they don't answer."

"Thirty minutes ago? Why am I just now finding—" He sucked in a slow, seething breath. "Show me en route."

He jabbed a finger toward them. "Take care of this and put his truck in the ditch with the other two. We'll bury them tomorrow."

Then Jessup heard footsteps and the sound of a vehicle driving away.

67

Windler looked over his shoulder, then back at his prisoners, and shook his head. "Hm, hm, hm. He is not a happy camper."

"Why are you doing this? We trusted you," Flowers said.

"A lot of people have made that mistake," the ranger said, climbing down from the hood of the Hummer. "Must be my boyish smile."

"It ain't your winning personality," Jessup said, twisting his arms and scraping at the ground.

"That hurts, but not as bad as you two are about to hurt. As for why, money, of course. Like I said, a Louisiana game warden makes about enough to pay his bills. I have to think about my future. And Jake you of all people should know, you can pull on those handcuffs all you want. They don't stretch."

One of the masked men glanced over his shoulder and said, "Hey, Houston, we're getting a lot of movement out there."

Windler threw him an annoyed look, then pulled what looked like a large TV remote from his shirt pocket. "Here's what's going to happen. I'm going to flip this switch and it's going to activate that gizmo up on the telephone pole behind you." He pointed at the black tube Jessup had noticed earlier.

"It's called a 'thumper' because, well, it thumps. Ninety beats per second. It's kind of like the Pied Piper story from when you were a kid. You know, where he plays his flute and the rats follow him out of town."

"I see three big rats standing here," Flowers snarled.

He chuckled. "You think we're big? You ain't seen nothing. *Sus scrof scrofa* is the Latin name; the Russian Boar. The largest, most powerful, and most aggressive wild hog on the planet. I don't know the specifics, but when our government friends give 'em a little tweak they are a wonder to behold. Twelve hundred pounds of pissed off pork. A half ton weapon that will mow down whatever it sees... and then eat it.

"And they do have an appetite. They go through a warehouse full of corn in a week, but what really excites them is meat. Once a day" —he glanced at his watch— "right about now, in fact, we load up our metal soldiers, turn on the thumper, and watch the show. It's frightening. It's even better when we add a little flavoring."

A man stepped forward, holding a garden sprayer. Dark liquid sloshed inside the opaque plastic container.

The color drained from Flowers' face.

"We save this for last," Windler said. "The smell really riles them up."

A thick copper smell permeated the air as the man sprayed down the slabs of meat with the blood.

Flowers gagged.

"I know it seems disgusting, but Larry actually did you a favor sticking that slab of meat in your lap," Windler said. "But just to make sure it's over with quick..."

He nodded, and Larry shifted the sprayer and doused the two prisoners.

"No!" Flowers screamed as she whipped her head from side to side.

Jessup sat still, his head down, his fingers searching for the bracelet as the sticky, foul liquid ran down his head, shoulders, and legs. He felt it and grabbed it.

"I lied though," Windler said. "There won't be much pain." He turned to one of the camouflaged men. "How long did Cleve last? One yelp?"

The guy chuckled.

Jessup stared at Windler. "Was that before or after the bridge?"

"Before. That was me on the bridge."

Flowers gasped.

He looked at her and chuckled. "You have no idea how shocked I was when I saw you on that boardwalk. And you can only imagine how pissed our government friend was when he found out you were still alive. That's the reason you're both here tonight. My recompense if you will."

She stared at him; her eyes filled with rage as blood dripped down her face.

"But all is forgiven... or will be shortly."

A loud snort came from the darkness.

Windler clapped his hands. "All right, folks, there's our cue. Suppertime. The boys and I will retire to the confines of the armored Humvee to watch." Then he leaned in and whispered, conspiratorially, "Just between you and me, those things scare the shit out of me even when I'm inside that vehicle. I can't imagine what it will be like for you two."

Flowers roared and kicked at his face, but he danced back, snickering. "Let's go."

The three men climbed into the Hummer and the doors shut with heavy clunks. The big diesel motor roared to life, the Hummer backed up fifty yards, and the lights clicked off.

Jessup frantically twisted his fingers around trying to insert the plastic hand-cuff key into the slot. Behind him, he heard a click. He looked back and saw a green light flashing on the black tube. It was synced with a rapid knocking sound, like someone striking a stick against a log.

He fumbled with the band, then dropped it again. "Fuck!" He twisted around to see where it fell.

"Jake."

"Hang on, April!" He twisted the other way and saw it.

"Jaaaake," she said, her voice rising.

He followed her gaze and saw the brush at the edge of the clearing move.

"Shit!" Jessup contorted his body and arms into an unnatural position, felt the braid, and snatched the bracelet. He fumbled with the cuff, got the tiny key inserted, fought the urge to quickly twist the fragile plastic key, felt the rachet give, and the cuff loosen.

"Yes!" he hissed, jerking his hand free.

He scrambled behind Flowers as the high beams on the Humvee flared on.

"How—what—" she stammered.

He stuck the tip of the key into her right cuff, twisted, and felt the plastic bend.

The truck motor roared to life.

Jessup yanked the key out and jammed it into the other cuff as tires tore into the gravel. From the corner of his eye, he saw the vehicle accelerate toward them as one of the masked men holding a rifle rose through the gun turret.

Pow, pow, pow!

Bullets zipped overhead and slammed into the telephone pole. The next volley wouldn't miss.

He said a quick prayer and twisted the key. The cuff slid open and Jessup yanked Flowers to the side just as lead ricocheted off the rebar frame where she had been cuffed.

"Run to my truck!" he shouted, half dragging her across the ground. They made it three steps when the Humvee slid sideways to a stop in front of them. The driver threw open the door and jammed an M-16 at them. Barely five feet away, he couldn't miss if he wanted to. His finger tightened on the trigger.

68

A massive shadow exploded from the darkness and smashed into the driver, crushing him between the door panel and the frame. Blood shot from the man's mouth, and the force of the blow knocked the door off its hinges. The shooter was dead before he hit the ground.

Jessup and Flowers bolted around the Humvee while several pigs ran past them and tore at the meat on the metal men. The man in the turret shot at the giant pig eating his now-lifeless friend. Seeing the bullets had no effect, he turned the weapon toward Jessup and Flowers just as they reached the Toyota.

With a loud squeal, something from a nightmare shot out of the brush, and scrabbled up the side of the Hummer. With a flip of its head, the boar hooked the gunman in the ribs with a foot-long tusk, reared back, and plucked him from the opening like a Cajun sucking a crawfish. The man screamed all the way to the ground, then fell silent as a massive hoof caved in his chest.

Jessup tore open his door, heard a yelp, and saw Flowers jump to the side just as a pig as big as the truck shot from the shadows and smashed into the passenger door. She grabbed the bed rail and flipped into the back as the truck rocked up on two wheels.

Jessup twisted the key and the old truck roared to life, but as he reached for the gearshift, he caught a flash to his left. He ducked instinctively as the driver's side window exploded, showering him with glass. He glanced and saw Windler pointing a rifle at them through the Humvee's gun port.

Windler shot another burst, and three holes stitched the side of the bed. Flowers yelped, but before the man could fire again, a pig jammed its head through the driver's door. Windler spun toward the animal and fired. The monster let out a loud squeal and backed away.

Jessup jammed the gearshift into drive, floored the accelerator, and shouted, "You okay?"

There was no reply.

"April!" He took his foot off the gas, ready to hit the brakes, and heard a tapping. He looked in the mirror and saw her kneeling at the back window.

"Thank God." He hit the button for the vent glass and the panel slid down. Flowers clamored into the back seat and crawled up to the front.

"Are you hurt?" he demanded, his eyes moving from the road to her and then back again.

"I'm good, just banged up. How did you get those cuffs off, MacGyver?"

He grinned, reached into his pocket, and held up the bracelet. "The survival bracelet Davie got me. The connecting clip has a built-in handcuff key."

Her mouth dropped. "When I meet him, I'm going to buy him a pony."

"Let's get out of here first. This road is shit—all mud—and we're going the wrong direction. Windler will catch us in no time in that Hummer."

"I'm not worried about Windler," she said, looking out the back window.

He glanced at the mirror and saw a half dozen of the monster boars charging after them. And they were gaining.

"Maybe this leads to another exit," she said.

"Fingers crossed." He shot her a look. "Did I hear you use the 'B' word back there?"

Even in the dimming light, Jessup saw the woman turn bright red.

"I've never heard you curse before."

She turned even redder.

"But you're going to have to up your game," he said, grinning. "On a scale from one to ten, bastard is about a three."

She rolled her eyes.

He looked up. "I see headlights." Then, "Oh, crap, hang on!"

Bam! A hog slammed into the tailgate and the truck lurched to the left. Jessup jammed the accelerator to the floor and fought to keep the wheel straight.

He looked at the speedometer. Thirty-five, and the creatures were gaining.

A second pig slammed its head into the side of the Tundra and rocked the truck. The glove box popped open and everything spilled onto the floor.

Jessup snarled, "I'm getting real tired of mutant animals."

Then he saw Flowers' eyes get big. He looked up and saw the end of the road—and the ditch.

He jammed down the accelerator and said, "Put on your seatbelt!"

"Jake, there's no bridge!" she screamed as she snatched the belt across herself.

Then they were airborne.

A split second later, the front tires smacked the far bank, and bounced over the lip. Jessup tried to will the back half to follow, but the undercarriage hit the ground just ahead of the rear axle. Momentum threw the four-thousand-pound truck forward and the spinning rear tires hit dirt, digging gouges into the berm as they sought purchase.

"Go, go, go!" Jessup chanted like the skipper of the *Andrea Gail* heading up the face of the rogue wave. But life imitated art. The bank crumbled, and before they could get the doors open to jump out, the truck toppled backward into the ditch.

69

The twenty-foot-long truck slid off the edge of the berm and smashed into the bottom of the pit. Flowers' head slammed against the headrest, and when she opened her eyes, she saw stars through the windshield.

"Are you okay—" she started to say, then the stars shifted as the Toyota slowly tipped backward.

"Hang on!" Jessup yelled as the truck pivoted across the ten-foot opening and smacked against the ditch wall.

"Whew! What a rush," he said as he lay sprawled against the interior roof and rear window rubbing his neck. "This would make a great ride at Disney World."

"I'll stick with Pirates of the Caribbean," Flowers said, hanging upside down by her seatbelt.

"If we get out of here in one piece, I'll take you."

"Deal. What now?"

"Grab hold of the steering wheel and I'll cut your seat belt."

After she joined him, he asked, "You hurt?"

"No, you?"

"Just my pride. I really thought I could make it."

She shook her head.

"Our guns are gone," Jessup said, grabbing his backpack. They crawled through the rear window and dropped to the ground. Their feet sank several inches into the bottom.

"Jake, your poor truck."

It was upside down, wedged in the pit at a forty-five-degree angle, the bed at one corner and the front end resting against the inside wall.

"Ah, winch it out, run it through the car wash a couple of times, it'll be good as new. I just wish it was leaning the other direction, then we could climb on it and get out of here." He reached into the backpack, pulled out the two headlamps, and handed her one.

The truck shuddered. Jessup peeked out from underneath and saw one of the giant pigs standing at the edge of the ditch nudging the front end. When the thing saw Jessup, it squealed excitedly and dipped its head over the edge, sending clods of dirt raining down.

A chorus of grunts and snorts followed, and soon the mutant creatures lined the bank.

He ducked back under the truck.

"Maybe if we're quiet, they'll forget about us and go away," Flowers whispered.

Jessup nodded.

They waited, and after a minute, the grunts and snorts faded.

Flowers let out a breath, then looked around. The ten-foot-wide tunnel was a black void in either direction, like a massive hallway lit by stars.

"Ugh, it stinks down here," she said, wrinkling her nose. She clicked on the light and shined it around. "What are all those clumps?"

Just then, they heard a splash. She flipped the light toward the sound but saw nothing. The splashing sound grew louder. The light flashed on a pair of red orbs, and out of the gloom came a monster.

Jessup added his light and illuminated a group of pigs surging toward them.

"Run!" he said.

"Where are they coming from?"

"There must be a ramp somewhere," he said as they slid through the muck.

"They live down here?"

"That would explain the smell."

"That means we're running in..."

"My truck should slow them down," Jessup said, just as the first pig slammed into it.

Almost in slow motion, the Tundra slid sideways, then fell on top of the pig. It squealed loudly as the other animals trampled over it, trying to squeeze around.

"Yeah, take that!" Jessup hollered. His triumph was short-lived as another boar clambered to the other side, destroying what was left of the old truck. It charged forward, followed by more pigs.

They slid and slipped through the mud as the horde advanced, their massive hooves finding traction in the muck like monster truck tires.

Flowers and Jessup slashed their headlight beams across the dirt walls, searching for a way out but found none.

"They're gaining," he said.

A beam reflected off amber.

"There!" Flowers shouted.

With renewed hope, they ran faster. That hope was dashed when they saw the battered remains of an old Dodge pickup lying on its side, blocking the ditch.

"Go, go, go!" Jessup said, stooping down with his fingers interlaced. She stepped into them, and he nearly threw her over the side of the truck.

He scrambled up just as the first hog slammed into the barricade. Jessup's mud-slick shoes went out from under him and he smashed down onto the truck, his legs dangling a foot from the monster's face. He kicked like a line dancer on meth until Flowers jumped up, grabbed his arms, and dragged him over the rest of the way.

He fell in a pile at her feet, then stood, the right side of his body covered in muck. "Thanks... I think," he said in a shaky voice as he scraped scum from his eye.

Crash!

More of the creatures slammed into the crumpled pick up.

"This won't hold them long." He pointed down the ditch toward another dark shape. "There's the other vehicle that asshole talked about. Let's get to it."

"Oh my God," Flowers said staring at the front of the truck and the air-brushed license plate that read 'Georgina.' "This is Enos Norton's truck."

"The missing kid?"

She nodded.

"Now we know what happened to them."

The truck shuddered from another impact.

"Let's go," she said.

As they got closer, she exclaimed, "I know that truck, too."

"Me, too," Jessup growled as he stared at the Chevy pickup lying upside down, its massive mud tires rising above the suspension like the legs of a rigor mortised cow. "It's the one that forced your car off the Lake Pontchartrain bridge."

"Very good," came a voice from above them.

70

They looked up and saw State Agent Houston Windler standing at the edge of the pit, a headlamp lighting up his leering face like a goblin.

"I'm shocked you made it this far." He was holding a rifle casually in the crook of his arm. "I thought Perkins was exaggerating when he said you two were resourceful."

There was a crash and Windler glanced over. "They're almost through. Won't be long now."

He looked down. "I could just shoot you, so you don't suffer, but after you made dinner out of my two assistants, I'm not inclined to be generous. Of course, you could just keep running around the ditch, but the pigs will get you, eventually. You'll just be more tired when they do."

"Better than being talked to death by you, asshole," Jessup snarled.

Windler chuckled. "You see how excited they are? That's my fault, I'm afraid. After I gave them a taste for live game, the slabs of meat just don't seem to do it for them."

"By live game, do you mean Enos and his friends?" Flowers said.

"They weren't the first, but they put on a good show. Enos almost made it out. Got all the way to the cattle gate." Windler shuddered. "That was a little gruesome, even for me."

"They were just kids," Jessup said, shocked by the man's callousness.

"Yeah, well, not my problem."

"But why?" Flowers asked.

"Our government friend said he needed a live demonstration. For what, I don't know, don't care. Pike said he could get them up here, so I told him to set it up. He didn't know what was going to happen, but that boy would have done anything to work back here."

There was another loud crash at the Dodge.

"Then, why did you kill him?" Flowers asked.

Windler looked surprised at the question. "Because of you. My people saw you talking to him, and the next thing we know you're snooping around the Rebel Yell." He shook his head. "Loose lips sink ships."

Her mouth dropped open.

"So, I used his truck to run who I thought was you off the road. That way, if word ever leaked back, we could say he did it and left town."

Her body shook with rage.

"Then you had to screw it all up and not be in the car."

"You son of a bitch," she snarled.

Windler chuckled. "Story time's over. It's suppertime, kids."

They snapped their heads toward Enos's truck and saw the first of the pigs push past it.

Jessup looked up at the big tires. If they climbed them, they might be able to jump to the far side of the ditch. He started up, but Windler lifted the rifle. "I will shoot you if you do that."

He grabbed Flowers' arm and dragged her under the overturned Chevy.

"Like I said," the game warden shouted, "you can run, but you'll just die tired."

The big truck sat nose high with its tailgate stuck a foot into the mud. That left a small triangle of space for them to crawl into. They squeezed in and put their backs against the rear window glass, using their headlamps to light up the cramped space.

Jessup looked at her and winked. She tried to smile, but it crumbled away.

He turned and shone his light through the window into the truck cab. The pigs would dig through to them in no time. Jessup knew their only hope would be to find a gun to use against the monsters, but after seeing what little affect rifle rounds had, even that seemed hopeless.

Suddenly, Flowers began clawing at the dirt around an overturned crate.

"Help me," she said as she tore into the thick smelly mud.

He started digging. "What are we doing?"

"Look." She pointed her light at the side of the box and lit up a spray-painted stencil of a skull and crossbones.

"What is it?" he said, digging faster. The ground shook as the monster boars got closer.

"Remember when Windler said he caught Pike using cyanide bombs to kill pigs? This is them! I remember seeing this box when I looked in the back of his truck at the store."

"You mean..."

She nodded. "Maybe we can use them to—"

A pig hit the truck with a thundering *crash!* and shook the chassis.

Windler cackled overhead.

The monsters clawed at the dirt around the sides of the truck and Jessup and Flowers clawed the dirt away from the box. A boar got its nose under the bed and snorted wildly. Jessup reached into his backpack and pulled out the stun gun he had at PIT City. He stabbed the pig in the nose and pulled the trigger. The electrodes sparked and clacked, and with a horrifying squeal, the hog tore away from the truck, causing the others to back off.

"That should buy us a second," he said with a deranged grin.

"I've got an edge," Flowers said. He grabbed hold and together they pulled the crate onto its side. She tore at the straps and the lid fell open, exposing road-flare-sized tubes. The sticker on the side said M-44 Cyanide Trap. An instruction card hung from a piece of string on each one.

"How does it work?"

Flowers pulled off the card and read while Jessup shocked another pig that had dug a hole almost large enough to squeeze through.

"They're pissed," he said.

"It's easy. You slide the little tube onto the big tube. The little tube has bait on it. When the pig bites down, the cyanide tube explodes in their mouth."

"We have to stick it in their mouth?" he shouted.

She shrugged, jammed one together and tossed it toward the closest boar. The creature snatched it up with its teeth as it continued to claw at the mud. There was a *pop* and the pig hesitated, then shook its head violently, squealed, and scrambled back from the opening.

They looked at each other in surprise, then snatched up more of the devices, armed them and tossed them out. Four more took the bait, bit down, bellowed, and ran off.

The siege suddenly ended. Jessup armed two more, reached from under the truck and tossed them out. "Just to be on the safe side. Maybe we'll get lucky."

A minute later, they heard another *pop* and a squeal.

"Yes!" Jessup said, throwing up a fist. "You think it kills 'em? They're awfully big."

"I don't know, but it definitely slows them down."

As if to answer his question, a shot rang out. A bullet zipped through the truck bed and slammed into the ground six inches from Flowers' leg.

"You assholes are killin' my pigs!" Windler shouted.

71

Bam! Another round penetrated and hit the cyanide box.

"You motherfucker!" Jessup snarled. He grabbed Flowers, pulled her close, then spun around and kicked at the rear window glass until it broke. He shoved her through the opening just as, —C*rack!* —a round hit the ground where she had been seconds earlier.

Crack! Another bullet twanged off the window frame.

He'll get us eventually, Jessup thought as he searched the cab for a something, anything.

Bam! Bam! Bam!

Jessup grit his teeth and waited for the pain. Then he smelled gasoline.

The fuel tank!

"Barbeque time!" Windler said. "You guys get to decide: Do you want to be sushi, or extra crispy? You got five seconds, then I'm going to drop this match. One..."

He looked at Flowers, who returned an angry stare. There was no trace of fear in her eyes.

"Two..."

"You said 'son of a bitch.'"

"Three..."

Her mouth twitched into a grin.

"Four..."

"On a scale of one to—"

Boom!

The explosion was followed by a scream.

"That was a shotgun!" Jessup said.

They huddled in the cab, unsure what to do as gas puddled around them. Then, "Jake, you guys okay?"

They looked at each other, their eyes wide.

"Geo?" Jessup said.

They scrambled out of the cab and cautiously peered up from the edge of the truck bed. The big man was standing at the top of the ditch clutching a twelve-gauge shotgun that looked like a toy in his huge hands.

"It's okay. The hogs have backed off, but you two need to get out of there before this thing catches on fire."

They scrambled out and heard a moan from the opposite bank.

"Shut up asshole, or I'll shoot you in your other arm," Palmer said. He looked down. "Your best bet is to climb up on the back tire. I should be able to reach you and pull you over."

A half dozen of the giant pigs grunted and snorted at them from twenty feet away. Jessup stepped over the body of one of the poisoned hogs. Flowers went to follow, but the creature swung its head up and sliced her across the right thigh with its ten-inch razor-sharp tusk. She screamed and fell to the ground.

"No!" Jessup shouted as he dragged her away from the half-dead animal.

Boom! The shotgun exploded in a flash of light as nine pellets of double-aught buckshot slammed into the creature's head.

"Aaahh!" Flowers cried as Jessup pulled her to her feet.

"You're going to be okay," he said as he boosted her onto the overturned truck. Blood had already soaked her pant leg, and he cursed silently as he peeled off his belt.

Smelling the fresh blood, the hogs surged forward.

"Keep 'em off me for a second," Jessup shouted as the gas fumes grew thicker.

He prayed the muzzle flash wouldn't set off an explosion as Palmer pumped two more rounds into the lead animals, driving them back.

Then he shouted, "I'm out!"

Flowers screamed as Jessup cinched the belt tight around her upper thigh. He grabbed her under the arms and stood her up. The gasoline fumes were overpowering as the liquid pooled around them.

Damn thing must have been full when they pushed it in, he thought.

"Get her up on the tire!" Palmer said.

"Can you climb?" Jessup asked, grabbing her arm.

She stepped onto the back axle, grimaced, then nodded.

He helped her onto the tire. Palmer, laying on his stomach, reached down, grabbed her arm, and yanked her onto the bank.

Jessup, his shoes slick with mud, stepped onto the axle and crawled atop the big mud tire.

"Just stand up and jump," Palmer said, holding out his hand.

Click.

They both turned and watched as a flaming cigarette lighter arced through the air and fell into the ditch.

With a *whomp!* the gas exploded. Flames shot up the walls, and in the conflagration, they saw the leering face of Houston Windler kneeling across from them, his right arm dripping blood and his left arm clutching the M-16.

"You motherfucker!" Jessup shouted as he clambered atop the tire and jumped.

The flames and heat forced his eyes closed, but he felt a powerful hand grab his wrist and jerk him upward. Both men fell onto their backs in the grass, sucking fresh air, along with the stink of singed hair.

"Move and she dies."

They turned to see Windler aiming the rifle at Flowers.

"Whew," the state agent said through gritted teeth. "You got me good, Geo. I never took you for the hero type. Gotta give you guys credit, you almost pulled it off. But never bring a shotgun to a machinegun fight."

Jessup shifted his gaze and nodded past Windler. "You might want to save those bullets."

Windler laughed. "You must think I'm stupid. There's nothing there. They're all in the ditch."

Suddenly, he paused, sniffed the air, then slowly turned his head.

"Oh, sh—"

The giant Russian boar swung its head and raked a tusk across the game warden's stomach. Windler screamed as his intestines spilled onto the ground. He was still screaming as they pulled away in Palmer's truck.

72

— ∘ —

Jessup was reading the latest Chase Gordon novel on his phone when Flowers woke up.

"Sleeping Beauty is alive."

"You sure?" she said groggily. "I don't feel alive."

"According to that squiggly line on that monitor next to you, you are."

"Hmm."

"Did you enjoy your helicopter flight?"

Her eyes popped open. "I flew on a helicopter!"

Jessup chuckled. "Yeah, all the way from Monroe to the Tulane Medical Center."

"Dang, I've never been on a helicopter before. I missed it." She hissed, closed her eyes, and laid her head back.

"Doc said you're going to be hurting for a couple of weeks. The cut was deep; scraped the bone. Plus, all the nasty stuff that was in that ditch."

She shuddered at the memory.

"You just had to be like me, didn't you, Flowers? I have a scar, so you had to have a scar..." He grinned.

"Uh, not quite.

"Thirty-seven stitches. Nice try, but not even close to my eighty-three."

"Trust me, that's not a record I want to break." Then she said, "We have to get that evidence before they can destroy it."

The door opened and Flowers' group supervisor, Jamie Reynolds, walked in. "Too late, they cleaned the place out."

"The pigs?"

"They had the world's biggest pig roast in that ditch."

Flowers dropped her head.

"And you, young lady, were not authorized to destroy government property," she said, nodding at the bandaged leg.

"Thought I was persona non grata with the FDA?"

Reynolds flipped a hand. "You know how they are in DC, the wind shifted."

Flowers' eyes narrowed. "What do you mean?"

"That means they compared the evidence you two recovered from the scene of the Berrymans' death with evidence from Rebel Yell and it matched."

"But you said it was destroyed."

"The big stuff was. The meat lockers, the electronics, the cameras, records, but you can't destroy all the genetic material in an area that big without a missile strike."

"I wouldn't have put that past them," Jake said. "So, they can prove the pigs that killed the Berrymans came from the Rebel Yell?"

"Yes."

"That's great," Flowers said. "We can grill the owner and his workers. They won't want to face a murder charge."

Reynolds frowned. "You don't know?"

Jessup and Flowers exchanged a confused look and she asked, "Know what?"

"Everyone at the hunt club that was involved with the operation is dead, along with an ambassador and his aide."

"What?" Jessup said.

Reynolds took in a deep breath, then explained what she knew of the situation.

"DC is calling it a diplomatic disaster of epic proportions. The worldwide press is asking why, after the deaths of Congressman Berryman and his wife, the government invited—no, encouraged—the German ambassador to go on a boar hunt. They're just thankful his son survived."

Jessup nodded slowly. "Let me guess. If the truth got out that Berryman was assassinated and then the German ambassador gets killed by the same animals, we'd be on the brink of war. So, the story is going to be that the animals escaped from the Rebel Yell, made their way to the game preserve, and killed the congressman and his wife. And since it's not against the law to breed wild hogs..."

She turned to Flowers. "You're right, he *is* smart."

Jessup looked at Flowers and cocked his head.

She turned red, then changed the subject. "Did they check for genetic markers?"

Reynolds smiled. "That's the good news. The DNA in the pig follicles show an absence of a gene called myostatin, which restricts muscle growth. The experts say the animals were definitely genetic mutations."

"Yes!" Flowers said, slapping a hand on the bed. "What about Greg and Carolyn?"

Her smile vanished. "In all my years with the federal government, I've never seen things locked down like they are now. Sphincter muscles are drawn up tighter than Scrooge's purse strings. Everyone's so worried about the diplomatic fallout that officially, both sides of the aisle are going with the escaped rogue animal story and have shut down all related investigations."

"They can't do that!" Flowers said with a grimace as she tried to sit up.

"They can, and they have. Cleve Pike lured Enos Norton and his friends to the breeding farm to rob them of money and weapons. When he thought you were going to expose him for the murders, he came after you, but killed Carolyn by mistake."

Flowers stared at her boss.

"Greg committed suicide after he learned the FBI was about to arrest him for espionage for tapping into three top-secret databases. The agreement, as it stands, is that no one will ever learn about the espionage charges, including Greg's family, friends, and colleagues, if we drop all inquiries and investigations into his death."

Flowers listened and tears ran down her face.

"Even if we could prove he was murdered, the charges can't be disputed, April. Though his intentions were honorable, Greg spied on the government."

"He did it for me," she said in a weak voice.

"You, among others."

Flowers looked at her. "What does that mean?"

"It seems Greg was tapping into secure government websites long before he met you. He started in college, searching for covert political activity, corporate espionage by the government, that sort of thing. He leaked the information to anti-government groups, but never did it for money." She chuckled. "The guy was so brilliant. It was a hobby. An ultimate 'screw you' to Uncle Sam."

She placed a hand on Flowers' shoulder. "Greg had good intentions and his heart was in the right place, but he brought this on himself. What happened to Greg was going to happen whether he helped you or not."

Flowers stared at a spot on the far wall and gave a slight nod.

"Does this information blackout include April's investigation?" Jessup asked.

Her smile returned. "Nobody with a pulse believes two giant pigs wandered thirty-five miles from the Arkansas state line to a federal reserve and killed two people. Behind the scenes, the people who liked Berryman are pissed. And the ones who know about the GENIT program are pushing to keep it alive. If anything, your fan base has grown."

Flowers sat up. She looked from Jessup to Reynolds. Her boss anticipated the next question.

"Unfortunately, due to budget restrictions, they won't fund the program beyond overtime and expenses. You can bring in task force officers from other law enforcement agencies and the FDA will cover their overtime and expenses, but they won't provide salaries and benefits, so no outside contractors." She looked at Jessup. "Of course, I'll help in any way I can."

Flowers nodded but was too disappointed to look at either of them.

"In the meantime, you get better. I'll check on you when I can." She stopped at the door. "Good job, April."

As the door eased shut, a single tear slid down her face.

"Hey, what's that for?" Jessup said, sliding his chair closer. "You just got some great news. We should be celebrating. Want to go dancing?"

Her shoulders hitched as she began to cry. Jessup pulled her close.

"I'm s-s-sorry, Jake," she said between sobs. "I t-tried."

"It's not your fault, April. Besides, you heard what she said. It all depends on which way the wind's blowing. You paid me a consulting fee before. Who knows, they may start it back up. I don't need much."

"Oh, Jake," she said mournfully as she buried her face into his shoulder. "I-I paid that with my own money."

Jessup sat back and looked at her. Then he threw back his head and laughed. "April Flowers, you are something else." Then he gave her a bear hug.

A few moments later, she scraped a Kleenex across her red, puffy face and sat up. "I'm not doing it."

"Not doing what?"

"This investigation. Forget it. I'd rather investigate salmonella outbreaks in northern Idaho. I hear it's real pretty up there."

Jessup smiled, remembering their conversation inside a police holding cell. "No, April, you have to do this. If you don't, all those people will have died for nothing."

"But I don't want to do it without you!" She began to cry again.

"I'll still be around, and I'll help you in any way I can."

"How?" she sobbed; her face buried in his shirt. "You don't even have a truck anymore."

"Yeah... that's true. You may have to come get me."

They both started laughing.

73

Dirk Blanton walked down the darkened hallway of his Georgetown town-house, entered the den, and walked straight to the bar. He grabbed a bottle of Wild Turkey and a glass and filled the tumbler half full of the amber liquid. He snatched the lid off the ice container, reached in, and felt water.

"Goddammit!" he shouted. "James! James!"

"I sent James home, Senator," came a voice from the corner.

Blanton squealed and spun around to find Derrick Flattner sitting in an easy chair, his legs casually crossed, and a slight smile on his face.

Blanton's eyes went to the operative's hands. They were empty. He shouted, "You scared the shit out of me, Derrick! What the hell are you doing here? Do you not realize how dangerous it is for me to be seen talking to you?"

Flattner put on a puzzled look. "Why?"

"Why? Because your creatures killed a foreign ambassador, after they killed a sitting congressman, that's why. Do you have any idea the shit storm that's hit Washington DC? It's just a matter of time before they track it all back to Section 17."

"No, they won't," Flattner said. "There's nothing to lead them to Section 17. Operation Tall Grass was a completely civilian operation. It had no direct ties to the military, other than a video link to a communications center at Fort Hood, which has since been severed and all records destroyed."

"But there are witnesses."

"Everyone with knowledge of the Tall Grass operation, besides you, me, and Dotson, are dead."

"But the Rebel Yell Hunt Club. People know I've flown in there. They're going to find out that I'm the one who arranged the pig hunt for the ambassador, for Christ's sake." Blanton turned to the bar, grabbed the glass of bourbon and knocked back half of it.

"Yes. They're going to find out because you're going to tell them you arranged it."

He spun back around. "What? Are you out of your mind?"

"Then you're going to tell them that after you heard about Berryman being killed, you tried to cancel the hunt, but that the ambassador wouldn't allow it. You asked him to reconsider, but he insisted. You pleaded with him not to take his son, but he refused to do even that."

"But—"

"Your friend, Earl Tanner, was present during the conversation and will verify it. He'll say that he, too, had planned to go on the hunt, but that you convinced him not to go. He's also going to say he allowed you to use his helicopter to get there, but that he regrets doing that."

"But, how...? Why...?"

"How? I talked to him," Flattner said. "Why? Because he knows you make a much better friend than you do an enemy."

Blanton swallowed the rest of the drink, poured another, then sat down. "This is a nightmare. It was a mistake, a terrible mistake."

Flattner looked at him. "What do you mean?"

"All of it, the entire operation. SPAAD, Section 17, mutant animals, killing Berryman, all of it."

"Consider all the soldiers we've saved, and those we will save."

Blanton waved a hand. "Yeah, that's great, but what good does that do me if I'm in prison?"

"Nobody's going to prison, Senator. In fact, things couldn't be better."

Blanton leaned back into his chair. "Are you crazy? How can things be any worse?"

Flattner smiled. "First off, they will credit you with trying to keep the ambassador from going on the hunt. At his funeral you'll eulogize him as the cameras catch a tear that escapes and rolls down your face. Then you'll stand up on the Senate floor and demand legislation targeting the feral pigs that took the lives of your good friends. After that, you'll get on national television and announce that in memory of your colleague, Representative Berryman, you're changing your vote to support the Okaloosa National Wildlife Refuge."

Blanton jumped to his feet. "What the fuck have you been smoking, Derrick? Why in the hell would I do that?"

Flattner shook his head. "Because you've already lost. Half a dozen senators have switched their votes. It's going to pass. You have to get in front of it and support it. That will take all suspicion off you."

"But all that money."

"Senator, you stand to make a lot more money off the sale of surplus animals to our private buyers. Tax free money. In fact, we just sent half a million to your offshore account. There's a pending order for four more dogs, which will mean another half million."

Blanton sipped his drink, then shook his head. "I just can't do this anymore. It's time to cut our losses, pull the plug on this entire thing while we still can."

Flattner looked down, chuckled, and shook his head. "I'm afraid that's not possible, Senator. We have too much invested and too much to lose. In fact, we're about to break ground on a cloning lab in Mexico. Which, by the way, I need to talk to you about funding for it."

Blanton's eyes hardened. "Son, I don't know who you think you're talking to, but I'm not one of your flunkies back at Fort Hood."

"Senator, what do you think people are going to say when they find out you allowed the transfer of the two mutant pigs to the Rebel Yell hunting grounds?"

His eyes went wide. "What are you talking about?"

"You know, when Gus Erickson called you and asked if it would be okay to move the two runts onto his property for the ambassador to hunt."

"You tapped my phones?"

"You, of all people, should know that the NSA listens to everybody and everything." He held up his cellphone. "Want to hear it?"

Blanton sat with his mouth open, then smiled ruefully and said, "And I have to assume that if you have *one* recording, you have others."

Flattner lifted a hand. "I would be surprised if you didn't have your own collection of recorded conversations, Senator, just to keep everyone... honest. That's all these are for. Not to hurt anyone, but to ensure the safety and security of the operation and everyone associated with it—including you."

"How noble of you, Derrick, but what about the FBI investigation?"

"The FBI is going to discover that the owner of the hunt club had powerful friends who stood to lose a lot of money if they shut down the Okaloosa Reservoir Project. That club owner, aided by a corrupt Louisiana Department of Wildlife and Fisheries agent, killed the congressman and his wife, then staged it to look like hogs killed them. Ironically, those same hogs then killed *them*."

Blanton drained the second drink, then rolled the glass back and forth in his hands. "So, where does that leave us?"

"Like I said, Senator Blanton, we're in good shape. We're right where we want to be. You're going to come out of this stronger than ever. You'll be seen reaching across the aisle trying to bring the country together in their time of sorrow. In the meantime, we will continue creating animals of war to protect and defend the United States."

"As long as I keep the government money faucet open."

"Yes, sir. And, in exchange, we'll keep the faucet flowing into your offshore account. It's a win-win."

"I've said it before, Derrick, you've thought of everything," Blanton said, his eyes dark and his lips drawn tight.

Flattner smiled.

"Well, I suppose I have some phone calls to make regarding my new position on the Okaloosa National Wildlife Refuge. You found your way in. I'm sure you can find your way out."

Flattner stood. "Senator."

· · · ● · ● · · ·

A black Chevrolet Suburban pulled up as Derrick Flattner reached the sidewalk outside the townhouse. He got into the back seat, shut the door, and the big SUV drove off.

Parked down the street, Carl Dotson sat up in the back seat of the van, switched off the recorder, removed the thumb drive, and thought about what he had just heard. Unintentional deaths during operations like this were unfortunate but inevitable. The murder of innocent civilians was another matter.

He had three options. Release the tape and blow the operation out of the water—basically, the suicide option. Walk away and let the organization implode. Or monitor the situation closely and try to control it.

He still believed in the overall concept. The program had saved the lives of hundreds of fighting men and women, and they had spent tens of millions of dollars getting to this point. Things had only started to slide when greed and personal gain became more important than the original mission.

Now that he knew what he was dealing with, he decided to go with option three, for now. He looked at the thumb drive and chuckled. It was ironic that he and his boss were using the same information to keep the program alive.

74

Three weeks later, Jessup was hooking up a water hose on his new-to-him diesel engine in the *Tortuga*. The rebuilt motor had less than a thousand hours on it and had come from a boat that caught fire and was deemed a total loss by the insurance company. The owner had given the burned boat to Stu Jones, the marina owner, in exchange for overdue slip fees. Jones salvaged what he wanted, then gave the motor to Jessup in exchange for helping around the marina. A win-win for everyone.

His phone rang.

"Hey, Frosty, what's up? We still doing the noon meeting?"

"Jake, something came up. I need you to get downtown, now."

He sounded upset.

"What's going on, Frosty?"

"I don't have time to explain. Just drop what you're doing, get cleaned up and come down to police headquarters. We've got a problem."

"Wait a minute, Frosty," Jake said, concern creeping into his voice.

"I don't have time, Jake. Just get down here quick." There was a click, and the call disconnected.

Jessup stared at the phone, then wiped his hands and got cleaned up.

· · · ● · ● · · ·

He walked into the lobby of Memphis police headquarters and showed the desk sergeant his ID.

"Where you goin'?" the man asked.

Jessup hesitated, then said, "I don't know." He pulled out his phone and sent Frosty a text. WHERE ARE YOU?

A few seconds later, 12TH FLOOR. GET UP HERE NOW!

Jessup's heart rate increased.

"Is something going on upstairs?" he asked the cop. The man shrugged and went back to his newspaper.

Jessup drew in a deep breath and took an elevator to the 12th floor.

Frosty was waiting for him, a grave look on his face.

"What's going on, Frosty?" Jessup's concern was morphing into anger. "Tell me."

Frosty pursed his lips and shook his head. "They got new information on that possession with intent charge from a couple of months back."

"What? That was all bullshit and everybody knows it!"

"What can I tell you?" Williams said, holding up his hands. "They just told me to get you down here. Try to keep your cool until we hear what they have to say."

"Keep my coo—" Jessup spat, his face turning red. "These motherfuckers..."

Williams raised a hand. "Just listen first."

Jessup clenched his teeth, nodded, then followed his friend inside.

Five men and three women were sitting around the conference table. He knew them all. His attorney, the police director, and the six members of the Civil Service Committee, the ones who had denied his reinstatement to the police department.

Jessup felt his blood boil. So that's what this was. One final slap. Official notification that he'd never get his job back. It wasn't enough to have his attorney tell him. They wanted to rub it in his face.

He looked at the union lawyer, who was staring at the table. *Why didn't he warn me about this?*

Everyone stood up and faced him.

Here we go.

"Sergeant Jessup," the police director said. "Thank you for coming down here on such short notice."

Sergeant Jessup? They were really going to rub it in.

He gave a curt nod, trying to do as Williams had said and not lose his temper.

The director gestured to the Civil Service Committee leader, a thin, balding man with large, round glasses that made him look like an owl.

"Sergeant Jessup, the members of the board wanted to personally thank you for your help in heading off what could have resulted in a major economic and political problem for our fine city, particularly considering what has happened to you the last two years. Criminal activity by three of our employees resulted not only in you losing your job, but also being arrested for fabricated felony drug charges. Despite that, you went to bat for Memphis, sparing the city the trauma of a major federal investigation. We are in your debt, Sergeant Jessup.

As of today, you are officially reinstated to your position as sergeant in the Memphis Police Department, complete with back pay and no loss of seniority."

The man held out his hand. Jessup stared at it, dumbstruck.

Williams leaned in and whispered, "Shake his hand, Jake."

Jessup shook it. Then each member filed by and shook his hand as they left the chamber. He looked from Frosty to his attorney, then to the police director. They were all grinning.

"Close your mouth, Jake. You're going to catch a fly," Williams said.

"What—how—?"

Jessup's attorney finally spoke up. "The mayor got a call from the US Attorney. Not the one across the street," he said, pointing toward the federal building, "the big kahuna in DC. He said he was very upset that one of his agents was falsely charged with narcotics trafficking and wondered what other types of criminal activity might be taking place in Memphis. He said he was about to send a hundred agents here to investigate everyone, from the dogcatcher to the mayor himself, when Agent Flowers came to him and said that it was an isolated incident and had been properly handled by the city. When the US Attorney told the mayor the only reason he was standing down was knowing that there were fine officers like Sergeant Jessup in the ranks, the city couldn't reinstate you fast enough."

Jessup looked stunned. Then he spun on Williams. "You asshole, you had me scared half to death."

Williams burst out laughing. "Dude, you should have seen your face."

Once the director swore him back in, she asked Jessup and Williams to wait in the conference room.

"Man, my head is swimming," Jessup said. "Please tell me I'm not dreaming."

"Nope, this is the real deal. Congratulations, Jake."

"Thanks, Frosty. I appreciate you." Then he shook his head and said, "April Flowers."

"What's the matter? You look a little glum."

"Nah, man, I'm floating, but I feel a little guilty. April did all this for me, but once I get back to the detective bureau, I won't have much time to help her with her investigation."

A somber look crossed Williams's face.

"What?" Jessup asked.

"You're not going back to GIB, Jake," he said, looking down.

75

Jessup stared at him for a second, then slowly nodded his head. "Oh, I get it. They're going to put me in some do-nothing spot. They can't get rid of me, so they'll hide me."

Williams lifted his hands in a helpless gesture.

Jessup blew out a breath. "Well, at least I'm back on the job. So, where are they going to send me? The property room? Hospital security?"

"Worse," Williams said. "The Feds."

The conference room door opened and in walked April Flowers, a huge grin on her face.

Stunned, Jessup looked from Flowers to Williams, then back at Flowers.

Then he spun back to Williams. "You did it to me again!"

Williams shook his head. "You are so easy. You're the most negative-thinking person I have ever known."

Jessup shook his head, then turned to Flowers. He looked at her for several seconds, then said, "Thank you."

Williams slapped him on the shoulder. "That's 'thank you, boss.'" He gave Flowers a wink and a hug, and as he walked out, he said, "Tonight, six o'clock. Early Thanksgiving of jerked chicken at EZ's. Informal, wear your favorite T-shirt."

The door clicked shut, and Jessup said, "I gotta sit down."

"Good idea." Flowers limped to a chair.

"How is it?"

"It's better. They said a couple more weeks and I'll be back to normal, whatever normal is."

He smiled. "I don't know what to say."

"You don't have to say anything."

"I take it this means you still have a job?"

"I do. After all the smoke cleared, literally and figuratively, the people in DC finally realized that the genetic manipulation of animals just might cause problems."

Jessup huffed. "Huh. You think?"

"Some congressmen are considering regulating it."

"That won't be a quick process."

"No," Flowers said, "which is why they want to keep the GENIT program going in the meantime."

"No pushback from your bosses or their bosses?"

"They're not happy, but the Berryman killing pushed everything into the light. They covered up the assassination for political purposes, but a handful of people know there's a rogue element within Homeland Security willing to circumvent federal law, and the bigwigs got a taste of what can happen when it blows up in their faces. It also doesn't hurt that we have another senator and a couple more congressmen on our side."

Jessup grinned. "We, huh?"

Flowers nodded. "That's right, we."

"All right, so what's our first step, boss."

"The first thing is to stop with the 'boss' stuff. I can't handle that. Then you need to come to New Orleans, get sworn in on the federal side, and sign a million documents. After that, we'll come up with a game plan. Maybe over coffee and beignets at Café du Monde."

"That sounds almost as good as sitting in a motel room with a beautiful woman, eating popcorn, and watching *Justified*."

She blushed.

"In the meantime, I need to go down to personnel and sign half a million documents for the city side, right after I hit a noon meeting."

She grinned. "Good. See you at EZ's?"

"Come over early. I'll show you my new motor."

Her eyes went wide. "You put a motor in that thing? It's sinking."

"Get out of here, Flowers, before I cut your other leg," he snarled.

• • • ● • ● • • • •

Black smoke was billowing up from *Tortuga's* transom as Flowers walked up. Jessup came out of the cabin, grinning. "What do you think?"

She grimaced. "I guess you don't have to worry about it sinking if it burns down."

He squinted at her. "It's not on fire. That's diesel smoke. It's been sitting for a couple of years, just a little oil in the cylinders. It'll burn off."

She looked dubiously at it but climbed aboard. "Where do you keep the life preservers again?"

He threw her a scowl, then turned off the motor. "Let me get cleaned up and we'll head over."

From the v-berth he said, "Water and Diet Cokes in the fridge."

She grabbed a water and plopped down in the lime green beanbag she'd sat in when she first spoke with Jessup a year and a half earlier.

He came out a second later wearing jeans and a Pink Floyd T-shirt.

"You know," she said, looking up, "since we're going to tell the guys what happened, you ought to wear that T-shirt you got from Transylvania."

Jessup nodded, "Hey, good id—" Then he paused and smiled. "I know what you're doing, Flowers."

"Huh?"

"Stand up."

She stood, looking confused.

"Open your jacket."

"What?"

"I can read you like a book, Flowers. You want us to show up wearing the same shirt. Come on, open up."

She rolled her eyes. "They cut mine off at the hospital, remember?" she said as she pulled back her jacket.

He saw the whale on the "Save The Oceans" T-shirt, and said, "Oh, yeah." He shrugged sheepishly, then went back and changed.

"Sure is peaceful out here," she said as they walked over to EZ's boat house.

"It is. Being right in the middle of a big industrial area turns a lot of people off, but it keeps the crowds down."

As they passed the marina office, Flowers said, "That water went right through me. I gotta make a pit stop."

While he waited, Jessup walked over to the old Chris Craft Commander, as a James Taylor song drifted across the water. He thought about the old ghost sea captain who lived there with his mermaid wife and smiled.

"Okay," she said.

They knocked and the old Jamaican yelled, "Come on in, mon!"

Jessup pushed the door open, stepped inside, and stopped dead in his tracks.

There, standing in the middle of the living room, were EZ Proctor and Frosty Williams, both wearing gray, Transylvania, Louisiana, T-shirts.

Jessup turned to Flowers, who was now wearing a matching T-shirt and a huge grin.

Just then he heard the sound of claws scraping against wood as Stella charged from the back. She too was wearing a Transylvania T-shirt.

Jessup dropped his head and sighed. "This is so sad."

Made in the USA
Coppell, TX
02 February 2024

28515985R00154